By TJ K

Published by DREAMSPINNER PRESS
http://www.dreamspinnerpress.com

into this river
i drown
tj klune

Dreamspinner Press

Published by
Dreamspinner Press
5032 Capital Circle SW
Ste 2, PMB# 279
Tallahassee, FL 32305-7886
USA
http://www.dreamspinnerpress.com/

Into This River I Drown

Cover Photo by Kyle Thompson, kylethompsonphotography.com
Cover Design by Paul Richmond

ISBN: 978-1-62380-408-4
Digital ISBN: 978-1-62380-409-1

Printed in the United States of America
First Edition
March 2013

For my father,
John Edward Irwin

May 27, 1955—June 27, 1987

For all the things I can remember.
For all the things I have forgotten.
For all the things I never got the chance to say.
For all the things I'll say when I see you again.

Every word that follows is for you.

If the relationship of father to son could really be reduced to biology, the whole earth would blaze with the glory of fathers and sons.

—James A. Baldwin

What was silent in the father speaks in the son, and often I found in the son the unveiled secret of the father.

—Friedrich Nietzsche

part i: grief

A man came to a river at the end of his life,
and there he met the River Crosser, who helped others to the far shore.
The man asked the River Crosser why he had to leave so soon.
The River Crosser told him it was because there was a design to all things.
"Where is the design in grief?" cried the man at the end of his life.
"What does it have to do with me? I still have family to care for! My son!"
The River Crosser looked at him with a melancholic smile that did not reach his eyes.
"You will see," he said. "Soon, you will see all things clearly."

you and i

TO MEET my father, you'd have to go for a bit of a drive.

The town I live in is not exactly the epicenter of the known universe. I can't even say it's on the outskirts. You know that type of place that you drive through on a road trip to more exciting places, the kind that you have to scour the map for just to find out where you're at? You pass a worn sign on a highway (that you don't know how you ended up on and you can't seem to find a way off)—*Roseland, Oregon Pop. 876. Established 1851. Elevation 2345 ft. Gateway to the Cascades!*

Exit 235A will be up on your right, almost buried behind pine trees. If you don't know it's there, chances are you might just drive right on by, never the wiser of the town that lies a mile to the north.

From 235A, you'll hit the only road into Roseland—Poplar Street. You'll probably notice that the road feels a bit bumpy under the tires of your car. It hasn't been repaved in God knows how long. The city council has said year after year that it's just not in the town's budget to have Poplar Street resurfaced. It's more important that we keep the town afloat in these trying times. It's hard to argue against covering pot holes as opposed to closing the library. In that, the council is always right.

"Council" makes it sound a lot more important than it actually is; really, it's just Mayor Walken and Sheriff Griggs making the decisions. And by *that*, I mean it's Sheriff Griggs; Walken hasn't had an original thought since 1994, when it was said he decided to quit chewing tobacco and take up smoking instead, because it was a healthier choice, especially if you smoked the ultralights. Now, the cigarette companies can't call cigarettes lights or ultralights anymore, as it seems they all still cause your lungs to turn black.

I TRIED a cigarette once, after asking my Aunt Christie for one when I was seventeen. She told me to take it around the back of the house so I wouldn't get caught. She slipped her bejeweled lighter into my hand with a smile and a wink. I hightailed it around to the back, put that cigarette between my lips filter first, and lit up, taking in the deepest drag I could. I swallowed the smoke with the intention of making it come back up and out my nose (because it would look so *cool*). But it only took a moment where my throat worked to push it down into my lungs, where the smoke hit my lungs, that I realized I was not destined to be addicted to nicotine. I started coughing painfully, smoke pouring out of my mouth in gray bursts. My eyes watered as I started to gag. I dropped the cigarette onto the grass with the intention of grinding it out with my heel, but my body had other plans, retribution for the poison I had put in me.

I threw up all over my shoes. The cigarette went out with a hiss.

Great gales of laughter poured down from above me.

I spit onto the ground, trying to rid my mouth of the excess saliva flooding my teeth. I wiped my face with my sleeve and turned to look at the cackling loons above me. In the window, staring down, were four faces, all so very similar, lit up with delight. What was different was the way they laughed. Aunt Christie shook her head as she snorted, her curly blond hair hanging down in her face. Hers was a low, throaty chuckle. On her left were two of her sisters, the youngest of the group, my other aunts Nina and Mary. Theirs was a high-pitched giggle, a sound that should grate the ears and cause the skin to prickle. But it never did, instead reminding me of bells. They shook their heads as tears sprang from their eyes.

They are the Trio, and they are mine.

But it was the last woman who was laughing at me that meant the most. The last woman, who I had not heard laugh in what felt like ages. Hers was a loud thing, a big thing. She laughed big for a woman her size. It was almost hard to believe that such a great noise could come from someone so small. It was wondrous to behold, like finding a treasure once thought lost.

Her name is Lola Green and she is my mother.

So I rolled my eyes up at them as they hooted down at me, asking me if I felt like such a big man now standing in a pool of my own cooling vomit. They asked if I had learned my lesson. They asked if I would ever do something like that again.

I didn't tell them but I told myself: yes. I would do it again. If it meant they would laugh, then yes. If it meant I could hear my mother laugh like nothing in the world mattered but that moment, then yes. Of course, yes. I would do anything just to hear her laugh like that.

MY AUNTS—Nina, Mary, and Christie—moved in the day after my father left. I was sixteen when they pulled up in Christie's big, loud SUV. They descended on our home, buried in grief at the sudden loss of Big Eddie, scooping up the pieces of me and my mother that had shattered to the floor. They tried to put us back together, holding the pieces in place until the glue they had placed upon us had hardened. But we were fragile still. My mother's sisters knew once something is shattered, it can never be put back together in its original shape. Undoubtedly some pieces are lost or fit into incorrect places. The whole will never be as strong as it was once before.

So they never left.

THE road is bumpy on Poplar, as I said. You'll see storefronts, lit up in the gathering dusk, and see a few people walking on the sidewalk, some glancing at your unfamiliar car as it bounces down the road. You'll think that Roseland looks like a place that time has forgotten, and you won't be wrong. I wouldn't call us *stuck* per se; I just think the rest of the world tends to move a bit faster. We're not forgotten. We're just behind.

I don't think I want it any other way.

As you enter the main drag, you'll see a banner across the road announcing the "Jump into Summer Festival" and think how quaint it looks, how fitting for a little place such as this. You might feel like going for a drive. You want to ignore how a passenger in your car snorts with laughter, joking about how creepy the sign is, that it's probably just a way for the town to get unsuspecting outsiders in to sacrifice them to the local god. You want to ignore it, but it *is* kind of funny, so you don't. You chuckle and continue on, the banner disappearing overhead.

Driving down Poplar Street will eventually take you past a gas station with a single gas pump at the front. In Oregon, you're not allowed to pump your own gas, so a thin black cord stretches out next to the pump, causing a bell to ring every time it's driven over. Inside the store, there are a couple aisles of chips and Twinkies. Suntan lotion, hot dogs rotating on a silver cooker. Coolers with beer and soda. Ice cream, if the mood should strike. There is a garage next door that can handle small repairs like oil changes and windshield-wiper replacement. And there is a sign that spins above the station slowly, one that lights up when darkness falls—Big Eddie's Gas And Convenience.

My father. Big Eddie.

But he's not here at the station. Not this spring eve. Not anymore.

If you continue up Poplar Street, past the old mill that sits crumbling like a giant who left behind its playthings, past the empty fields that used to belong to the Abel family before the bank foreclosed on their house, over the Tennyson Bridge, the Umpqua River roaring underneath, and hang a left onto Memorial Lane, you'll find my father.

You'll pass under an old stone arch emblazoned with the legend *LOST HILL MEMORIAL*. No one can tell me how this name came to be. There are no hills here; it could be said that they are lost, although no one can say where they went.

You'll travel past the Old Yard section of the cemetery, where the stones are crumbling, their markings faded and illegible. Some dates stick out still, reminders of impossible times—1852, 1864, 1876, 1902. But if you continue past those, you'll see a form that sticks out above other stones. If you stop your car, get out, and walk toward the west end of the cemetery, the form comes into sharper focus. It's as tall as a normal man, but much smaller than the man it's supposed to represent. Nothing in this world could be as tall as him.

Stone wings surround a form that always causes me to ache. Gray hands reaching out. Head slightly bowed, the eyes cast down. Gray hair, falling in waves onto smooth shoulders, forever frozen. An angel, you see. An angel watching the ground beneath her. She's beautiful, even if she is made of stone. If you lean down, you'll see words below her perfect feet, carved in fine, clear writing. Here, finally, in this place, is where you will find my father:

EDWARD BENJAMIN GREEN
"BIG EDDIE"
BELOVED HUSBAND AND FATHER
MAY 27 1960—MAY 31 2007

Fifteen words. Fifteen words is all there is to describe the man who was my father. Fifteen words are all that is left of him. Fifteen words that do nothing. They do nothing to show what kind of man he was. They do nothing to show how when he was happy, his green eyes lit up like fireworks. They do nothing to show how heavy his arm felt when he'd drop it on my shoulder as we walked. They do nothing to show the lines that would form on his forehead when he concentrated. They do nothing to show the immensity of his heart. The vastness that was his soul. Those fifteen words say nothing.

The only time my mother and I ever really quarreled in our lives, with any heat behind it, was deciding what his marker would say. She wanted it to be simple, to the point, like the man himself. He wouldn't want the superfluous, she told me. He didn't need more.

I railed against her for this, anger consuming me like fire. *How dare you!* I shouted. How dare she keep it so short? How could she not make it go *on* and *on* and *on* until those who made such markers would have to harvest an entire *mountain* for there to be enough room to say what he was, what my father had stood for in his life, all that he had accomplished? How could anyone understand the measure of a man when those fifteen words said *nothing* about him?

She watched me with an angry hurt that I tried to ignore. My throat felt raw, my heart pounding in my chest. My blood roared in my ears. My eyes were wet. My hands clenched at my sides. Never before had I felt such anger. Such betrayal.

The measure of a man, she said finally, is not the words that mark his end, but everything he's done since his beginning.

She walked out of the room and we never discussed it again.

But she knows. Those fifteen words?

They do nothing.

The angel who watches over him must feel this is enough, though, because she never has anything to add. She just stands there over him. Watching. Waiting.

Sometimes I wonder what she is waiting for.

MOST out-of-towners who pull into Big Eddie's Gas And Convenience will probably expect a man with a name such as Big Eddie to walk out, larger than life, a massive presence that cannot be ignored.

They can't know that Big Eddie died when his truck ran off the road and flipped into the Umpqua. What they'll find instead is a short man, just recently twenty-one years of age. Most people in Roseland have a problem believing I came from Big Eddie's loins, given my size. I was small for my age as a kid, and I'm small for my age now. But any words to the contrary about who I came from were always put to rest when people saw my eyes. *Big Eddie's eyes*, they always said. *Emeralds. Bright, like fireworks.* There is no question I am my father's son, even if physically the rest of me takes after my mother. I'm small, like her. Our coloring is the same—light skin, brown hair that curls when it gets too long. And my hair was always long before Big Eddie became trapped in his truck, most likely knocked unconscious when his head hit the window as the cab of his truck began to fill with water. It was always long before he died, and he died not because of the impact caused by someone who then fled the scene and has never been found, but because of the water that rose, filling up the cab where my father lay, still strapped in by his seat belt. My hair was always long before my father drowned.

Big Eddie liked to shave his hair short, until there was just scratchy stubble covering his scalp. I can still remember how it felt under my fingers when I was a child, how it prickled against my fingers, how it felt when I rubbed it against my cheek.

Four days after he died, and one day before I fought with my mother over fifteen words, I stood in front of my bathroom mirror, Big Eddie's clippers in my hand, his towel around my shoulders. I didn't flinch when I turned on the clippers. My hands did not shake. My lips did not tremble. I did not shy away from the sight of myself— shadowed, hollowed-out eyes, skin devoid of color. I didn't flinch as I brought the clippers up to the left side of my head and pressed them against my skin. It only took minutes before I was shorn and there could be no doubt that I was my father's son.

Green eyes like fireworks. Hair that prickled against my fingertips. Sometimes, I let it grow back until it starts to curl. Then I shave it down again.

My mother and my aunts didn't say a thing when they saw what I'd done that first time.

I love my mother. I love the Trio.

But I am my father's son.

SO IF some spring evening you were to pull into the station, this is what you would see:

Perhaps you're lost, and needing to fill your tank before finding your way back to I-10. Perhaps you're visiting relatives in town, or in the next county over and just driving through. Perhaps you know me, though I doubt it.

You pull up to the pump, causing the bell to ring from somewhere inside the store. The door to the convenience store opens. You see me, young, and you laugh quietly to yourself. *Is this supposed to be Big Eddie?* you wonder. *Talk about misrepresentation!*

You roll down the window. "Fill it up?" I ask, my voice low. Quiet. *It's not rude*, you think. *Just reserved*. I look shy. I look tired. I look distant.

"Yeah," you say. "Unleaded. Regular. Thank you."

I nod as you lean forward and hit the latch, releasing the cover to the gas tank. "He's cute," one of your passengers might say as soon as I am out of earshot.

"He's creepy," another one says, shuddering. "This is so going to be one of those horror movies in the direct-to-DVD bin. He'll ask us if you want him to look under the hood and he'll break something and we'll be stuck in this town. Ninety minutes later, all of us will be dead except for one, and *that* person will be chased into an abandoned meat-packing plant while the gas jockey chases you with a chainsaw and a hook hand."

The people in your car try to muffle their laughter. You don't say anything. But if you did, there are only a few words you think of when you look at me. There's only a few things that you could possibly think. So, while your friends laugh, you think *sad*. You think *depressed*. You think *blue*.

But, most of all, you think *lonely*.

And you'd be right.

The tank fills. "That'll be $32.11," I tell you when I come back to the window. You hand me your card and I take it inside to run it. It's almost full-on dark now. Bugs are buzzing near the neon sign. You hear birds off in the trees. A breeze ruffles your hair. Somewhere, a dog barks. Another joins in, and another. Suddenly, they stop.

And then….

Do you feel it?

There's something else. Something, just out of reach.

Gooseflesh tickles its way up your arms. The hairs on the back of your neck stand on end. Lightning flashes down your spine in low arcs. There's something else, isn't there? Something else in the air. Something else carried on the wind. Something… unexpected. Something… different. Something is coming, you know, though *how* you know is a question you cannot answer.

I don't feel it. Not really. Not yet enough to name it. I'm still buried in grief. Lost in myself.

But soon.

I walk back to you and hand you your card. Our fingers touch for a moment, and you feel like you should say something, *anything*. I smile quietly at you as I tell you to have a good night, and I'm about to turn and walk away when you stop me.

"What's your name?" you ask, your voice coming out in a rush.

I appear startled at this. Hesitant. Something flashes behind my eyes and again you think *lonely*. You think *blue*, but it's the color, not the emotion, and you don't know why. Everything is *blue*.

I tell you my name. Slowly.

"Big Eddie?" you ask faintly, wondering why you are saying anything at all. Your passengers listen raptly, as they feel it too now, though later none of you will admit it to each other.

I glance up at the neon sign circling above us. And I smile. You see much in that smile, illuminated by the light. There seems to be a measure of peace there, if only for a moment. There is strength, you think. Hiding somewhere under all that sadness.

And expectation. Like I'm waiting for something. Something to finally happen. Something to come along and say *you are still* alive, *you are still* whole. *There is no reason for you to be alone because I am here with you.*

Then the moment passes. "That was my father," I say. "Have a good night."

You nod.

"Let's get out of here," one of your passengers whispers. "I found a way back with the GPS on my phone."

You nod again and watch as I go back inside and sit down behind the counter on a stool. I'm watching my hands when you finally pull away.

YEARS from now on a very ordinary day, something you see triggers a memory of a time you stopped in Roseland, Oregon. You'll think of me for the first time in years. You remember my name, but only just. You'll wonder, as your heart starts to thud in your chest, if something finally happened. If things changed for me. If that look of longing, of *waiting*, led to something more. You'll think on this fiercely, a slight ringing in your ears that you won't be able to ignore. But then you'll be distracted by something mundane and I will slip from your mind. An hour later, you'll have forgotten that racing of your heart, the sweat under your arms. You'll have forgotten the little things you saw, that feeling of *knowing*, knowing something was about to occur.

But I have not forgotten.

My name is Benjamin Edward Green, after my father, our first and middle names transposed. People call me Benji. Big Eddie wanted me to carry his name, but felt I should have my own identity, hence the switch. I never minded, knowing it bound us further. It was a gift from him. Because of him, and everything that is about to follow, my time of waiting is almost over. Events have been set in motion, and once started, they will not stop until it is finished.

This is at once a beginning and an end.

This is the story of my love for two men.

One is my father.

The other is a man who fell from the sky.

in this town i live,
in this house my father built

I WATCH your taillights fade as you leave. Part of me wonders where you are going, but like all things, these thoughts come to an end. It's dark now, and getting late. I'm tired and want this day to be over so the next one can begin.

I go back into the store and pull the till from the register and take it to the back office. The money is counted and logged and put into the safe, ready for pick up by the bank tomorrow morning. The receipts are separated and placed on top of the money. I close the door, and the electronic keypad flashes at me. I enter the code and it locks.

I leave the office and lock the door. I set the alarm. I turn off the spinning neon sign. I turn off the lights inside and it goes almost dark, the only light from a streetlamp. I stand in the dark and take a deep breath as I close my eyes. I wait, to see if it will happen.

It does.

A hand drops on my shoulder. I know I'm imagining things. I know it's not real. It can't be real. But then there's a puff of air on the back of my neck, warm and soft, like a gentle caress. The hand on my shoulder squeezes gently, and as I open my eyes, wondering why I am not scared, standing in the dark with someone behind me, I see a flash of blue, like light, like lightning. But it's gone before my eyes are opened all the way and the hand on my shoulder departs. I turn, already knowing there's no one there. There never is.

The store is empty behind me, of course.

It's not the first time this has happened.

It's not uncommon, I've been told (over and over again), to feel a loved one nearby after they pass. They are not *really* there, of course, but a manifestation of what our mind begs us to feel. We hope for this to be true, that they aren't actually gone. That they are some kind of guardian angel, with nothing better to do than watch over us. It's a stage of grief to wish that those we loved never actually left us.

It's the stage I've been stuck in for five years.

The first time I felt that presence, I figured I was losing my mind, having just returned home for the first time in over three months. The second time, I decided my sanity was long gone. But then it happened again. And again. And again. Eventually, I accepted it, even if it's just my imagination playing tricks on me.

It is always the same. A hand on my shoulder. A breath on my neck. The gentle grip on my shoulder. A flash of blue. It doesn't happen every day, or every other day.

It's not even once a week. But when I am at my darkest, when I am sure I can't take another step, it happens. Every time I don't think I can go on, it happens.

I lock the front door of the station and get into the 1965 Ford F-100 that my father and I restored painstakingly. Lovingly. Light blue with white trim. Whitewall tires. White interior. Original dash and radio that never gets any reception. My father's old coat is always draped along the back of the seat. "It's cherry," Big Eddie used to say.

"So cherry," I agreed.

"So cherry," I say now to the empty air around me.

Except it doesn't feel empty. It feels heavy, like anticipation. Like expectation.

I wait for it to depart, but it doesn't leave.

Eventually, I fire the truck up and head for home.

ROSELAND is quiet this late at night. Granted, it's always quiet, but when the sun falls and the stars come out, the quiet becomes a palpable thing. A slumber that can only be erased by dawn.

I think a normal person would probably go insane living out here. There's no excitement. There's nothing to hold you here, unless your roots are entrenched deep into the earth like mine are. I feel lost in cities like Portland or Seattle. Buildings rise up out of the ground like metallic trees, impersonal and cold. People that you have never seen before and will never see again pass you by, ignoring you in favor of themselves. You bump into someone and get a scowl even as you fumble with an apology. I don't handle that very well.

I drive past Rosie's Diner on the corner of Poplar and Bellevue. Rosie herself moves around inside. An old guy in a tweed jacket and fedora who only goes by Mr. Wade sits in a corner booth, sipping his coffee and eating his pie as he does every night around this time. They both wave as I drive past. I wave back as I continue into the night.

The other shops are dark, closing before the sun goes down. The Safe Haven, a bookstore owned by a pair of old dykes. A hardware store owned by Mayor Walken. An Italian restaurant owned by Mayor Walken. A secondhand clothing store owned by an Armenian immigrant family. Doc Heward's office. A real estate office, owned by no one, boarded up and empty. A gift shop where I'd gotten—

A blue light flashes behind me in the rearview mirror.

My breath catches.

But then the blue light is followed by a red one, spinning in a lazy circle.

Dammit.

I pull over to the side of the road, the whitewall tires crunching the gravel near the ditch. The lights continue to swirl behind me as the car pulls up within kissing distance of the Ford's back bumper. He's doing this on purpose, I know.

The door on the car opens, and I can see the seal on the side, *DOUGLAS COUNTY SHERIFF* written in the middle. Boots hit the ground with a thud and he lifts himself out of the cop car with a grunt. He shuts the door and flicks on his high-powered MAG flashlight, sweeping it back and forth. He pauses to look in the bed of the Ford. There's nothing there. It's sparkling. It's immaculate. He knew it would be.

"Sheriff," I say as he reaches my rolled-down window.

"Benji," Sheriff George Griggs says, his voice a deep bass, filled with undeserved authority. The definition of his face has been lost to fat, his cheeks soft jowls covered in black stubble. His balding head is hidden beneath the wide brim of his hat. "You're out late."

"You know I'm not. I just closed up the station, like I do every day at the same time."

He narrows his eyes. "Is that so?"

I barely can contain the urge to laugh. "Yes. Why do you care?"

"Someone's got to keep an eye on you, boy."

"I'm not your boy."

He ignores the harshness in my voice. "Been drinking tonight?"

Now I laugh. "You're kidding, right?"

He's not kidding. Or, he's just trying to fuck with me. "No," he says.

I can play this game. "No, I haven't been drinking."

"Is that so?" he says again, the beam of the flashlight piercing my eyes. I squint and look away. "I thought you were swerving a bit back there. You high, Benji?"

"No," I say, trying not to grit my teeth. "I've never been high. I've never been drunk. I've never done a damn thing wrong."

He leans in, resting his arms on the door to the Ford. He smells like sweat and aftershave. His scent invades my space. "Everyone's done something," he says. I can feel his eyes on me as I look straight ahead.

"What have you done?" I ask before I can stop myself. I don't miss how he flinches, a subtle intake of breath, the beam from the flashlight wobbling before it steadies.

"You know," he says finally, "a smart mouth like that is apt to find its owner in trouble one day."

"Oh?"

"Serious trouble, Benji."

"Can I go, Sheriff, or is there something else you needed?"

He watches me for a moment more before he knocks the flashlight against the door: a sharp rap that I know will have chipped the paint. "You be careful, you hear me?"

Before he can move away, my mouth opens on its own again as I turn to look at him. "You find out who killed my father yet, Sheriff?"

His eyes are hard, his face reflecting red, then blue. Red. Blue. The skin under his eye twitches; he tightens his jaw. "It was an accident," he says quietly. "Big Eddie lost control of his vehicle and flipped into the river. Simple as that."

"That simple?"

"Yes."

"Have a good night, Sheriff."

He's been dismissed and he knows it. His mouth opens as he grunts. I think maybe he'll say more, but he spins on his heel and walks back to the cruiser, opens the door and spills back inside. We sit there for a moment, me watching him in the rearview mirror, the lights twirling.

Eventually, he spins out behind me and leaves me in the dark, the ticking of the Ford's engine the only sound I can hear.

I stay still for a moment. I breathe in and out.

A hand falls on my shoulder again, there in the cab of the Ford. Another flash of blue.

"I know," I say to what does not exist. "I know."

I TRIED to leave for college after I graduated high school, but it didn't take.

I hadn't even wanted to go to begin with, but Mom somehow wrangled a promise out of me that I would at least *try*. Lola Green is not above guilt and manipulation in order to get what she wants, especially if she feels it will benefit those around her. On the 167th day before I graduated high school, I told her no way was I leaving her alone with the store—I was the man of the house now, I meant to take care of her, and this discussion was over.

Many things ran across her face before she spoke: fear, laughter, horror. Love. So much love through it all. But then her eyes hardened, her mouth narrowed into a thin white line. Little lines appeared around her eyes and on her forehead. I knew that face. That face said that I had overstepped my bounds. That face said fifteen words were enough. That face said I had no choice and I would be going to college in the fall.

"Now you listen here," my mother said with a snarl. She is a little thing, just coming up to my chin, and I'm only five foot nine. But when she needs to be, she's all spit and fire and teeth and claws. Big Eddie always said if he ever had to brawl, he'd only need her at his side. "Your father and I worked our *asses* off to make sure you would never want for anything. You are not going to sit there and tell *me* that you're not going to school. You're going, end of discussion."

I glared down at her as she tried to get up in my face, poking me in the chest with a lacquered nail. "I'm doing nothing of the sort," I growled at her. "You can't watch the store all the time. You've got other things going on." And she did. She had run a small bakery out of our house for years before Big Eddie died. He always pushed her to go bigger, to think beyond Roseland. Word of her talent had spread to other towns around us and she seemed poised to break wide open. But then, of course, her husband drowned in six feet of water and put a hold on her future. It wasn't until the Trio had arrived and put us back together as best they could that she started up again. At the time of our... *discussion* about my future, she and the Trio had just launched a website for the bakery *Lola's Goods*. It was getting more popular by the day, which meant less and less time for anything else. She knew this. But even better, *I* knew this.

Her eyes flashed. "Oh, no," she said. "There's no way in *hell* you're using the station as an excuse. I don't care if I have to send one of the Trio down there, or hire a townie back on. I don't get why we just don't *sell* it. The bakery is doing—" She stopped herself. She'd gone too far, said too much. This was a thing never discussed, and never was to be discussed. A sort of unspoken truth had come after Big Eddie died: she would handle her end and I would take over for my father. Big Eddie had always planned on me taking over for him one day. I'd been there with him at the station since I could walk: in the garage, the store. I helped him with the pump. He lifted me up to wash the windows with the scrubber. The first time he'd left me at the store to handle things by myself, I'd been fourteen. After a stern lecture of no goofing around and no giving my friends any pop for free, he'd rubbed a rough hand over my hair and told me how proud he was.

"Starting today," my father had said in that deep voice of his, "you're officially my partner here, okay? It's you and me from here on out, Benji. Think you can handle it?" He held out his hand toward me, waiting.

I was thrilled. Elated. Moved to the point I thought that if I opened my mouth, tears would fall and my voice would break. But Big Eddie was telling me I was a man. Real men didn't do any of that. So I grunted, snapping my head up and down once, twice. I reached out and shook his hand. His grip was tight, his hand warm.

The next day, he had old Mr. Perkins (the only attorney within fifty miles), draft up the paperwork. I didn't know then he also made a change in the event anything should happen to him. If it did, the store would pass to me.

Which, of course, it did. And my mother knew this.

"It's *my* store," I reminded her.

"I'm *your* mother," she snapped, and the argument was over.

I was in Eugene at the University of Oregon for three months before I came home. I didn't speak to her the entire time I was there. I studied. I went out. I got laid. I took tests, read books, stayed out until the sun was coming up. When I figured enough time had passed and my point had been made, I packed up my things, said good-bye to the few friends I'd made, and drove back to Roseland. She didn't look surprised when I showed up at the door, my arms crossed. The Trio ran over, squealing, covering me with fluttery kisses, their mingled perfume so much like home I had to blink the burn away.

My mother watched me for a moment from her spot by the sink in the kitchen while the Trio backed away, waiting to see what would happen. "You tried?" she said finally. "And?"

"It didn't take."

"No?"

"No."

She pursed her lips. "I suppose you'll be wanting Little House, then?"

No. I don't know if I could handle that.

Little House had been built by my father. He had thought it would be a place for a workshop, a garage where he could have his own space to do with what he wished. But the moment he started building, he knew it was going to be bigger than that. Set further down the road than Big House, it had become my father's life work. And since life doesn't stop because he had something that he loved doing, it took us six years to finish. The hardwood was placed and varnished, the white paint with blue trim completed. Electricity and plumbing done. When finished, it was two bedrooms, one bathroom. An office. It was small. But then it too became mine. After.

"It's like a littler version of our house," I'd said once he'd finished.

"Oh, is it?" he'd said, grinning at me. He reached over and grabbed me, putting me into a headlock while he rubbed my head with his knuckles. "A little house, huh?"

"Size doesn't matter," I managed to choke out in laughter.

He'd lost it then, and by the time he was able to wipe the tears from his eyes, Little House it had been named.

I gestured toward the Trio, unsure of what they'd want. Unsure of what to say. Mary and Christie had been staying there since they arrived. I couldn't find the words to say *no, no I don't want Little House. I can't stay there. I can't live there. I don't want to live there.*

She shook her head. "They can stay here with me."

I balked. "There's not room here for all of you. It'd make more sense to just let me go back to my old room. They can keep using Little House."

"Benji, it's okay to—" Christie started, but she stopped when Mom raised her hand toward her, causing her to fall silent.

"It's yours," my mother said, her voice hard. "Big Eddie built it for you. You're obviously grown up enough to gamble with your future, so you will take the house and you will live in it. You will clean it, you will handle the upkeep. You will pay for the utilities. You want to grow up so fast, fine. You'll act like an adult. That's what you want? Fine. Have at it. Do what you want."

The Trio tried to leave the room quietly, but Nina, ever the klutz, ran into the door, causing it to fly open, smashing into a kitchen chair that fell over and skittered across the tile. My eyes never left my mother's and hers stayed on mine. "Sorry," Nina said hastily.

"Good God, Nina!" Mary huffed. "So much for a smooth exit. We're trying to not make this any more awkward than it already is!"

"Really," Christina said. "Do you have to run into *everything*?"

"I didn't see it!"

"You never do," Mary said, their voices fading as they left the kitchen.

I waited.

Lola Green broke eye contact first and moved to the center island and pulled open her knickknack drawer. She dug through it for a moment, her brow furrowed. She sighed when she found what she was looking for and placed it on the counter in front of her and stepped back again.

She waited.

The silver key reflected a beam of sunlight pouring in from a window and flashed over my vision, and it was like my father was standing next to me. I could hear him chuckling on his way to breaking into full laughter. Everything about him reflected back at me from that key, that tiny key that was meant to be mine.

A little house, huh?

Yes.

I sighed and closed the distance to slide it into my hand. For a moment, I felt as if there was a warmth there, a flash of heat. I shook my head. Just from sitting in the sun, I told myself.

I didn't know what else to say, if there was anything left that would make things right again. I had turned and started to walk away when she grabbed me by the wrist, her touch gentle but firm. Insistent.

I said nothing.

Finally, she said, "It's good to see you."

I breathed my relief. "Yeah?"

"Yeah."

"I missed you," I admitted. "I missed everything about this place."

She stroked the back of my hand. "I love you. You know that, right?"

"I know."

"I wish you hadn't come back."

"I know."

"You're too good for this place."

I shook my head. "This is my home. You're my home. That will always be enough."

"You should never have just *enough*."

"I don't want anything more."

"Look at me," she whispered.

I did. I had to. I couldn't say no.

Her grip on my hand tightened as my gaze again found hers, and, as she searched my face, I could see that even in those three months, even in that short amount of time, she'd aged. There was no flash behind her eyes. The lines around her mouth looked deep. Her hair was dull as it fell onto her shoulders. She had been grieving, the same as me. And I knew then that while she had hoped I could make something of myself away from this place, and she'd spoken true that she had wanted me to become something my parents had never been, the real reason she had sent me away was so she could grieve. So I wouldn't have to see her when she was lost. She had been thinking of me, yes, but for her own selfish reasons.

A shadow crossed her eyes for a moment, but then it was gone. Her breath caught in her throat as she choked out a watery laugh.

"What?" I asked her quietly.

"I see him in you," she said, her voice atremble. "God, those eyes...."

I didn't stop myself then as I gathered her up in my arms, this tiny woman who was a shell of her former self. She was stiff against me, startled at my brazenness. It was awkward at first, but then I felt pieces of her that had come loose start to break away, and she collapsed against me and shook, clutching at my back with her hands. Pulling, clawing.

I held her, for a time.

I PULLED up in front of Little House, switching off the truck. I sat there, staring up at the house, for an unknown length of time, willing myself to go in, telling myself that enough time had passed, that Big Eddie would no longer be a part of Little House, that he'd no longer be infused into every corner, every nook and cranny of the house he'd built. I told myself that I'd moved on. Those three months in Eugene where I'd let myself go, where I'd drank to the point of blacking out as much as my body could stand it, where I'd wandered rather than attending class.

I didn't have the heart to tell my mother that I'd already been flunking out of the U of O, even only after three months. I couldn't tell her about the rathole of an apartment I'd moved into off campus. I wouldn't tell her about the nameless men that I'd brought to my bed almost nightly, more for the touch of something human than the sex. I wouldn't tell her how feeling skin against mine was the only way I maintained my sanity—the soft trail of a tongue at the base my spine, a quickened breath in my ear as someone thrust above me.

I couldn't tell her how I had obsessed over the accident. I couldn't tell her that I'd called Shirley who worked as dispatch for the sheriff's department. She and I had gone to school together, and she was sympathetic. I'd gotten a copy of the police report on my own, its contents telling me nothing more than I already knew. Shirley was able to get me scene photographs, showing my father's truck upside down in the river at mile marker seventy-seven, showing his tire marks on the road and gravel, the scarred boulder down at the river's edge that had struck the left front tire of the truck, breaking the axle and causing the truck to flip. It also showed a second set of tire tracks on the road, but noted no other debris was found. The river would have washed away any paint transfer as the truck stayed upside down underwater, the tail end sticking in the air at an angle.

I read my own statement that had been provided, and my mother's, both of us saying Big Eddie had no enemies, that everyone worshipped the ground the man had walked on. I don't remember speaking with the police, but I could see the anger in my words, could feel the heartbreak I'd felt, the denial.

But it was the coroner's report I was most interested in. The coroner's report that showed my father had suffered a broken clavicle from the impact and broken ribs, one of which had punctured his right lung. He had a splenic abrasion, a ten-centimeter laceration on his right forearm. Another, smaller laceration on his forehead. A broken bone in his left ankle. None of which were life-threatening. No drugs or alcohol were found in my father's system. His heart, the coroner said, was slightly enlarged, but otherwise he was a healthy forty-seven-year-old man when he died.

Cause of death: asphyxia due to suffocation caused by water entering the lungs and preventing the absorption of oxygen to cerebral hypoxia.

Which is a fancy way of saying that my father was alive when his truck came to rest upside down in the Umpqua. We were told that most likely he was unconscious as the water levels began to rise in the cab of the truck. It would have been fast, they said. He wouldn't have felt a thing, they said. That the accident didn't kill him, but that the river had. My father had drowned.

The longer I looked, the more I was sure my father was awake when the cold water filled his nose and mouth. His lungs. This thought became an obsession.

The police investigation had concluded it was a single-vehicle accident. There was no evidence of another vehicle involved. The black skid marks on the roadway had been partially washed away by rain that had begun to fall shortly after the accident would have occurred. Given the amount of water in my father's lungs, the coroner thought he'd been in the water anywhere from four to six hours before he'd been discovered by a motorist who just happened to look down at the river as he passed by.

Possibly he'd fallen asleep, they'd said. After all, he'd gotten up at four that morning to head up to Portland to meet up with some friends.

Possibly he'd gotten distracted, they said.

Possibly he'd swerved to avoid a deer.

Possibly it was weather-related, given how great the storm was that day. Everyone was surprised it hadn't flooded. They were sure it would. The town's contingency plan had been put on notice. Sandbags were made ready. The Shriner's Grange had been made available in case people needed to escape the rising waters. None of that had happened, of course. The river did not flood anyone or anything. Except my father.

So many possibilities, they said. We may never know, they said. But it didn't appear to be foul play, they said. There was no evidence to suggest that. Everyone loved Big Eddie.

I didn't tell my mother I thought that was a lie.

I gripped the steering wheel and stared up at Little House.

He's gone, I told myself. *He's gone. He's not here anymore. There's no reason for him to be here anymore. He's gone.*

I opened the door, grabbing my bag off the seat next to me. I closed the door to the Ford and clutched the silver key in my hand as I forced one foot in front of the other. I ignored the way my hand shook as I slid the key into the lock. And for the first time since Big Eddie had died, I opened the door to Little House and stepped inside.

I didn't know I was holding my breath until I realized I wasn't breathing. I let it out slowly and reached over to flick the light switch. The lights flashed on overhead. The entryway lit up in front of me. Living room off to my left. Kitchen, off to my right. Hallway ahead led to bedrooms. I waited. I listened.

Nothing except the normal settling of Little House.

It hurt to be in there, yes. It hurt because I could look at the walls and tell you the exact day they'd gone up. It hurt because I could look up and see the exposed beams overhead and tell you how I'd held the ladder for him while he hammered away. I could tell you about everything having to do with Little House, the house my father built.

My heart thundered in my chest.

I hung the key on a key rack. I closed the door behind me. I set my bag down. I took a step forward.

And a hand that wasn't there touched my shoulder.

I closed my eyes as I trembled. *No,* I thought. *He's gone. He's not real. This isn't real. Big Eddie died and this is my house now. Little House is mine, and oh my God,* someone is *breathing* on me—

I spun around.

For a moment, I could have sworn I saw a flash of blue, deep and dark. But I blinked and it was gone and I couldn't be sure it'd been there in the first place. I blinked again, my breath ragged in my throat. No one was behind me. The door was still closed. I thought about opening it and running up to Big House and cowering in my old bed, the covers pulled up and over my head, waiting for daylight, waiting for everything to make sense, for the world to brighten again, to lose the haze it had fallen under. But somehow, I stayed.

"I felt…," I said out loud, not knowing who I was speaking to. My face grew hot and I shook my head. "Forget it," I muttered. "I'm—"

haunted

"—home. That's all that matters. I'm home."

Little House shifted, the creaking of the wood its only reply.

SHERIFF GRIGGS'S taillights have faded into the dark behind me.

An accident. That's all it was.

Sure, I think. *Why not? Everyone else thinks it was an accident. The cops. The staties. The town. The Trio. Even….*

Even Mom.

It's easier, I think, for her to believe it was an accident, that there was nothing more behind Big Eddie's death. Maybe that's what she needed to move on. Maybe that's what she needed to be able to fall asleep at night. Maybe that's the only way she could stay sane.

I'd be lying if I said it doesn't make me wonder if I loved him more than she did.

Sheriff Griggs isn't coming back, so I start up the blue Ford and pull back out onto the road, headed for home. The truck feels empty now, like whatever is (or isn't) with me has gone.

I think about stopping at mile marker seventy-seven. But I was there yesterday, and I need to try and stay away. It's getting to be too much again, seeing that place. It's starting to follow me into my dreams again as well: a flash of a river, then brake lights pointing toward a grayed-out sky as rain pours down, lightning flashing blue and bright. A flutter of massive wings from some bird I can't see somewhere in the distance. A hand always rests on my shoulder. The scene and sounds before me fill me with horror and I open my mouth in a silent scream, but the hand grips me tight. There is comfort there, near the river. Even so, I wake up sweating, a strangled noise dying on my lips as the roar of the river fades from my ears.

No. I need to stay away from seventy-seven tonight. It's getting late as it is, what with Officer Friendly pulling me over. Even after all these years, I can't pinpoint what it is about Griggs that bothers me. He and Big Eddie went to school together, were friends of a sort, along with my mom and the Trio, only four years age difference separating all of them. But they went their separate ways after high school, and when they all returned to Roseland after college, things had just been different. Dad had married Mom. The Trio lived in Seafare, on the coast. "People grow up and grow apart," Big Eddie had said once when I asked.

Which is true, I guess. None of my friends, what few there were, stayed in Roseland after we graduated from Umpqua High over in Wilbur. They'd all talked about getting out of here and going to far off mythical places, like California or New York. I pretended to ignore the looks I received when I mumbled that I was perfectly happy right where I was. The world is too big for someone like me. I worry about getting lost. At least here, in Roseland, I know where I am. People know who I am. It's enough.

If you were to ask me if there was something else buried in the anger, in the depths of my grief, I'd look at you funny, not understanding what you meant. There's nothing else besides grief. Besides anger. But it's a shelter, a haven that I have amassed around myself to protect me, to focus my thoughts and energy away from the inevitable truth.

I have no qualms admitting that Big Eddie was my best friend. Most sons and daughters would probably shudder at the idea of admitting it out loud, and maybe they're right. But I'm not normal. I never have been. I was the nerd. The geek. The weirdo. I had friends, sure, but no one close. No one like my father. No one I felt like I could tell everything to, even the greatest secret I carried with me for months before

I finally broke down and told him one day toward the end of building Little House. Toward the end of his life. Even that I could not keep from him.

"Spit it out," he growled at me when I handed him the wrong-sized nail.

"What?" I asked, my eyes wide.

"Something's been on your mind for weeks, Benji," Big Eddie said, pulling himself to his full height. It might have been intimidating to most, and usually it wasn't for me (he was my *dad*), but I couldn't look up into his eyes.

"Oh," I said, shuffling my feet. "That."

He dropped a big hand on my head and ruffled my hair before sliding his hand to my chin and gripping it gently, pulling up until my gaze was locked onto his. "What do men do when they have important business to discuss?"

"They look each other in the eye," I whisper out loud, pulling into the driveway, almost home and lost in memory. "They look each other in the eye because it shows respect." I barely acknowledge the blue flash that skates off somewhere to my right in the dark.

"That's right," my father said, dropping his grip from my chin, then putting his hand on my shoulder and squeezing gently. "And I respect you, and you respect me, right?"

"Right," I said, never turning my gaze away.

"Now, what's going on, son? It isn't like you to keep things from me. Not for this long."

"I'm scared."

His eyes widened. "Of me?"

I shook my head. Then shrugged. I didn't know which was true.

"Benji, what on earth would make you scared of me?"

"I don't know," I said, my voice cracking. Still, I couldn't look away.

"Did you break the law?"

"No, sir."

"Did you hurt someone?"

"No, sir."

"Did you hurt yourself?"

"No, sir."

"Then why are you shaking?"

He blurred as my eyes burned. "Because I'm afraid you won't look me in the eye anymore. That you won't respect me."

Big Eddie leaned over, so that our faces were only inches from each other. He studied me and I let him. "I will always look you in the eye," he finally said. "I've raised you to be honest and kind. I've raised you to be brave and strong. If you can become the man I think you'll be, then you and me will always be eye to eye. You get me?"

I nodded, because I did. "Deep breath," he said, his hand still on my shoulder. I took in air. "Let it out," he said. I did. "Now, tell me."

"I think I might… be… you know. Gay. Or whatever."

He cocked his head at me and squinted his eyes, which would have been funny under normal circumstances. But this was not normal. I couldn't breathe. He tightened his grip on me. His nostrils flared. He dropped his hand and stood up straight, still looking me in the eye. I followed him as he went up. "You *think*?" he said, crossing his arms across his chest.

I shook my head. I knew what he was after. "I *know*," I told him.

He nodded. And then, unbelievably, he laughed. "Jesus *Christ*, boy! Where the hell do you get off scaring me like that!"

My heart sunk. *He doesn't believe me,* I thought. That hurt worse than any kind of fury from him could have.

"I thought you were going to tell me something really bad!" He laughed harder, slapping his hand against his thigh. He caught my eye again and something passed then between us, and he must have felt my fear, my pain. His laughter bled to chuckles and he wiped his eyes and leaned down before me again, putting his hand back on my shoulder.

"You sure?" he asked, a small smile on his face.

I nodded, tears on my cheeks.

"Benji, do you know me?"

"Sir?"

"Do you know who I am?"

"You're Big Eddie," I said.

"And?"

"YOU'RE my dad," I say in the cab of the blue Ford as I approach Big House. I'm lost in years and it's like my father is next to me.

BIG EDDIE nodded. "You're damn right I am. So you should know by now that I don't give a rat's ass if you're gay or straight or one of those tranny guys that likes to dress up in a slutty skirt and pretend you have a vagina."

My eyes bulged.

"You are my son," my father said, ignoring my fierce blush. "The only one God saw fit to give me. As long as you grow up to be a good man, the rest doesn't matter. We clear?"

I nodded.

"We clear?" he asked again.

"Yes, sir," I whispered.

I thought that was it, I thought we were done. But then Big Eddie stood up, pulling me to his side. I wrapped my arms around him as he patted my back. "Dad?" I asked finally.

"Yeah?"

"You're really not mad?"

"Really."

"Okay."

We stood there for a moment longer, watching leaves fall from the tree in front of Little House. My breathing evened out, my eyes dried, my heart stopped pounding a million beats a second. I didn't know then that less than a year later I'd be standing under gray skies as my father was lowered into the ground, a stone angel his only guardian.

If I'd known... well, I don't know what difference it would have made. I'm sure I would have held on for just a moment longer. I'm sure I would have done everything I could to put myself in the oncoming path of Death so it would not take my father. Time is a river, I've learned. Always moving forward. But for people like me, people who have loved and lost, the river is something we fight. We swim against the current, trying to get back to the way we once were, trying to hold onto anything to keep us from getting swept away. It's exhausting and eventually we tire. Still we push on. I can't let him go into the river and be swept away.

I can't let him go.

I finally calmed down enough to drop my arms, but we stood there, side by side, for a bit longer, his arm on my shoulders.

Eventually, we got back to work on Little House.

I REACH Big House and waiting for me, as she always is, is Nina. She sits on the porch steps, the headlights of the truck washing over her worried face. I stop, trying to ignore the blue flash that flits off out of the corner of my eye. More and more frequently this has been happening, and I wonder if I should be worried. My luck, it's not a ghost I don't believe in, but a malignant brain tumor pressing against my occipital lobe. Eh. It's probably too late as it is.

I stop the truck in front of her and she skips down the remaining steps, her sandals slapping against the heels of her feet. "You're late," Nina scolds me as I open the Ford's door, her sweet face marked with lines that belie her condition. I often wonder if Mary ever felt guilty that she was not born with Down syndrome like her twin sister. Nina and Mary are fraternal twins, which is why Nina has Down syndrome and Mary doesn't.

"You're late," she says again, poking me lightly in the chest. "Why were you late? I was waiting."

I sigh. "Got pulled over," I mutter, not thinking of my words before I speak them.

Her eyes go wide and she covers her mouth, her words muffled when she speaks. "Oh *no*! Did you get a ticket? Did you get in trouble? Did you get *arrested*?" She's starting to get upset, her chest heaving slightly, the intake of her breath sharper.

I reach out and pull down her hands from her mouth. Tears are already glistening on her cheeks. I rub my thumb over her palms, the only thing that calms her when she's upset. "It's okay," I say softly. "Nothing wrong. Sheriff Griggs just wanted to chat."

She startles me when she sticks out her tongue and blows a raspberry. "I don't like that man," she snaps. "He was never nice to me when we were kiddies."

I smile. "Can I tell you something?" I ask her.

She nods eagerly, the tears forgotten, curling her hand into mine as she pulls me forward to whisper it in her ear. She smells like strawberry shampoo. I kiss her head once before I whisper, "I don't like him either."

Nina turns to me, searching my eyes to make sure I'm not fooling her. I show her my sincerity with a small smile and she giggles, putting her hand up to her mouth again. "He's a bad man," she says in her laughter. "Bad, bad man!"

"Bad man," I agree. I'm about to ask how her day was when she suddenly stops laughing and looks above me, her eyes wide. I turn, but there's nothing there. "What is it?" I ask, looking back at her.

"Wow," she says in awe. "It sure is bright today."

"The stars?"

"Oh, no," she says, a beautiful smile growing on her face.

"The moon?"

"Bless the moon," she says, "but no. What did you do today?"

"I was at work, Nina. You know that. At the store."

She shakes her head. "No, Benji. What did you *do*?"

"I... I don't know what you mean, Nina." Goosebumps sprout on my arms. "Nina?"

"Oh, Benji," she whispers in reverence, her eyes sparkling in the moonlight as she watches the space above me. A wind picks up, blowing through the trees.

"What do you see?"

"Blue," she says. "There is so much blue." She sighs. "It's been around you for a long time, but now it's just so *blue*. You did something. It's why I wait, you know."

"Is it?" I choke out.

My aunt glances at me before looking back up. "Yes. Every night you come home, there's a bit of blue that follows. Sometimes it's faint. Sometimes it's bright. But it always dances, Benji. It always dances after you. I'm not sure if…." She becomes distracted again.

I don't believe this, I think. *This isn't real. There's nothing there. I see nothing. I feel nothing.*

But that in itself is a lie. That which I do not believe has been there ever since I returned to Little House. The hand I don't feel on my shoulder. The breath I don't feel on my neck. The flash of blue that isn't there. Ever since that night, I've come home to find her waiting on the porch, her hands folded in her lap, waiting for me. She's always delighted when I pull up in the Ford, clapping her hands and laughing. I always thought it was me, that she'd been happy to just see me. And while that may be part of it, it seems, for her, there is more.

This isn't real. This can't be real. Reality isn't flashing blue or disembodied hands. Reality isn't the feeling that someone is always there, that I'm never truly alone. Reality isn't—

I stop, cutting myself off.

Nina giggles and claps her hand. "Whatever you did," she tells me, "it sure is something. I've never seen it so bright."

"Nina?" I croak.

"Benji?"

I can't ask. My throat works.

She waits.

I have to know. I can't not know.

"Is it him? Is it…." I can't find the words to finish.

She appears startled as her gaze finds mine. She takes a step toward me and reaches up to cup my face, her hands soft and cool against my flushed skin. I stare down at her wide eyes and tell myself the flash of lights I see reflected back aren't there, that I'm hallucinating. I'm tired. I'm sad. I'm fucking lonely and I'm making up shit that isn't *there*. I'm seeing things that aren't *there*. I'm losing my fucking *mind*—

"Big Eddie loves you," Nina says, rubbing her thumbs against my cheeks. "Sometimes, I think he's closer than even you could imagine. But this? This is *blue*, Benji. Different."

"I don't understand."

Her brow furrows. Then, "Secret?"

Secret? This game we played when I was a child? This word I haven't heard from her in years, and hearing it now knocks me off my axis. She flexes her fingers against my skin. "Secret?" she insists.

I nod.

"Cross your heart?"

"Hope to die," I tell her as I make an X shape on my chest with my finger.

"Stick a thousand needles in your eye," she finishes solemnly. She pulls on my face until I'm lowered to hers and her lips are near my ear. I shudder as she breathes.

Finally, she says, "The blue follows you because it worries. The blue dances to make you notice. The blue flashes to make you smile."

"Worries? About what?" Not that I believe a damn thing she's saying. This is ridiculous. I shouldn't be feeding these fantasies of hers. She's obviously deluded herself into thinking—

"You, Benji. It worries because of the river. You're drowning."

I jerk my head back out of her hands, and for a moment she leaves them outstretched in front of her, as if she's offering herself to whatever it is only she can see. I take a step back, because she's too fucking close, and I can still feel her breath on my skin.

Nina lowers her arms and opens her eyes, those damnable, intelligent eyes. She'd been born with Down, yes, but fell into a category that only affects a small portion of those afflicted: mosiacism. During her gestation, some of the cells in the Down's embryo were able to revert back into their normal chromosomal arrangement. Which essentially means that while she still has Down syndrome, her intelligence is above others with her same condition. I've grown used to her insights, knowing she is much smarter than most people will ever know.

But this?

"What did you *do*?" she asks again, but as if she is speaking to herself. "What changed? Why today? Why now and—" She stops suddenly, a sharp intake of breath. She slowly raises her eyes again, passing over my face until she's looking above me. She's silent. Then, "I see." Pause. "And you would do that? For him? Oh. Oh. Yes. Oh, yes. So lonely. Like you? Like… you."

I am rapt, unable to look away. A tear slips from the corner of her left eye and down her smooth cheek. I reach up and rub it away and she comes back to me, whatever conversation going on in her head now over. Or at the very least on hold.

She grasps my hand and says, "You see it, don't you?"

I shake my head before I can stop myself. "Nina, I don't know what you're talking about. It's not real. There's no blue. There's no light. It's just a trick your mind is playing on you." *Because that is what I must believe. Please believe it too.*

She gives me a knowing look.

"There's nothing up there," I tell her, trying to keep my voice level. "There's nothing there. You know this. You're better than this. You're smarter than this."

"Apparently the smarter of the two," she retorts.

I sigh. "Nina—"

"Benji, it's here, no matter what you do. Open your eyes."

"My eyes have been open for years now," I say bitterly, not expecting her to understand. "They're open. You can take my word on that."

She suddenly rushes forward and throws her arms around my shoulders and buries her sweet face in my neck. She starts to cry quietly and I hold her while she lets it out.

After a time, she looks up at me with bright eyes and a watery smile. "Oh, Benji," she says. "I'm sorry you feel so lonely. I didn't know. I didn't know it was that bad."

A tremor threatens to rise through me, but I push it away. I kiss her forehead instead. "How can I be lonely when I have you?" I ask her.

Nina laughs as she pulls away, wiping her eyes. "It's my bedtime," she tells me suddenly and turns back toward Big House. I watch her reach the porch and am about to head back to the truck when she calls out my name.

"It won't be much longer," she says. "Pretty soon, I think you'll see."

Chills flash down my spine. "What's soon, Nina? What will I see?"

She smiles and it's kind. She thinks for a moment, as if trying to carefully decide what to say. Finally, she decides on a single word and says it aloud before she turns back and opens the door to Big House, then closes it behind her, leaving me in the dark, the sounds of crickets and the wind through the pine needles fading, as the one word echoes back to me, the only thing I hear.

Everything.

LITTLE HOUSE is empty. Nina spooked me more than I care to admit, and I go room to room, turning on the lights, checking under beds, in cabinets. Closets. Drawers. Nothing. There's nothing here. No one. Little House is empty.

And at the same time, it's not.

I can't help but feel someone behind me everywhere I turn, like I'm being followed. I catch myself in the mirror, my skin white, my eyes blown out, black overtaking green. I look detached. I look like I haven't slept in days. Weeks. I look insane. I look unreal.

"It's empty," I mutter to myself. "This whole place is empty."

I'm lying to myself.

Without letting myself think about why, I leave the hallway light on and my bedroom door cracked, so a little sliver of light lands on my bed. I'm exhausted. My head hits the pillow and I think I'll drop off immediately. I'm ready for today to be over.

Twenty minutes later, I'm still awake.

Blue. There is so much blue.

You're drowning.

Into this river—

You are my son.

Cause of death: asphyxia due to suffocation caused by water—

It isn't true! He can't be dead! He's not gone, you bas—

Do you know who I am?

You're my dad—

I sigh and roll on my side, trying to shut my brain off.

I open my eyes.

A river runs next to my bed.

As soon as I see it, the roar of it hits me, assaulting my senses. Water crashes against rocks, rapids carrying chunks of debris onward. Mist hits my face. I lift the blanket from my body and put my feet on the ground. Grass beneath my toes. Stones. Dirt. Mud.

I stand.

Little House collapses around me with a groan and suddenly it's an early gray summer morning, weak light shining through the thickening clouds. Rain starts to fall, and fat drops splash on my shoulders and head. *Dream*, I think as I stick out my tongue, catching a raindrop, clean and fresh, free of grit. *This is a dream.* I turn on the riverbank. My bed is gone. The embankment stretches up behind me at a steep incline, and at the top, just over the rise, a rectangular green sign peeks out. A mile marker. I can see the tops of two numbers, two horizontal lines. Seventy-seven.

"Benji," a voice says quietly, deep and rough. It should startle me, but it doesn't. I feel warm. Alive. The voice makes me feel alive. More than I've felt in years.

I turn and there's a flash of blue, and a great noise, like the flutter of something huge. I look up, rain falling into my eyes. A single feather, a foot in length, falls toward me. I raise my hand out in front of me, palm skyward. The feather lands on my hand, brushing against my fingers. It's a deep navy blue that causes my bones to ache. It feels like the softest silk against my fingertips. I lift the feather to my nose and inhale. It smells like the rain around me, wet and wild. Full earth. Pungent. Strong.

"Benji," a different voice says, and the warmth I'm feeling vanishes. This voice is dark and wet. My name is gargled on its tongue. I clutch the feather in my hand as I look up.

"Benji," the river says again.

I take a step toward it, the feather hardening in my hand.

Then, above the rushing water, above the rain, above the voices calling out my name, comes a different noise. It is low, guttural. An engine roars. I hear brakes squealing, the crash of metal against metal. I spin around, my feet sliding on mud and grass. There's another crash, this sound greater than anything around me.

A red truck sails over the embankment, rolling to the left in midair, its engine racing. It lands seven feet from me on its left tires, before it crashes down onto all four. But the momentum is too great for it to stop and it bounces toward the river. A great boulder rests on the river's edge. The truck starts to veer right, as if trying to avoid the impact, but it catches the left front tire. There's a loud crack as the axle breaks apart. The truck flips and lands in the river, water splashing high over the banks. The tires continue to spin seconds later, until they slow to a stop, the truck on its back and nose down in the water, the tail end sticking up at a sharp angle against the gray sky, the brake lights at odds with the fading light.

The feather is burning in my hand.

Without thinking, I run toward the river's edge. The water is fiercely cold when I jump from the bank, knee deep. The second my feet hit the soft riverbed, mud rises up around my ankles and begins to pull me down. I fight it, wrenching my left leg up, feeling pain as the muscles in my legs shriek from the strain. My right leg follows. But every time I bring my foot down again, the mud wraps around me.

"Dad!" I shout through the rain.

The engine floods and cuts out. The truck shifts within the current and scrapes against rock. The sound causes my jaw to clench, my ears to ring. I stumble when my foot becomes stuck, splashing my face down into the water, the cold a numbing thing, immediately forcing its way down my throat. I scrabble into the riverbed with my left hand, but it too becomes entrenched in mud. I gag and start to choke. I force my eyes open, blinking away the sting, but I can't see, the water is moving too swiftly. The more I fight, the more tired I get. Lights begin to flash behind my eyes as the water enters my lungs.

My right hand floats up near my face. The feather is still there, clutched tightly. The silky blue flutters slowly. It brushes my face. *Oh, please*, I think. *I'm drowning. Oh, please. Help me.*

A big hand clamps down on my shoulder, the grip tight and biting, and all I can see is *blue* and all I think is *blue* and all I can hear is *blue*. My head breaches the surface, water spraying in all directions. I vomit a thick stream of river and begin to gasp for air. I open my eyes and the sky around me is *filled* with feathers, all dark, all blue, all raining down from the sky.

The hand slips from my shoulder and wraps around my chest, pulling me back until I'm pressed against something large and warm. I look down at the arm around me, thick and strong, a fine layer of auburn hair running up to the back of the gigantic hand. I'm lifted up with this one arm, pulled up the body behind me, through a shower of blue feathers that continues to fall. I struggle, but the strength around me is too great, and I catch a last glimpse of the truck upside down in the river before my vision is blocked by a moving wall of dark blue from either side of me that carries a rustling that sounds like wind over bones. I'm wrapped into this cocoon and I breathe it in. *Earth*, I think.

"You shouldn't be here," a voice says in my ear, the arm around me clenching tighter. "This is not a place for you. You are not ready to cross. You will drown. I cannot allow that to happen." As he speaks, his lips scrape against my neck and I shiver, droplets of water falling from my hair.

"But—"

The two sides of the cocoon flash open in front of me, and even as I recognize them for what they are, there is a bright flash of blue and I am flung upward, toward the gray clouds above me, the sky bending inward, to a point, as if being pulled from the other side. I fly up through this apex and feel a flash of extreme vertigo as my world flips upside down and I fall from the ceiling of Little House and land in my bed with a crash, the frame groaning beneath me.

I sit up, gasping, my eyes flashing open, kicking the covers away from me, pushing up against the backboard.

A dream. It was just a dream.

My skin is slick with sweat, not wet with river water.

My legs are not covered in mud.

I did not almost drown.

I did not just witness my father's accident as if it just happened.

I was not pulled from the water and wrapped in a cocoon.

But even though I know this, know *all* of this, even though I am a rational person living in the real world where nothing extraordinary ever happens, even with *all* of this, I am at a loss to explain what is in my right hand.

A large feather, of the deepest blue.

Not a cocoon.

No.

Wings.

the man who fell from the sky

"ARE you coming down with something?" my mother asks me the next morning in the kitchen of Big House as she puts a cup of coffee in front of me. "You look really pale." The Trio stop their chatter and lean in closer to me, trying to determine themselves if I am sick.

"Oh," Mary says, glancing at her twin. "You do look ill."

"Ill," Nina parrots with a giggle. "So deathly ill. Sickly."

"He just needs to take a day off," Christie decides. "How many days have you worked in a row now?"

"Not that many," I grumble. "I'm not sick. I just didn't sleep well last night." *And apparently I was saved by a bird-man that I took a feather from and it became real. So...* that's *a thing too.*

"Thirty-two," my mother says as she rifles through the desk calendar. "You've worked thirty-two straight days. No wonder you're getting sick."

"I'm not sick!"

"You need to take a break," Christie says.

"Take a break and get laid," Mary says as she sips her coffee.

"Totally get laid," Nina agrees.

"Do we know any homosexuals? To help him out?" Christie asks her sisters, much to my horror.

"Like, on TV? Or in real life?" Mary asks.

"Real life," Christie says. "I think we should attempt to start local before trying to go after celebrities. Maybe by the time he's ready, Tom Cruise will have come out."

"He's too old," Mary says with a frown. "Benji needs someone younger. And far more hip."

"I don't know any gays," Nina says sadly. "I must not be very hip."

"You are very hip," Christie reassures her. "And you do too know some gays! You know Benji here. He's obviously a gay. And what about that lovely he-she that used to do your nails back in Seafare? What was his-her name?"

"It depended on what day it was," Mary says. "Sometimes he was Joe Workman. Other times she was Quartina Backhand, the most dangerous woman in captivity."

"What a lovely name that is," Christie says. "She-males are so amazing."

"I don't think Benji wants a lady-man," Nina says.

"You're probably right," Mary says thoughtfully. "He probably wouldn't know what to do with him-her."

I groan and lay my head down on my arms. "Please, just shoot me now."

The Trio laughs.

Mom rubs her hand over the back of my head. "Girls, you're embarrassing him. You know Benji's a bit of a prude."

"A bit?" Mary snorts. "He's the biggest prude we know."

"I am *not* a prude," I snap at them, still hiding my face, knowing I'm blushing.

"How come your neck is turning red?" Nina asks. "Are you hot?"

"What about Carl!" Mary says excitedly. "He's strapping *and* available *and* only one town over."

"We tried that already, remember?" Christie asks. "It turned out he was into some very kinky things."

Understatement. Over dinner, Carl told me that he was into fisting and wanted me to wear his arm and be his puppet.

"A prude," my mother says lovingly. "You are taking the day off today. One of us can take the store today."

I shake my head as I yawn. "I can't. I've got two oil changes and Abe is convinced that there's a rattling sound under the hood of the Honda, even though there never is. Today is busy."

My mom sighs. "Then tomorrow."

"I've got—"

"Benji," all four women scold at once.

I throw my hands up in the air. "Fine. Tomorrow."

Mom grins at me as she takes my cup from my hand and pours the coffee into a travel mug. All four women then stand in a line and I kiss their cheeks, the Trio telling me not to worry, that they will find a homosexual or two, even if they have to think on it all day.

I shake my head as my mom hands me my mug and motions for me to turn around. I do, and she lifts my backpack up and sets it on my back. They treat me like I'm twelve, but I like to think it's more for their benefit than mine. Mom's fussing with the zipper on the back of my bag when alarms start ringing in my head. I'm about to turn when she opens the bag to see what the zipper is caught on.

A feather falls to the floor.

I bend to scoop it up, but Mary beats me to it. "Where in the crap did you find this?" she asks, holding it close to her face.

Christie plucks it from her fingers. "This has got to be the biggest bird *ever*."

My mother grabs it. "Benji, where did this come from?"

I make a move to take it back, but she holds it away from me. "Near Little House," I say defensively. "I just like it, okay? Give it back." I can't tell them the thought of anyone other than me touching the feather makes me want to snarl and lash out. I can't tell them I spent the remainder of last night sitting in a chair in the corner of the room, my knees curled up against my chest, watching the feather as it lay on my bed. I can't tell them where it came from, but somehow I know it is *mine*, that it is for *me*.

"Can I see it?" Nina asks quietly.

My mother looks to me. I shrug, every fiber of my being screaming for me to take it back, that no one else should touch it, but I don't want to be forced to explain these ridiculous feelings, seeing as how I don't understand them myself.

Not so ridiculous, I tell myself. *It's mine. It's* mine *because it came from* my *dre—*

She hands it over to Nina, who moans softly as it touches her fingers. "It's so pretty," she whispers. "And so, so blue." Her eyes flick to mine at this last. I look away. "Did you see him?" she asks me.

I close my eyes.

"See who?" Christie asks, baffled.

"The bird?" Mary asks, confused.

"It must have been huge," my mom said.

I open my eyes. All are watching me. But it's Nina I look at. "No," I say. "I didn't see him."

She nods as if she's received the answer she expected. She watches me for a moment longer before handing the feather back to me. There's a burst of heat as it touches my fingers, and I know she can feel it too when her eyes widen, when a coy smile dawns on her face. "It's *blue*," she says after a moment. "Isn't that right, Benji?"

"Yes, dear," Mary says, smiling at her sister. "The feather is blue. That's very good!"

I shove it in my backpack and turn to walk out the door, unable to take her knowing eyes on me anymore. My mother calls after me, reminding me that I'm taking the day off tomorrow, that she'll open the store. I wave without looking and then am out the door into the cool morning air.

"THIS whole area used to be gold!" Abraham Dufree tells me a few hours later, standing above me while I lean under the hood of his '89 Honda Civic. "That's why Roseland was founded, you know!"

I know only because Abe tells me the same thing almost every single week when he brings in his car for a rattling he's sure he hears under the hood, or how his tires seem to be low, or he's sure there's a brake problem because they feel squishy to him. More often than not, there's nothing wrong with the car. "He just needs someone to talk to," my father had told me once. "After Estelle died, he got lonely. It's what happens when you're with someone for over sixty years, Benji. When that is suddenly gone, you're lost. He just needs help finding his way back." After Big Eddie, Abe still brought his car in and transferred all his stories over to me. I don't know when it happened, but I suddenly found myself with a best friend who was an old man.

"In 1851, right?" I say, tightening the spark plugs that I loosened only moments before to make it look like I was doing something.

"That's right! This place was just empty fields and hills, and then they found gold! Over the next year, over two thousand people made their way up here, thoughts of riches flashing through their eyes, wouldn't you know. O'course, once the railroad moved south, the town pretty much dried up along with the veins buried under the rock."

"But somehow it's still here, right?"

"Oh, sure. There's something special about this place. There's something about Roseland that kept it alive, even when everyone else thought it would die."

"What makes it special?"

He laughs, as he always does at this point. "The people, o'course! I've lived here all my life, Benji. It's always the people. They're the ones that kept it alive. You and I have kept it alive."

"And what was it Estelle always used to say?" I ask him, even though I can tell him verbatim. "What did she used to tell you about the gold?"

He grins and nods, his dentures sturdy and slightly yellowed. "She used to say, 'Abe, there's still gold up in those hills, I can just feel it! I've almost a mind to head on down to the hardware store and pick up a shovel and a pickax and just start hitting rocks to see what I could find!' That's what the missus used to say. Sure as I'm standing before you, that's what she said."

I don't know why, but I choose to deviate from our usual conversation. I'm supposed to tell him that I wouldn't be surprised if his late wife was right on the money, that there were nuggets of gold the size of footballs just waiting to be discovered. Then we'd move on to the weather and how it seems to get hotter and hotter every summer and the season approaching should be a *doozy*. It was March and already in the seventies? Gosh!

But I don't. Somehow I know things are changing, and I can't stop myself. I'm thinking of the feather when I say, "And did she ever?"

The grin slides from Abe's face. He looks confused. "Did she ever what, Benji?"

"Did she ever get a shovel? Did she ever get a pickax? Did she ever head into the hills and split rocks until she found gold?" My hands feel cold, even though it's warm; wet, even though they're dry.

His old face wrinkles further as he frowns. I wonder if I've made a mistake. I wonder if things are supposed to always stay the same. I wonder if it's too late to take it back. Then, in a quiet voice, he says, "No. She didn't. It was just something she always said. She liked to talk big sometimes, you know. I think we all do." He sighs as he looks out the front of the garage, sunlight dancing through the trees. The shadows sway along the ground. "But that was her talking, the old girl. Something she said when she was dreaming out loud. Do you ever dream out loud, Benji?"

Now *he's* changing the script. I'm immediately on the defensive, attempting to resist the blinding, fiery urge to run into the shop, to check my backpack to make sure the feather is where I left it. *It's probably gone*, I think. *It's probably gone because it was never there to begin with. It was just a dream. It was only real to me because I dreamed it out loud. I dreamed it real.*

I stand up and close the hood of the Honda gently, pressing down until it latches. I grab an old rag off the workbench and wipe a smear of grease off my left hand. Some of the black is caught under my thumbnail.

And still he waits. He pulls out a pocketknife and starts twirling it deftly through his fingers. It's an old thing, scuffed and tarnished. Estelle had given it to him on their first wedding anniversary he told me once, reverence in his voice. They didn't have a lot of money, he said, but she knew they would only ever have one first anniversary. So she had taken some of her savings from her little jar on top of their old green fridge and marched out one pretty fall morning and had come back with the beautiful knife. Engraved in gold on the side were the words *I love you, my husband. Forever, Este.*

My heart is a little sore at the thought, but I can't ignore his question. Not now.

Do you ever dream out loud?

"Sometimes," I say. *All the time*, I really want to say.

Abe nods. "I thought you might. You and I are the same, you know."

"How do you figure?" I ask, even though I already know the answer.

"We've lost," he says simply, but what I hear in those two words is *my half is gone, my everything is gone, and Big Eddie... wasn't he almost the same to you? Wasn't he just almost the same? There's a hole, isn't there? Some hole in your chest or at the pit of your stomach that is not filled, that won't ever be filled.*

A bell dings overhead. Someone at the gas pump.

Abe glances out the windows. He narrows his eyes. "This can't be good," he mutters.

"What is it?" I follow his gaze out the window. A nondescript black sedan is sitting next to the gas pump, its engine ticking loudly as it cools. There's no movement that I can see, but the tinted windows are just dark enough to block any views to the inside.

"Government," Abe says.

I laugh. "What? Abe, you've watched too many movies. Let me go take care of them and we can finish up here. They're probably just lost."

"Not like us," he says as I walk out the front of the garage.

The driver's door opens and a man climbs out of the car, maybe in his late thirties, early forties. The sleeves of his dress shirt are rolled up to his elbows, his tie loosened around his neck. His black hair is short, his eyes hidden behind mirror shades.

"Help you?" I ask.

"You the owner?" he asks, his voice higher pitched than I would have thought.

"Yes, sir."

He sizes me up and down and glances up at the sign spinning overhead, and I wait for it to come, as it does with all outsiders. "Big Eddie, huh?" he says, sounding amused.

I shrug. "My father."

"Is he around?"

Sometimes I think so. "He's dead."

"My condolences."

"Sure. Thanks. Did you need gas or…."

"When did he die?"

"I'm sorry?"

"When did he die?"

I pause. It seems outside has gotten brighter and I squint. "Who are you again?"

A thin smile reaches his lips before he reaches back down into the car and then stands back up, closing the car door. He walks toward me until only a few feet separate us. He raises a badge. Joshua Corwin, it says. FBI.

You win that one, Abe.

"Your name?" Agent Corwin asks.

"Benji. Benjamin Green."

"How'd your dad die, Benji?"

My throat is dry. "Car accident?"

He hears the inflection in my voice. "Are you asking me or telling me?"

"Car accident."

"Oh? When?"

"Five years ago. Five years this May." A little over a month away.

"That right?"

I'm uncomfortable, unable to see his eyes. "Why?"

He ignores this. "Sheriff Griggs still around, huh?"

"Sure." It comes out bitter.

"Not friends, I take it?"

"Long story."

"It usually is. Was your dad a good man, Benji?"

A short bark of laughter is out before I can stop it.

An eyebrow arches above the sunglasses. "Something funny?"

"If you knew him," I say, my voice growing hard, "you wouldn't have asked that question. He was a good man."

"Oh? He would have done the right thing, you think?"

"Always."

He nods.

"Look, did you need something? I've got a customer waiting on me, so...."

"Old-timer? Yeah, he hasn't stopped staring at me since I got here." Agent Corwin waves at Abe, who is still standing at the window. Abe doesn't wave back. "Nice guy," Corwin says.

I wait.

Finally, "What's the word on the wind, Benji?"

"I don't know what you mean."

He cocks his head at me. "This is a small town, right? Doesn't everyone know everyone else's business here? Rumors usually spread like wildfire."

"Maybe," I say slowly. "But I've never been one to care about that sort of thing."

He reaches back behind him, and I think for a moment he's going to go for a gun, or handcuffs, and I think that maybe I've done something wrong, that I shouldn't have looked into things like I did. I want to tell him I've left it alone for a while now, even though it is still there in the back of my head, white noise that won't ever disappear.

He hands me a business card instead. The FBI seal. His name. His phone number is listed, and for a moment, I zero in on the last two digits: seventy-seven. "You call me you ever start to care about that sort of thing," he says. He's mocking me, but he doesn't know that I know.

"Sure," I say.

He asks me to fill up the car and I do. He pays me and leaves without another word. I return to the garage.

"What'd he want?" Abe asks me, sounding worried.

"I don't know," I say honestly, showing him the card. "Just asked about Dad and... I don't know."

Abe shakes his head. "Big Eddie?" he asked, his eyes wide. "Why'd he want to know about *him*?"

"Just... he asked me if I thought Dad was a good man."

Abe snorts. "Good man. Big Eddie was the *greatest* man. Don't you dare believe otherwise. I loved that man as if he were my own. Blast it all, he *was* my own. And the only thing you need to concern yourself with is to keep doing what you're doing. He'd be proud of you, Benji. I just know it."

I nod, unable to speak.

His eyes soften. "We're the same, you and I," he says again.

We are. I really think we are.

I assure him I'm okay.

I can tell he doesn't believe me.

THROUGHOUT the afternoon, a spring thunderstorm etches its way across the Cascades. It looked like the mountains would hold the storm off from dropping down into the valley, lightning flashing near the peaks, but as I start to close up the shop for the night, the air smells of rain and ozone. Ripples of thunder peal through the air, crashing and causing the ground to vibrate underneath my feet. There's no rain, and the air is heavy with static.

My father was a great man.

It's this I think as I sit at a stop sign. The wind is picking up around me, and the thunder has begun to sound angry. Arcs of electricity travel along the surface of the clouds, light up the world in purples and white. And blues. So many shades of blue.

My father was a great man.

Straight ahead is the way home. To turn left is to head toward Lost Hill Memorial.

To turn right? To turn right is to go to the highway. To mile marker seventy-seven.

I told myself I wasn't going to go there anymore, that there was nothing left at the river for me to see. There was no longer any trace that a man had ever died at seventy-seven. Someone (I don't know who) had put up a small white cross on the river's bank shortly after the accident. I saw it for the first time four days after the funeral. It confused me. *BIG EDDIE* had been written in a childish scrawl across the horizontal bar. I knew what had happened there. I knew now where my father lay. I was certain that having *two* memorials would trap him, that he'd be stuck between the two, forced to return to the river over and over again, unable to leave.

I tore the cross from the earth. I broke it in half, then in half again. I threw the pieces into the river.

No one ever put up a cross again.

But they could have, I think now, irrationally. *These are strange days and strange nights. There are feathers and blues. Dreams and storms. There are things Nina sees that aren't really there. The script has been broken with Abe. The FBI wants to know if my father was a good man, and I think Little House is haunted. I think I'm haunted and it's not real. It can't be real. I am drowning in this river and I don't know how to stop. I haven't been to seventy-seven in days. Weeks. Someone could have put a cross back up again.*

It's no question, of course. I turn right.

IT ONLY takes ten minutes before I am at mile marker seventy-seven. I pull up in front of the sign and turn off the truck, the flares of lightning above illuminating the white numbers. They reflect back at me with each pulse from above and it's like they're calling me. Beckoning.

Just gonna make sure there's no cross, I tell myself. Once I see there's no cross, I can go home. I can go home and forget about all of this. I need to move on. After tonight, it's time for me to move on. Just gotta check one last time. Make sure there's nothing there.

I hesitate with my hand on the door handle. Before I can stop myself, I reach into my bag and grab the feather, then open the door out into the storm.

The wind is howling in my ears, almost drowning out the roar from the river below. Another arc of electricity shoots overhead, and I count to two before another crack of thunder blasts the world around me. *Just gotta see,* I tell myself. *I'll be quick.*

I slide down the embankment, careful not to fall on my ass and roll down the hill. I reach the bottom as another gust of wind blows against me, almost knocking me back. The feather begins to slide from my fingers. I grip it tighter. It pokes into my flesh, giving me a small cut. I ignore it.

I am at the river's edge. There is no cross. There is nothing here.

I breathe a sigh of relief.

Lightning flash.

There's a truck in the water. Upside down. Back end sticking up, at an angle.

Another flash and it's gone.

Another flash and the cry of an engine roaring down the embankment.

Lightning above and there's nothing behind me.

I close my eyes.

I open them and there are thousands of crosses on the river's edge, all white and glaring and blazing. *Big Eddie!* they shout. *Big motherfucking Eddie!*

I close my eyes. I open my eyes.

The crosses are gone, but the world around me is filled with feathers, billions of them falling from the sky.

A hand on my shoulder. A breath against my neck. A flash of blue.

I fall to my knees and cover my ears, the feather in my hand stabbing my skin. *I can't do this anymore,* I think, my own voice almost lost in the storm. *I can't do this anymore. I can't face this on my own. I am* drowning *in this river and I am* haunted *in this house my father built and my mind is breaking. It is* shattering. *I am broken and alone and afraid. Please. Please. Help me. Help me. Oh. Oh, someone please help me. I can't do this on my own. Not anymore.*

Please.

There is a final crash of thunder and then silence.

I open my eyes.

The river flows in front of me, the surface covered in feathers.

The ground around me is covered in feathers.

A sharp pain pierces my head and I cry out, my eyes burning. I lower my head to the ground as my skull threatens to explode. Feathers press against my face. They smell of earth.

And just as suddenly as it appeared, the pain is gone.

I open my eyes.

The feathers are gone.

There are no crosses. There is no truck.

The river moves forward.

And from above comes a blinding flash of light.

BIG EDDIE and I sat on the porch of Little House, a few days after it had been completed. He handed me a beer with strict instructions never to tell Mom as she'd kick his ass. I promised I wouldn't. He knocked his can against mine and we both took long drinks and sighed. We sat side by side in a couple of lawn chairs. Every now and then, I'd feel his arm against mine.

We were quiet, each lost in our own thoughts. It got like that every now and then, when no words were necessary, more a hindrance than a help. Mom said she'd never known any other people who could just be content to sit next to each other and not say a word. It would drive her nuts, she said, all that quiet.

But there were times when important questions needed to be asked. And when they needed to be asked, we asked them.

He asked, "Benji? Do you believe in the impossible?"

I thought for a moment. "I believe impossible things can happen, though we may not always get to see them."

He turned my words over in his mind. Then my father said, "I thought this house would be impossible to finish. On the day we started, I thought it would never get done." He paused. "I thought the life I have now would not have been possible. Your mom. You. None of this seemed like it could be real. Like it could be mine. It seemed impossible."

I looked at him funny. "But we're real," I told him. "We're yours. Right? Me and Mom?"

He looked out across the yard, up toward Big House, a king surveying his domain. He must have liked what he saw, because the sigh he gave sounded of peace. "Yes," he said quietly. "You are. Impossibly. Improbably. You are."

DO YOU believe in the impossible? my father's voice whispers in my head.

I do. I do believe in the impossible.

I believe because high above the treetops, high above the mountains, the clouds have parted and a brilliant blue light is falling toward the earth. The sounds of the world around me are gone. I cannot hear the wind blowing through the trees, causing them to creak as they bend and sway. I cannot hear the sound of the river flowing in front of me, even though I'm only feet away. I cannot even hear my strangled breath, though my chest surely heaves. The world has gone mute, bowing to the blue fire in the sky.

The light moves like a comet, and the trail it leaves behind is almost as bright as the light itself, leaving an incandescent streak that seems to divide the clouds and the stars left above. There is a low *hmmmmmmm* that floats through the air, as if it's vibrating as it falls. The light begins to reflect off the river as it gets closer, the waves throw off flashes of blue and white.

Oh sweet God, I think wildly. *What... what?*

Impossible. Improbable.

As the falling light gets closer to the earth, the *hmmmmmm* gets louder and the ground beneath my feet begins to vibrate, the river rocks near the edge clacking together, bouncing off of one another. The vibration worsens and my teeth start to chatter together. The light becomes too bright to look at, and I lower my gaze in fear that I will be blinded. The river rocks rattle violently before they rise into the air, floating four feet above the ground. Thousands of them, as far up and down the river as I can see. There's a crack across the river as massive pine and maple trees groan against the earth, pulled up, their roots snapping underground.

Coming from the previous silence, this destruction is ear-shattering, massive. The world begins to roar around me and I can do nothing but watch. The boulder that my father's truck had struck, causing him to flip, begins to split, the divide running down the side like a fault line. It breaks in half and both sides rise into the air.

The light is brighter now, and I hazard a glance, terrified, but unable to look away. For the split second I allow myself to look at it again, my mind registers the light for what it is—fire. Blue fire tinged with arcing lightning, snapping and sizzling. The *hmmmmmmmmm* has become *HMMMMMMMM.* My teeth vibrate in their sockets, my bones quake in muscle. The noise crawls along my skin, hairs stand on end, my spine straightening as if electrified. I cry out as I squeeze my eyes shut. I don't know how much more I can *take*, I don't know how much more I can *stand*, because I'm about to be blown apart and I'm sure all that'll remain of me, my only mark on this earth, will be a fine red mist that falls into the river.

It gets worse before it gets better, a cacophony where all my cells and the *membranes* of those cells are pulsing and screaming and boiling. My flesh is alive as it crawls, and behind the blackness of my eyelids, the blue light penetrates and explodes, at its brightest now, fireworks blasting in the dark.

I hear the light smash into the ground and feel the earth roll underneath me harshly as if absorbing the blow. A second later, I'm pummeled by a hot blast of air that knocks me off my feet, end over end. I cry out as something scrapes up my back, and then there's another bright flare in the dark. I land sitting upright, my back pressed against the embankment.

Open your eyes, I tell myself, panting.

No.

Open your eyes!

No! Just my luck, that was a fucking nuclear bomb and there's a mushroom cloud forming right in front of me and I'll—

OPEN YOUR EYES!

I open my eyes.

Trees have been uprooted and lay on their sides, their needles and leaves smoking, but not burning. The ground is littered with stones. The river is covered in debris, ever flowing. And across the river, a pillar of smoke is rising just inside a clearing beyond a hill. My shirt is singed. In my right hand, impossibly—

improbably

—is the blue feather. *My* blue feather. From a dream so far away from now.

A meteor? Was it a meteor? That's all it was.

But a sense of urgency befalls me. I want to see it, whatever it is. I want to find out what causes the sky to light up blue and fall to the earth. I want to find it first. Others will have seen it. Others will have heard it. Others will come. I don't know why, but I know I need to see it first.

The nearest bridge is ten minutes away. I won't make it in time. People are probably already piling into their cars and trucks, wanting to collect themselves a piece of space rock for their very own. *Did you see that?* they are asking each other excitedly. *Did you* feel *that? Load up, boys! Let's go see what the* fuck *that was!* More and more of them will come and whatever it is that fell will be for everyone and not for me. I don't know why I think it's important for me to find it first but—

oh someone please help me i can't do this on my own

—I can't shake the feeling that I must get there. I must get there now.

No time to cross the bridge.

The river. The river is shallow here. Unless you're trapped.

I can do this. I can do this.

I strip down to my boxers, fold the clothes, and hold them under my arm, the feather safely tucked inside. I leave my shoes on the bank. The night air should be cool, but there's heat radiating from across the river. The water is cold, freezing really, still carrying a melted winter down from the mountain. My nipples pebble and my teeth chatter. The water is up to my knees. I pause as a thick tree branch floats by. Heat pulses against my face. The rocks are slippery against my feet. Another step. The water rises to my groin, and the cold against my testicles is mind-numbing, wiping out all thought in a wave of ice and pain. I gasp… but take another step. And then another. And then another. The water is up to my chest. Another piece of tree floats by, a long thin branch reaching out and scratching my right cheek before I can turn away. It stings.

Another step. Mid-chest, halfway, and through the cold, through the thought of pushing toward a light that fell from the sky, and although I have so many memories to choose from in my twenty-one years of life, only one thought occurs here, midway through the river.

I'm standing where my father died.

Pain threatens to rise, and I'm so cold that I almost let it. There's still heat against my face, but it's nothing compared to the cold of the river. I think… I think about dropping my clothes and letting them drift away. I think about lowering my arms. I think about submerging myself in the water, the river closing up and over my head. I think about opening my eyes under the water, opening my mouth and lungs underwater. I think about lifting my feet and letting the current sweep me away. I am here now. I am here, having chosen to walk into this river, and I could drown. I could so easily drown. It would be simple, really. It would just take a moment. And then it would be over.

Another step. I take another step and then another and another until I'm pushing through the river as fast as I can, the water spraying up all around me. The current is swift against my legs, trying to pull me back, telling me to stop running, to just *stop*, but then it lowers from my chest, to my stomach. From my crotch to my ankles. And then I'm on the other side, shivering, the warmth of the fallen light like a blanket. I take a shuddering breath. The knot in my chest releases.

I dress quickly and shove the feather into the waist of my jeans. There can't be much time left.

Whatever it is, it has to be big. As I jog up the hill to look down into the clearing, I can see the trees that have been uprooted from the impact, having collapsed in an outward circular pattern as if blown out. My breath quickens. My heart races. I reach the crest of the hill. I close my eyes. The air smells of dusty earth. It's overwhelming and it invades my senses, but all I want to do is inhale the scent until I'm intoxicated from it, till I'm high off of it. Another shudder rips through me. My head is pounding. I feel inside out. Sweat drips down my face. I open my eyes and look down.

The earth is scorched and smoldering, smoke rising out of a small crater in the center of the clearing. Black char radiates outward through the clearing, long streaks of black against the green and brown of the forest floor. Flecks of orange and red flash but don't ignite. Toward the center of the crater, the scorch marks change, become less random, more defined. The lines across the crater are angled. Each line looks to serve a purpose, like it has meaning, a distinct reason for being. I view each line, moving my eyes faster, only to realize I'm looking at it too small. I'm focusing too closely. My gaze widens. And now I see the full picture.

Stretched out from the center of the crater, charred into the earth, are the imprints of wings, great wings that appear to be fifteen feet in length each. The tips are jagged and sharp, the width greatest at the end, spilling out from the crater, black lines slashed into green. I look down the length of them, toward the center of the crater.

And there lies a man.

Not. Fucking. Possible.

I almost fall down the hill, I'm leaning so far over. I catch myself before I roll head over heels to the bottom of the steep incline. I can't process what I'm seeing as it's so far fucking *beyond* the realm of possibility, so far fucking *past* the *idea* of probability, that my mind can't fathom it. Without thinking about why, I reach back and pull the blue feather from my jeans and clutch it in my hand. It feels hot. It feels like it's shaking, but that might just be me.

Do you believe in the impossible? my father's voice whispers in my head again.

I don't. I don't believe in the impossible. It's not real. A man did not just fall from the fucking sky and land in the middle of the forest in Roseland, Oregon. I did not just see this. This did not happen. And even if it *did* happen, there is a fucking logical explanation for this. The FBI agent. The government. Of *course*! They're testing some weapon. Some kind of flying weapon thing and it just crashed and that is all. The pilot is probably hurt and needs my help.

That's it, I tell myself. *Also, ignore the feather in your hand that came from a dream. Plausible deniability.*

I stumble down the hill, half running, half sliding on the grass. I reach the bottom and stutter to a stop, unsure what to do. That wild, earthy smell assaults me and I'm horrified as it makes me hard, going straight to my dick. And it *is* an assault, because I can't stop it, and I don't want it. So much is crashing through my head that I can't focus, I can't make sense of anything, and that smell is making it worse. I stop myself from opening my mouth and sucking in as much air as possible.

I walk to the edge of the crater. Even this close, I can still make out the shapes burned into the ground, and it shorts my mind again. But this close I'm able to see the man. My gaze falls upon him and I am lost.

Fiery red hair, cut close to the scalp, almost buzzed short. Eyes closed, dark lashes against pale skin. His nose is flat and angled, like it was broken at some point and not set correctly. There is a smattering of faint freckles across the bridge, dotting to the cheeks. Lips slightly parted. Dark stubble covering his cheeks and chin, above his mouth, like rust. Neck exposed, pale skin that is almost like milk.

Clothes? There's… *something*. A vest? A cape? Sleeveless, strong arms spread on the ground. A bronze band strapped around the left arm near the shoulder. Clear definitions of ropey muscle under deep red hair that grows thicker toward his forearms and then thins on the back of his hands. Hands that are twice the size of my own. His legs are exposed mid-thigh down, covered with red hair that looks like fire covering muscle. Feet as large as his hands.

Who is this? *What* is this?

A groan comes from the red mouth, low and rough.

I scramble back as quickly as I can, suddenly sure that I don't want him to see me, sure if he does, I'm dead. My mind is screaming at me to run, to run so very fast. Why the *hell* did I think it was a good idea to follow something that had fallen out of the sky? I turn and plan to do just that, to run until I'm back up that hill and down the other side, until I'm at the river that I'll cross so fast it'll seem like I'm walking on water. I'll get in my truck and get the fuck out of here and go back to Little House and pretend none of this has happened, that this is all some fever dream that I'll eventually forget as I get back to my perfectly quiet and mundane existence. It doesn't matter that I'm clutching a feather in my hand that came from a nightmare, squeezing it so that the bristles poke against my flesh. It doesn't matter that I'm haunted by something I don't believe in. It doesn't matter that I'm drowning in this river. None of this can be real.

Another groan comes from the man (*Man?* I think desperately. *Man?*). Even though I've convinced myself to run as fast as I can, I hesitate at the low moan, my feet seeming to stick to the ground. *Run!* I shriek at myself. *Run, you son of a bitch!* But I don't. I slow as I approach a tree that has been partially uprooted on the edge of the clearing. It's tilted at a precarious angle, its thick trunk looking as if it would only take a gentle push to send it the rest of the way down. It's this tree I stand behind, pressing my back up against the rough bark, hearing the high-pitched whistling sound coming from my mouth. My skin, still damp from the river crossing, feels like it's crawling with electricity. *This can't be happening*, I tell myself. *This isn't happening. I'm dreaming. I've fallen asleep at the store and I just need to wake up.* I hit the back of my head against the tree. A dull pain. It's not enough. *Wake up.* I hit my head again, harder. *Wake up.* Again, the pain bright. *Wake up!*

I'm still in the clearing.

Then there's movement, from behind me.

I follow the angle of the tree toward the ground until I come to the partially exposed roots. I crouch down and peer through the maze of dirt and roots, seeking protection. The shallow crater is visible, and as I watch, the man sits up. Incredibly, the black lines that had been burnt into the ground around him also rise from the ground, as if they're attached to him. Flecks of scorched earth fall to the ground, like it's snowing ashes. They look like burnt bones, remains of something that should be glorious instead of ominous. A feeling of dread rolls through me and my teeth begin to chatter. Sure he can hear them even from the distance that separates us, I grab my jaw to hold my mouth still, ignoring the way my hand shakes. My grip bites into my skin and I know I'll be bruised there tomorrow, but the pain pushes through the fog that had descended ever since I decided to come to mile marker seventy-seven. It's like a light has pierced through the shadows and covered me completely, to the point that it's like I'm blazing.

He grunts as he pushes himself up from the ground, looking massive and terrifying. The burnt black rises with him, cascading down his shoulders, fluttering and twitching. He's big, far bigger than I first thought. He has at least six inches on me and outweighs me by a good hundred pounds. The vest that had been covering his torso falls to the side, exposing half of his chest. Deep auburn hair covers the skin on his pectorals, and I have a brief moment to wonder what it would feel like to touch him before my heart starts jack-rabbiting as he opens his eyes and looks straight at where I'm hidden.

Sure he's seen me, I freeze, still clamping my hand over my mouth. A tiny whimper escapes me and he narrows his eyes. But then he looks away, over his shoulder, at the black suspended behind him. He reaches up with one gigantic hand and touches the left one (*wing, wing, wing*) and cocks his head. Then, an oddity: he rolls his shoulders as if working out a kink and proceeds to shake his whole upper body like a dog shaking off water. Another sound escapes me, a short bark of hysterical laughter that is immediately silenced when the burnt black behind him breaks off and swirls up behind him like it's caught in a tornado. It spins briefly before exploding outward, then raining down and landing on the forest floor.

He looks toward me again. And begins to walk up the side of the crater.

It would probably be a good idea to run, I think to no avail. My feet still won't move.

He reaches the top of the crater and stands there scanning the clearing before him. He looks skyward and closes his eyes. His lips move and there's a low rumbling sound coming from him, but I can't make out the words. I strain to hear because it suddenly seems important that I know what he is saying, that I should know each of the words pouring out of his mouth. My father's voice whispers in my ear, telling me to *listen*, that I just need to *listen*. I lean forward further and my nose brushes against a paper-thin root strand. It tickles. My nose scrunches up. *No. No! You don't—*

Too late. I sneeze. It sounds as loud as a gunshot.

I look back up. The clearing is empty.

Alarms begin ringing in my head. *Get the fuck outta here!* I scream at myself. *Run and don't look back*! I spin around and stand, looking over my shoulder as I begin to run. One step, two steps, three—

I crash into something amazingly solid, knocking me off my feet and onto my back. My head raps against the ground and there's a bright flash. I groan and reach up to hold the back of my head.

A deep chuckle from above me. I open one eye in a half squint.

The man from the crater stands above me, peering down at me like I'm the most interesting thing he's ever seen. His head is turned slightly to the left, his dark eyes appearing black in the moonlight that is poking through the clouds. He's grinning, showing strong teeth, and for a moment I wonder if he's going to eat me alive. Then he speaks and turns my world upside down.

"Benjamin Edward Green," he says, his voice flowing over me like warm water. He sounds absurdly happy and this causes my stomach to twist in knots. "Twenty-one years of age. Born February 17, 1991 under an amethyst moon at 2:32 in the morning. Parents are Lola Ann Green and Edward Benjamin Green." As he says my father's name, a brief shadow crosses his eyes, but it's gone before I can be sure it's there. I can't be sure any of this is happening. "Grandparents are Gerald and Linda Green and Mark and Sarah Fisette." He stops and watches me.

"Uh." That's all I can say because my mind has begun to fracture a bit. As much as I don't believe it to be so, as much as the last twenty-four hours has been surreal (*Oh, it goes back further than that,* I think, detached), I can't ignore the man standing above me. I can't ignore his voice, that voice that I refuse to believe is familiar, but know to be so. It comes from some far-off place, like it's a dream—

you shouldn't be here

—that I can't be sure I've woken up from. He's still watching me, waiting for some kind of response, but I'm somehow at the river in my dream, still feeling his arm wrapped protectively around my chest, his massive body pressing against my back—

you will drown

—like I need to be saved, like I'm precious and need to be held. My eyes begin to burn because—

i cannot allow that to happen

—part of me doesn't *want* this to be a dream. Some small, secret part of me wants this to be real, to have him standing above me and be *real* because it would mean I am not alone anymore, that even though I'm pretty sure he's going to kill me, I wouldn't be *alone*. My thoughts are suddenly getting muddy, a light haze falling over my vision. *Too much*, I think. *This is all too much.*

He leans over and his grin widens. So many teeth. "Benji," he says, and he sounds so fucking *happy* that I ache down to my bones, causing me to shudder. He reaches out and touches my right hand, a look of wonder on his face, his dark eyes flashing. I follow his gaze and see the feather still in my hand, bent oddly and ruffled, but still there, somehow.

He looks about to speak again, but then he snaps his head up as he rises quickly, staring off to the west toward Roseland as if he's been spooked, like he hears something I cannot. I half expect his ears to twitch and stand up away from his head. He's tense now, his shoulders stiff. I want to ask him what's wrong, but I don't dare. That sharklike grin is gone, replaced by a growing scowl.

"What is it?" I hear myself ask hoarsely as my vision begins to tunnel. "What's wrong?"

"Others," he snaps, his ire evident on his face. "They're coming. I can see their threads. It's time to leave."

"I'm tired," I say quietly, and my voice sounds so far away. "I'm sorry. I don't think I can make it back across." I close my eyes and start to fall.

Before I'm gone completely, I feel strong arms gather me up, clutching me tightly. As I'm swallowed by the dark, I hear a voice that says, "I will take you safely across the river." And it follows me down until I'm gone.

IN THE dark, this is what I hear:

Big Eddie says, "By the time we finish, it'll be so cherry. You just wait and see, Benji. When we're done, she'll purr and gleam, and when the sun hits her just right, your heart will jump in your chest and you'll know what love really is. And it will *shine*."

Nina Fisette says, "There was a time that was *blue*, when the air around me just *blew*. We knew he was *blue*, and knew what to *do*. I see it, all around. What did you *do*? He's blue and what did you *do*?"

A new voice, a strange voice. "Gonna get you across the river and get you away because they're coming and I can't tell who they are. Why can't I tell who they are? Why is nothing working? Oh, Father, can you hear me? I am but your humble servant. Help me protect Benjamin Edward Green. Help me to do what I must to keep him safe."

A woman says, "This is Janet Tadesco with Channel Four Action News. I'm at mile marker seventy-seven on the Old Forest Highway just outside Roseland. As you can see behind me, emergency crews are working to remove a pickup truck that appears to have lost control and flipped into the Umpqua River. We're told the driver and sole occupant was forty-seven-year-old Edward Green from Roseland, who was pronounced dead at the scene. At the moment, it is unclear just how long Green was in the Umpqua and whether or not his death was caused by the impact or if the river played a factor. We'll have more as this story develops."

My father: "Ten years old already, Benji? Pretty soon, you're going to be all grown up and will probably be bigger than I am! You're going to be a big guy and you will take this whole world by storm. Just you wait."

Pastor Thomas Landeros says, "Into the ground we lower a man who was a husband. A father. A friend, both to us and this community. God's plan may not make sense to us right now, and it may even make us angry, but rest assured there is a reason for all things, even if that reason is hidden from our eyes. Isaiah 41:10 reads: 'Fear thou not, for I am with thee; be not dismayed, for I am thy God; I will strengthen thee; Yea I will help thee. I will uphold you with the right hand of my righteousness.'"

A deep voice, a strong voice that is already growing more familiar: "That water was *cold*! Shit. The truck. Oh, I love that truck. Looks like I'm going to have to drive. Unless you want to wake up and take over. That would be great, right about now. I'm not sure how good I'm going to be at driving. I get the idea, but sometimes things are harder than they look."

My mother says, "He's gone, Benji. Oh my God, Big Eddie is *gone*. I don't know how it—oh, *Christ*. This isn't real. This isn't real. My heart—oh, how my heart *hurts*."

Christie Fisette says, "You can sleep now, finally. We're going to stay here as long as you need us. Sometimes it's harder to ask for help the more you need it. So there is no need to ask us. We know what you need. You sleep and let us carry you for a while."

Big Eddie says, "And then I got down on one knee and—Lola, you stop hitting me! Ha ha ha! Benji should hear this! He's old enough now! So, as I was saying, I got down on one knee and I said, 'Lola Fisette, I don't have a ring right now. I don't have a lot of money right now. I actually don't have a lot of *anything* right now aside from my big dick, but if you promise to marry me, I'll take care of you for the rest of your life.' And you know what she said? She looks me straight in the eye and says, 'Your dick ain't *that* big!'"

Sheriff Griggs: "I'm sorry, Lola. There just doesn't appear to be evidence of foul play involved. It looks like Big Eddie just got distracted on his way out of town and lost control. There's just not any indication that he was run off the road, and believe me when I say we looked. I'd not close the book on this matter if I wasn't 100 percent sure. You've known me since we were kids, and Big Eddie knew me longer. We all grew up together, along with your sisters. You know I am a man of my word. I promise you."

Mary Fisette, overheard: "I know he loved you, Lola, but he *worshipped* the ground Benji walked on. There is nothing Big Eddie wouldn't have done for him. But he's not here and you are. And you need to help him. You're losing him, Lola. It's been almost two years since the accident, and Benji is pulling further and further away. You've got to do something before it's too late. He's drowning, honey, and I don't know how much longer he can last. You lost your husband, but he lost his *father*, the only one he will ever have."

That strong voice: "Okay, how hard can it be? You've seen people do this for decades. Just put that key thing into the slot thing and move the stick thing to the 'D' thing. I can do this. I am a driver. I can do this. Bless me, Father. Please."

Big Eddie says, "You are my son, the only one God saw fit to give me."

Big Eddie says, "You must be strong. You must be brave."

Big Eddie says, "Wake up. You gotta wake up, Benji. He's come down from On High because *you* called him and you've got to wake up. He's been waiting, yes, but *you* helped bring him here, down to this place. You've got to help him. He's going to act *big*, he's going to talk *big*, but deep down, you two are the same. You must remember this. You are the same. You grieve. You think yourself alone. He will need you as much as you'll need him. It's almost time for you to stand. It's almost time for you to stand and be true."

I—

Wake up.

Dad, I can't just—

Wake up.

I miss you so damn—

WAKE UP!

I—

—OPEN my eyes. I'm in the cab of the blue Ford, and we're *flying* through the dark, the engine of the truck roaring as the headlights illuminate the road before us. I'm covered in my dad's old coat, my skin still slightly chilled.

I look over at the man who fell from the sky, his big hands wrapped tightly on the steering wheel at ten and two, just like I was taught at sixteen. His eyes are wide, his forehead scrunched up in concentration, his lips pulled back in a grim smile. I gasp and reach for the passenger door, trying to put as much distance between us as I can.

"Uh," I say articulately.

He glances over at me, dark eyes flashing, his smile growing wider. "I'm driving!" he says with an excited rumble. "I didn't think I could get the hang of it, but I'm *driving*." His gaze never leaves my face.

"Watch the road," I whisper.

He ignores me, his eyes still on mine. "Sure as shit, I didn't think I'd get it that fast. I mean, I've *seen* you people drive before, and I thought, how hard could it be? I mean, *you* obviously weren't going to do it, because you decided it was a good time to pass out."

"Slow down," I say.

"I mean, I've seen you drive this old truck before, but you *never* go this fast. You drive like Abe does in that little car of his—"

"*Slow the fuck down!*" I scream at him.

My sudden outburst startles him, and he jerks the wheel to the left and the Ford follows with a groan of metal and rubber, the rear beginning to fishtail and swing to the right. There's a moment when all the weight of the truck seems to be on the passenger side and I think we're going to flip, but then that passes and we're spinning out. The truck comes to a halt in the middle of the two-lane highway, having spun in an almost complete circle before stalling in the road. The only sounds are the ticking of the cooling engine and our panting breaths.

Then, "You've got a loud yell for such a little guy," he says, arching his right eyebrow in appreciation. "I don't think I've ever heard you yell that loud before, Benji. Not even when you were *really* angry."

My brain can't compute this, this intimacy, him speaking as if he knows me. My brain doesn't seem to be computing a whole hell of a lot, now that I think about it. *It's probably because I've completely lost it,* I tell myself. *I've gone completely and utterly batshit insane. It's the only thing that would make any sense.*

"Who. The fuck. Are you?" I ask, ignoring the waver of my voice

He rubs a hand over the rusty stubble on his face. He appears to be trying to choose his words carefully before he speaks, but seems to be having difficulty doing so. This, of course, only makes it worse. People who choose their words can choose to lie. "Calliel," he says finally, averting his eyes from mine. "My name is Calliel and I'm the guardian angel for Roseland and its people. And I'm here because of you. You called me, Benji. You called me and I came. Oh, and I've always wanted to tell you, because it hurt me to see you so. I've always wanted to tell you how sorry I am about your dad. Big Eddie was a great man. He was a great man and I'm sorry."

I wish he'd lied.

corporeal

SO, EITHER he's certifiable, or I am, or we both are.

That's the only thing I can think as I stare at him as he starts up the truck again, the grin back on his face at the purr of the Ford's rebuilt eight-cylinder engine. He straightens out the steering wheel, pulling us back into the right lane. I am astonished when I feel mildly amused on top of everything else kicking around in my head when he keeps the speed below thirty miles an hour, grumbling under his breath that he's doing Abe proud. He keeps glancing at me out of the corner of his eyes, but he's trying to be sneaky about it. It does no good for him to try and hide it as I am still plastered against the far door and facing him, refusing to take my eyes off of him.

Him. Calliel.

I'm the guardian angel of Roseland and its people.

And I'm here because of you....

"How did we get back across the river?" I ask finally, unsure what else to say.

He stops muttering to himself about speed and starts watching me again until I remind him to pay attention to the road. "I'm not going to crash," he says, his brow furrowing. "Have a little faith, huh?"

Faith. That's funny, coming from a man who claims he is an.... Jesus Christ. This is not a real thing. *He* is not a real thing. He's just a man. He's just a normal—

"I carried you across," he says. "You're light and I'm big, so it wasn't that hard."

"How come I'm not wet?"

He snorts. "I carried you above the water."

My eyes bulge out of my head. "You can walk on water?" I whisper.

"What?" He laughs. "Of course not. I waded across and carried you over my head so you wouldn't get wet." He laughs again. "Walk on water. You're funny."

I didn't think it was funny. At all. "Why didn't you just fly over? Angels have wings right? If you were really an angel, you would have just flown over." Logic wins every time.

He shakes his head. "Can't seem to pull them out here. I tried. I stood there on the riverbank for a minute or two, but nothing happened. I don't know if it has to do with me becoming corporeal or what."

"Cor-what?"

He shrugs. "Physical. Real. Here."

"Did anyone see you crossing the river?"

"No. I got you back in the truck in time. There were people coming, though. I could hear them. I came down from On High with a crash, so I'm not surprised. I didn't think it was going to be that loud, you know? Or that bright. We passed a couple of cars before you woke up, but no one tried to stop us. I couldn't tell who they were like I normally could. I couldn't *feel* them. I didn't want to take any chances. I kept you safe, just like I said I would." He says this last in a growl, like he expects me to contradict him. I'm too overwhelmed to even really consider his words.

"Oh." Then, sudden panic, clawing at my throat. "Where is it?" I gasped, rubbing my hands over the seat frantically, my dad's coat falling off me. "Where did you put it? Did you leave it behind? Don't tell me you fucking left it!"

He glances at me, a worried expression on his face. "Where's what?"

"The feather, dammit! Where did you put the feather!"

"Benji," he says quietly, pointing at the seat next to him. "It's here. It's right here."

It is. In the dark, in my panic, I couldn't see it. I snatch it up, sure he's going to try and take it from me. It warms instantly in my hands. I watch him with wary eyes, wondering how I could have possibly gotten to this point.

"You know where that came from, right?" the man named Calliel asks me.

I dreamed it real. "Just found it outside," I mutter, looking away.

"Sure, Benji. Okay." He doesn't push it, but he's not fooled.

Silence, for a time. Then, "You're just fucking with me, right? This is a joke?"

He laughs, a deep thing that sounds like it comes from the pit of his stomach. "No. No joke. I'm not that big of a joke-teller. I hope that's okay. But I sure like driving this truck. This is cherry, right, Benji? This ride is so cherry. Isn't that what Big Eddie used to say?"

I can't speak.

We drive on in the dark, a hand of ice wrapped around my heart.

THE fact that Calliel knows where he is going should surprise me, but with all that has already happened, it seems to be the least of my worries. We pass Poplar Street in silence, where I'd sat at the intersection only ninety minutes before, trying to decide if I was going to go to the seventy-seven or go home. Ninety minutes is all it has taken for my reality to change. We don't speak. I still sit with my back to the door, watching him. The occasional car driving by illuminates his face. Sometimes he's looking ahead, focused on his driving. Other times, he's glancing over at me, his mouth opening like he's going to speak, but then closing like he's thought better of it.

He's been waiting, yes, but you *helped bring him here, down to this place. You've got to help him.*

I've got to do no such thing. The fact that he's now pulling into my driveway means nothing. The fact that the small smile on his face is growing as Big House comes into view means nothing. Do I call the police? Do I wake up my mother and the Trio? What do I tell them? Where do I tell them he came from? He's certifiable, to be sure. Can I even be sure I saw what I remember seeing? The more logical explanation is that it was dark, that there was a huge storm going on over me, thunder and lightning. The light I saw falling from the sky was just some aftereffect of the storm. A freak thing. Maybe ball lightning. This man got struck and now he's crazy. The electricity has done something to his neurons or synapses or whatever they are. And I'm just tired. Sitting beside a stranger who drove directly to my house without needing directions.

"It seems so different seeing it from this side," he sighs, slowing as Big House looms above us. "It seems so real."

"It's always real," I mutter. "Everything about it."

"That's not what you normally think," he says without looking at me.

Fear again. "How do you know what I think?"

Calliel shrugs. "It's just something I did. It was part of my job."

"What am I thinking right now?" *Tell me the truth. Who you really are. No more bullshit. No more crazy. Tell me who you are. Tell me the truth so I know this is just a dream that I can't seem to wake up from.*

He catches my eye again, and for some reason, I can't break away. For a moment, I can imagine him doing just as he said he would. That he's reading my mind and in a moment he'll tell me what I'm thinking. But even worse, he'll be able to tell me the things I'm *not* thinking, the things buried so far down that dragging them into the light will break me in half. I hold my breath as his gaze bores into me. *Who are you?*

The moment shatters as he sighs again and looks away. "Can't do it," he says, sounding frustrated. "Being down here isn't the same as being up there looking down."

I deflate, feeling strangely disappointed. I'm about to tell him that I can give him a few bucks if he's looking to get something to eat since he'll be on his way (I'm hoping), when he slams on the brakes in front of Big House, the headlights illuminating the front steps.

I follow his line of sight. "No," I tell him, already struggling to open the door. "No, you don't even touch her—"

"Nina Fisette," he says happily, watching my aunt waiting patiently on the steps for me to come home. "Born September 14, 1964 at 3:34 in the afternoon under a sapphire sun. Sister Mary Fisette born thirty-four minutes later. Suffers from trisomy 21 caused by the presence of an extra partial twenty-first chromosome. Daughter to Michael and—"

I grab my dad's coat from the floor of the truck and I'm out the door even as Nina rises from her spot on the steps. She looks hesitant as she sees me rushing toward her, but then her gaze flickers over me, back to the truck, and the smile that blossoms on her face causes me to stumble in its beauty. I've never seen her wearing the look she has on her face now, and it's enough to cause the world to shift on its axis again. I stop as she walks past me, not even acknowledging my presence. I reach out to grab her, to stop her from whatever it is that she's about to do, but she pulls away, never looking back. "Nina," I say, but it comes out choked.

The man has gotten out of the Ford, and as she walks toward him, the rational world as I know it disappears like sand through my fingers.

Calliel stands in front of the truck, watching the small woman walk toward him. He's changed. There are flashes of blue whirling around him, sparking off into the darkness. His eyes are alight with something I can't place. Elation? Unbridled joy? Love? I don't know. I've never had anyone look at me the way he's watching her. I can hear a soft exhalation as she reaches him, a sigh of peace. The blue is brighter now, spinning faster. It molds around him, beginning to take shape. It only takes seconds when the lights make a faint outline, clinging to his back and rising up and down around him. The feather in my hand vibrates, heating until it's almost too much to hold on to.

Before I can shout a warning, my aunt reaches up with her little hands that can't quite reach what she's trying to hold onto. Calliel lowers his head and she cups his face in her hands, rubbing her thumbs gently over his cheeks. He closes his eyes, and, remarkably, hums a contented sound that causes the hairs on the back of my neck to stand on end. The blues (Prussian and cobalt and azure and indigo and so many, many more) spin in tighter circles and the shapes behind his shoulders become more pronounced until I can no longer deny the outline of great wings that stretch around him.

The night has gone silent around us, as if we three are the only living things left on the planet. I'm aware of every breath I take, every beat of my heart, every thought that rushes through my head. It's not as if my ears are plugged, no; it's as if I can hear clearly for the first time and I've focused on every single little thing that ever was and ever will be. Bright flashes of light burst behind my eyes, but I can't look away.

"Hello," Nina says, her voice filled with awe.

"Hello, Nina Fisette," the stranger says, turning his face in her hands so it rests against her left palm.

"You came," she says. "I didn't think you would. I didn't think you *could*."

"He called for me," he tells her, never taking his gaze from hers. "He called for me and I would not say no. I made a promise. To him. To you. You know this, little one."

"Promises are made to be broken," she says, her voice breaking. My heart stutters in my chest. "Promises aren't always kept, even if they're meant to be."

"Not mine," he says, reaching up to his face to place his hand on top of hers. "Not to you. Never to him."

"Does he know yet, you think? Does he realize?"

Calliel glances up at me, the blue dancing around him causing his eyes to spark. The feather in my hand grows hotter still, but I can't look away. Much is said in his eyes, but I can't decipher any of it. My breath hitches in my throat and my eyes start to burn, and all I can hear is my father in my head saying, *Wake up. Wake up, Benji.*

He's come down from On High and you need to wake up. Open your eyes and see. Wake up.

"Not yet," Calliel tells my aunt as he watches me. "But he will."

"He'll be difficult," she warns him gently. "He won't know what to do. You know this, yes?"

"I know," he says, looking back down at her, the blues beginning to fade. "I've watched for a very long time. I can see the patterns. The shapes. The design that connects you all."

She chuckles. "And are you in the design? Can you see yourself there?"

He shakes his head. "It's hidden from me. I don't remember much from up there. I remember knowing the call was coming, knowing it would be soon. I just don't…." He squints his eyes shut. "There is much I don't remember. Pieces. Large pieces disconnected because parts are missing. I think I knew this would happen. I think I didn't care. I've been trying to put the pieces back together so the shapes make sense, but it's still too soon. Little one, what if I don't belong here?"

"Then we'll deal with it as it comes," she says, patting his face gently. "But you'll never know unless you try. Your blue is so lovely. So warm and so beautiful. Lonely, but beautiful."

He grins and preens under her hands.

The night is slowly returning, darkness filtering back in. Crickets are chirping. Wind is blowing through the trees. Off in the distance is the high-pitched yip of a coyote. My heartbeat slows. My breath evens out.

When the final blue fades into the night, Nina drops her hands and takes a step back from him. "There is much you can teach each other," she tells him quietly. "But he is trapped too."

He nods. "I know."

"I think I shall call you Blue," she announces, clapping her hands together. "But I still want to know your real name."

"Calliel."

"Calliel," she repeats, tasting the word on her tongue. "Very pretty. And strong. It suits you. Can I still call you Blue?" She sounds like a little girl, shyly asking for what she thinks she'll never get.

He smiles. "You can call me what you like, little one."

She giggles and holds her arms out, spinning in circles, her laughter spilling out in all directions. When she stops, she's facing me. "Hello, Benji," she says. "Didn't I tell you?"

"I don't know," I say hoarsely. "I don't know what's going on."

"Soon," Nina says. "I told you soon you will see. And you will. Soon, we all will." She turns again and stands on her tiptoes, then reaches up and plants a kiss to Calliel's red beard. She spins back around, a gentle blush rising on her cheeks, evident even in the dark. She rushes toward me, a determined look on her face. I open my arms and she collides with me, breathing heavily against my neck. "There is a point to grief," she whispers fiercely. "But there is also a point to opening your eyes and living."

I nod, not knowing what else to say. Disbelief washes over me again.

She lets me go and pushes past me. "Nina, wait. You can't...." I stop.

She looks at me over her shoulder expectantly.

What do I tell her? That everything we've both just seen is a figment of our imaginations? That this man (*Blue*, I think; *Calliel*) isn't what she thinks he is, whatever it is she's thinking? I can't say those words—they would sound false to the both of us. I don't know *what* I'm thinking. I don't know *what* he is.

"Just... don't tell Mom, okay?" I say finally. "Or the rest of the Trio. Not until—"

"Nina? Benji? What's going on out here?"

Oh fuck.

Without thinking, I turn and toss the coat at Cal. He stares at it for a second until I hiss at him to put it on so he doesn't look like he's ready to do battle in a gladiator coliseum. He does, smiling quietly to himself.

My mother opens the screen door to Big House and Mary and Christie pile out behind her. They're looking at us curiously until one by one they see the gigantic man still standing next to the Ford. "Hello," my mother says uncertainly.

Calliel takes a step and starts to smile, and we're only seconds away from, "Greetings, Lola Green, born December 15, 1962 under a corporeal moon and take me to your leader" or some other fucking crazy bullshit.

"Uh," I override him loudly. "This is just... a friend of mine. You know. Just... hanging out. And stuff." He looks at me curiously, and I try to put as much murder in my gaze as I possibly can, but he seems amused, nothing more.

"A *friend*?" Mary says, starting to grin. "Well, he's certainly quite the specimen for a *friend*."

Oh goddammit.

"Yes," Nina says, somehow picking up on the growing awkwardness. "I was just waiting for Benji to come home and he introduced me to his friend and nothing more. Nothing more at all is going on, so no nosy nellies."

"What's his name?" Christie asks.

"Blue," Nina says, as he says, "Calliel," while I say, "Cal."

The three women on the patio stare at us.

I cough. "Calliel Blue," I manage to say. "Everyone calls him Cal."

"They do?" Calliel asks, sounding extraordinarily baffled. "I have not heard this before from—"

"What he means," I say, interrupting him, "is that he has a lot of nicknames and Cal is just one of them. Or Blue. Or... whatever." *Yeah.* That should convince them.

"Really," Mom says, sounding like she doesn't believe a single word that's falling from my mouth. "Hello, Cal. Or Blue. Or Calliel. I'm Lola, Benji's mom. These are my sisters, Christie and Mary. I think you've already met Nina."

He waves jovially at them (and everyone except for Mom starts waving right back), looking at me, begging with his eyes to speak. I shake my head quickly once and, unbelievably, he grunts at me, calling me ridiculous without saying the words.

"Cal Blue?" Mary whispers quite loudly, still waving. "That sounds like a porn name. He looks like he does porn too. Big bad ginger-man porn."

"That's not a porn name," Christie scoffs. "Calliel sounds… Hispanic. Or Greek."

I groan.

"I am not Hispanic," Calliel assures her. "Or Greek." Mary and Christie titter quietly at the sound of his voice, rough and wonderful.

He tries again. "I'm actually—"

"He's actually Californian," I say, as if that explains everything. To Mary and Christie, it seems to suffice; they nod as if that makes perfect sense. My mother is not buying a damn thing. Even worse, she's starting to get that look on her face that means she's going to start asking questions I have no idea how to answer. Making a decision, I walk over to him and take his hand in mine. Even though it can't possibly be real, there's a moment when our fingers connect, that feeling of skin against skin. An even brighter blue bursts across my vision. His palm feels calloused, his fingers soft and dry. My toes curl in my work boots. I look up at him and find him staring down at our intertwined fingers, wonder playing across his face. He raises his gaze to mine and smiles again. Fuck it all.

"Not what you're thinking," I say under my breath. "Don't you say a damn word until I tell you to." He nods, looking back down at our hands. He gives an experimental squeeze and then does it again.

Great. Fantastic.

I take a deep breath and look back to the porch. Mary and Christie watch us, dumbfounded. Nina looks like she wants to tackle us and kiss our faces off. Mom looks like there are at least four hundred more questions she must ask right at this moment. I need to end this now. "Cal's going to be staying with me in Little House for a while." *Uh, what?* He squeezes my hand again, harder. "There's some stuff he and I need to talk about, so… you know. Maybe we can do this whole thing later?" I direct this last at my mom, trying to put enough emphasis on my words that she feels no need to say anything else.

She can see right through my attempts, but small wonder. She nods tightly, pursing her lips. Mary and Christie stand behind her, waggling their eyebrows obscenely, but it's wasted on my apparent new best friend, who is still looking down at our hands, squeezing again and again like he's never held hands with another person.

Maybe on whatever planet he comes from this is frowned upon, I think, trying to avoid going into hysterics.

"We'll talk later," my mom says finally, the tone in her voice letting me know in no uncertain terms that there *will* be a later. I almost want to tell her that I'm fucking twenty-one years old, but realize how that would sound and there's no fucking way that's going to happen. "Remember, you've... you've got the day off tomorrow, so...."

"So make sure you get plenty of *sleep*." Mary giggles, sounding so much like her sister when she laughs.

"Yeah, *sleep* in," Nina says, although I'm not sure she understands what she's saying.

"Ladies," Christie says, "into the house. Let's leave Benji and Gigantor alone so they can do whatever it is two guys do when they are all by themselves in an empty house where no one can hear them scream."

My mom shakes her head and turns and walks back into the house, followed by Christie and Mary. Mary asks her older sister if it looked like Cal was wearing a skirt, and Christie replies that it must be a Californian thing. Nina waits until they're all inside before she looks back at us. "I promise I won't say anything," she whispers hurriedly. "But these things have a way of getting out all on their own. Be careful, Benji. And Blue?"

He looks up from our hands, where he's nearly turned mine into mush. "Yes, little one?"

Her eyes sparkle. "I am so very happy to meet you." She blushes again and runs up into the house, then closes the door behind her, shutting off the porch light and leaving us in darkness.

I stand there, staring after them, trying to collect my thoughts.

"Benji?" he finally says, sounding bemused.

"What?" I say tiredly.

He hesitates. "They seemed nice," he offers.

Oh dear God. I drop his hand and move back toward the truck. "Let's go, Blue or Cal or whatever your name is. We have a shitload to talk about."

"I can't wait to tell you things," he tells me seriously, which causes me to roll my eyes. "Well, what I can remember, anyway."

I reach the Ford, ignoring the tingling in my hand and just how empty it feels.

it came from outer space!

THE ride to Little House is quiet. I don't know what I would say even if I could speak. Two thoughts are running through my head, both of which are cause for panic. First, if I've gone insane, then apparently I've pulled Nina into my delusional psychosis, since she seems to see the same things I do. Beyond that, she apparently has seen it (him?) *longer* than I have (*what did you* do?). She didn't seem to fear the outline of wings that had formed on Calliel as she held him. Although I don't know what there was to fear besides the fact that there *were* the outlines of wings.

The second thought?

The second thought is one I'm trying to push away. The second thought is one that I'd rather not focus on because it doesn't make any sense. I don't even know *why* I'm having this second thought. Out of everything that has happened in the last twenty-four hours, why is this on my mind?

The second thought: the way my hand felt in his. Engulfed. Sheltered.

This is a thought I don't want to have. I *can't* have it. I tell myself it has been the lack of human contact lately. I tell myself it's because really he's not unattractive (though the moment I think this, I am horrified and shove that away). I tell myself it's because it's been a while. I tell myself maybe it's time I take a trip to Eugene. Roseland isn't exactly filled with available men, not that I would be looking if it was. There's too many other things I need to focus on.

And I don't even know if he's gay. Or human.

It's a good thing I just told everyone he's staying with me.

"Little House." He grins, stopping the Ford and then turning it off. He seems to hesitate for a moment but then reaches over, handing me the keys. "You going to let me drive again?" he asks, almost shyly. "I do like driving, I think. Even if you make me drive way too slow. What's the point of having the dial go up to seventy if you can't go that fast? It seems ridiculous."

I take the keys from him. "We'll see," I mutter, unsure why I'm not just saying no flat out, why I'm not telling him to get the hell out of my truck and out of my life. I seem to be unsure about a whole hell of a lot. I'm pressed up against the passenger door again, trying to put as much space between me and him as possible. It doesn't help that I have to clench my fists together to keep from taking his hand in mine again. It doesn't help that in the dark, in my father's jacket, his shape is familiar, almost surreal. *Yeah, I don't have daddy issues at all.* I shake my head.

"What?" he asks me curiously.

"Nothing," I say. I reach for the door handle.

"This would be so much easier if I could still read your mind," I hear him grumble

He follows me up the porch and into Little House. I hang the key on the rack and flip on the light, then hold open the door and wait for him to walk through. He seems to hesitate at the entryway, which of course leads to the most random thought (*you always have to invite them in first*), but then he takes a deep breath and crosses the threshold, his gaze taking in everything, everywhere. His hand goes to the door as he passes it, letting his fingers run across the wood, tracing the bumps and whorls from the cedar my father crafted and shaped. The look on his face is one of such reverence that I have to look away before it has the chance to become something more.

He closes the door behind him, then immediately opens it again, swinging it back and forth before closing it a final time and latching the lock. I start to head down the hallway, assuming he'll follow. But he speaks in a low rumble and I stop, keeping my gaze toward the floor. "I was here when you and Big Eddie broke ground that first day to build this house, you know."

Fear returns, thunderously bright.

"Oh?" I manage to say.

"Yes. That first pick he took to the ground to break up the earth. You sat on a cooler just a little bit away from him." He sighs. "He said you couldn't help just yet because your mother would tan his hide if she saw you with the pickax. He told you not to worry because there'd be plenty of work to do. But you still helped. Every time he stopped to catch his breath, you ran over to bring him some water from the cooler. He'd smile at you and you'd smile back at him and it would start all over again."

I shudder.

Then a hand falls on my shoulder.

A breath near the back of my neck.

I whirl around. For a moment, I'm sure there is a flash of blue, but I only see Calliel standing right in front of me, our bodies almost touching. He's looking at me closely with an intensity I can't quite accept. The hand on my shoulder, the feeling of someone always just out of reach that I've experienced ever since I returned to Little House. That touch I've ignored, passed off as a figment of my imagination. That touch that happens here, and at the station, in my truck, in my room.

Everywhere. It happens everywhere and only when I need it.

I take a step back, unable to keep the distress from my face. Calliel sees it and looks as if he's going to reach up and grab me, to stop me from moving back, but he apparently thinks better of it and drops his hands back down to his sides. I stumble and fall back, hitting the wall and then slumping against it, trying to stay standing. He doesn't move.

"I'm not going to hurt you," he says finally, sounding almost hurt. "Why would I?"

"I don't fucking know what you are," I snarl. "I don't care what Nina says or what she sees or what anyone else sees. I don't know you."

"But I know you," he says simply. He takes a step toward me.

"No," I gasp. "You stay right where you are. I want some goddamn answers. Tell me the fucking truth."

Calliel cocks his head at me and frowns. "I already told you, Benji. I told you almost right away."

"Just tell me the truth," I say weakly.

He closes his eyes and takes a deep breath. With that breath comes a feeling of heat bursting softly throughout the room, the air growing thicker. When he opens his eyes, he seems taller somehow. Bigger. His eyes are almost completely black, the white peeking out around the edges. For a moment, I think I see an outline of wings again, but I blink and they're gone.

He speaks, almost as if in recitation: "I am the Throne Angel Calliel of the second Heaven, in service of God, our Father, descended from On High. I am the Guardian of Roseland and its inhabitants. These are my people, my charges, the ones who have been entrusted to me. I protect them. I carry their fears. I lift up their prayers. I hear their calls and I answer if it is within my power. I do not pass judgment for I am not God. God judges sin and the follies of man, not I. I do not intervene with the plans of God. I do not avenge the plans of God. I am an extension of him and his will, for he is my Father and he is divine." He pauses, almost glowering at me, daring me to refute him.

"Oh," is all I can think of to say.

The charge gathering in the room dissipates as quickly as it arrived, cold sweeping back in.

HE FOLLOWS me as I move down the hall toward my bedroom. He touches everything he sees with that same wonder, as if he's never felt such things and he finds them extraordinary. There are little grunts of pleasure at particular things that seem to tickle him for some reason: the thermostat on the wall that he cranks up to ninety before scowling at the vent that blows down from the ceiling; light switches which he flicks on and off, the light above flashing bright then going dark. I am almost horrified by this, a cold feeling in the pit of my stomach as I mull over asking him if they have light switches and heating ducts where he comes from.

Because, I think as I watch him study himself in a mirror, *he obviously doesn't come from around here. And if he's so fascinated by something as simple as a light switch, chances are he's probably not from around anywhere else, either. I wonder if there is still a chance that this is a dream.*

"Isn't that a sin?" I ask him as he stares at his reflection, obviously pleased by his appearance. He runs his hands over his head, touches the auburn scruff on his face.

"What?" he asks as he pulls his ears out and grins at himself in the mirror.

"Vanity."

He rolls his eyes, which seems unbecoming of someone in his position. "Everything is a sin if you think about it," he says, looking somewhat surprised at his own words. "Nobody is perfect."

"So says the man who claims to be an angel."

He glances over at me. "Perfection is a flaw in itself," he says. "And I don't *claim* to be anything. I *am*." He looks almost insulted. "Nina believes me. Why can't you trust like she does?"

"Nina's… different," I sputter. "She's different from the rest of us."

"You speak of her triplicated chromosome?"

"Sure," I say, suddenly forming a plan. "Why not? Let's speak about that. Why would your God allow that to happen to her? Why would he let her be like that?"

He looks confused. "Like what?"

"Disabled."

"She looked perfectly able to me."

I scowl at him. "You know what I mean. She has a mental handicap. Why would he allow that to happen? Why would God do that to her?"

"Is she not happy?" he asks, leaning against the wall, my father's jacket bunching up as he crosses his arms.

"This isn't about her happiness," I snap at him. "Answer the question."

"I just did," he says. "I asked you if she was happy, and you implied by deflection that she was. If she is happy, who are you to say she's not how God wanted her to be?"

"She doesn't know any better!"

"And how can you? Do you think you know better than she? Than God? That *is* a sin, to presume the will of my Father. For all you know, she's exactly the person she is supposed to be, even if she is different. You of all people should know that, Benji."

Tears sting my eyes. This is too much. All of this is too much. "Don't you dare talk to me like you know me, you bastard." He takes a step toward me, but I shake my head and take a step back. "I don't know who the fuck you are, aside from your creepy-stalker bullshit. I want to go to bed so I can open my eyes tomorrow and see that this was all a dream, because it *is* a dream. I'm going to wake up and I'll still be at the station, or I'll be lying by the river, but you will be gone, because you're just a fucking figment of my imagination. Things like this don't happen. Things like this aren't real. You're not fucking real."

"And yet, I'm here. Because *you* called me," he says, his voice hard. It sounds like an accusation.

"Don't you *dare* put this on me. I don't fucking know you!"

A memory, rising: *Oh, someone please help me. I can't do this on my own. Not anymore.*

"You're lying," he says, dawning comprehension lighting up his eyes. "This is you lying."

"Get the fuck out of my house."

"But—"

"Get the fuck out of my house!" I bellow at him. Without waiting to see what he does, I go into my room and slam the door behind me.

MEMORY.

My earliest memory is from when I was three years old. My father had taken me to the park, affectionately named the Blue Park, given the color of all the equipment. It sat on the edge of the Umpqua about ten miles upriver from where he would drown thirteen years later. I don't remember going there. I don't remember getting out of the car or walking to the park. I don't remember what happened after we left. I can't even be sure what my next real memory is. What I can be sure of is my father sat me on his lap on the merry-go-round, kicking his feet in the sand, causing us to spin slowly. In his other hand, he held a paper cup that was orange and white, containing a vanilla milkshake. He put the straw to my lips as we spun in a lazy circle and I took a deep drink. Cold flooded my mouth and a sharp pain pierced my head, a brain freeze from the ice cream. I cried out. My father whispered soft words that I can no longer remember, then pressed a large hand against the top of my head and rubbed the pain away.

We kept on spinning.

FOR some reason, it's this memory I think about as I lie in my bed, still fully clothed, unable to sleep six hours after I've slammed my bedroom door. Nothing about that day pertains to anything that's happening now, but it's the only thing I can focus on that makes sense. That flash of pain I felt that day has never slipped from my mind and even now I can remember what it felt like, blinding and cold. It let me know I was *alive*, that I was *real*. It tethered me to my father in such a way that only death could break. Maybe not even then.

I don't know why I thought the touch on my shoulder that I knew wasn't there was my father. I don't know why I assumed the breath on the back of my neck that wasn't real was his. I don't know why I hoped it would be, even though I knew it couldn't be real. For someone who spent a lot of time actively denying what he hoped to be true, the disappointment I feel is a surprisingly palpable thing. Some part of me had to have believed that Big Eddie still roamed this house in one way or another.

I've strained to listen for any movement coming from the house, but I hear none. I don't know if Cal's gone or if he's still in the house. The truck hasn't started up again, so I know at the very least he hasn't stolen that. I immediately feel guilty for thinking such thoughts, ignoring the little voice that wants to know *why* I feel guilty about *anything*. But Little House is quiet aside from its usual creaks and groans.

For all I know, he could still be making faces at himself in the mirror, I think, squashing the smile that quirks the corner of my lips.

It's almost five o'clock in the morning. I've been up since six the previous day. I should be dead to the world right now. But I'm not. I'm trapped in a memory while struggling to hear the telltale signs of a man who claims to be a guardian angel. Finally, I can't take it anymore and walk to the door. I press my ear against it and wait. Aside from the subtle creaks of the house, nothing. No footsteps, no voices. No sounds of Cal smooshing up his face in the mirror, no light switches being flicked on and off. Images in my head of him finding the gas stove and flicking *that* on and off dance through my head, and I open the door to try and find him before he burns the house down.

The hallway is empty. "Hey," I call out, my voice carrying a slight waver.

Nothing.

I move down the hall. The spare room is empty, as is the bathroom. The kitchen is not on fire, but it too is empty. As is the living room. I call out again, louder, but receive no response. I ignore the twinge that sparks in my chest, because it means nothing. It does nothing for me. It's not pain like memory; if I focus on it too much, it *could* become memory, therefore making it real because I'd felt it.

He's not in the house. He's nowhere. He's gone, and now I can go back to my room and climb back into bed and pull the covers up over me and lie there in the dark and drift away. I'll sleep in for the first time in forever and wake up, already forgetting the night before. I'll go into the station at some point in the afternoon, ignoring the way my mom or one of the Trio threatens me, telling me to leave, that I'm supposed to have a day *off*. I'll shrug their concern off and take over for the rest of the day and then come back to Little House and start my life over again. I'll start the routine of work and obsessing over my father and the suspicions about his death I can't prove, and it'll go on until the day I can no longer get out of bed. From there, the river will cover my head and I'll drown. I'll drown because that is what I'm meant to do.

Instead, I open the front door and turn on the porch light. It's cold and I shiver. The yard seems to be empty other than the Ford and a faint flicker of light in the distance that is Big House. I open the screen door and step out onto the porch and then down the steps. The truck is still unlocked, and when I open the door, for a moment I can smell him, that deep earth smell that reminds me of walking in the forest after it rains. The feather sits on the seat where I left it, slightly bent and twisted from all it's been through. It warms in my hand.

Fuck. He's really gone. I can imagine him wandering around, telling people their names and when they were born and who their parents were and getting himself arrested and ridiculed. Crap, what if he gets hurt? What if I see him on the news one day as the cops are trying to identify the homeless man they found frozen to death? A dozen scenarios play through my head, each more damning and melodramatic than the last, and I curse myself for losing my temper so easily.

I've turned back toward the house, determined to get my keys and drive until I find the bastard when he says, "That's such a cherry ride, Benji. You think I'll still be able to drive it even though you're mad at me? I really like that truck."

I look up.

It takes a moment for me to find him, but then the moon pokes through the clouds that remain from the spring thunderstorm and I see him. Cal is sitting on the roof of Little House in my father's coat, a big imposing figure perched near the edge above the porch like an oversized gargoyle. He's watching me with a curious expression on his face.

"What are you doing up there?" I sigh.

"You told me to get out of the house. You didn't say anything about being on it."

"Of course," I mutter. "And why would you need to be on it? Or in it, for that matter?"

He shakes his head. "Can't leave you here."

"Why? What are you doing?"

He looks at me like I'm stupid. "I'm a guardian angel. I'm guarding."

"Guarding what?"

"You."

"Why?"

"You sure ask a lot of questions for someone who doesn't believe me."

"I never said I don't...." I trail off. "How'd you get up on the roof?"

"I climbed."

"No shit, Cal. Where'd you climb up at?"

"Or maybe I flew up here."

I snort, unable to stop myself. "Bullshit," I tell him. "You don't have your wings."

He grins. "True, though I can still feel them there. They itch. I don't know how to get them back, but I'll figure it out." He points to an old wooden ladder propped up against the side of the house, hidden in the shadows.

I nod, unsure if I should go up after him. I lean against the hood of the truck instead, waiting until I either decide to join him or he comes down.

Now that I know where he is, I'm starting to get pissed off at myself for being worried about him. Why the fuck should I care what he does or where he goes? Why should I be worried about who he talks to or if he ends up in a goddamn ditch? I shake my head, trying to clear my mind before it overwhelms me.

"So," I say.

He waits.

Say it! "You're an angel." *Still sounds ridiculous.*

He nods once.

"And you fell from outer space."

He chuckles. "If you say so."

"And you crashed in Roseland."

"I didn't *crash*," he growls, sounding offended. "I was *pulled*."

I wave him off. "Right, my bad. You fell because I called you, right?"

"Yes."

"How? How did I call you?"

"You prayed," Cal says. "Your prayers were getting louder and louder, and at the river, you almost split the sky. I had no choice but to come."

Immediate guilt. "I forced you here?" I say in a small voice, even as my mind shrieks that this whole conversation is ludicrous.

"No," he says immediately, standing like he's going to jump off the roof and come toward me. I shake my head again and cross my arms against the cold. He looks unsure, but he crouches back down, the shadows from the trees covering most of him. "You didn't force anything, Benji. You might have hurried up the timetable, but I chose to come."

"What do you mean 'hurried'?"

"You went to the river," he says with a frown. "I told you to stay away, but you went anyway."

Sharp pain, behind my eyes, like a brain freeze. It's cold. "But... that was just a *dream*."

He shakes his head. "Nothing about that place is a dream, Benji. The river can hurt you."

I could so easily drown, I had thought.

"I crossed it to get to you," I blurt out without meaning to, noticing how he flinches at my words.

"I know," he says quietly. "I know what happened when you reached the middle. I could hear your thoughts then. They were the last thing I heard before everything went black. You thought about drowning. It was a test. One I never would have agreed to had I known it would happen. I would rather have watched you from far away for the rest of your life than see you cross the river." By the end of his declaration, his mouth has curled up in a snarl, his shoulders tensing, and though his voice never rises, I can still hear the anger behind his words.

A billion questions float across my mind, and I can't seem to pick out the ones that should be asked first, the ones that are the most important. There's too many ideas, too many grandiose thoughts, and they jumble together into an incoherent mess. "What's Heaven like?" I finally ask, not sure why that question comes the easiest.

He looks at me funny. "I don't know," he says. "I've never been."

"What? But... you're an *angel*."

"Yes, but Heaven is for mortals, for humans. I am not one."

"Oh." What do you say to that? I'm sorry? "What's God like?"

"Never met him, though word is he's a control freak."

I narrow my eyes. "Are you making fun of me?"

He chuckles. "Kind of. Only the upper echelons get an audience with him. I'm pretty far down on the totem pole."

"Why?"

Calliel looks embarrassed. "I'm still sort of new at this," he mutters, averting his eyes.

"New at what?"

He waves his hands from his crouched position. "You know... this whole *thing*."

I'm confused. "Falling from the sky? Not having wings?"

He sighs and glares at me for a moment, as if my incomprehension is somehow causing him pain. "I'm new to being a guardian angel," he grumps at me.

"You're *what*?"

He scowls at me. "Why're you laughing at me?"

"I'm not," I say, even though I am. I can't help but think it would be just my luck that my guardian angel would be brand new to the job. *Wait*.... "What do you mean you're new? You said you've been around since construction on Little House started and that was years ago. How long have you been the guardian to Roseland?"

"Since it was founded. New guardians are always assigned to the small towns first before they can work their way up to the larger cites."

I feel the blood drain from my face. A buzzing picks up in my ears. "That," I hear myself say, "was almost two hundred years ago."

He laughs, a low gruff sound. "I told you I'm new."

"That's *new* to you?" I ask, starting to wheeze again. "How old are you?"

Cal looks worried again, as if my mental breakdown is splayed clearly across my face. "We don't keep track of years like you do, Benji. But if I had to put a number on it, it would be 186 years, 247 days, nineteen hours, six minutes, and fifty-five seconds. Fifty-six seconds. Fifty-sev—"

"I get it," I interrupt. "That's when you were born?"

He moves closer to the edge of the roof, peering down at me. "We're not born like you. I don't have parents. He had need of me and I simply came into being."

"What? Who?"

"God. Who do you think?"

I feel dizzy. "So God just thinks of an angel and they pop into existence?"

"I'm pretty sure you're oversimplifying, but okay."

"And then you're assigned to a town to watch over them?"

"Yes."

"For how long?"

Calliel looks away, toward the brightening horizon. "As long as it takes," he says softly.

"Takes for what? Is it like some sort of test?"

His shoulders slump. "Yes. We're all tested. Every one of us." His voice grows slightly menacing.

"When is your test?"

"I don't ever remember you asking this many questions. That's all this is with you. Questions, questions, questions."

"It's not every day you meet someone who is an angel," I say honestly.

The grin is back, though smaller than it was before. I'm almost scared to ask. "What?"

"You believe me," Calliel says.

"I wouldn't go that far," I assure him. "What about—"

"Hush, Benji. It's starting. Come up here and look."

—my father? What about my father, Calliel? If you are supposed to be a guardian, if you are supposed to watch over and protect the people of Roseland, what about my father?

For a moment, I almost refuse. Too much has been laid at my feet and I need time to process it, away from him. I need to figure out what the fuck I'm going to do. In my heart, pounding with a ferocious ache, I know I believe him. My rational mind is telling me, *No*. It's saying, *No, how could it be? How could something like this actually be?* But my heart is winning the war and I am beginning to believe. Still, I need to think. I need to focus.

I'm at the ladder before I realize I'm even walking. I'm on the first two rungs when he peers over the edge of the roof down at me. He waits for me to climb up another rung or two before he extends his hand, watching me. He must see the hesitation in my eyes. He must see the conflict in my soul, the way the battle wages. So he waits, hand extended but unmoving. I hesitate, but not for long. I reach up and put my hand in his and I'm pulled up in one fluid motion onto the roof. He lets me go as soon as my feet are set. He turns from me and sits back down on the roof, facing east.

I am slow to follow, unsure what he's asking of me. I don't know if he's dangerous. I don't know what his purpose is, his point in being here. I don't know anything, it would seem.

But all that goes away when the golden flash appears over the Cascades, the sun rising on a new day. It's not something I've taken the time to watch in a long time. I sigh and move to sit next to Cal, not touching, but close enough that I am aware of him. He seems to be in an almost religious rapture as the sunlight touches his skin. He closes his eyes and breathes in deeply, and I want to know what his thoughts are right now, right at this moment, this second.

I shiver, because it's still cold. He hears me and opens his eyes again before he takes off Big Eddie's coat and drapes it over my shoulders even as I protest. The vest he wears still leaves part of his chest exposed and his right nipple pebbles against the cool air. The sun hits the deep red curls on his chest and looks like fire.

I have to ask. I have to. "Cal?" I say quietly.

He smiles. "Yes, Benji."

"Couldn't you… could you not guard my dad?"

He bows his head, the sun dancing off his hair. I feel him shudder next to me, and when I look over, a single tear slides from his eye and catches the sunlight, refracting it until it's almost too bright to look at. It takes forever to fall and there's a sharp pain in my head like a cold explosion, but then, like all things, the moment passes. I want to take my words back but I don't know how. No one has cared about my words in a long time. I've forgotten how to use them correctly.

"Even I can't stop death," the angel Calliel says hoarsely. "No matter how much I wish it so."

The sun continues to rise on a new day so very different from the ones that have come before.

part ii: black

The man at the end of his life did not want to cross the river.
Others had come to the shore and crossed with smiles on their faces.
The River Crosser came back each time and held out his hand to the man, but the man always took a step back because the hand scared him.
Once, while the River Crosser was on the opposite side of the river, the man at the end of his life went to the edge to look at his reflection in the water.
He kneeled on the bank and leaned over as far as he dared, careful not to fall in.
He saw that he did not have a reflection. Everything was black.

the woven design

By THE time the sun is completely over the mountains, I can barely keep my eyes open. Cal has been quiet ever since I asked him about guarding my father, but the sunrise seems to soothe him, at least partially. He smiles at me as I yawn big, my jaw cracking. My eyes droop and my chin falls to my chest before I jerk awake.

"I gotta get some sleep," I mumble at him. He nods and pulls me up. He makes me wait while he goes down the ladder first and then holds it as I step down each rung, staring up at me intently. *He's guarding*, I tell myself sleepily, ignoring that twinge in my chest. We are in the house and down the hall before a thought occurs to me. "Are you tired?" *Do you even sleep?*

He shrugs. "I may need to rest my eyes," he says.

I resist the urge to have him explain further. I don't think my brain can handle anything more than what I've already been told. Part of me is still convinced this is the world's longest dream and that I'm going to wake up in my bed in an empty house, Cal already fading from my mind, forgotten in a week's time. I show him the spare room across from mine, which has a large bed with clean sheets. I tell him to check the drawers because I'm pretty sure there are some of my dad's old clothes in there. I tell him it's probably a good idea for him to change out of his skirt/tunic thing until we can figure out something more appropriate. He nods, but doesn't go into the room.

"You're not going to leave, are you?" I blurt out before I can stop myself.

He watches me for a moment. "No, Benji. I won't leave."

I nod, my eyes starting to close on their own. "Just don't leave the house yet," I mumble to him as I turn. "And if someone knocks on the door, just ignore it. Don't need you telling them everything about themselves and that you know God personally or some bullshit."

"Then what should I tell them?" he asks, sounding confused.

"I'll be up in a while," I say. I close the door behind me.

"Good morning, Benji," I think I hear him say quietly through the door, but I can't be sure if I have imagined it.

My EYES open and I'm standing at mile marker seventy-seven. Rain falls from a gray sky. Thunder rumbles in the distance. The river looks swollen against the banks, the water dark and choppy.

I look up to the sky and say, "I am not here." Rain falls into my mouth and I choke.

There's a flash and the rain has turned to feathers.

Flash. Feathers turn back to rain.

"I'm haunted," I say, my voice flat.

And I am. I know this. I am haunted here at this river.

There's another flash and I'm down by the riverbank, mud squishing up against my boots. There's a cross, starkly white. Then there are a million of them. Then there are none. Another flash. Feathers on the river, covering the surface. Then there are none.

The river beckons. I take a step toward it.

A truck on the road, the engine roaring. The sound of metal striking metal, grating and sharp. The truck sails over the edge, bouncing on the bank behind me. It strikes a large boulder. It flips, landing upside down into the river, its back end angled up toward the sky. The rear tires spin lazily until they stop.

There's a flash and I'm knee-deep in the water, the current pressing against my legs, my feet sinking in river mud.

I've been here before. I've been at this moment before.

An arm, a strong arm, will slip around my chest, and a voice will tell me I cannot cross, I cannot be allowed to drown. I turn my head swiftly, but there is no one behind me. Movement catches my eye up on the road.

A figure silhouetted against the gray-white clouds, staring down at me.

"Help me!" I scream as I wave my arms over my head. "My *dad* is in there!"

But the figure does nothing. They don't call back. They don't wave back. They just watch. They just watch as the cab of the truck behind me slowly fills with river water. They do nothing. They say nothing.

I turn back toward my father. I'm going to get him out. I'm going to change this. I'm going to fix this. The future will be changed because I am here. I am here. I am—

"No, Benji," a strong voice says from behind me. An arm wraps around my chest, pulling me against a large body filled with so much warmth it's like he's burning from the inside out. "You'll drown. You'll drown here and I can't watch that. I can't let that happen. Not now. Not ever."

I struggle against him, but it's no use. I scream at him to let me go, but he doesn't. He won't. He's too big. Too strong. I moan and sag against him, the fight draining as quickly as it has come.

"I will help you carry this burden," he whispers in my ear. "I will carry you."

There's another flash and the roar of the river and I—

will carry you

—open my eyes to a sunlit room. *My* sunlit room. My heart thumps against my chest, my breathing is rapid. *A dream*, I think. *Everything was a dream.* I'm sure of this now. None of what I remember happening *did* happen. I know it didn't. There was no storm. No light fell from the sky. I did not cross the river. I did not find an angel.

Calliel. A name that causes a twinge in my chest.

I sit up and put my feet on the floor. I listen to Little House. It tells me nothing. But that *means* nothing. He—

could be on the roof again

—was nothing more than a figment of my attention-starved imagination, something my lonely mind created, someone big and solid who said he came here because I called him, because *I* drew him here. Things like that don't happen, not in real life.

So why am I still listening for him?

I find my resolve buried deep. I stand, my knees popping. I glance at the clock. It's almost noon. I reach for the doorknob, hesitating. Only the silence of Little House allows me to move forward. I open the door.

Calliel is splayed out on the floor in the hallway outside my bedroom door. He's taken the comforter and a pillow off the bed in the spare room and dragged them into the hallway. The blanket has been kicked around in his slumber (*I guess angels* do *sleep,* I think). He's found sweatpants to change into, from somewhere, and they're a little too small for him, clinging tightly to his thighs. He's not wearing a shirt, his biceps tight against the top of the comforter. He lies on his side, facing the door. I am mesmerized by the smattering of freckles scattered down his shoulders and his side, light brown and evenly spaced, as if they are forming a pattern. They disappear into the curls of his chest hair. I lose count of them once I reach thirty. I lift my gaze to his face and his dark eyes are open.

"Hello," he says.

"Why are you on the floor?" I ask, though a billion other things are on my mind. "I told you that you could use the bed in there."

He sits up and stretches, looking surprised when his back pops loudly. He stands, letting the blanket fall to the floor. I'm hyperaware of how close he is to me and take an involuntary step backward as I struggle to breathe. "I was doing my job," he says, his voice pitched low, almost defiant.

"Guarding?" I ask.

He nods.

"I don't need to be guarded."

"You do," Cal assures me.

"From what?"

He gives me that exasperated look I'm starting to recognize. It's almost endearing now. "You know."

The river. "You can't read my thoughts but you can go into my dreams?"

He says nothing.

"Why won't you let me...?"

His eyes harden. "It's dangerous, Benji. You don't know what you're looking at."

Truer words were never spoken, I think as I stare up at him. I need to change the subject. I can't let him go on with this. It suddenly seems important, this dream. I'd gotten further into the river than I had last time, seen more—the tires spinning on the truck, the figure standing up on the road in the rain. I need to distract him somehow. An idea, something I'd considered as I fell asleep the night before. "What about the others?" I ask.

This confuses him. "What do you mean?"

"The other people of Roseland. You said you were the guardian angel to Roseland, right? How can you be protecting everyone if you're here?"

He studies me before he speaks, as if gauging my sincerity. Somehow, I don't think I've fooled him. He seems, at times, to have an almost simple demeanor. But other times, like now, the intelligence that flares behind his eyes is a breathtaking thing. He knows my game, but he's letting it slide. For now.

"There are shapes," he says. "Patterns to follow. Designs to read. It's… hard to explain."

I wait.

He sighs and steps back, leaning against the wall near the spare bedroom door. I try to focus on what he's saying instead of looking at the muscles carved into his stomach, the lines of his hips, the white that is his skin. "I can't tell the future," he says, sounding almost frustrated, as if this fact is the bane of his existence. "I can't speak to God's plan. I don't think anyone can, even the higher-ups, the archangels. Sometimes I wonder what exactly Michael knows, or what Raphael or Gabriel or David can see, but I don't think even they know what the future will bring. Metatron may have known, but no one has seen him in generations, so I can't say for sure."

My head is starting to hurt again. "Metatron?" I mutter. "More than meets the eye?"

Apparently he doesn't get my feeble attempt at a joke, the seriousness never leaving his face. "Metatron is the highest angel, supposedly the first. But he disappeared and no one knows where he went. He's more legend now than fact."

My weak understanding of any kind of religion is fairly evident. My dad and mom were never ones to go to church. About half of Roseland goes to Our Mother of Sorrows, the local Catholic church. Different faiths head to nearby towns to worship. I asked Big Eddie once why we didn't go. He told me that a man should be free to choose to do as he pleases on Sundays, even if it meant watching the Seahawks. I never argued with the logic of my father.

The names are familiar (Raphael and Michael, Gabriel and David) but he might as well be speaking in Latin for all I understand. It might be too early for an angel hierarchy lesson. I shake my head, trying to clear my thoughts. "What does this have to do with Roseland?"

"It's the pattern," he explains. "I can see threads weaving out from Heaven and down toward Earth. They form shapes. An outline. A design for each human being on the planet. Think of it like… like a loom, and these threads are woven, a plan for an individual. While I can't see them being woven, I pick up the ends of the threads and follow them. There are signs in them, signs that I have to watch for, of actions that I must take, or actions that I must *not* take. And they're all connected, some way or another. You humans are more connected to each other than you could ever realize. You may not see it, but I do. I see it every day."

"And this is God telling you to do this?" I ask, incredulous. "How can you know if you've never even seen him?"

"Faith, Benji," Calliel says, like it's that simple. And maybe to him it is. "I have faith that my Father knows what he is doing, that he knows what is right. That he has a plan for the way things will turn out." His eyes darken and he frowns at this last, but the moment passes. I almost call him on it, but I don't know what he'd do. He still scares the royal fuck out of me.

"And God does this for *everyone* on this planet?"

He laughs, and it's a big sound. "Everyone here and everywhere else."

"What do you mean 'everywhere else'?"

"Questions," he growls at me, but there's a small smirk there. "Always with the questions. There are more… *places*… than this one."

I hold up my hand. "I don't want to know. I've already got too much going on inside my head to know that there are aliens."

He grins at me. It's almost feral.

"Can you see *my* thread?" I ask, feeling ridiculous.

His eyes light up. He nods. "Started again this morning. I can see them. Feel them."

"What does it look like?"

"It's blue," he says immediately. "It's blue and strong. Far stronger than you could ever know. It's so bright. So bright and strong."

"Oh," I'm unsure what to do with that.

It's blue. Everything I have is blue. I don't know where the thought comes from.

The river, my father's voice whispers in my head. *It all comes back to the river.*

"One last question," I say, considering.

Calliel sighs, but waits.

"You said I called you and you came, right?"

He nods, his eyes starting to cloud over.

"Have others done that before? You know, other angels?"

At first there's nothing, and I think I'm not going to get an answer, but then he shakes his head, just once.

"You're the first?" My skin feels cold.

He nods tightly. "That I know of."

"How did you—"

"No more questions, Benji." He boils over, showing anger for the first time. It's a deep thing, a dark thing. I shiver again. "I'm doing what I have to do. So many damn questions, all the damn time. That's all you do. That's enough for today." He glares at me, flexing his crossed arms, as if daring me to ask another question.

"We've got to see about getting you some clothes," is all I say.

WE'RE seated at the table, his mood suddenly shifted toward happiness again (which might or might not have to do with the Lucky Charms in front of him). My stomach growled as I got dressed and I realized I hadn't eaten anything since the previous day, and it was now almost noon. Trying to keep it light and from sounding like a question, I asked him if he ate food. He was still glowering at me after I made him put a shirt on while he told me that he consumed a "sort of energy" around him when he was On High (I started singing "Angels We Have Heard On High" in my head for the hundredth time). I told him I was flat out of "sort-of energy" and told him I had cereal. He scowled at me as I placed a bowl of Lucky Charms in front of him, poking at it with a finger until I told him to stop it and use a damn spoon. I thought he was going to chuck the silverware at my head or shoot me with some kind of angel laser death beam. He did neither, instead gripping the spoon tightly, scooping up a green clover, and touching it with his tongue tentatively. He licked it a few times before he finally put it in his mouth. The look on his face and the sounds that followed suggested he had either never tasted anything so wonderful, or he was literally having an orgasm in my kitchen. This unfortunately led to a billion more questions in my head, wondering if angels could *have* orgasms, and if it would be like some kind of celestial goo. Then I realized what I was thinking about and immediately put a stop to it.

"God," he moans now, milk dribbling down his lips to his beard. "This sure is good. I think I would like some more, please. Can you just give me the green ones this time? I think I'd like a bowl of just those. The other ones are getting in the way of the green ones on my tongue."

"I don't think they make Lucky Charms that way," I say, somewhat disgusted by the way he's eating, but still unable to turn away. It's a sugar disaster in the making.

"They should," he says seriously, grabbing the box from my hand and then peering inside. He reaches in and snags a handful and proceeds to pick out the green clovers. One sticks to his lip as he chews and the look he gives me is one of such pleasure that I can't help but chuckle at him. He flicks his tongue out to snag it and I stop chuckling.

No. No fucking way that's going to happen. I'm not even going to—

He stills, then jerks his head to the left. His jaw twitches. His eyes are wide as he stares out the kitchen window to the front of Little House. "Pattern," he whispers. "Shapes. Design."

I'm alarmed. "Cal, what is it?" I look out the window but can't see anything, not that I should be expecting to. Even with my doubt, for a moment I think maybe I'll see threads falling from the sky, woven intricately with a shining material that causes the heart to ache. But there's nothing. "What's going on?"

"He's coming here," Cal growls. "He's coming here and he should stay away."

"Who? Who's coming here?"

He glances over at me, eyes hard. "You let me handle this," he says suddenly.

I snort nervously. "Like hell. I don't think you're quite ready for visitors just yet."

"I'm your guar—"

"I was just fine before you got here," I remind him, even though we both know it's a lie. "I don't need you speaking for me. Not when I can speak for myself. Who's coming?"

He doesn't need to answer—I can hear a car now coming up the drive. It passes by Big House. It stops next to the Ford near the porch, the sun reflecting red and blue off the lights on the top. Sheriff Griggs opens the car door. Cal stands quickly, tipping over his chair.

"Shit," I groan. "What the hell is this, now?"

"George Griggs," Calliel spits out through gritted teeth. "Fifty years of age. Bastard. Born May 4, 1961 under an emerald moon at 7:45 at night. I must not be blasphemous. Parents are Brian and Jennifer Griggs. I must not decide the definition of sin. Grandparents are Gerald and Molly Jackson. I am a guardian. I am a servant. I am not the judge. I am not the jury. I am not the executioner. I do not decide fate." He's snarling by the end.

And little blue flashes are starting to appear around him, growing in brightness, here on a spring afternoon in Little House.

Sheriff Griggs pulls himself out of the car, looking back toward the main house.

I stumble over to Cal, nearly tripping on his overturned chair. I stand in front of him, pulling the curtains shut over the kitchen window while the sheriff's back is turned. I reach up and cup Cal's face in my hands, like Nina had done. His red stubble is rough against my palms. His lips are still moving, saying something that I can't quite understand. I can't even be sure it's in English. I pull on his face until he looks at me, and I almost reel away. There is fire in his eyes, but it is so much more. It's as if he is burning from the inside out, his body ready to explode. The blue flashing lights get brighter and begin to take their shape behind him, a shape now becoming familiar. If I don't stop this now, it'll only get worse from here. The sheriff will be able to see the heavenly explosion occurring in my kitchen and I won't have words to persuade him otherwise.

"Do you see me?" I ask Calliel, not knowing how much time we have.

He growls at me, the outline of wings taking shape.

"Do you see me!"

"I see you," he snarls into my face.

"Then you need to calm down. You need to stop this." I drop my voice lower as I continue, hearing the sheriff's boots crunching in the gravel as he walks toward

Little House. "If he sees you like this, we won't be able to explain it away. Do you understand me? He'll try to take you away. You've got to calm down."

"He can try," Cal snaps. "I can make it so he goes away. I could do it if I really wanted to. Send him to the black. Send him in deep."

"You are *not* judgment," I whisper harshly, throwing his words back at him. "You are *not* jury. And you are *not* the executioner. You are the *protector.*" I breathe a sigh of relief as the blue lights begin to fade, as the fire begins to die in his eyes.

"I am the protector," he says to me. He reaches up with one big hand and places it over mine still holding his face. "Benji, I am the protector."

"You are. But you need to let me handle this, okay? I need you to trust me. Can you do that? For me?"

He nods as the blue lights disappear. There's a knock at the door.

"Stay here," I tell him as he looks at me like that is the stupidest idea he's ever heard. I'm not surprised to hear him follow me as I walk to the front door. He pauses in the entryway to the kitchen and I almost snort with laughter as he puffs himself up, trying to look as big as possible. He scowls at me.

I open the door, blocking Cal from view, leaving the screen door between us. "Sheriff," I say, keeping my voice light. "Two times in two days. Beginning to think you're stalking me."

"Benji," he drawls. "Stopped by the store to speak with you. Was surprised when Christie told me you had the day off. Good for you. Late night last night?"

"No later than usual," I say evenly.

"How about you open the screen so we can talk?"

"Aren't we talking fine the way it is?"

"Benji," Sheriff Griggs says, shaking his head as if he's disappointed. "There's no need to have an attitude. You know I'm an old friend of the family. I've known you since you were born. Hell, I knew Big Eddie since we were both four years old. Thick as thieves, we were."

"Funny, that," I say, my voice hardening. "Especially since my father's not here to say otherwise. I guess I'll just have to take your word on it, huh?"

He changes tact suddenly. "What were you doing out near seventy-seven last night, Benji?"

He's trying to catch me off guard. "I never said I was out there."

He narrows his eyes. "Mayor Walken swears he saw your truck hightailing back toward town on the old highway."

Dammit. I should have known it wouldn't be that easy to have gotten back unseen. "Does he? And what was our illustrious mayor doing out there so late?"

"Surely you've heard by now," he scoffs. "Lord knows this town is full of busybodies who have nothing better to do than talk."

"Slept in this morning, Sheriff. First day off in long time, remember? I just got up. No one has told me anything."

He's watching me, looking for deception. I stare right back, unwavering. I might not know what the hell I'm doing and I might believe this man to be the ultimate liar, but he's still only Griggs and he doesn't intimidate me in the slightest. "A light," he finally says. "Fell out of the sky."

Calliel finally breaks, emitting a low growl that causes me to shiver. *Oh crap,* I have time to think before the door is ripped open the rest of the way. He maneuvers himself so that he's put himself slightly ahead of me. I should be annoyed at this (and maybe I am, a little) but it's almost worth it to see the look of surprise on Griggs's face as he takes a step back at the sight of the big guy before him. Cal is scowling at the sheriff and still growling, the rumbling in his throat getting louder.

Griggs recovers from his surprise and stands upright again, imposing but still shorter than Cal by an inch or two. Cal is obviously not impressed with the man before him. I elbow him sharply, keeping my eyes on the sheriff. Cal ceases his rumbling and throws a glare my way before looking back at Griggs.

"And you are?" Griggs asks curiously. I don't miss the way he raises his hand subtly to his side, flicking off the leather strap to the holster that houses his service pistol. I try to push my way back up in front of Cal, but he raises a big hand and presses me back, trying to force me behind him completely.

"I am Calliel," he says flatly. "Benji is my friend. Your tone is not appreciated, Griggs."

The Sheriff looks bemused. "Christie mentioned Benji had a new... *friend*," he says snidely. "Cal Blue, was it? From California?"

Goddammit, Christie. Keep your fucking mouth shut for once!

"Whereabouts in California you from, Cal? Or is it Calliel?"

"Not your concern," Cal says, starting to growl again.

"He's just visiting," I say, pushing past him again. "He's a friend from out of town. Not that it's really any of your business, Sheriff."

"So he was the one driving the Ford last night, I take it?" Griggs asks, already knowing the answer. "I had wondered why the mayor sounded confused. To tell you the truth, it scared him out of his mind a bit." The sheriff chuckles, his mouth twisting into a sneer. "Says he thought it was Big Eddie driving the Ford again, coming out of the dark like a bat out of hell. Isn't that something?"

Cal tenses next to me, and I bend my arm behind my back, grab his hand, and squeeze. The growling subsides and he squeezes back. We say nothing.

"Where you boys coming from last night?"

"Just a drive," I say.

"That so," he says, rubbing his jaw. "And you didn't see any lights?"

"Oh sure," I say. "I saw plenty. It's called lightning. Quite the storm last night, right, Cal?

"Quite the storm," Cal repeats.

"Well," the sheriff says, "whatever hit the ground caused quite a show! I saw it from all the way in town, so I'm a bit surprised you boys didn't see it. You know, just driving around in the dark." He spits off the side of the porch. "Made quite the racket when it landed too. Blew the hell out of the ground, knocked down a bunch of trees." He looks me in the eye and says, "Right about where your daddy died, Benji. Just *yards* away."

I'm about to launch myself through the door, but Cal tightens his grip on my hand to the point where I'm sure my bones are going to snap, the pain clearing the fog of fury that has settled around my mind like a gray haze. It's what the sheriff wants, I know. He wants to get under my skin, to cause me to lose control, to lash out and give him just cause to arrest me. He wants something from me, but I don't know what.

But Cal holds me back, the tightness of his grip telling me if I won't let *him* lose it, then the same goes for me. The sheriff sees his hand on me, the glare on Cal's face. Griggs's gaze darts back and forth between the two of us. A small smile forms on his face as he takes a step back. "Cal Blue," he says slowly. "Cal Blue from California. I'll have to keep that in mind. Well, since you boys *obviously* didn't see anything last night, I best be on my way." He raises his hand and tips his hat toward me. "Benji, as always, it's been a real pleasure. I'm sure we'll see each other again soon. Maybe I'll stop by the store." It comes out like the threat he means it as, and a chill floats down my spine. He turns and walks down the steps.

"Agent Corwin," I suddenly say.

He stops, but doesn't turn. "How's that now?" he says, his voice soft.

"An Agent Corwin stopped by the store yesterday," I say. "Said he was with the FBI. Asked about my dad. Wanted to know how long he'd been dead." I pause for effect. "Asked about you too. Seemed surprised you were still the sheriff. Told me to call him if I thought of anything interesting. Town gossip, you know. Spreads like wildfire."

The sheriff leans over to spit again and I can see the sweat on his brow. He takes another step toward his car, running his fingers over the Ford. "Man, Benji," he says, his voice light. "I sure do hope you know what you're doing. I'd certainly hate to see something happen to you. Or to your ma. Or the Trio. Nina's so trusting, isn't she? She most certainly is. Why, I bet she'd get in a police car if she was asked. Such a sweet, *sweet* lady." He taps the hood of the Ford, the ring on his thumb scratching against the paint.

"If you touch her," Cal says quietly, "I will take you and yours into the black. If you touch *any* of them, darkness is all you will see."

The sheriff laughs. "Well, how about that!" he says, slapping his knee. "Boy, you wouldn't be threatening a county sheriff, would you?"

"The black," Cal promises him, shutting the door slowly. He turns back to me and I have to fight myself from taking a step away.

a meeting of the minds

MOST people don't realize that being hunted is just one step away from being haunted.

It's this thought I have when I wake in the dark, struggling to catch my breath. I sit up in the bed and look at the clock. Just after midnight. I shake my head, trying to clear the dream away. But something feels different. Off.

After the sheriff left, it had taken a while to calm Cal down. I could tell he was just one word away from bursting through the door and hunting down Griggs to tear him apart piece by piece. His dark eyes had grown darker, and he ground his teeth together. He clenched and unclenched his hands repeatedly.

I was unsure what to do, as he ignored my entreaties to move away from the door, to stop glaring out the window. Griggs was long gone, I told him, and besides, didn't he want to go back to the kitchen and have more Lucky Charms? I picked out all the green marshmallows for him. He ignored me.

And since I didn't know what else to do, I just stood near him, hoping my presence would be enough to calm him. There was a tentative moment when I touched his back through the old white shirt he'd found in a drawer that pulled tight across his shoulders. He said nothing and I began to rub my hand in a slow circle at the base of his spine. Eventually he sighed and I felt the tension bleed from him and he bowed his head.

"He's just talking," I told him quietly, meaning the sheriff. "He's made empty threats before."

There was a flash of fury in his eyes, and he turned and gripped my shoulders. "He will not threaten you while I stand before you," he snapped. "Do you understand me?"

"Cal...."

"*Do you understand me?*"

"Yes."

He scowled at me and turned to look out the window.

We spent the rest of the day on opposite sides of the house. Cal had still been at the window as night had fallen, but I'd heard him making his nest outside my closed door right before I'd dropped off to sleep.

And now that I'm awake, in the middle of the night, Little House feels different. It feels emptier.

I move from my bed and open the door. His blanket is there. His pillow is there. He is not.

He's not in the spare bedroom. He's not in the bathroom. He's not in Little House. Sunrise is still hours away, but I tell myself I have one last place to look. I open the door and climb up the ladder.

There is no one on the roof.

I will take you and yours into the black.

I slide down the ladder as quickly as I can, my heart starting to thud in my chest. *He wouldn't do that*, I think. *He wouldn't hurt anyone.*

But, I realize, I don't know a damned thing about him. I don't know what he is capable of. I grab the keys to the Ford off the table near the door. I slip on my work boots and grab my father's coat from the rack on the wall. It smells of earth, of feathers. I shut the door behind me and head out into the night.

POPLAR Street is dark as I drive through town. I pass the station as it sits silently. No one's out this late. Some shops have low lights that reflect in the front windows. The banner for the "Jump Into Summer Festival" glows briefly as my headlights hit it, but then I pass under it and it is dark again. I leave the main drag behind, turning onto Old Valley Road, which winds up through the hills that surround Roseland. I'm trying to remain calm, but not knowing where Calliel might be is doing nothing for my nerves. I almost expect to get to the sheriff's house and see it razed to the ground, Calliel standing above it like some dark avenging angel.

I'm a guardian, he whispers in my head. *I guard.*

Yes, but he also protects. And he's found someone he's deemed a threat.

I switch off my headlights as I round the final corner, familiar enough with the road to drive it in the dark. The house is not destroyed as part of me had anticipated, but rather is lit up, as if someone is still awake this late on a Tuesday. I pull the truck into a copse of trees off to the side of the road well away from the house, hiding it in case someone passes by.

I hurry up the side of the road, feeling slightly ridiculous at being crouched over, but I need to make sure nothing has gone horribly wrong, or at least find out what happened. I cross a ditch rather than head directly up the driveway, then cut across the yard. The lights inside are bright in the dark, but still muffled by curtains pulled across the picture windows, three cars in the driveway. One I recognize as the sheriff's SUV. The other two I don't know. There's enough visibility for me to see a floodlight attached to the front of the house. I go toward the rear in a wide arc to avoid setting the light off. There's another light on in the house at the back. The ground around the house drops off. There must be a cellar, a rarity in Oregon. The light at the back is coming from a window just overhead that I can't see into, but it's propped halfway open. I smell cigarette smoke.

Then I hear voices.

"I told you to blow that shit outside," Griggs rumbles. "I don't know why you gotta smoke inside my house."

"What can I say," a male voice I don't recognize says, "it's an addiction."

Laughter. Several voices. All male.

"I don't care," Griggs says. "Blow it out the window."

"Someone's in a mood tonight," another man says. "This has really got you spooked. I don't think I've seen you like this before. Not even when Big Ed—"

"I told you not to mention that around me," the sheriff snaps, cutting him off. "Look, I don't know how much of what he said was bullshit. Nothing has come through the police station, and the field office in Eugene and Portland said they haven't sent anyone out this way."

"Would they tell you if they had?" the smoker asks. "Seems to me if they were investigating, they wouldn't tell you a damn thing."

"I've got a guy who owed me a few favors," Griggs says. "He called around, checked some stuff out. Nothing."

"We still going to move operations?"

"I don't know yet," Griggs says. "I don't want to, but if someone is poking around, we may have to."

"What is your timeline, then?" a new voice says. *That* one I recognize. Mayor Judd Walken. My mouth goes dry.

"Give it a few weeks," Griggs says. "If need be, we could do it on the day of the festival, when everyone is distracted. I hate to lose our position now, though. It's prime fucking real estate. No one even knows about it. But it's whatever the boss wants."

"This whole thing has bad mojo written all over it," the smoker complains. "First the guy in the river. Then that fucking meteor thing falling right near there. Jesus, Griggs! It's like the universe is telling you to get the fuck out, and you're saying we need to *wait*?"

"Now, now," the mayor says over the sheriff's angry growl. "It's just a bunch of random occurrences. Let's not assign this to some higher cosmic power. I've already reached out to the community to assure everyone that it was *just* that, a meteor that fell and that the science department at the University of Oregon has already come to pick it up. People seem to be excited that such a thing happened in our little town. They won't question it."

"That's great and all," Smoker says. "Just one thing: *there was no fucking meteor*."

"Bah," Walken says. "Semantics. That's what it could have been regardless. It could have just burned up upon entry and then fell apart when it landed."

"Or, it could have been one of those drones they've got along the Mexican border," Smoker says coldly. "You've supposedly got an FBI agent in town out of the blue, and then something falls out of the sky on the same day? I'm not a believer in coincidence, Walken."

"A drone, you say." Walken laughs. "If that's the case, it must have gone the way of the meteor, then, wouldn't you agree? I assume a drone would have left debris."

"Unless that kid got to it first," Smoker snaps. "You were the one who saw his truck."

"I can't be sure of what I saw," Walken admits. "It looked like the Ford, but I was in such a hurry. And besides, it didn't look like Benjamin driving."

At hearing my name upon his lips, my blood freezes.

"It could have been that other guy," Griggs says. "That big fucker that tried to start shit at Little House."

"What did you say his name was?"

"Blue. Cal Blue. Or Calliel or some shit. Supposedly from California. Still waiting to hear back from the DMV to see if there is any record of him on file there."

Oh, Jesus. Cal. Fuck, what if he sees my thread? No. Stay away, Cal. In my fear, I try to push Cal as far away from my thoughts as I can.

"And if there's not?" Walken asks.

"Then obviously he's lying," Smoker says. "Which means he has something to hide. And this close to a moving date, I don't deal well with unknown variables."

"Speculation, all," Walken says. "He's probably just Benji's ass buddy. Lord knows that boy has been alone for so long. Maybe he's just found someone to give him attention. Big Eddie's death was hard on him."

"Fucking faggots," Smoker spits.

"Quite," Walken says, sounding amused. "We'll keep an eye on him, and this Cal Blue. Actions can be taken if necessary. I've sunk too much money into this... *venture*... to let it fail."

"I say we just take them out now," Smoker snarls. "Kill the fucking faggot before he goes any further with this. He's already—" He's cut off suddenly, a gurgle coming from his throat.

There's movement above me from the window, and, for a moment, my panic is bright and all-consuming; I'm sure I've been spotted, that people are staring down at me from above. I snap my gaze upward and see the back of a balding head pressed against the window sill, a hand wrapped around his throat. I recognize the mayor's ring as it flashes in the dark, a gaudy ruby on his pinkie finger. The hand is squeezed tight, but no one is looking down at me.

"You seem to forget, Traynor, that you are operating in *my* town, with *my* permission, which makes me *your* boss. You would do well to remember that. I'd hate to think that you'd do anything outside the scope of your employment. Remember, while you are here, I *own* you. Do you understand this?"

Smoker—or Traynor, I guess—nods, unable to speak.

"Good," the mayor says as he releases the other man's neck. Traynor takes in a gasping breath. "Besides, I'd hate to think of what *my* boss would do if you acted without authorization. Doesn't seem like a good idea for any of us. I will say, though, that if there are any... *issues* with the boy, I believe getting permission to hunt him down won't be as hard as we all think. Until then, we watch. Is that understood?"

"Yes, sir," voices rumble in agreement.

"And you," he says, though I can't tell to whom he's speaking. "I expect you to keep a close eye out. Are we clear?"

A grunt of consent.

"Now, then, shall we check the maps? I'm sure there are plenty of places we could look at should we have to move. Sheriff, would you do the honors?"

The voices and footsteps fade as they start to move away. I release the breath I hadn't realized I'd been holding.

And then I run.

I DON'T turn on the headlights until I'm almost back to Poplar Street. I consider, for a moment, still trying to find Cal, but he could be anywhere. He could be gone, for all I know. If he's going to come back, he'll go to Little House and I need to return anyway to make sure no one else is there.

I pull up the driveway at almost two in the morning. Big House still stands. My mom's little car is parked out front. I know the Trio's vehicles are parked in back. The house is dark, no movement. There doesn't seem to be anyone else around. I stop in front of the house, consider knocking on the door and waking them up, but then decide against it. Much, I'm sure, can be seen on my face at the moment, and I haven't had time to process any of it. I put the truck in drive and head toward Little House.

The lights catch a flash, like animal eyes, on the roof.

Cal.

I release a trembling breath and grip the steering wheel, trying to ignore the overwhelming relief I feel at finding him safe and sound. With so much else screaming through my head, I can't even begin to understand *why* I feel such relief, or *why* I have to stop myself from tearing out of the Ford and demanding he stand before me so I can make sure he is okay. This is something I don't yet comprehend, but it seems to be growing stronger.

I switch off the truck and open the door. I can feel his eyes boring into me as I lock it behind me. I glance up at him; his body is tense, his dark eyes bright with something I can't quite make out. He seems rigid. His gaze follows me as I move to the ladder. I take a deep breath and start climbing. I look up when I get halfway. He's not there, waiting to pull me up with him. I sigh and climb the rest of the way.

He's perched at the edge of the roof, wearing a white T-shirt and jeans. If he got them from the house, then they are my father's old clothes. The muscles of his arms strain against the sleeves of his shirt. The red stubble on his head and face looks dark in the starlight. I walk the few steps it takes to reach him, unsure if I should touch him in some way. Surely he's aware of my presence. I decide against it and sit down on the roof, a few feet away. I'm suddenly very, very tired. I have to be up in a few hours.

We sit in silence for a while. Then, in a deep-throated grumble tinged with anger, he says, "Where were you?"

"Looking for you. Where did you go?"

He doesn't look at me. "A thread called to me. I had to follow it to make sure I did my duty. When I returned, you were gone." This last comes out as a harsh accusation.

I'm getting angry. "When I *woke up*, you were gone," I snap. "I thought you'd gone away. What was I supposed to do?"

"I have a job to do, Benji," he snaps. "Even if I am here for you, that doesn't mean I can neglect my other duties."

"I never asked you to. I was just… worried. I needed to make sure you were okay."

"I am fine," Cal says stiffly. "Except for when I returned. You were not here and I could not find your thread. I panicked. There is still a lot I can't remember about the day you called, or even the time before. I don't know why I can see certain things and not see others, why I can remember pieces but not the whole."

"I'm sorry." I don't know why I feel so ashamed.

"Do you know what I did, Benji? Do you want to know what I did when I could not find you?"

"What?"

He finally turns to look at me. Much is said in that look, but I can't decipher any of it. "I prayed," he says. "I prayed for the first time since I've been here. And you know what response I received?"

"No."

"None. I didn't receive a response. It was like no one heard me. It was like my Father wasn't listening. I prayed as hard as I could, asking for help to find you. And no one answered my prayer. It feels like I'm being tested. Or being punished, but I don't know why. I can't remember why. I can't remember what I did. I don't know what I'm supposed to do. All I know is I prayed and he didn't answer. When I was watching Roseland from above, I would pray and he would be there. Even at my loneliest, I would get a response. Now? Now there is nothing."

"But… maybe you did get an answer," I say slowly.

He looks at me sharply. "How do you mean?"

"I'm here, right? With you? We may have gotten separated, but I'm here now. Maybe you were heard after all."

Calliel looks like he wants to argue with me, like I've completely missed the point he was trying to make. Instead, he sighs, then chuckles to himself as he shakes his head. "You are here," he agrees quietly.

"And can you see my thread?" *This is the weirdest conversation of my life.*

He nods. "I can see it well." The relief in his voice is a palpable thing and it almost knocks me flat.

"And you're okay, and the person you had to help tonight is okay, right?"

"Yes, Benji. She is fine."

I want to know who it is and what he did, but it doesn't feel like it's my place to ask. "Okay, then."

"Are you?"

"What?"

"Are you okay? Where did you go tonight?"

For a moment, I think about telling him everything, just to see what he says, or what he thinks. I want to see if he knows anything. If he's the guardian of Roseland, then he might have an idea about what happened in the sheriff's house tonight. The worst he could tell me is that he can't remember. I'm about to ask, but then I catch the worried spark in his eyes, the way he starts to frown. He's got too much on him already, I realize, probably something more significant than I could ever understand. To him, my problems would be nothing because, in the reality of the cosmos from which he comes, *I* am nothing.

"I'm okay," I say, my voice steady.

He starts to say something, but then shakes his head.

So we sit there, on the roof, he and I. Every now and then, I feel his hand graze against mine. Eventually, my head starts to bob, my eyes heavy. I don't protest when a strong arm wraps around me and pulls me over. He is so warm, and I bury my face in the crook of his neck and breathe deeply, smelling earth. He keeps his arm around me as he rubs his chin on the top of my head. Eventually, I drift off to sleep.

I do not dream.

SOMETIME later, I awaken to a gentle voice. "Benji. Benji. Open your eyes. Open your eyes and see."

I do. He's staring down at me, cradling me in his arms, a small smile on his face. "The sun is about to rise. You must see this. It is a beautiful thing." He looks toward the horizon.

But all I can see is him.

a man about town

I MAKE him shower before we leave (a scowling "I don't think I'm going to like this" turns into a loud "Hey, this is pretty neat!"). He dresses in the same clothes he had on before, the white T-shirt and jeans, pulling on an old pair of work boots. I tell him with no small amount of dread that while I'm at work he's going to need to go shopping for some new clothes.

"Why?" he says, looking down at what he's wearing. "Is there something wrong with this? I don't think I'm going to like shopping."

"You know, you say you aren't going to like anything, yet you end up liking everything," I remind him. "I haven't yet steered you wrong, right?"

"Do you like shopping?" he asks innocently enough.

I'm unable to stop the look of disgust on my face. I try to hide it and say, "Sure. Well, some of the time."

He nods. "I wish someone had told you that you're a terrible liar so I wouldn't have to be the first one. I feel bad now."

"You don't feel bad at all," I growl at him.

Cal's eyes dance. "I do," he promises. "But I'm not going to go shopping. I will stay with you until it is time to leave. But if there are any threads, I will follow them and then come back."

"You have to go," I sigh. "You can't keep wearing that."

"Why?"

I struggle with the answer. "Those are… my father's. It's just… weird for me. To see it."

His eyes go wide as he looks down at himself. "I'm sorry," he says, sounding wounded. "I did not think. Benji, please forgive me." He starts to lift the shirt over his head, and I catch a glimpse of his stomach, wonderfully muscled under the auburn curls. I almost think about letting him continue, but that probably makes me a bit of a pervert, so I stop him, pulling the shirt back down.

"It's okay for now," I assure him, even though he's trying to unbutton the jeans. I slap his hands away. "It can wait until you're done shopping."

His face turns red and he looks down at the ground and mumbles something.

"I can't hear you," I tell him.

He speaks up. "I don't have currency," he grumbles, glancing up at me before looking away. "I can't buy things without it, right? That's how it always is. You need money and I don't have any."

"You mean God doesn't pay you?" I tease.

He looks horrified. "No! All I do is for him. He is the Creator; he is my father. His will is word and I must follow for he is divine—"

"Right, okay," I cut him off before he goes into a sermon. "I've got money, no worries."

He looks miserable again. "I haven't a way to pay you back."

I shrug. "We're friends, right?"

He hesitates, but then he nods.

"And you're going to be sticking around? At least for a while?"

He nods again, quicker this time. I ignore the relief I feel.

"Well, then, my friend, you're going to need new clothes. And since you are my friend, there is no need to pay me back."

He looks suspicious. "I don't know," he says.

"I'll let you drive the truck into town today."

His eyes light up. "You will? Wow. That truck sure is cherry. You'll let me drive it and all I have to do is take your money that I can't repay and go shopping, which I'll probably end up hating because *you* don't like it, to buy clothes like the ones I'm already wearing?"

Jesus Christ. "Uh. Sure."

He grins. "Alright, hey, that's great! Thanks, Benji. I sure do love that truck. It's so cherry, right?"

I smile back. "So cherry."

IT'S four hours later and I'm regretting letting Cal out of my sight.

I sent him off with strict instructions (*You can't go up to people you don't know and spout off their names and birthdays and families and whatever else you want to say. Why not? People will just find it weird.* But that's how I remember everyone! *I know, but if the whole idea is for you to remain incognito, then you can't give yourself away on the first day. Let people introduce themselves to you should they want to.* You act like I don't know how to talk to people, Benji. *Cal, you* don't *know how to talk to people.* Have a little faith, huh? *Coming from an angel, that's hilarious.*) I found him an old wallet that I hadn't used in years and gave him a wad of cash. I knew I was hovering when I asked him if he knew how to use money. "Oh, I don't know, Benji; I've only watched humans for two centuries." The bastard can be very sarcastic when he wants to be.

Which in and of itself is a paradox. Even after two days, I can see that there are so many sides to him. Maybe too many. There's times he exudes such strength that it threatens to knock me flat. Push him into a corner and he will lash out. Make him angry and you will see it on his face, and God help you should it be directed toward you. Those are the times that I *do* believe he is an angel, that I *do* believe he guards us as he says he does.

Then there are his other sides, most specifically when he seems unsure, hesitant. While most of his insecurity has to do with things that I take for granted, it's strangely amusing watching his attempts to adapt. His wonder is almost childlike in its mien. He sees things I no longer can because it is as if he's experiencing everything for the first time. And what catches his eye seems to be inconsequential at first: marshmallows, a sunrise. The look on his face as the sun breaks over the horizon is one of pure wonder, and he closes his eyes as the sun's rays first strike and warm his face. I try not to think about what his life must have been like On High. It sounds like it's a cold, lonely place, even if he is working for God.

And then there's the darker part of him. *I will send you and yours into the black.* I don't want to think about that part. I don't want to know what "the black" is. It's only been two days since he fell from the sky, but those two days have shown just how little I really know about the world. What would happen if he turned that anger on me or my family? This town? For every story of an angel I've ever heard, there's always been a counter to it, an avenging angel. Dark prophecies. Swords of fire. The devil was an angel at one point. There are things he's keeping from me, I know. I don't know how much of it falls under his supposed memory loss. It seems almost too convenient for me. But doubting him shames me. I don't know if I can trust him, but how can I doubt him?

It's not helping that my mind is completely jumbled from the conversation I overheard at the sheriff's house. Maybe I've gotten too complacent about what happened to Big Eddie. There was a fire inside of me, after his death, a fire that burned so brilliantly it threatened to consume me. Maybe like any flash fire, it had grown so bright and hot it burned itself out, leaving only charred remains. But buried under my grief, I can feel the remains still smoldering, waiting for a spark to ignite them again.

I'm under no illusions about what the men in Griggs's house were referring to last night. I might not be the smartest person alive, but the blatant way they referred to me left no room for misinterpretation. I don't know how their so-called "operation" connects to my father, but it has to. Somehow.

The FBI agent's card sits in my wallet, hidden away.

Three days ago, life was quiet. Life was routine. Solitary. Secluded, even. I knew what to expect from the world, at least my little corner of it. I knew it had teeth and could bite off my outstretched hand when I wasn't looking. I knew it was easier to run and hide and bury myself in sorrow. At least there, I could let my soul bleed as much as it needed to. I knew I was drowning, but I was okay with that.

Now? This is how things are now:

Thirty minutes after Cal leaves, I am having serious doubts about letting him go off on his own, kicking myself for even suggesting it. He's a grown man, I tell myself. A grown man who just had Lucky Charms and took a shower for the first time. I step out in front of the store, looking up and down Poplar, but that already familiar red hair isn't anywhere to be seen. I go back inside.

And it starts.

Eloise Watkins comes into the store. She had been the librarian until the library closed due to budget cuts. She usually comes in on Fridays for a pack of Virginia Slims 120s, telling me each time this will be her last pack, she's serious this time. She'll proceed to smoke the cigarettes through the weekend, finishing the last one on her porch on Sunday evening. Monday she'll tell everyone she's quit smoking, that she doesn't even feel the cravings, and why did people think it was so *hard* to quit? Friday will come around and she'll back in for her smokes.

Which is why it's weird when she comes in on a Wednesday, her eyes sparkling.

"Oh, Benji!" she exclaims, coming up to the counter. "You've been talking about me?"

I smile, not sure what she means. "You're a couple of days early. And what do you mean talking about you?"

"I just *had* to come see you and say well done," she says with a grin, reaching over the counter to rub me on my head. "He's absolutely magnificent!"

I'm confused. "Uh, what?" Then: *Oh, this can't possibly be good.*

"Your gentleman!" she says, the curve of her smile turning a bit wicked. "He stopped me on my way to the salon and asked me where the pants store was."

"Oh, crap," I groan. "What else did he say?"

She laughs. "He said that he wasn't supposed to tell me, but that he knew my name and when my birthday was. And that *smile* he gave me…." Her eyelids flutter as she stares dreamily at me. "I didn't even know you knew when my birthday was. Or that you cared," she purrs, reaching over to rub her hand over mine.

I snatch my hand away as if she'll set it on fire. "Eloise, you are sixty years old. And I'm gay."

She sighs as she pulls back. "Yes, there *is* that," she says. "And if I had a specimen like that man, I wouldn't be looking for any on the side either."

I blush furiously. This is not something I talk about openly. Ever. "I'm not… we're… he's not… I don't know what you mean."

She arches an eyebrow at me. "Well, at least one of you is sure. He told me that you belong to him and that he came because you needed him here."

I groan again, laying my head on my hands. She laughs and runs her hand over the back of my head. "Love is so hard, isn't it?" she asks.

"We're *not*—"

"Anyway, I just wanted to stop in and say you have *impeccable* taste, my dear. Who knew you had it in you?" She turns and leaves.

I've just about made up my mind to close the store to hunt the bastard down when Mrs. Taylor Clark, of Clark's, the medium-sized grocery down at the other end of Poplar, comes into the station. It would seem she's met a certain large individual outside her store, opening and closing the door to the freezer that holds ice out on the sidewalk. When she asked what this gentleman was doing, he pointed out that he was just experiencing the difference between the warm spring air and the sudden burst of cold from the freezer. He pulled her next to him with his rather large arms and made her experience the same blast of air. He laughed, and she couldn't *not* laugh with him, so she did. It would seem this gentleman was off to buy clothing, as Benji had ordered, but just between him and her, he thought he was just going to *hate* shopping. But, he said, it was what Benji wanted, and he would do *anything* for Benji, so off he went, if she could just point him in the right direction of the pants store?

"I wanted to climb him like a tree," she tells me, blushing furiously, undoubtedly thinking of *Mr.* Clark, back at the store.

Ten minutes later, Jimmy Lotem from the hardware store stops in, telling me he just helped a peculiar fellow pick out a pair of boots. Apparently this fellow had told Jimmy that he needed a good pair of boots because he was going to work with his friend Benji, and if he needed to help others in town, he would, especially when he was called to. Oh, and how was Jimmy's mother? the fellow asked. Jimmy, a bit surprised, had asked how this fellow knew about his mother. The fellow was quiet for a moment, then said that Benji had told him. Jimmy, unable to stop himself (and, admittedly, touched like he hadn't been in a very long time), told him that his mother wasn't doing so well, that the cancer had returned and his mother was no longer well enough to handle any more rounds of chemo. This peculiar fellow had stood and taken Jimmy's hand in his own and said, "You will mourn when she passes, but just know that when she does, she will be taken to a place where she will be celebrated and revered for the life she led. And you will be with her again, one day."

"It was like he *knew*, Benji," Jimmy says, fighting back tears. "It was like he *knew* how scared I am. He was gone before I could say anything. You'll thank him for me, won't you? Or maybe he'll be around?"

I nod, speechless.

But that's not the end of it.

More come. Some in pairs, some in small groups. But most individually. The majority of the people who come in are here for curiosity's sake, wondering where the redheaded man had come from. He had just introduced himself on the street, letting people know he was with me now. Many took that to mean more than it did, and I struggled to clarify our relationship over the way they grinned at me, watching me with knowing eyes that knew not of what they spoke. He was sweet, they said. He was kind. A bit odd, sure. But happy. And bright. Oh, he was so bright.

A few others say he spoke with them longer. He told John Strickland that he was sure his crisis of faith would pass, and that God would be there waiting for him. John tells me that, for the life of him, he can't remember how the topic came up but he's glad it did, because the few words Cal has spoken to him make more sense than anything he's heard in years. "I think I want to pray on it," he tells me, looking astonished at his own words.

Then there's Margaret Sims, a young slip of a woman who works as a secretary for old Doc Heward. Cal spoke with her as she sat out in the spring sunshine, taking a break. He told her that he sure was happy that he wasn't alone anymore, that it had been a long time since he'd had anyone to talk to. "But then Benji found me," he supposedly said, even before he'd told her his name. "Or I found him. I'm not quite

sure yet. Maybe we found each other at the same time. I don't know that it matters."
He sat with her, in the sun, and told her that he didn't want anyone to be alone again.
She confessed to him that she missed her grandmother since she'd passed away last
year, and that she felt alone too. "She wouldn't want you to feel that way, I don't
think," Cal had told her. "Life is for the living. It's time for you to live." He'd then
kissed her on the forehead and stood and waved as he walked away.

Life is for the living.

And others:

Terry Moore, who says she could see kindness in his eyes, but that they looked
sad.

Larry Roberts, who says Cal shook his hand and told him about the sunrise he'd
seen this morning, and how the colors had been so alive.

Janice Evans, who is at a loss to explain what he'd said to her, just that she's
been able to see through a fog of despair for the first time since her daughter died last
year.

Rosie Duncan, of Rosie's Diner fame, calls to tell me Cal stopped in and asked
for a bowl of the green things from Lucky Charms. When she told him she didn't
have any, he smiled at her and told her that was okay. She was so taken by him that
she'd sent one of her waiters down to Clark's to buy a box and then Cal sat at the
counter while he picked out the green clovers.

And still more. So many more, in all a total of forty-three people I count over the
space of four hours. But it's the last one that almost causes me to break.

My mother walks into the store.

"Hey," I say, glancing out the front windows for the tenth time in a minute,
trying to see if Cal is on his way back.

"Benji," she says in greeting. She makes her way back to the cooler and grabs a
bottle of water before coming back to stand in front of the counter. She studies me,
though I'm not sure what she's hoping to find. "So," she says.

"So," I say, playing her game, hoping it isn't going to be what I think it is.

"I was in town making a delivery to Rosie's," she says. "Also picked up an order
for the Jump Into Summer Fest."

"Oh?"

"Yep."

"Big order?"

She shrugs. "I guess. The coordinators want pies. Lots of pies. More than last
year. Apparently summer means pie."

"That's good," I say, glancing out the window again, craning my neck to see
down the street further.

"Looking for something?" she asks. "Or someone?"

I eye her warily. "I'm pretty sure I don't know what you mean."

"I'm pretty sure you do."

I groan. "Did he get you too?"

She shakes her head. "No, but he's made quite the splash. It's all anyone would talk about. And imagine my surprise when everyone started asking *me* questions. Questions I had no idea how to answer. How did Benji and Cal meet? How long is Cal staying? Are they serious?"

"Mom, it's not like—"

She interrupts me. "Do you care for him?"

"Well... yeah, I guess. He's my friend." *My weird, weird friend who fell out of the sky.*

"Friend?" There's too much emphasis on that word. I know what she means.

I blush. "It's not like that," I try again.

"It's not?"

"No."

"Does *he* know that?"

"Cal's just... really friendly."

"Friendly isn't going around telling people that you belong to him," she points out.

I wince. "He has a tendency to speak like he doesn't know what he's talking about."

"Oh?"

"Yeah."

"And he was out... what? Shopping for clothes that you told him he needed to get?"

I hate small towns. "Mom, it's not what you think." Then I stop and think about it for a moment and allow myself to get angry. "And even if it was, what business is it of yours? I'm twenty-one. I live in my own house, under my own roof. My life is my life."

"I'm not questioning that, Benji," she sighs. "I know that. Trust me, out of everyone in the world, I know that probably better than anyone. And I'm not trying to.... Benji, I'm just worried."

"About what?"

She turns and looks out the window, staring down Poplar Street. "Regardless of our standing in this town, regardless of what goodwill your father left us, this is *still* a small town. There's going to be prejudice here. You have to know that."

"There will be prejudice wherever I go."

"That's not the point," she snaps without looking at me.

"Mom, no one gives two shits about me. They could—"

fucking faggots why don't we just kill them now

"—care less what I do."

"Maybe before, but this? Benji, how well do you even know this guy?"

"We're not doing anything!" I'm getting pissed off now.

"But you want to," she says, turning back to me. "Benji, I can see it in your eyes. Even now, there's something there. Something I haven't seen in a long time. Not since…." She can't finish.

I look down at my hands, scraping my thumbnail against a chip on the countertop. "And you're questioning it?" I ask bitterly. "You see me happy and you want to stop it? How fucking fair is that?"

"Benji—"

"And since when did you give a rat's ass about me being gay? It's never been an issue before. Or at least it wasn't for Dad."

"That's not fair," she says, looking hurt. "I am just as much on your side as your father was."

I feel like a bastard, but she was trying to push me into a corner. "You've got a weird way of showing it sometimes."

"But—"

I wave my hand at her. "It doesn't matter. Nothing's going to happen. You don't have anything to worry about. We're too different." *Understatement.*

She hesitates, looking unsure. But then she reaches out and covers my hand with her own. "I just want you to be safe," she says, her voice cracking. She shakes her head angrily when I look up, obviously pissed at herself for breaking down in front of me. "You're all I have left."

"You have the Trio," I say, trying to stop myself from pulling my hand away.

"You're all I have left of *him*," she says, and I understand.

"Mom," I sigh, not wanting to think about it anymore. "Cal's a good… guy. Just give him a chance, okay?"

She nods, rubbing a hand over her eyes. "Everyone seems to like him," she says with a soft chuckle. "I just worry about you."

"Yeah. You are my mom, after all. It's kind of in the job description."

"And you better not forget it," she says, bending over and kissing my hand on the counter. I look away before my own eyes start to water.

She grabs her bottle of water and turns and heads for the door. "I'll expect you both for dinner soon," she calls over her shoulder, our rare display of emotion held like a secret between us. "If he's going to stick around and cause you to gaze out the window with that look in your eyes, I need to get to know him." She pushes out the door before I can respond.

"I'm not *gazing* out the window!" I shout, even though I totally was. She waves her hand like she hasn't heard me.

I scowl after her.

And I'm still scowling when he walks into the store thirty minutes later, numerous bags in his hands. "Benji," he says with a grin.

"You," I growl at him, "are in so much fucking trouble."

He cocks his head at me, not looking particularly intimidated. "Why is that? Hey, I didn't hate shopping like I thought I would. It was actually pretty okay. I got some pants from the pants store and there were these boots that almost didn't fit my feet and I almost didn't buy them because why would you need to wear boots when you can just walk bare—"

"I am pretty sure I don't need a rundown of your entire day, since *everyone you spoke to has already told me all about it.*"

He has the decency to look somewhat guilty. "Ah. About that. See, I didn't want to be rude and people were looking at me like they didn't know me, so…."

"It's because they *don't* know you," I remind him through gritted teeth.

"Well, yeah. And I felt bad, because I know *them*, so I thought it would be rude if I didn't introduce myself. And then we got to talking about stuff, and before I knew it, I had talked to a lot of people. I still went shopping, though, like you asked," he says, showing me the bags in his hand. "Even though I didn't want to."

I am incredulous. "Are you trying to guilt-trip me?"

"Is it working?"

"No!"

"Oh."

"Cal!"

"Benji." He smiles, and it causes my heart to stutter. He puts the bags on the floor and takes a step toward the counter. "You're looking at me differently," he says with great interest.

I take a step back. "I am *not*," I snap at him. "I was just worried is all. You can't go around being like you are!"

He frowns. "How else am I supposed to be? If there's one thing I've learned about human nature, is that it is imperative to be who you are."

"You're not human," I say, instantly regretting my words as his face falls.

"I know," he says, looking down at his hands.

"That's not what I—"

"It's okay, you know. You're right. I'm not human. I shouldn't be expected to act like one." He shakes his head. "But of all people in this world, Benji, I thought it would be you who'd understand what it's like to be different."

Shit. I've hurt him. I think. "I just don't want anything to happen to you."

He looks up at me again. "Nothing's going to happen to me." He tries to reassure me, the small smile returning, as if he hopes what he'll say next will please me. "You know what I found today?"

"What?"

He leans onto the counter, flexing his big arms, the fabric of the shirt straining against him. "I'm pretty much bigger than anyone here," he says confidently. He flexes again. He watches me watching him and the smile grows. "Many people told me how big I am. How strong I look."

"Did they?" I manage to choke out.

"Yes, there was one lady who wanted me to take her to dinner. She told me to call her. I told her I don't have a phone and she said that was okay, we could just go around back where no one could see us."

I see red. "*Did* she?" I snarl, unable to stop myself. I bet it was that stupid *bitch* Suzie Goodman who works at the pharmacy. That fucking *slut*—

"No," he says, eyes sparkling. "That was a joke. I found out today that I enjoy humor and I can tell jokes after all. It turns out I am pretty funny. Isn't that great?"

I look away. "Bastard," I whisper.

"Look at me," he says, his voice changing, becoming deeper, stronger.

I can't stop myself. I don't want to stop myself. He looks into my eyes and I hold my breath. "Yeah," he finally says with surety in his voice. "You're looking at me differently."

Dammit.

"Why were you telling people I belong to you?"

Cal grins. "Because you do. All of you here do. I am the guardian angel of Roseland. It is my job. You all belong to me."

"Oh," I say, unable to stop it from sounding like I'm disappointed.

He turns away from the counter to pick up his bags. "But especially you," he says over his shoulder as he heads for the small office in the back.

I stare after him.

I can see it in your eyes, my mother whispers in my head. *Even now, there's something there.*

He will need you as much as you'll need him, Big Eddie says.

You're looking at me differently.

I am so fucking screwed.

revelation

I AM at mile marker seventy-seven.

The gray sky opens up and rain falls down.

I stand on the river's edge.

Feathers. Crosses.

A truck crashes and flips into the water, its rear angled up.

I am in the river.

A shadow of a figure stands on the road, watching.

"Benji," a voice calls. It is not my angel.

My angel, I think, confused.

The water is up to my chest. It's cold, causing my teeth to chatter. The mud in the riverbed is up to my ankles and is as strong as it's ever been. Each step is nearly impossible. My legs strain against the suction and current.

"Benji," the voice calls again.

It's coming from the truck.

A strong arm around my chest and I'm pulled away, away, away.

I AM wary of him over the next few days. There are times I wake up in the middle of the night and he's gone, following threads only he can see, the nest outside my bedroom door empty. These are the moments I feel relief I won't admit to out loud, a small part of me thinking it might be okay if he doesn't come back. This can't last long, I tell myself. People will begin to ask questions. My mother and the Trio will begin to ask questions. How long can the name Cal Blue and the person behind it hold up to inspection? He can only end up bringing my carefully constructed world crashing down, and I don't know if I have the strength to build it up all over again. So it's good, I think, looking down at the blankets on the floor outside my door. *It's good he's gone. He doesn't belong here. He's an angel. I am a little speck of dust that means nothing. This won't be any more than that. He is big and bright and strong and powerful. And I am nothing.*

But that's only a small voice.

Inevitably, I'm up and pacing the floor in the living room in the dark, glancing out the front windows every few moments into the night, hoping to see a large figure ambling up the driveway toward Little House. The longer it takes, the more I begin to eye my keys hanging on the rack. *What if he's hurt?* I ask myself more than once. *What if he's lost? What if he's trying to find his way back to Little House and he can't? What if he needs my help?* And, as if he can hear me thinking, as if he understands I'm about to break, that is the moment I see him, a flash of the red rust on his head, his creamy skin illuminated by the moon and stars. Relief washes over me. These are strange feelings, new feelings, feelings I don't think I can or even should be having. I watch him for a moment as he moves toward me. I think how handsome he is, how strong he looks. I think how the small voice that wants him to leave is undoubtedly right, but I will ignore it for as long as I can, because I don't think I can go back to the way things were. Being alone, being haunted. I allow myself to think these things for just a moment, because any longer will be too much for me to handle.

As he approaches Little House, I melt back into the dark, down the hall, stepping over his blankets and then shutting the door behind me. I crawl into bed and lie on my side, facing the door. Moments later, I hear footsteps walking down the hall gently, as if he is trying to be quiet so he doesn't wake me. Shadows shift across the floor as he stands in front of my bedroom door. And then his voice, softly saying, "I'm back, Benji. I'm here."

The first night he said this, I was sure he'd seen me in the window, that he knew I was awake. But then he said it again the next night. And the one that followed. And the one after that. Finally, on the seventh night, I stayed awake as long as I could, to see if I could hear him when he left. It was just after midnight when he stirred. He stood and leaned against the door. "I'll be back, Benji. I promise. I will come back."

But regardless of when he leaves or when he comes back, he knocks on my door shortly before dawn, waking me from a fitful doze I've just fallen into. "Benji?" he says. "It's almost time." And then he walks down the hall and out the door.

There are moments when I tell myself to stay in bed, that I don't need to put myself into this any further. *It doesn't mean anything*, I argue with myself. *It can't mean anything.* But then my feet find the floor and I'm standing before I can even think about it. I walk down the hall. I take my father's jacket from the coat rack and slip it on. I put on the old work boots by the door. I go outside, the sky already beginning to lighten in the east. The grass is slick with dew. The stars are still visible overhead, though they are now fading.

I reach the ladder and climb up one rung, and then two. There is movement above me and I look up. The angel Calliel is there, hand outstretched. There is no hesitation now as I reach up, his big paw engulfing mine. He pulls me up the rest of the way and then moves back to his perch at the edge of the roof. I sit a few feet away from him, but by the time the sun shoots itself above the horizon, with that first blinding ray over the Cascades, I'm pressed up against him, his arm heavy across my shoulders, my head in the crook of his neck.

I asked him once why he wanted to see the sun rise every morning, what it was that caused him to be out here at the crack of dawn every day.

He watched me for a moment before looking back at the horizon. "Its beauty," he said. "It reminds me every day that there is beauty in the world. That even though it may feel like we are alone sometimes, we are never truly alone." The sunlight hit his face and his red hair and beard turned to fire. He looked down at me again, pressed up against him. "Why are you here every day?" he asked.

I looked into his dark eyes and said the first thing that came to mind. "Because you're here." I immediately blushed, realizing how the words sounded. The smile that bloomed on his face was bright and knowing. I looked away, but not before he pulled me tighter against his chest.

The times he disappears during the day are more difficult, because those are the times I worry most about his visibility. He tells me he'll be fine, that he isn't doing anything that will bring more attention to himself, but that does little to calm me. Whenever the threads call, he follows. There are times we're in the middle of a conversation when he breaks off, staring off into the distance. "I have to go," he says after a moment of silence. "I'll come back, I promise." Sometimes he asks for the keys to the Ford, but most of the time he takes off on foot. I watch him and contemplate following. I even tried to, one time, but he moved so quickly I lost sight of him within minutes.

He never tells me what he did, and I never ask. I don't feel it is my place to, nor do I think I have a right to know. But things happen around Roseland that I can no longer associate with normalcy. The Wallace family was displaced after their house burned down one night, a freak electrical thing. They escaped through the window. The house burned to the ground, but the Wallaces were safe. Mr. Wallace later said that he'd awoken because of what he thought was a hand on his shoulder, but no one had been there.

How lucky! breathed the town. How fortunate! said its residents. God *must* have been watching over the Wallace family that night—it's the only explanation!

I thought there might be another explanation, as Cal had come home that night smelling of smoke.

Little Becky Newhall went missing after she went outside to play two days after the Wallace fire. Her parents were frantic, and a large mass of people gathered, ready to comb the woods for any sign of the girl. But even before they could all set out, she was discovered on the porch swing at her house, covered in a blanket, her arm clutched to her chest. She'd fallen into a small sinkhole, she said later. The fall had broken her arm. She cried for a long time and screamed for someone to get her, but she grew tired and tried to sleep. She woke sometime later and she was being carried by someone who told her everything would be okay. She went back to sleep and when she woke again, she was on her porch at her house.

Who saved her? the town cried. Surely the hero would come forward and receive the praise and blessing of Roseland? No one came forward. It's the will of God, some said. He works in mysterious ways, others whispered. Little Becky Newhall surely had her guardian angel watching over her, all agreed.

"It's the threads," Cal tells me when he comes home, slick with mud and grime. "I follow the threads."

I say nothing as I turn on the shower, getting the water scorching hot, knowing he likes it that way.

IT'S been over a week since Cal arrived. I can't even tell which way is up anymore, in a dizzy, antigravity kind of way. Floating is probably the best way to describe it. I feel like I've been floating in a haze of deep blue, something that is pleasant and at the same time alarming. It's been eight days since he fell out of the sky, and I'm already having a hard time imagining the way I lived my life when he *wasn't* here. It was routine wrapped in grief. It was monotony disguised as security. I feel like I was blind and am now able to see for the first time in years. Everything is bright. Everything is shiny.

And it scares the hell out of me.

It seems like everyone has met Cal in one way or another. People still stop by the store daily, either to see him and chat him up, or to tell me something that he's done. Of course, a lot of the news is still of the Wallace fire and little Becky Newhall. I'm waiting for a single person to make the connection between Cal and those two events, but so far no one has said a thing. The people of Roseland will typically say whatever they are thinking, so I don't believe anyone is trying to hide it, but I still feel some anxiety every time the bell dings in the store.

I can feel the FBI agent's card burning a hole through my wallet. I've taken it out every now and then and stared at it, trying to work up the nerve to dial the phone number and relay what I heard at the sheriff's house to him. I don't know why I think it's important that Agent Corwin knows about Griggs and Walken and Smoker, but the timing of the agent's visit and what I heard can't be coincidence. What stops me, though, is the sheriff's voice in my head: *Nina's so trusting, isn't she? She most certainly is. Why, I bet she'd get in a police car if she was asked. Such a sweet,* sweet *lady.* I see her in my mind, the way she looks at the man she calls Blue every time she sees him, her smile so brilliant, her eyes dancing. I can see the way she waits for us every night, the way she rushes out to hug me first and then him. "Blue," she always sighs. "Benji and Blue."

Agent Corwin's card goes back into my wallet. But I know it's there.

So almost everyone, it seems, has met Cal, with the exception of the one I knew would probably get the biggest kick out of him. Abe didn't even call to schedule his usual appointment. Instead he just walks in this morning and looks around, trying to be nonchalant, but failing miserably.

"Looking for something, Abe?" I ask as I unload cartons of cigarettes and slide them into the racks, trying to keep a smile from forming.

"Oh?" he mutters, looking down each aisle. "What was that, dear boy?"

I roll my eyes. "Thought you'd be in here a lot sooner than this."

"Yes, well," he says distractedly, peering around the counter where I stand. "I had those doctors' appointments in Eugene, you know. Specialists that need to poke and prod to tell me what I already know so they can charge Medicare up the wazoo: I'm an old man, and I'm not getting any younger."

I'd forgotten about his appointments. "How's your blood pressure?" I ask as he opens up the cooler, peering between the shelves to see back into the freezer.

He scowls as he closes the door. "Nothing my lisinopril won't be able to handle."

"And your heart?"

"Beating like I'm twenty-five!" He cups his hands to his face and looks through the window into the empty garage.

"And how's your colon?" I ask, trying to keep from bursting out laughing.

He turns and narrows his eyes at me. "Benji, the day you ask me about the status of my colon is the day I know you are trying to keep something from me."

I shrug. "I'm pretty sure I don't know what you mean."

"Benjamin Edward Green!" he hollers as he walks menacingly toward me. "You are still not so old that I won't bend you over my knee and tan your hide!"

I can't hold it in anymore and I bellow out my laughter. "I'd like to see you try it, old man."

He tries to keep the serious look on his face, but gives himself away when his lips twitch. "It's different here," he finally says after he's regained some control.

"What do you mean?"

He looks around the store before his gaze finds me again. "It feels... lighter. Calmer."

I snort. "They gave you the good meds this time, huh?"

Abe smiles quietly, seeing right through me. "You seem lighter too, Benji."

"Abe, I think you might be seeing things." But even I don't believe my words. I feel lighter, somehow, and I wonder why I'm just noticing it now.

"So, where is he?"

I sigh. "Getting sandwiches from Rosie. She told me to send him from now on because at least *he* doesn't complain about her egg salad."

Abe arches an eyebrow. "He hasn't tried it yet?"

"Oh, he did. He just doesn't complain to her face about it. He told me it was like eating sadness." I pause, considering. "Word gets around, I guess," I say, asking a question without actually asking a question.

Abe nods. "Oh, it does. But nothing but good. People seem to be falling all over your Cal."

My Cal. That thought zings right through me. "He's not mine," I mutter, feeling heat rising in my face.

Abe watches me with knowing eyes. "Uh-huh. Is that why you've got that dreamy look on your face right now?"

I groan. "Abe, it's not like that."

"Really? Who are you trying to convince here, boy? Certainly it's not *me*, because I can see right through your bullshit."

"I'm not—"

The bell rings overhead. "Benji!" Cal booms, bags in hand as he enters the store. "Rosie gave me pie but your mom's is better. I almost told her that but then I realized that would hurt her feelings so I said it was the greatest ever."

"That's great, Cal," I say, waiting for the inevitable.

He smiles at me, then seems to notice Abe. "Hello," he rumbles. He furrows his brow, and I know his mind is firing, making the connection. When he does, a grin splits his face and I know what's about to come out, regardless of how many times we've had this talk.

"Cal," I say, interrupting him, "this is my friend Abe Dufree. Abe, Cal Blue." Cal shoots me a look over his shoulder, obviously annoyed that he wasn't able to tell Abe which moon he'd been born under. I shrug.

"Abe!" he says, moving forward and wrapping the old guy in a hug. Abe squawks in surprise, but then he chuckles and brings his arms around Cal's shoulders and pats his back solidly. He glances at me over Cal's shoulder, a wry smile on his face.

"Cal!" he exclaims just as loudly.

Calliel sets him down, then steps back and puts his hands on Abe's shoulders. "It sure is great to meet you!" he says. "You're probably the fourth or fifth person I wanted to meet the most. Maybe even the third."

Abe grins up at the big guy. "Maybe even third?" he echoes. "Then I shall count myself as being blessed."

"You *are* blessed," Cal tells him seriously. "Extraordinarily so."

Abe opens his mouth then closes it, speechless for the first time since I've known him.

"And thank you," Cal continues, his hands still on Abe' shoulders, "for taking care of Benji as you have. It means more to me than I could ever say."

Abe shakes his head, and his eyes look brighter. "I didn't—" His voice cracks and he shakes his head again as he clears his throat. "I didn't do much," he tries again. "You're certainly an odd one, aren't you?"

Cal glances over his shoulder at me. "I like him," he says.

I nod, not speaking for fear I'll break.

He lets go of Abe and picks the plastic bags up off the floor and comes over to me. "Rosie said you need to eat more, and I agree," he announces. "So you will eat all of the sandwich and the salad I brought, and I will sit here and share mine with Abe and watch you until you finish."

And he does just that.

"All the mountains here were filled with gold!" Abe says excitedly a little later, talking with the angel like they're best friends. "And you mark my words, Cal, someone is going to find a nugget the size of your fist up in those hills, and there will be a huge rush of people trying to get rich!"

"I have really big fists," Cal says, showing Abe and me just how big they really are.

Cal watches me as I put the last bite in my mouth, while he talks to Abe about gold nuggets the size of fists. Then he cleans up our lunch and tells me he's going to throw it away and take the trash out back while he's at it. I nod as he pulls the trash bag from the big plastic can near the doors. He winks at me while he walks toward the office in the back.

Abe watches him go. "He's wonderful," he says quietly.

I sigh. "You too, huh? Just like most everyone else in town."

Abe arches an eyebrow at me. "Just like you too, then?"

I shrug and avert my eyes. "He's my friend," I say, but who I'm trying to convince, I don't know. There's something there, sure, and it sparks in my chest like a mini sun going supernova every time I see him, but it can't matter. I'm just a guy from a small town in the middle of nowhere who doesn't plan on doing anything else with his life but what he's doing now. Cal is… Cal. He's a guardian angel, for God's sake. He can't belong to just one person. He has to belong to everyone, even if they don't know it. And besides, even if he *could* just belong to one person, it wouldn't be me.

Abe has known me too long, it seems. "Now you listen here," he says, his voice stern. "I already know what you're thinking, and you need to knock it off. You're a better man than most anyone I know, and you learned that from your father. How do you think Big Eddie would feel if he could see you doubting yourself like this?"

"That's not fair. You can't bring my father into—"

The bell tinkles overhead as someone walks into the store.

He's a young man, probably not much older than me. He's dressed in jeans and a hoodie, both of which look crusted with filth. His skin is pale and sallow, and his eyes look like heated black coals bored into his skull. He's twitchy, darting nervous looks around the small store, his hands shoved into the front pockets of the hoodie.

Abe glances at me then back at the man.

"Help you find something?" I ask, keeping my voice level.

The guy shakes his head, pursing his cracked lips, and walks down one of the aisles.

"Security cameras still up?" Abe asks under his breath.

"Yeah," I mutter, relieved that he feels it too. "Why don't you head out the front door?"

"And leave you alone?" he says. "Hardly. You got your cell phone?"

"It's back in the office."

"Gun?"

Now I feel guilty. "Back in the office. I was cleaning it. Forgot to bring it back up."

"Of course you did," he murmurs. "Well, this should be interesting."

The guy has done a tour of the store, not stopping to pick anything up. I know he's casing the store, trying to see if anyone else is in here. I don't know how long he's been watching outside and whether he saw Cal before he came in. I don't recognize him, so he's not a townie. But I *do* recognize the way he's moving, the rigidity behind his steps, the way he jerks his head back and forth. He's high, or was high, or has been high on something hard-core. Drugs have never been a problem in Roseland, as far as I've seen. Most of the underage kids here resort to cheap beer cadged from their parents' refrigerators. But you'd have to be blind not to see the signs of a habitual user.

Cal hasn't come back yet, but that doesn't mean anything. For all I know, he's distracted by something outside, as he's prone to be. Worse, he might have seen a thread that is not my own and been pulled toward it. *It'd be pretty great if my thread was screaming for him about now*, I think. *Or however it's supposed to work.*

Our new friend licks his lips again as he walks by us, glancing our way before looking out the front to the street. Abe starts forward, as if he's going to clock the guy from behind, but I grab his arm, shaking my head when he turns to scowl at me. I raise my hand at him, mouthing *wait*. His lips pull together in a thin line. *Cal!* I scream in my head as the guy reaches up and latches the lock on the door. *I could really use your help right about now! If you can see* anything, *see my fucking thread!*

Time seems to slow as the lock clicks into place. The guy seems to explode, pulling his hands from his pockets in a jerky motion, a handgun in his right hand. He raises it up, his eyes wide, his hands shaking, mouth moving. "You know what this is! Give me all the fucking money in the register! Do it now!"

"Okay, son, okay," Abe says, his voice low and smooth. "We all just need to take a deep breath here. No one has to get hurt."

The guy snarls as he takes a step closer, waving the gun between the two of us. "Shut up, you old fuck!" he cries. "Get the money out of the register before I blow your fucking head off!" He glances behind him, out the front window. The sidewalk is empty this far down Poplar Street. "Where's the other guy?" he snaps when he looks back.

Shit. "What other guy?" I ask, tapping a button on the register, opening the till drawer.

"The big one! Where'd he go?"

I shake my head, grabbing the bills that make up the hundred or so bucks I've got in the drawer. "He left out the back a while ago. Had some errands to run."

He looks toward the back of the store. It's empty. "You got a safe back there?" he asks, jerking his gaze back to me.

"Nothing in it," I tell him. "Bank pickup came yesterday afternoon."

"Fuck!" he screams. "All I wanted was a fucking hit, man! Traynor *told* me I could get it, that fucking bastard!"

Traynor. The name is familiar, but I can't place it right now.

"What did Traynor tell you that you could get?" Abe asks gently.

He swings the gun back and points it at Abe. "I told you to shut the fuck up," he says coldly. "I will kill you, man. I've done worse. I don't fucking care."

"I've only got a hundred bucks," I say loudly, trying to get the guy's attention off Abe and back to me. "It's yours if you take it and leave now." I hold it out to him across the counter, both of my hands visible.

He twitches again, the gun coming back in my direction. He takes a step toward me then stops, narrowing his eyes. I can see something stirring in his mind. Whatever it is can't possibly be good. *Cal!* I scream again. My heart is starting to pick up in my chest and my palms feel clammy. But I'm also pissed, maybe more so than I've been in a long time. This is my store. This is my father's store. He worked his ass off to make sure this place stayed afloat and I've done the same since it became mine. Who the fuck does this guy think he is, walking in here, waving that fucking gun around? This place was my father's. It is now mine. This is my *home*.

"Maybe I don't believe you," the man says slowly, as if choosing his words carefully. "Maybe I don't believe you about the safe."

"The bank comes the same time every week," I tell him, a sneer on my lips. "Just because you're tweaked out of your mind doesn't mean I'm lying to you."

"Not a good idea to upset the guy with the gun," Abe mutters.

"There's no money in the back," I tell him again, my voice hard. "Either take what I'm offering or get the fuck out of my store."

"I'll fucking shoot you, you goddamn asshole!"

"Take the money and get out."

"Benji," Abe pleads.

I look the guy straight in the eye and say, "Get. *Out.*"

I think, *Cal.*

I can see it all, those next few seconds stretched out so that they feel like days. His finger tightens around the trigger, the hammer inches back. A bead of sweat drips down his forehead, slides between his eyes and off the side of his nose, leaving a track like a tear under his sunken right eye. His lips tremble. His shoulder shakes. His finger jerks and the gun fires, the sound surprisingly muffled in the store. *Cal*, I think again.

The world around me suddenly darkens with a loud rush, and I smell earth, raw and pungent.

Silence.

Then:

A low snarling noise rumbles near my left ear.

"Holy mother of God," Abe whispers.

The would-be gunman moans.

I open my eyes, unsure of when I closed them.

It's dark, which confuses me for a moment. Wasn't it just daylight? And then I wonder if I've been shot in the face and am blind. There's no pain, but I've never been shot in the head before, so I don't know if it's supposed to hurt. Maybe I should be relieved there's no pain. If there is no pain, then there can be no sorrow.

The earth smell hits me again. It's overwhelming and a lump forms in my throat. I don't know why. *This earth is my home*, I think, not knowing where it comes from. Then the black ruffles against my face, light and soft scratches. The rumbling near my ear gets louder. *Oh*, I think. *Oh. This? This is…. He's….*

Wings.

The darkness parts in front of me, light forming down the middle and spreading toward my face, the cocoon splitting, the shelter cracking in half. The ruffling of feathers is almost as loud as the rumbling from behind me. They part, the great wings rising above me. Blue. The feathers are so blue, so deep and dark and wonderfully blue that the lump in my throat grows bigger and my eyes burn.

The rumbling turns into a full-on growl and I turn my head to the left. Only inches from me is the face of the angel Calliel, coming slowly into focus. His head is so close to mine I can smell my soap on him, even through the scent of musty earth. The stubble on his head blends into a sideburn that turns into the light beard across his face, a deeper red than I've ever noticed before. His eyes look almost completely black. His lips are parted, his teeth bared in fury. The rumbling is coming from him. His chin scrapes my shoulder, and only then do I notice his arms around me protectively, his right across my right shoulder and chest, his left around my waist.

Something catches the corner of my eye and I look up, over his head. The wing above me seems massive, pressed against the ceiling and bending back down toward the floor. A tip of the wing, which I now see is the left, falls toward me. It stops moving down about a foot overhead. The wingtip is still for a moment, but then it starts to shake, twitching back and forth. Something falls. I reach up with my only free hand and catch the object. It's hot in my hand. I lower it to see.

A round disc of burning metal, squashed flat.

The bullet.

The growl is turning into a roar.

I turn from Cal and look ahead. The tweaker is standing frozen, his face pale. Abe is staring slack-jawed, his eyes wide. I wonder what they see. I think for a moment, my mind disconnecting from the reality in front of me, that what they see must all be blue.

I turn back to the angel. I reach up with my free hand and grab his chin, turning his head toward mine. There's a moment when the sound coming from his throat gets louder, and his eyes get blacker, but then something sparks within him and a semblance of humanity returns.

He can't have humanity, I think wildly. *He's not human.*

"Hey," I whisper.

He snarls at me.

I shake his chin with my hand. I struggle to free my left arm, twisting as I pull. He tightens his grip around me, and for a moment, I think he won't let me go, but I slide my other arm loose and he moves his hands to my back, clutching me tightly. I reach up and cup his face in my hands. He tries to pull away and I dig my fingers into his skin.

"Hey," I say again, louder. "It's okay."

Cal shakes his head. "He needs to go into the black!" he roars, his voice far deeper than I've heard it. His breath is hot against my face, contrasting with the chills down my spine. "He will suffer for trying to take what's mine!"

"No," I say, trying to ignore the way his words slam into me. "You need to listen to me. Can you do that?"

I think he's going to refuse, he's going to pull away and launch himself at the gunman, sending him into the black, whatever or wherever that may be. He surprises me then, as a shudder rolls through him, rippling up through his body and extending through his wings. He squeezes his eyes shut tightly, and when they open again, they are dark, but the overpowering black is gone. He nods.

"You are not the judge," I tell him. "You are not the jury. You are not the executioner. Since you are none of those things, what are you?"

"I am the protector," he whispers.

In the distance, a bell rings, but we ignore it.

"And you have protected me," I tell him, relaxing my grip on his face, tugging gently on the auburn hairs on his face. From up above, bright lights swirl and the wings begin to fade.

His face grows dark again. "But… but he—"

"No," I tell him. "Me. You and me. Okay?"

He watches me for a moment. I don't look away. He sighs and the lights above grow brighter, obscuring the feathers, which are growing fainter. He hugs me tightly, his face going to my neck. He breathes me in and lifts me, my feet leaving the floor. He trembles again before he sets me back on the ground. The wings have almost completely disappeared, the blue lights flashing, but growing dim. A moment later, they're gone completely.

"You had your wings," I tell him, almost laughing at the absurdity of the sentence.

His eyes flash. "Your thread is very bright. And very loud. I heard you screaming my name. I was angry." This last comes out heatedly, as if he's getting riled up again.

"At me?"

He shakes his head. "No. At myself. I should have been here sooner. I got distracted. You must forgive me." He reaches out and grabs my hand, clutching it in his own. His eyes search mine, pleading.

"There's nothing to forgive," I say, entwining my fingers in his.

He looks like he doesn't believe me, but I don't know what else to say. Today has been a very weird day. Getting shot at can do that to you, I guess. I'm ready to go home and it's not even two in the afternoon.

I look back out to the store. The gunman is gone.

"Looks like we're about to have some company," Abe says from the window, his voice thin. "People must have heard the gunshot or seen the guy running. Rosie's marching her way down with a shotgun. She looks determined."

"She probably just wants to make sure I made you eat the sandwich," Cal says. "She was really insistent about that." He looks worried at the thought of Rosie with a shotgun. Hell, *I'm* worried about Rosie with a shotgun.

"Abe," I start, unsure how to finish.

He waves his hand at me. "Boy, I've known you since you weren't nothing but a twinkle in your father's eye. I may not completely understand what I just saw, and I may not even believe it, but it's not mine to tell. Though, if you can, I'd like to hear more about it later. I think you've got one hell of a story."

I hang my head in relief mingled with sorrow. "Thank you," I whisper, not knowing what else to say.

"And you," Abe says, pointing at Cal. "I don't care if you're angel or demon. Just promise me you'll protect him."

Cal stiffens next to me, and for a wild moment, I think he's going to refuse. I look up at him and his eyes are almost black again and something crosses them, a shadow darker than the black. But then it's gone and he nods and says, "I promise."

Abe watches him for a moment, as if gauging his sincerity. He frowns. "All right, then. Look alive, boys. The posse's almost here. We've got some explaining to do."

the last time,
the first time

THIS is the last time I saw my father alive.

He said, "I've got to make a trip to Eugene in the morning. Going to meet up with some old friends. I'll be back in the afternoon."

The way he said it gave me pause. For one, he did not say who the friends were, and though I didn't think to ask, it would strike me later as being very odd. It was as if he was attempting to hide something, something he wasn't ready to say. That was unlike my father, for hadn't he taught me there was to be truth in all things? That, even at the expense of someone's feelings, it's better to be honest than to tell a lie? Lies, he said, could come back to haunt you, no matter how small, or how good your intentions might be. We were never to lie to one another, given that he was raising me in truth. That might be why I didn't think anything of it at the time.

He leaned against the doorway upon making this announcement, crossing his arms in front of his chest. He seemed tense, slightly nervous, which caught my attention almost right away. Yes, I would think about why he said the word "friends" instead of saying who later, and I'd kick myself for not thinking of asking, but it was his stance that I remember the most. His shoulders were slightly hunched, his face lined. He looked older than I'd ever seen him, and I wondered if he was getting sick. I wondered if he needed sleep. I wondered if he shouldn't just stay home.

But I said none of this. My biggest regret is that instead I said, "Do you need me to open the store tomorrow, then? It's Saturday. I don't have plans." I did have plans, with some buddies, but I would cancel for him. My father asked me and I did. It was that simple.

But it's never as simple as we think. It's never as simple as we hope. I should have done more. I should have demanded he tell me what he was doing, who he was going to see. I should have screamed that he tell me everything, why he was so anxious, why there was that look in his eyes. That look that said he wasn't sure what he was doing. I should have begged that he take me with him, let me tag along. Mom could open the store, I should have said. Or we could close the store for a day. Just let me go with you. Please, just take me with you. Tell me what's wrong. Let me help you make it right. Don't do this on your own.

I should have said all of those things. And more.

Big Eddie smiled, but it looked forced. "That'd be great, Benji. I think it's going to be slow tomorrow. Supposed to be a storm coming in, so you can take your school work with you and get some studying done. You've got finals coming up in a few weeks."

I made a face as I muttered, "Don't remind me. I don't know how I'm going to pass this stupid algebra final. Who cares about *x's* and *y's* and what stands for what? The alphabet shouldn't be in math."

He laughed, and with that simple action, he seemed freer. Lighter, somehow. He moved from the doorway and came to where I sat at my desk. "Can I tell you a secret?" he said, putting a hand on my shoulder.

I grinned as I nodded, waiting for my line.

He didn't disappoint. "Cross your heart?"

"Hope to die."

"Stick a thousand needles in your eye," he finished.

I waited.

He leaned closer and whispered, "Nobody uses algebra in the real world. Learn it, pass it, then forget it."

I laughed. "Unless I want to be a nuclear scientist," I said. "Or a mathematician."

He rolled his eyes. "You aren't gonna be no damn mathematician. Green men have no need for math. We're hands-on. We get dirty."

"Unless you're balancing the books for the store. Or building a house."

He waved his hand in an easy dismissal. "Just the basics," he said. "That's why we have an accountant. And a contractor to help with the logistics."

"Sure, Dad." I turned back to the book. He lifted his hand from my shoulder and ruffled my hair. I didn't know it then, but that touch, those fingers in my hair, would be the last time I would feel my father alive. I would see him again, but he'd be cold under my hand, life long since departed.

Had I known then what I know now, I would have clung to him. I would have looked him in the eyes to see that spark of mischief, that undying intelligence that belied his gruff exterior. If I'd known the inevitable, I would have said everything I felt in my heart and soul. I would have told him thank you for being my father. I would have said that if I'm ever going to be a good man, it's going to be because of the way he'd raised me. I would have said that building Little House together and fixing up that old Ford until it was so cherry were the best times of my life. I would have said that I didn't think I'd be able to go on without him.

I would have told him I loved him.

But I didn't. I didn't because I didn't know. I didn't even say good night. Or good-bye.

My father's last words to me were, "I'll see you when I get back, okay? Don't study too hard. Live a little, Benji."

I nodded, not looking up. *I'll live a little once I pass my sophomore year*, I told myself.

He left my room.

Twenty hours later, my mother would arrive at the gas station in the pouring rain to tell me he was gone.

ROSIE and her shotgun aren't the only ones that show. After she arrives, more townsfolk start pouring into the store, word of the attempted robbery spreading quickly. Their faces are filled with concern, which quickly turns to anger that such a thing could happen in Roseland. This is such a safe place, they say. Things like that don't happen here. What the hell is going on?

Sheriff Griggs arrives the same time my mother and Christie do.

"Benji," my mother gasps as she pushes her way through the crowd, wrapping me in a hug. "Christ, are you okay?"

"I'm fine," I say, my voice muffled against her shoulder. She pulls away, and as mothers tend to do, checks for herself, not satisfied until she knows I haven't actually been shot.

She asks what happened just as Griggs walks into the door. He looks around the store wearily before announcing loudly that the store needs to be cleared. Roselandians grumble but comply. They gather out near the one gas pump, whispering excitedly.

I tell the sheriff and one of his deputies the same thing I would have told my mother. The guy had come in, demanding money. I'd attempted to give him everything out of the register, but he wanted more. The bank, I say, picked up the funds from the safe the day before as they do for all the businesses on Poplar Street. The robber had flashed his gun around, and it'd gone off accidentally. We didn't see where the bullet had gone, but there didn't appear to be any damage. Maybe it misfired, I say. I didn't know. But the shot seemed to scare him. He fled.

"That so?" the sheriff says. "Sounds like you got lucky, Benji. You and your friend Cal, here."

Cal keeps his face blandly schooled and says nothing.

"Very lucky," the sheriff repeated. "You got a security setup here, don't you, Benji?"

"Eh, sorry, Sheriff," a voice says from behind us. Abe walks out of the back office and down the aisle to where we stood. "Just went back to check the tape myself and there seemed to be a malfunction. The tape is completely blank. Didn't record a darn thing. You should really get that checked, Benji. Hate to think something could happen again and there'd be no evidence of it."

The real tape is out behind the store smashed to pieces and buried in the trash, but the Sheriff doesn't need to know that.

Griggs frowns. "Well, isn't that just something. Awfully convenient that happened. A shame there's no video to back up what you're saying."

My mother scowls. "You sound like you don't believe him," she accuses Griggs. "What the hell else would have gone on here, Sheriff? My son was just *attacked* and you're making it sound like he had something to do with this!"

Griggs shrugs. "Just asking questions, Lola. You know I have a job to do. If it makes you feel any better, the guy was caught very easily. Apparently someone saw him ditch the gun a few stores down and one of our very own residents made a citizen's arrest. He's heading over to the station as we speak."

The words chill me, but I show nothing on my face because Griggs is watching for any reaction. "That's good," I say. "I'm glad he was caught so easy."

Griggs laughs. "I bet. He's also shooting off his mouth like you wouldn't believe!"

"Oh?"

"Yep. Seems to think there was a monster in the store."

"A monster?" my mother asks, sounding flabbergasted. "What on earth?"

"One of my deputies radioed me on my way here, letting me know that he'd packed the guy into the back of a squad car. Seems he's shouting to anyone who'll listen that there was a monster in this store. That the big guy here had grown wings and was going to kill him." He sounds strangely amused, as if it is the funniest thing he's heard in a long time. He glances over at Cal. "Well, how about it, big boy? You sprout some wings?"

"That's ridicul—" I start until the sheriff raises a hand to silence me.

"No, sir," Cal says quietly. "I don't have wings."

"You sure about that?" Griggs asks. "Seems the guy saw *something*."

"I think if you'll take a blood draw, Sheriff," Abe says coldly, "you'll find he was high as a kite. I wouldn't be surprised if he didn't know *what* he saw. Seems to me we've got a drug problem in Roseland. He's not the first one I've seen lately. I doubt he'll be the last."

"That so, old-timer? Well, I may do just that." He cocks his head at Abe. "And you make sure you call the station if you ever see someone with *drug problems*. I'll be sure to take care of that for you. The streets of Roseland are no place for tweakers and burnouts."

"You do that," Abe replies flatly.

"You've caught the guy, Griggs," my mother says. "Plenty of people saw him running from here, or so I'm told. That should be enough for you. I'm closing the station and taking Benji home."

"And what about Cal?" Griggs asks. "Gonna take him home too?"

Cal looks unsure until my mother steps in. "Of course. He's staying at Little House. I'm going to take care of both these boys, you can count on that."

The sheriff nods, tipping his hat in our direction. "Well, then, I'll take my leave." He looks me up and down, his gaze staying on my feet for a moment, then looks back up at me. He turns to walk out the door. He stops before stepping outside. "Say, Benji," he says, looking over his shoulder, "you wouldn't happen to wear a size nine boot, would you?"

"Yes, sir," I say.

"Funny thing, that. Found some size-nine boot prints outside my back window a few nights ago, like someone had been prowling. You wouldn't know anything about that, would you?"

I laugh, though my stomach is sinking. "Sheriff, I would think between running the store and everything else that I wouldn't have time to be paying you a visit. I'm pretty sure I'm not the only one who wears these boots. It's all they sell at the hardware store." My heart thuds in my chest.

"Is that all, Sheriff?" my mother asks icily. "Seems to me you have a suspect to go speak to."

"That I do," he says with a grin. "I'll let you know if I have any other questions. And, Benji, watch yourself out there. Seems like you're attracting all kinds of attention these days." He winks at us and walks out of the store, the little bell ringing overhead.

"MOM, I'm *fine*," I tell her in Big House as she tries to check me over yet again. "I'm just worn out. I think we're going to head to Little House to take a nap, okay? I just want to put today behind me and start over again tomorrow."

She looks like she thinks that's the most ridiculous idea she's ever heard, but I'm already standing, motioning to Cal to follow me out the door.

"You're getting that security system upgraded," she says, standing to poke me in the chest. "I don't care how much it costs. You know better than that, Benji."

I sigh. "I'll start researching first thing tomorrow, okay? We'll see what we can get and how soon."

She narrows her eyes.

"I promise," I say. "Cross my heart."

"Hope to die?"

"Stick a thousand needles in your eye," I say gruffly. "Cal, let's go."

He follows but I feel his absence behind me as I reach the door. I turn and see he's standing in front of my mother. She's looking up at him, unsure about his presence so close to her. I think about calling out to him, but I wait.

He reaches out and touches her shoulder. "Lola Green," he says quietly, "I know you are worried. I know sometimes things can seem scary. And maybe sometimes they *are* scary. But I will tell you this, okay? I will watch Benji. I will protect him. I will keep him safe. This I promise you. I will keep Benji safe. It's my job."

My mother gasps quietly, bringing her hand to her mouth, her eyes growing bright. She makes a little strangled noise from behind her hand and shakes her head. "Who *are* you?" she whispers. "You come out of nowhere and you stay here and you say things like that to me? Who the hell are you, Cal? Why are you here?"

For a moment, I think he's going to open his mouth and spill everything, and I think about what that would do to her, what that would mean. There would be surprise, I'm sure. Shock. Disbelief. Confusion. And *if* she believed him? *If* he did something to prove what he would say is true? There would be anger. Rage. Fury. She would demand answers I'm not ready for. She would ask him, if he was a guardian as he claimed, then where was he the morning Big Eddie died? Where was he then when he was supposed to be protecting the people here?

He would tell her that he couldn't remember, that pieces were still lost to him. He would tell her that he was like a puzzle that had yet to be made whole. He would tell her how sorry he was, but he just couldn't remember.

And it would sound like a lie.

Instead, he says, "I am Cal Blue. I am here because I care about your son. I care about all of you, but I care about him more. I am here to protect him, and I will do my duty."

She trembles, tears welling in her eyes then spilling over onto her cheeks. She sniffs and brushes her face angrily. "Then you better do your job," she says bitterly. "If something happens to him, I am coming for you. Do you understand me? If anything happens to him, I will hunt you down and make you pay."

"I wouldn't expect any less," he says, squeezing her shoulder.

She glances at me, her expression unreadable, and then she turns away, leaving the kitchen. I hear her going up the back stairs and wait until her door slams shut. He stares after her for a time before I call his name, my voice rough.

He seems so big when he walks toward me, as if there are parts of him, just under the surface, that add to his mass. For a moment, I think I see the faint outline of wings stretching out behind him, the tips dragging along the floor. A flat disc of metal feels like it's burning a hole in the jeans pocket I placed it in earlier. My skin feels electrified. My heart pounds. I don't know what all of these events mean, but it feels like things are changing and I can't do anything to stop it. I don't know that I want to even if I could.

He towers so far above me that it seems impossible. His eyes are like pools of oil, liquid in the way they shift. He reaches down and takes my hand in his and carefully pulls me out of Big House and toward home.

HE TAKES me to the bathroom in Little House and turns on the shower, telling me to strip. I do, trying to decide if I should be shy in front of him. My shirt goes up and over my head. I hesitate when I reach the fly to my jeans, but the earnest expression on his face is not mocking me, nor is it filled with any kind of deep hunger. I take off my boots and flip the buttons on my jeans and drop them to the floor. Something stutters across his eyes then and there's a quick flash as he looks me up and down just once, and I think I hear a sharp intake of breath, but I can't be sure over the noise of the shower. He parts the curtain, closing it behind me when I am under the water. I can see him through the plastic as he picks up my clothes and folds them, then puts down the toilet seat lid and sits. Waiting.

The water scalds my skin. The steam is heavy in the room. I feel detached, like I'm above myself, looking down. This moment feels almost like a dream. I lean my forehead against the tile, the water cascading down my back. I close my eyes and I'm tired, suddenly exhausted. My knees feel weak, and I open my eyes, my vision tunneling. I inhale, but I choke on the steam. It's hard to catch my breath and I just want to lie down. I just want to close my eyes and not think. It's not a bad thing. I know that desire to want to escape, to not have to worry about the things I no longer have control over. So I let go. The release is almost shocking in its simplicity. I let go of all of my confusion and jumbled thoughts because I just want to float on my back and look up at the sky and go wherever the river will take me. I let go and fall.

But before I fall completely, strong arms wrap around me, holding me tight. A worried voice says my name. Lips brush against mine, and in my secret heart (crossed, hoped for death, a thousand needles stuck in my eye), I know I'm safe as I disappear into the dark.

THERE is no seventy-seven in this place. There is no river. There are no crosses, no trucks that crash down embankments. No voices call my name, no shadow figures standing on the roadway above. It smells of earth and there is only peace because all I have is blue.

CONSCIOUSNESS creeps in slowly. I don't want to wake up, but I feel that I must. I'm warm, and comfortable. I know I'm in my own bed even before I open my eyes. I crack open my left eye and it's dark in my room. The sun has set since I passed out in the shower. Moonlight is soft through the window, splaying shadows from the trees onto the floor.

I am alone, and I try to ignore the ache that causes. I'm not too successful.

The bedroom door is shut and I hold my breath for a moment, trying to hear anything in Little House, to see if he is somewhere near or if a thread has called to him and he is gone. I don't hear anything. Little House is quiet. But don't I feel something there? Isn't there something, just beyond the door? All I have to do is open the door and he will be mine, because isn't something there?

There is, and he calls to me. My blood sings, the cells almost boiling. My skin prickles. I feel like I'm vibrating and my teeth chatter. I sit up and put my feet on the floor. I'm wearing only my usual sleep shorts. I try not to think how I got into them. "Things are changing," I whisper frantically, my voice hoarse.

Things have already changed, is the reply.

I stand and take a step toward the door and it's—

blue

—easier than I thought it would be, as is every step that follows. The floor is cold against my feet, the air in my room cool against my hot skin. My nipples pebble as I reach the doorknob, and I give myself one last chance to stop this, to stop all of this. I could. I could crawl back into my bed and pull the covers up and over me and hide there until morning, when things would make more sense, when things would be rational and I wouldn't have to—

I open the door.

Calliel has made his nest on the floor outside my room, a pillow under his head, a blanket covering his waist and legs. He's still wearing the same white T-shirt from earlier in the day, or so I think. For all I know, he could have any number of white ones. I rake my gaze over the muscles visible in his stomach and chest even below his shirt. They seem to go on for miles, and it's all I can do to keep from falling down on top of him to find out just how far they go. His neck is strong, the rusty stubble beginning just under his Adam's apple. The small cleft on his chin. The parted lips, full and pale. Those dark eyes.

He's awake and looking back at me, his eyes glittering in the dark.

We're silent, for a time.

Then:

"No threads tonight? No one to go save, Superman?" I say this lightly.

He shakes his head, a twitch to his lips.

"I'm sorry," I say, unable to think of anything else.

"For what?" he rumbles up at me.

"Falling asleep." I think I mean to say something else. I don't know.

"You were tired."

"Yeah. It's been a… strange day."

"These are some strange days," he agrees, arching his back. He looks like he's stretching, but his shirt rides up his stomach and I see the red fur there, the hard planes of his hip bone jutting in sharp relief.

I tear my eyes away. "Cal… I—"

"You need your rest." He looks toward my bed. "Go back to sleep, Benji. We can speak tomorrow. You've been through a lot today."

Disappointment tears through me, and it's harsh. "Okay," I say in a small voice. I reach out to shut the door, but then I don't want to. I don't want it closed. It's a barrier between me and the outside world. It's a barrier between him and me and I don't want it there anymore. I push it open even further so that it's against the wall and I glance down at him defiantly before I move back to my bed.

He says nothing.

I climb in and lie on my side, facing the open door. I can make out his faint outline, the red hair on his head and face, the tip of his nose, the part of his lips. I can't tell if his eyes are open or not. His chest rises and falls, and I wonder about things I've never thought before, like if he needs air to live like I do, if he breathes wherever it is he came from. I don't know if I've ever felt his heartbeat. Does he have one? Is there a pulse in his neck, hidden under the red stubble? *I want to find it,* I think before I can stop myself. *I want to find it with my tongue.*

Logic sets in then, along with my dismay at having thought such a thing. Angels might breathe, and their hearts might beat, but how can they want someone the way I do? And even if they—

he

—could, why would it be someone like me? I am nothing. I am no one. I am a small-town hick who will always be a small-town hick because I'll never leave this small town. I will live here and I will die here. I won't ever be someone he could want. I could never be enough for him.

But I want to be. I'm scared, but I want to try.

When did this happen? When did this start?

"Cal," I say, my voice stronger than I thought it would be.

He sighs, like his name on my lips is something wonderful to him. He moves until he is lying on his side, facing me. I can see his eyes now, the whites reflecting back at me. My breath catches in my throat. Even in the dark, I can see how he's not human. There's something about him that feels far older than I could possibly imagine. Again I think I'm insignificant, nothing more than a fleck of dust flung far in a gust of wind. Before it can overtake me, I push the thought away.

I don't reach out to people, not anymore. I don't even let most people come to me. I push them away so I can remain buried in myself, in my own pity.

So I push most all of them away. The ones allowed in are only trusted because they have been here with me since Big Eddie died. They understand my pain even if not its depths. I don't know how deep their own pain goes, but I know it's nothing compared to my own. Selfish, yes. I know. I know that through and through. But pain is selfish. Grief is selfish. It demands attention, and the more you focus on it, the more it wants from you.

"Do you want me?" I manage to say.

Please. I can't do this on my own. Help me.

He's silent for a moment, continuing to watch me. I want to look away, embarrassed by the need that echoes in my voice, but I can't seem to break the connection. Something is holding me there, and though I can't name it, I don't want it to go away.

"I shouldn't," he finally says, and I am ready to shatter into a billion pieces, but I hold my tongue and wait. It feels like I wait forever. "I shouldn't because it's not what I was made for. It's not why I came to be. But yes, Benji. God help me, yes. I don't want anything more than you. I want nothing less than you."

I take this for what it is. This is the eighth day since he fell from the sky, since I found him in the crater. Eight days since I found out what he was, since I began to believe there might be something else out there watching over us. Over me. I don't know if I can believe it all, because I don't think enough time has passed for my mind to process the monumental implications of Cal's existence.

But none of that matters now. I sit up on my bed.

"Cal?"

"Yes, Benji?"

"Will you…." *Say it, say it, say it.* "Will you come here?"

There's no hesitation on his part. He rises from the floor, shaking the blanket off. He looks even bigger than before. Little House creaks under his weight as he walks toward me. I am aware of each breath, each step. He finally stands above me, and I'm tired of waiting. I'm tired of wondering. I'm tired of being alone. I reach up and grab the front of his shirt and pull his lips down to mine.

He grunts in surprise but doesn't pull away. He's tentative at first, barely moving. His movements seem shy and unpracticed. It's only then that I realize he's probably never done this before, that this is his first *anything*, and I have to stop myself from groaning. It's slightly awkward, this kiss; the angle is almost too much, and we're not quite synced up. But then my tongue touches his lips and he sighs again. His breath goes from him into me, and it tastes like he smells, earthy and strong. There's a touch of something spicy in there too that I chase after.

He keeps his hands at his sides as if he doesn't know what to do with them. I let go of his shirt and wrap my arms around his neck as his tongue touches mine for the first time. A shock rolls up through me and he shudders along with me. He breaks the kiss and presses his forehead against mine, panting as we watch each other. We're so close together that I can see myself reflected back and I want more. All I want is what he can give.

It's like he hears me, like he knows what I'm thinking. One moment he's leaning against me and the next he's all hands and collapsing. He falls against me, pressing me back onto the bed. His mouth is on mine again, and gone is the reticence, the inhibitions. He's still a novice, but it doesn't matter. His weight is pressed against me, it's crushing me, but I don't want him to move away. He moves his lips from mine and drags his tongue down my neck to the hollow of my throat as I play my fingers over the red stubble on his scalp. His breath is hot against my skin and I'm harder than I've ever been. I groan when he grinds into me, his stomach against my hips and dick. He pulls back, a look of shock on his face. He grinds again and I cry out. The smile that follows is not one I've seen on him before. It's wicked and dark, as if he knows what he is doing to me and enjoys the hell out of it.

I want more.

I reach down to pull his shirt up and over his head. It catches on his chin and he snorts in laughter before pulling it off the rest of the way and then dropping it to the floor. He props himself up above me on his hands. I'm about to snarl at him to lay on top of me so I can feel his skin against mine when he looks between us and then back up at me, the shyness returning.

"What is it?" I ask breathlessly, running my eyes over his torso, matted in auburn curls that start on his chest and trail down to his stomach and into the top of his jeans. "What's wrong?"

He shakes his head. "I've never done this before," he says, sounding frustrated.

I can't wait any longer to touch. I reach up and run my fingers through the hair on his chest, rubbing my thumbs along his nipples. The muscle is hard underneath and I explore lower, touching his stomach, his navel. He groans as I roam my hands over him, but my exploration turns into something I never would expect to hear from him: a slight chuff that becomes a giggle. He's ticklish there, on his sides near his hips, and this realization is something so endearing that I feel like I have the wind knocked out of me.

I reach the start of denim, and I need to be crushed again under his weight so I hook my fingers into his belt loops and pull him back down on top of me. The first thing I notice is the heat of him. Then it's the hair on his body, soft and delicious against my own hairless torso. He is still chuckling when he kisses me again and his laughter pours from him into me and I can taste it like it's a palpable thing. I wrap my legs around his waist and press my heels against the back of his legs, pushing him further into me. We rock together, and I don't know how much longer I can last if we keep going this way. He's obviously a quick study. He twists his tongue against mine and begins to reciprocate, moving his hands up and down my exposed chest.

"Never done this before?" I gasp as he latches his teeth on my neck. "Could have fooled me."

His only answer is a low rumble as he kisses my shoulders, my arms, my sides. His tongue slides over my nipples, first the left, and then the right, leaving them wet, the cold air a shock after the warmth of his mouth. He's going lower, gripping my sides with his big hands, kissing my stomach, swirling his tongue near the top of my shorts. My cock strains against the fabric, pressing up underneath his chin.

"You don't have to," I say, arching my back as he reaches under and squeezes my ass. "You don't—" But he's already mouthing me through the cotton. I can feel the sharp graze of his teeth, the swipes of his tongue. He pulls the shorts down over my hips and then his mouth is on me, hot and harsh. There's too much saliva, yes, and his teeth get in the way, but it's still like nothing I've ever felt before. Either he's doing something so very right, or everyone I've been with was doing it wrong. I'm approaching the edge already, and I don't want to lose control now. I don't want it to be this way. I need more. I need so much more.

I reach down and push him off me, and the look he gives me would be almost comical if not for the swollen lips, the saliva on his chin. He looks like he is going to protest, but I shake my head at him and he stills.

I pull him back above me, my dick straining against my stomach. I brush my fingers over his chest and stomach and with a practiced twist of my hand, I unbutton his jeans. He's watching me again, and when I wrap my fingers around his cock, his eyelids flutter gently. I brush my thumb over the slit, rolling my fingers around the head. "I want more," I tell him as his eyes widen. I pull my hand out of his jeans and spit into it, then reach back down and get him wet. He groans again.

"I don't want to hurt you," he pants.

I laugh softly. "You're not *that* big," I tell him, even though the weight in my hand suggests otherwise. He's also uncut, which is something I've never experienced before. There seems to be so much more skin than I'm used to and I have to keep from hyperventilating at the thought of angelic circumcisions. There's so much I don't know about him, but at the moment, it doesn't matter.

He's trying to be serious, even though his eyes keep rolling up in his head. "I can't hurt you," he says as I use my feet to push his jeans and boxers down to his knees. "I'm supposed to protect you." He falls forward and bites gently into my neck again.

"You won't hurt me," I say, writhing against him. "You won't let it happen. Please, Cal. Please."

He pauses against my neck and I hold my hand still. His muscles tense. His length in my hand is hot and his shoulder is pressed against my mouth. There are those freckles there, the ones I saw the night he fell. I count them with my tongue, first one, then two, and three and so many more. "Please," I whisper.

He growls, low, and without warning, I'm flipped over onto my stomach and Cal falls against me, pressing his cock against my ass. His tongue is in my ear, his teeth catching the lobe. He rubs his dick in the crack of my ass, and I can feel him leaking against me.

"Do I scare you?" he whispers hotly. "Are you afraid of me?"

"No, no. No, you don't. I know what you are. You don't scare me. You don't. You can't." I'm babbling, I know, but I can't find a way to stop.

"Do you trust me not to hurt you?" he rumbles in my ear, grazing his lips against the shell.

There's no question, and not just because of what he's going to do to me. "Yes," I groan. "Yes."

"And you know that I am here to protect you?" he says, rutting against me harder.

"Yes, I know! Please!"

"You called me here, and I came for you."

"I know, oh *God*, I know!" My own dick is digging into the mattress, the pressure a thing of beauty. But it's not enough. It's nowhere near enough. I reach up and slide my hand into the drawer, finding an ancient tube of slick. I don't know how long it's been in there, or even if the stuff expires, but I don't care. My fingers brush against a box of old condoms, and I grab one and hold it over my shoulder. "Do you know what this is for?" I ask as he pauses.

"Yes, Benji," he says, sounding amused and annoyed. "I'm not an idiot."

I press my right cheek into the pillow. "I know you're not. Do you need to wear this?" *This has to be the weirdest conversation of my life.*

Hurry, hurry, hurry.

He scowls. "No. I've never been with anyone but you. This is my first everything."

I figured that, but it still annihilates me to hear. "But I've been with—" I try, only to have him cover my mouth with his big hand.

"I don't want to hear about anyone else," he hisses in my ear. "I don't want to hear it from your mouth. I don't want to know. I never did. I never watched because I couldn't take it. I couldn't. It hurt my heart. You can't hurt me now. I don't need that."

"Cal...."

"Do you trust me?" he snaps.

"Yes," I say quietly, because I do.

"Then put that down. You won't hurt me. I won't hurt you."

I drop the rubber back in the drawer and hand him the lube.

He uses his fingers first, and he's slow and careful, heeding my warnings that it's been a while. He's quiet while I tell him what to do, no doubt listening for any sounds of discomfort from me. There is pain, but it's negligible. There is burning as I'm stretched, but I welcome it. He kisses the base of my spine and adds another finger when I tell him to. He kisses my back again when I start to shake at his intrusion.

It's enough.

He props me up on my knees when I tell him I'm ready, that it needs to be now. There's a moment when he pushes himself in when I think it's going to be too much, I'm not going to be able to take him, and I grit my teeth. But I crash through that ceiling, and when his hips are pressed against my ass, there is no more pain. There is only him rising above me, beginning to move back and forth. He's grunting, holding me at my shoulders, grazing my neck with his fingers. I cry out at a particularly deep thrust and he leans on top of me, his face in my hair, his breath on my neck, and I'm reminded of the days when I felt that breath alone in Little House. Those days of coming home to nothing but memories like ghosts, drowning in a river I couldn't see. I can remember those feelings, but even after this short amount of time, it's like peering at them through a murky haze.

But he's here now, with me. He wraps his arms around my chest and pulls me back up onto my knees, my back against his sweaty chest, forcing me to sit in his lap. He rolls his hips underneath me, and I turn my face until my lips find his.

As he rises and falls beneath me, one arm around my chest to hold me to him, the other starting to jerk me off, I close my eyes and lean my head back against his shoulder. There in the dark, I see the blue, I *feel* the blue, and it's overwhelming and it's huge and it's overtaking me. I can't handle it anymore and spill over onto his hand. He feels this and hears my cries and snaps his hips once then twice, and then there is warmth erupting in me and it's like nothing I've ever felt. His groan becomes a whine in my ear and I tremble against him.

I can feel it, then. His heartbeat. It's strong as it pounds inside his chest. This causes my eyes to burn and I don't know why. Maybe because it's unexpected. Maybe because it makes him more human. He was alive before, but now I *know* he's alive. He takes a deep breath behind me and then lets it out.

As we collapse on the bed, him still lying atop and inside me, pressing his lips against the back of my neck, I have a moment to think that things aren't changing.... No. It's not like that at all.

As he wraps a big, gentle hand around my throat, finding my lips again, I realize that everything has *already* changed completely and I can't go back to the way things were. Not after this night. Not after knowing what this could be like.

The angel Calliel kisses me again, and I begin to think about the future. About the possibilities that lie ahead. About the fact I no longer seem to be alone, because I know he will choose to stay. We'll continue as we are now and things will be better than they were. I think these things. I think of these things and more.

But....

Even as he gives a contented sigh in my ear, even as I pull him closer, isn't there something at the forefront of my mind? Something aside from the postcoital glow, aside from my wishes for the future and my hopes of the present. Things have changed, oh yes. Make no mistake about that. But that's the funny thing about grief and anger combined; even while buried in newfound happiness, it claws and it whispers. It begs. It howls.

It screams.

It doesn't let go. And it demands retribution.

cross your heart
hope to die

I AM surprised, when I finally pull myself out from under Cal to get something to clean us up with, to find it's not even ten o'clock at night. It feels like days have gone by, the violence in the store this morning a distant memory. It could be the postfuck glow, or it could just be everything piled on top of everything else. I don't know.

I need to talk to Abe tomorrow, though for the life of me, I don't know what I'm going to tell him. The truth seems like a good place to start, but since I'm not completely sure of the full truth, I don't want to end up making this worse.

I just need to figure out what to say to him.

But first, I need to figure out what to say to myself.

Always with the damn questions, I can hear Cal growl already.

No. I have to push through it.

I clean myself in the bathroom, a pleasant ache in my ass that I haven't felt in a long time. I look at myself in the mirror and try to see if I've changed outwardly to match the hurricane on my insides. I can't tell. I still look like me. I look closer. There's a small, dark bruise above my clavicle on the right side of my throat. I touch it, and it burns slightly. Cal likes to mark, it seems. There are red marks on my hips that stretch toward my back. His handprints, from digging into my skin, holding me to him as he thrust into me. They are fading already, but each finger is still clearly outlined against my pale flesh.

Changes, even on the outside.

I take a wet cloth out to the bedroom, light from the bathroom spilling out. My mouth goes dry and I almost stumble at the sight. Cal nude, stretched out on my bed, his white skin almost glowing in the dark. He has his arms folded up behind his head, the hair under his arms as dark red as the curls on his chest. His chest and stomach rise slowly with shallow breath. His dick lays spent against a thatch of pubic hair. He has long, hairy legs, muscled and relaxed. For a moment, I wonder if he's posing and I want to scold him again about vanity, but I can't seem to make any words come out.

I reach him to find his gaze on me, watching every step I'm taking, my every movement. There's a low huff of air as I clean him off, the remnants of spunk caught in the red trail on his stomach, the muscles there clenching. I let my gaze trail up his body, and once he's sure I'm looking at him again, he flexes his arms behind his head. I still my hand on his stomach.

"You like that I'm big," he says knowingly, his grin all teeth.

"Vanity," I accuse him weakly. I drop the cloth on the floor and climb onto the bed, suddenly unsure about where to put my hands, where to lie down. This hesitation only lasts a moment as he reaches up and pulls me down on top of him, pressing my face in his throat, his chin against the top of my head. My dick finds this a wonderfully interesting place to be and stirs, but there are other things on my mind.

Cal rubs my back slowly, making lazy circles that cause my skin to tingle. He kisses the stubble on my scalp and rumbles underneath me, a low sound I can feel in his chest.

So many things to say, to ask, and I can't seem to focus on a single one.

But apparently there's been something on his mind too, because he's the first to break. "Benji?"

"Yeah?"

"Why were you at his house?"

I'm confused. "What? What are you talking about?"

"Griggs."

Oh. That. Fuck. "Why do you think that?" I ask, trying to buy some time. For what, I don't know. He's surely felt me tense against him.

He doesn't sound fooled in the slightest. "Because you lied to the sheriff earlier today. You might have fooled him, but I can tell when you're lying."

He's said this before. "Because you're an angel?" I ask, unsure if that's a stupid question or not.

He shakes his head above me. "No. Because I know you, Benji."

"You say that," I say slowly. "You say you've watched me for I don't know how long and—"

"Since you arrived here," Cal interrupts, pressing harder against my back. I almost arch into it.

"What?"

"I've watched you since you were born," he says. "You were mine from the beginning, just like the rest of the people in Roseland. The moment you crossed back into the town after coming home from the hospital, you were mine. That was a good day."

I swallow past the lump in my throat. "It was?"

"Yes. I was very happy that day. But you haven't answered my question. Why were you up at that house?"

"That was the night I was looking for you," I say guiltily. "Griggs had come by the house and made those stupid threats, and I thought…."

"You thought what?"

Now I do try to pull away, but he doesn't let me go. In fact, he pulls me back down to him and tightens his grip on my back. I put my face in his neck and inhale his earth scent. "I thought you might have gone up to his house. I thought you might try to send him away."

"To where?"

"The black."

Cal tenses beneath me. "So you thought I was going to attack him because of what he said?"

"I didn't… I don't know, Cal." *Like I don't know anything about you.* "You were pretty scary when you said that to him."

A sharp intake of breath. "Do I scare you?" He sounds scared himself.

Does he scare me? If he does, it's only because of the unknown, which I hate to admit makes up a big part of who he is. I tell myself I wouldn't have just slept with him if I had feared him, but something inside me disagrees, telling me I probably would have done so regardless. He's kinetic, dynamic, a moving storm over an open plain. He's dry lightning, ozone-sharp and devastating. If there is fear there, it's so wrapped up in everything else I don't know how to separate it.

But I've waited too long to answer and he's starting to breathe heavier underneath me. I prop myself up so I can look into his eyes. He's wary, but doesn't look away. "Should I be scared of you?" I ask him.

He opens his mouth and closes it again almost immediately. He furrows his brow and frowns. "I don't want you to be," he says finally. "But maybe you should be. Regardless, you shouldn't have gone to his house, Benji. He could have hurt you. You need to stay away from him." This seems like a slip on his part and he winces.

"Why do you say that?" I ask him, refusing to ignore it.

"He's not a good man, I think."

"You *think*? Or you *know*?"

He looks away and I can't stop myself from leaning down and brushing my lips against his rough cheek. "I've been trying," he mutters, leaning into my lips.

"Trying what?" I say against his face.

"There's this… knot… in my head. I'm trying to untangle it, but the more I pull, the tighter it gets. I can remember certain things. I can remember *many* things. I remember Roseland becoming mine, only seven people here. I remember watching it grow. The buildings. The houses. The people. Many were good. Some were not. But it didn't matter, because they were *mine*. I wasn't made to judge. That is not my job. I was made to assist them, because sometimes, people need a little help. Just a nudge." He shakes his head. "You think that God is some all-powerful being, and maybe he is. But I don't understand. If he's supposed to be, then why is there a need for someone such as me? Why is there need for other guardians? Or why is there need for any angels at all?

"If he really wanted it, nothing bad would ever have to happen. There would be no need for someone such as me. The threads are knotted in my head and chest and I want them to separate, but I don't know what that would make me. What is God doing? Why do I exist, Benji? Why must I follow these threads? Why do I have control over certain things, but can't stop others?"

He's getting worked up, his chest rising rapidly, his heart thumping wildly under my fingers. I try to quiet him down, to tell him it's all okay, but he shakes his head angrily. "You want to know, don't you? What happened to Big Eddie? You want to know so bad, don't you?"

Yes. Yes, I want to know more than anything. I shake my head. "No, Cal, I don't need to—"

"It's there, Benji," he says angrily, knocking his hand against his head sharply. "It's all in there somewhere. The threads. The pieces. I just can't find them. I don't know how to start. I don't know where to begin. I am not Death. I cannot control it, but I am *aware* of it. There's a difference between what I do and the inevitable."

"Like the Wallaces? The fire?"

A short bark of harsh laughter. "You knew?"

"You smelled like smoke."

"You were smelling me?" he asks, surprised and pleased.

"Uh… sure. The fire?"

He nods. "Sometimes, Death can be avoided. The thread isn't completely black, though it's getting there. It still pulses with life, but time is short. Only when I find a thread of complete black do I know there's nothing I can do. The Wallace family still had color. Greens and reds and little Emily was this bright pink, so alive. It wasn't their time."

"But… my father?"

"I can't remember," he says hoarsely. "Benji, you have to believe me. I wouldn't keep this from you. I promise you I wouldn't."

A dark part of me wonders at this, wanting to berate him, poke him further until he cracks. It seems awfully convenient, this dark part says, that of course he wouldn't remember. An angel fell from the sky and couldn't remember the people he was supposed to protect? What are the chances of that?

I try to push the doubt away, but it's latched on and wants to burrow. "What do you remember?"

He closes his eyes with a heavy sigh. "I remember… On High. It's beautiful, Benji. Beautiful like you wouldn't believe. It's warm and bright. It was supposed to have been made by God himself during the seven days of Creation. It's a lovely place. But it's also a lonely place. We rarely interact with each other, the guardians. The other angels. Decades could go by without seeing another one. Whenever one of my people traveled away, they would be watched by whoever's jurisdiction they fell into, and vice versa. If an outsider comes here, I must protect him or her as if they are my own. There was never a need for me to speak with another guardian, so time would pass. I remember being busy. All the time. There was always something to do, some thread to be followed. But since I've been down here, it hasn't been like that. There've been times I've been called, but not as much as I was used to.

"Your father is in here," Cal says, pointing to his head and chest. "Tangled in this knot. I don't know how to pull him out. I can't remember that day. I can't remember many of the days that followed. It's there, somewhere, but I can't find out how to fix it. I want to fix it so bad, but I'm scared to see it too. I'm scared of what it will show me."

"Why, Cal?" I ask, not knowing if I want the answer or not.

He reaches up and cups my face, lifting his head to kiss me sweetly. I feel blind against him. "Because," he says as he pulls away. "Because if I untangle it, I'll see what really happened. I'll see why I couldn't save Big Eddie. I'll see what I did wrong and why I didn't do more to try and stop it. I'll see the truth, and you'll hate me for it. Out of everything I can remember, it is you I see the most, Benji. The day Big Eddie left is gone. It's in the black. But after? Oh, the day after and every day that follows, there are pieces I can touch, things I remember and it's all *you*. I hurt because *you* hurt. All I wanted to do was make it all better, to make it all go away, to wrap you up so you wouldn't hurt anymore. You carried the weight of the world on your shoulders, and I just wanted the burden to be easier for you, to help you carry it so you would realize that you weren't alone."

"Stop," I croak, my eyes burning. "Just… don't." I don't want to hear this. I *can't* hear this.

He ignores me, kissing me again. "I broke the rules, I think. I would come partway down, just so I could touch you, just so I could take some of your pain away. But it wasn't enough. You were sinking further and further into the river, and I couldn't let that happen. I couldn't let you drown. So I…."

Like you let my father drown? I think before I can stop myself.

I press my head against his chest. "So you what?" I say, my voice muffled. I'm trying to regain some of my composure, but it's a losing battle.

"I don't know," he whispers. "It's there, in the knot. I remember you calling for me, and not just the night I fell. Even before that, I could hear your aching, because it was too much like my own. I was lonely up there. I was lonely without you and I had to come down. You finally called for me. You *screamed* for me. I had to come. I… I just don't remember how."

"You bastard," I mutter weakly. "You bastard."

"I'm sorry, Benji. I don't know… I don't know what else there is."

He looks miserable when I raise my head from his chest. I am angry, yes, but I don't know if it's at him. I'm trying to believe him about what he can and can't remember, but it seems to be too much of a coincidence. The one person who can answer every question I've had about that day also happens to be the one person who can't remember any of it?

"What about Griggs?" I push. "What about him? Or Mayor Walken? Or the smoker? The smoker who—" I stop. The name. What was his—

Memories, rising.

Walken: *You seem to forget, Traynor, that you are operating in* my *town, with* my *permission, which makes me* your *boss.*

The gunman: *All I wanted was a fucking hit, man! Traynor told me I could get it, that fucking bastard!*

"Traynor," I whisper. Was it something as simple as that? Drugs? Was that a connection? A hit of what?

"Benji?" Cal asks me, looking worried.

"Do you know a man named Traynor?" I ask. "Do you recognize that name? Is he one of yours?" I hadn't recognized his name or his voice, so he didn't seem to be a townie.

Cal closes his eyes, and they move quickly behind his eyelids. "No," he says after a moment. "I don't know him. I don't know that name. He's not one of mine."

"But you would have to know him if you saw him, right? If he's in your jurisdiction?"

Cal shakes his head. "Only if something were to happen to him. Only if I could see his thread."

I didn't know where to find Traynor, much less cause something to happen to him so Cal could track him. "Why should I stay away from Griggs, Calliel? What are he and Walken doing? What is going on in this town?"

He squeezes his eyes shut. "I don't know."

I roll off him and he doesn't try to stop me. I sit up on the side of the bed and put my feet to the floor, my back to Cal. "I think you do," I say bitterly. "I think some part of you knows and you're just not telling me. I think you know far more than you're saying. I believe you when you say it's tangled up in you, that you haven't pulled it apart. But I don't believe you *can't*. I think you're scared and you're hiding behind it."

Blue lights begin to flash in the dark.

"That's not—"

"How did you come here? You said you were the first. You told me you fell because I called you. How did you do it, Calliel?"

"Oh, Benji," he whispers. The blue lights are brighter.

I stand up and look down at him, scowling. "You said that angels are tested. That all of you are tested. Maybe this is your fucking test, Cal. Maybe you don't remember because you're being tested. Maybe that's why you exist. Maybe that's why God needs angels and that's why you see the threads. Because it's just some fucking *game* to him. His tests are nothing but *games*. You see patterns. You see designs. But you don't see what's right in front of you. You're being played, Cal. God doesn't give a damn about you. He doesn't give a damn about me. It's all a fucking game!"

Cal leaps up from the bed, the flashing lights following him and starting to form behind him. "*Nothing* about this is a game," he snarls at me, a look of pure fury on his face. I'd be scared by it if I wasn't so angry. *Just an hour ago we were fucking,* I muse darkly. "I am here because of *you*. I came here because of *you*. All I want to do is keep you safe! To keep you away from the river!" The accusation in his voice is loud and clear. *You did this to me. You brought me here. This is all your fault. You tore me away from the only home I've ever known and now you're pushing me away.*

It only succeeds in making me angrier. "Can you say the same thing about my father?" I shout at him. "Where were you when he was drowning? Where were you when he was dying? Did he call for you? Did you promise to protect him too? What about *him? Why did you let him die!*"

The blue lights explode and the room is suddenly awash in a flash that causes my eyes to burn. Afterimages dance along my vision as I blink, trying to make sense of the darkness falling again in the room. My eyes start to adjust and I see Cal leaning over the opposite side of the bed, curling his hands into the comforter, great blue wings extending from his back, curling against the ceiling, dragging along the floor. Again, they take my breath away. They are surreal. My mind argues with itself, telling me they can't be real, this is nothing but a nightmare I can't seem to escape, but I hear them dragging on the floor, and that rustling sound can't be anything but real. It can't be anything but here in this room.

Wake up, my father whispers from a fading dream. *You gotta wake up, Benji. He's come down from On High because you called him and you've got to wake up. He's been waiting, yes, but* you *still brought him here, down to this place. You've got to help him. He's going to act big, he's going to talk big, but deep down, you two are the same. You must remember this. You are the same.*

"You're right," the angel Calliel says, standing. His hands are fists at his sides. His voice is something I haven't heard yet before. Angry. Deep. Cold. His wings shift around him, the deep blue catching the moonlight. "I should have done more. I should have *been* more. You have every right to be angry. I will try to remember what I did and what was done. You will know as soon as I do."

The wings begin to fade, as does my anger. Now, I'm just unhappy. "I shouldn't have yelled at you like that," I say quietly. "It's not fair to you. I'm sorry."

He shakes his head, but he won't look at me. The wings are growing dimmer. "No need to apologize. I am a protector, and I need to do my job. I've allowed myself to become distracted. I need to be working more on remembering. On trying to figure out how I came to be here and why. I need to know who allowed it. The reason they did."

"But... I thought you came here for me," I say, backtracking, wishing I hadn't said a goddamn thing. My chest hurts. "Don't you...."

The wings are gone now. He slides into his jeans and shirt. He moves toward the door. I reach out and grab his arm as he tries to move past me. He towers above me, fully clothed. I'm still naked. I tremble at the heat of him. "Where are you going?"

"Out," he says gruffly, finally looking at me. He looks sad. He looks like he's been betrayed. "Away. I need to think. I need to focus. I need to make this right. Some of us have lost our Father too."

The sting of those words overwhelms me. "Will you be back to watch the sunrise?" I ask quietly.

He looks like he's about to speak, but doesn't. He pulls himself from my grasp and I'm still standing there when the front door to Little House opens and then shuts behind him.

I WAIT on the roof as the sun rises. He doesn't return.

I'm still there when I see Mary and Nina walk out the door of Big House and get into the car, going to open the store.

I'm still sitting there when Christie leaves a few moments later, going only God knows where.

I'm still sitting there when an old Honda rolls up the driveway. It rolls past Big House and a minute later brakes squeal as it pulls next to the Ford. I'll have to remember to check the pads next time. Abe opens the door and gets out. He looks up at me. "Benji," he says.

"Abe."

"Where's our friend?"

I shrug.

"Is he here?"

"No. He's gone."

Abe looks around. "He left?"

I nod.

"He coming back?"

"I don't know." *I hope. Oh, how I hope. I'm sorry. I'm so sorry. Please come back.* I've been praying like this for hours. Nothing has happened.

"Boy," Abe says, narrowing his eyes, "what did you do?"

"I told him that God didn't give a shit about him," I say honestly. "I told him he might as well have been the one that killed my father, since he didn't protect him. I told him I didn't need him here." Those words hurt. I ignore the way my voice cracks.

"Did you mean it?"

I shake my head. "He's my friend. I was mad. He was hurting and frustrated and I took that and made it my own. I lashed out. I drove him away. I drove him away and I don't know if he's going to come back."

"You're going to make me climb that ladder, aren't you?" Abe asks, sounding resigned.

"Had to watch the sunrise," I tell him, hoping he'll understand even though I know he won't. "It's kind of a tradition now. Abe, what if he doesn't come back?"

But Abe doesn't answer, he's already moving toward the side of the house, to the ladder. I try not to think as I wait, but I fail miserably. *You've only known him nine days,* I chide myself. *Nine days is* nothing *in the scheme of things. Nine days is* minuscule *compared to how long you've gone without him. Grow a pair.*

I almost believe my own lies. Almost.

Abe finally huffs his way to the top and comes to sit beside me, his knees cracking as he lowers himself. He doesn't speak for a time, and we watch the morning take shape around us. It's okay, this silence. It's easier to drown when it's quiet.

But I should have known it wouldn't last long. "Wings, huh?" Abe finally says.

"Yeah. Angel, even."

"That's…. something new."

"That's what I said."

Silence. Then, "Did you mean it?"

"No," I say roughly. "I didn't mean a word of it. It's not his fault. He's right. I'm the one who called him here. Even if he wanted to come, I still called him."

"That light everyone was talking about. Last week? The meteor. Out by seventy-seven where Big Eddie… oh my God, that was *him*?"

I manage a weak smile. "You should have been there. He made quite the entrance."

The blood has drained from Abe's face. "I just never thought… not here. Not in my lifetime."

"He's a guardian. Supposed to be our guardian angel. The whole town's guardian angel. That's what he says."

"Guarding from what?"

"Everything, I think. I still don't know quite how it works. He's… different. I think he's even different than any other guardian angel. I don't know why I know that. But I do."

"Big Eddie? Does Cal know…."

I shake my head. "He can't remember. Something happened to him. Something that made him forget. He's not supposed to be here. Something broke when he fell and he doesn't know how to fix it. And I just made it worse."

Abe's quiet for a moment, gathering his thoughts. "You know," he says after a minute, "we both hurt, sometimes more than I think we'd care to admit. I lay awake all night last night, thinking I would know what I would ask when I drove over here. You know what I was going to ask him, Benji?" He looks out into the forest. "I was going to ask him about Estelle. If he was an angel like I thought he was, I was going to ask him about my wife. I was going to ask him why she had to leave when she did. Why she had to go before I did. Ten years, it's been now. We weren't young when she passed, but she was young enough that it shouldn't have happened. I'm told an aneurysm is like that. It's one of those things that shouldn't happen, but it does anyway."

I bow my head, fighting back against the tears that threaten.

"I was selfish, you know. A long time after she died. Years. I was angry at her for being the first one to die, leaving me behind all alone. I always figured I would go first. I was older. She was in better shape than I was. I smoked for thirty years.

She never so much as had a sip of wine. She didn't do *anything* to deserve...." He trails off, watching the rising sun.

Eventually, he sighs. "So I was furious that she went first. That she was at peace and I was left alone here. I was so mad at her and I stayed that way for a long time.

"I was going to come here and ask your angel if he knew of Estelle. It sounds ridiculous, right? I told myself that all night as I tossed and turned. But I got up this morning determined to ask him if he knew her. If he could see her, because, boy, there are times when I swear to God that I can feel her near me. I was going to ask if he was there when she left me. Do you remember what happened? You might be too young, but that's okay. She was walking across Poplar Street. Just a normal, sunny day. She was going to get her hair done. That's all. She was going to get her hair done and instead she died in the middle of the road, her face pressed against the asphalt. I was going to ask Cal to give her a message for me. Do you know what that message was, Benji?"

I'm unable to speak.

"I was going to have him tell her I'm sorry," he says quietly, putting his arm on my shoulder. He doesn't pull me toward him, just lets me feel the weight of him. "I was going to say I'm sorry for being so angry for so long. That I missed her and I'm sorry for acting like I didn't. Grief is like that, Benji. It masks the anger until anger is all you know. Until you're buried in it. You're not the only one grieving here. I am too. I loved your dad. Loved him because he *was* mine too. Love him still, even after all this time. He's not an easy person to forget. Your mother grieves. Your aunties grieve. And your angel sounds like he grieves as well. And maybe it's worse for him, because maybe he *should* have done something. Maybe he *did* fail. But it sounds like he doesn't know, and you can't blame him for that. You can't blame anyone until you know the truth. Big Eddie would have expected more from you, boy. I do too, for what it's worth."

A watery laugh escapes me. "He would have told me to stop acting like such an idiot," I say, wiping my eyes.

Abe smiles. "And he would have loved you no matter what. This man. This... angel. Cal. Calliel. Is he... do you care for him?"

I know what he's asking. I can't lie to him. I won't. "Yes."

"And does he feel the same?"

Yes, Benji. God help me, yes. I don't want anything more than you. I want nothing less than you.

"Yes," I whisper. "More than I probably know. He's... watched me. For a long time."

Abe nods. "Things like these always have a way of working themselves out. You'll see. It'll be right as rain before you know it. You just have to have a little faith."

He might be right. And before I can think otherwise, I'm spilling the details of the argument Cal and I had, details I didn't think I'd share when Abe had arrived. But it's out and when I finish, he squeezes my shoulder. Relaying it out loud makes me want to kick myself for how ridiculous I'd been. I never should have pushed him. I never should have let it come to this.

"He's right, you know," Abe says after a time.

I snort. "About which part?"

He turns to look at me, his face stern. "About messing around with Griggs. You saw the way he looked at you yesterday, Benji! He *knew*. He is not a man to cross, believe me. I've seen men like him before. No good can come from it. Let someone else handle it. You call that government man who came by last week. That FBI agent. What was his name?"

"Corwin."

"You call Agent Corwin if you think it's important. Or let me do it for you. You let them handle it. But you let it alone, you hear me? You don't want to be in their sights, boy. Not a single one of them. I don't know what they've got going on, but you need to separate yourself from it. Don't let it become your problem. For all we know, that's what happened—" He cuts himself off before he goes any further.

But I heard it, and the words I've never dared to speak aloud are given life.

For all we know, that's what happened to your father. For all we know, he crossed them. The Sheriff. Walken. A man named Traynor. Whoever their boss is. For all we know, he found out what they were doing and it became his *problem, which then became* their *problem. Griggs has certainly made enough veiled threats, hasn't he?*

"I can handle Griggs," I say, feeling less sure than I sound.

Abe shakes his head sadly. "That's where you're wrong. I don't think anyone can. I stopped at Rosie's on my way over to get a cup of coffee. She had some interesting news."

Dread washes over me. "What?"

Abe looks like he'd rather say anything than what he says. "Apparently our twitchy friend from yesterday, one Arthur Davis from Hillsboro, hung himself last night in the sheriff's jail barracks, waiting for a bond hearing that was supposed to happen this afternoon. A deputy found him strung up from the edge of one of the bunk beds, a sheet wrapped around his neck. He's dead, Benji. Our lone gunman is dead."

the strange men

APPARENTLY, dead drug addicts don't warrant much attention. There is a small blurb online, a ten-second mention on the news: *A man under arrest for suspicion of armed robbery at a convenience store in Roseland hanged himself sometime between midnight and 6:00 a.m., when his body was discovered at the Douglas County Sheriff's Office barracks during the morning shift change. He apparently was a known drug user with a history of petty offenses. Any further information pending notification of next of kin.*

Griggs releases a statement, saying, "While the sheriff's department does its job to keep the streets safe, it is always difficult to understand why an individual would feel the need to take his own life. Our thoughts are with the family of Arthur Davis."

Apparently it was cut and dry. No further investigation required.

These are some strange days, Cal said.

I can't sit at home and stare at the walls. Not while I can sit in the store and stare at the walls there. People ask where Cal is. I tell them he went back to California for a bit.

I pray. I do. I really do. I pray even though I'm not very good at it. I pray because that is how Cal said he came down the first time. I feel foolish at this, now that I have knowledge of what I'm trying to do. When I called him originally, it had been out of horror and fear and the need for someone to hear my pleas.

Now, it's just for him.

Cal. Please come back. I've only known you thirteen days and you've been gone for the last four of them. It's been under two weeks since you fell but it might as well have been forever that I've known you. I need you to come back. Please. Please just come back. See my thread. Hear me now. Please.

But there's no reply. Like any time I've ever prayed before, there is nothing. I come to the conclusion that no one is listening, that no one ever did. Angels exist; that's been proven by the one who fell from the sky. But there is nothing else. I believe in the impossible. I believe in the improbable. I do not believe that my prayers matter. Not for the first time, I realize just how small I really am, just how petty I sound.

That fear doesn't stop me from closing up the store every few hours to rush back to Little House, only to find it as empty as when I'd left it. It doesn't stop me from sitting on the roof every morning, watching the sunrise, searching the long driveway for that familiar figure in the dawn, ambling up to say he's hungry, to ask if we can go for a ride in the truck because it's so cherry.

But there's nothing.

EVERY time I close my eyes I see blue and hear the rustle of feathers. I hear his warning about the river and I jerk awake, flailing around for someone that isn't there. My bedroom door is left open, and every time I wake, I look to the floor there, to see if he's made his nest.

It's always empty.

I trudge up to Big House shortly after sunrise, exhausted but still unable to get any real sleep. My mother is in the kitchen with the Trio. They are quiet as I walk in, and I get the distinct feeling that it's only because I've entered the room, that any conversation they'd been having ceased at my entrance. Nina watches me with big eyes, looking like she's going to speak but then thinks better of it. Christie looks away. Mary attempts a smile. My mother hands me a cup of coffee, full of sugar and cream so it's a light brown, the only way I can drink it. I take a sip. It's hot.

I shouldn't be like this. I went twenty-one years without knowing he existed. I've spent the last five focusing on one day at a time. I've relied on no one but myself. Yes, there is this little family that stands before me, watching, obviously waiting for me to say something, anything to explain away the bags under my eyes, the hangdog look on my face. But even with them, I've been alone. Granted, the lonely island I have become is by choice. So why am I acting like such a goddamn pussy? Why do I care so goddamn much?

Because he's gotten under my skin. He wormed his way in and I can't figure out how to get him out. I'm haunted. I'm haunted by memory. I'm haunted by the scent of his skin against mine, the scrape of his stubble against my cheek. The way his mouth moves, the way his heart beats in that impossible, improbable way. That feather in the bag on my back. The way it feels like silk under my fingers. The way it's blue. I need—

No. No. I don't *need*. I don't want to *need*. Fuck this. Fuck him.

My mother is the first to break the silence. "You getting any sleep?" she asks, even though she knows the answer already.

"I'm fine," I say, my voice more rough than I'd like. "I'm fine," I try again, clearing my throat. It doesn't sound any more believable.

"Haven't seen Cal around," she says carefully.

"He's back in California," I mutter, taking another sip of coffee. "Went home for a bit."

I don't miss the shared glance between the sisters.

"When is he coming back?" Mary asks.

"I don't know. Does it matter?"

"It looks like it matters to you," Christie says. She sounds dubious.

"Benji, what's going on?" my mother asks.

I set the coffee mug down on the counter, ignoring the way it sloshes over. "It's nothing," I say, trying to keep from snapping at them. "He's not here, he's gone. So why don't you just stop with the questions. I didn't know you guys cared that much about him. I'll be sure to send him up here should he decide to make an appearance again." I glare at each of them before I spin on my heels and walk out of the kitchen, heading for the front door.

I'm being childish, I know. It's rude. They're just worried about me. But I can't take it. I can't take their pity, that look on their faces, the one that says *poor Benji. Poor, poor Benji.* It's the same look I've gotten over the past few days, more and more people coming in to ask about Cal, more and more people getting turned away in my increasing frustration. For the short amount of time he's been here, he's certainly affected a lot of people, and I hate him for it. I hate him for leaving me alone to fend against them all myself. That fucking ass—

A hand latches on to my arm as I am about to descend the porch steps to the Ford. The touch is familiar and I sigh. She's the only one who hasn't said a word. I don't turn because I'm worried I'll snarl at her too.

"Benji?" Nina asks carefully.

"What," I say, defeated.

"He'll come back, you know."

It hurts to hear. "Oh?"

"Yes. And you should know that better than anyone."

I shake my head. "It turns out I don't know a whole lot, Nina. Not anywhere near what I should."

"Do you care for him?" she asks. It's the second time in only a few days I've been asked this question and my answer is the same. I nod. "Then you know *enough*," she says, sounding far wiser than I ever could. "If you care enough for someone, then you give them the time to know what they need to do for themselves."

"He won't come back," I say, suddenly sure. "I said things. I said some horrible things to him. He won't come back. I wouldn't if I'd heard those things said to me. I'd hate me. Every single part of me. I'd turn and walk away and never look back."

"No," she says, rubbing my arm. "I don't think you would. You're better than you know, and so is he. Promises were made."

"Not to me," I remind her.

"Not out loud," she counters. She moves to stand in front of me. I try to look away, but she doesn't let me. "Not here," she says, touching my lips. "But here." She touches my head. "And here." She touches my chest. "Sometimes it's the promises we don't say that are the ones that are the loudest."

I can't help the small smile that forms. "How did you get so smart?" I ask her as I lean in to kiss her forehead.

She giggles and returns the kiss on my cheek. "One of us has to be. Lord only knows what goes on in that foolish head of yours."

I watch her for a moment. "A promise, huh?"

She nods and looks out into the brightening morning. "Benji, you have to remember that even though you've been sad, he's been the same. You think you've been alone, and so has he. But it may have been harder for him. You didn't know he was there, not really. He knew *you* were there. And he did what he could, but it wasn't enough for him. You might have called him, Benji, but he didn't have to come. I felt what he felt. He showed me. There was despair. There was sorrow. And then there was you, so bright within him."

My vision blurs and I don't speak, knowing my voice would be broken.

She sees this and reaches up to wipe my cheeks. "So you keep your head up. You stand tall and proud like Big Eddie did. And you will see. You'll see. Things will be okay, I promise." She kisses me again and then heads back into the house, shutting the door behind her.

IT'S just after three when Rosie comes into the store. It's been quiet today, the number of people asking after Cal reducing to a trickle. I've taken Nina's words to heart, but it's still rough to hear his name coming out of someone's mouth. I'm thinking how I haven't visited Big Eddie in a while and should probably go see him when the bell dings overhead. Rosie enters, looking grim.

What now? "Hey, Rosie."

"Benji," she says in greeting. She glances back over her shoulder, her shoulder-length ponytail flipping around. There are more streaks of gray in her brown hair than I remember seeing. Her normally youthful face is now lined with something I can't quite place. She scans Poplar Street before turning back to me. "Anyone been in here you don't recognize?" she asks me.

I shake my head. "Regulars today, no out-of-towners. Why? Everything okay?"

She gnaws on her bottom lip. "Maybe. I don't know. I could just be overreacting. Two men came into the diner today. They seemed… strange. I don't know how else to explain it. They looked normal. They were in black suits and black ties, but… I don't know, Benji. Something just struck me as off. They almost reminded me of Cal, but he's so much more… I don't know. Cal's warm. He's peculiar, but he's endearing. Does that make sense?"

I nod, only because that describes him perfectly. He is an oddity.

She looks relieved. "But these two, they just felt cold. That same oddity, but cold. I've been in this town a long time, Benji, and I've seen a lot of people come through here. But never something like them."

A buzzing noise starts in my ears. "Did they say who they were?"

Rosie shakes her head. "I tried to get names, but they ignored me. I thought at first that maybe they were police or something, but the more I think about it, the less I'm sure."

FBI? I think, remembering Corwin's card in my pocket, and his earlier visit. With all that's gone on lately, he's been the furthest thing from my mind. Maybe he sent someone else to follow up here in town. I tell Rosie this, but she's shaking her head again even before I finish.

"I don't think that's it, Benji. They weren't asking about Big Eddie or Griggs." She glances over her shoulder again out onto the street. It's empty. She turns back to me. "They were asking about Cal."

I can't prevent the shock on my face. "Cal?"

She nods. "They called him Calliel. They described him perfectly, asking if anyone in the diner had seen him. I had a few of my regulars in there. The doc, Julie from the mayor's office. Worley had come down off the mountain for a cup of coffee and a burger like he does every week."

I'm horrified. "They all know him," I whisper.

She snorts. "We do, yes. But you should know us better than that, Benji. They let me talk, and I didn't say a thing. I told them I hadn't seen the person they described. I asked them who they were and what they wanted, but they just said they were trying to find their old friend Calliel. They looked around the diner like they thought I was hiding the big guy somewhere. Then they left and started walking down Poplar Street, store to store. I got the doc and Worley to start calling the businesses to warn them, and I took the back alley from the diner down to here."

Her loyalty is almost enough to cause me to crumble. "Rosie... I—"

She heads me off. "Oh, no. Don't you even do that, now. You know we take care of our own here. Big Eddie always did right by us, by me, and you've done the same since you've stepped up in his place. And I don't think I've seen you as happy in that whole time as you've been in the last two weeks." I start to sputter, but she glares at me and I subside. "Do you trust that man?"

I don't hesitate. "Yes." The answer surprises even me.

"Then that's good enough for me. I liked him the moment I saw him. I don't need to know what he did, if he even did anything. I don't know where he is right now, and for some reason I've got a feeling you don't, either. But if you speak to him, you tell him old Rosie's asking about him and that he'd better get his ass back here before I hunt him down."

"I miss him," I admit. "I don't know...." I allow myself to trail off.

Rosie hears the bitter notes in my words. She reaches over the counter and grabs my hand. "He'll be back," she says, her gaze softening. "You should see the way his eyes light up when he's talking about you. It's always 'Benji this' or 'Benji that'." She grins at me. "Remember when you guys came in for dinner a few days ago?"

I nod. It had been the day before the gunman. The day before I called him to my bed.

"When you weren't looking, he'd steal these little glances at you, out of the corner of his eye. I don't think he knew anyone saw him, but we all did. Everyone except you. And that look? Oh, Benji. That look was everything."

My heart hurts. My bones ache. "I—"

The bell rings overhead. The door opens.

Two men walk in, unfamiliar to me. The room immediately goes cold. Both are wearing matching black suits, white dress shirts, and skinny black ties. They are big men, almost the size of Cal. Both have cropped dark hair, and for a moment I think that they might be twins, but one has darker skin, almost bronzed, while the other is a pale white. The darker-skinned man appears younger than his counterpart, who has lines around his eyes and mouth. Their eyes are the same, though, and I can see why Rosie had said they were like Cal. Their eyes are like black pools of oil, almost without any white around them. They look like Cal's eyes, but even from here, they seem darker. Older. Emptier. The strangers cause my stomach to twist.

The younger man, in the lead, looks around the store, jerking his head erratically, like a bird. He stares at the ceiling for a moment, narrowing his eyes. I follow his line of sight, seeing scratch marks against the ceiling tiles overhead. It takes me a moment to place them, only because I can't imagine what could cause those marks ten feet overhead. Then it hits me and my blood runs cold.

Cal's wings, wrapped around me, protecting me from gunfire.

I drop my gaze to find the pale-skinned man staring at me. "Help you?" I say, my voice somehow even.

He ignores me, averting his eyes to Rosie. "From the diner," he says, his voice oddly flat. There's no accent to it, no lilt to his words. Each word down to the very letter sounds exactly the same. Even in Oregon there's a specific cadence to the speech. This voice sounds like it comes from nowhere.

Rosie grins cheerfully. "Came to say hello to my friend!" she says, her voice booming. For an old broad, she's got some balls, that's for sure. "Why am I not surprised to see you boys again. Say, I didn't catch your names earlier."

"We didn't give them," the darker man says, his voice just as strange. "What happened there?" He points to the ceiling with the scratch marks.

I glance up just for a moment, pretending to study what he's showing me. "Don't rightly know," I finally say, slowly. "Can't say I spend much time looking at the ceiling."

Rosie frowns as she looks up. "Probably the electrician," she says. "These old buildings are wired like you wouldn't believe. Looks like tool marks to me."

I shrugged. "Could be right."

"Big Eddie," the older one says, and I squeeze my hand into a fist. "That's the name out there on the sign. Big Eddie."

"Sorry, gentlemen. If you want to speak to my father, you'll have to communicate with the dead. He's bones in the ground."

They glance at each other, and for a moment, I swear I see their eyes twitch back and forth rapidly. I blink, but it's over and I can't be positive it happened. They both turn back to me.

"You're Benjamin Green," the older man says. "Benji."

I raise my hands. "You got me there. How'd you know that?" Sweat trickles down the back of my neck into my shirt.

"We're looking for a... man," he says, ignoring my question. I hear the hesitation on the last word and know they're flat-out lying. They know what he is. They know who he is. "Goes by the name Calliel. Big. Red hair. Beard is red. Like fire. Like so much fire. Has he been here?"

I shake my head. "Guy like that'd stick out around here. Can't say I've seen him. And a name like Calliel? Sounds Hispanic... or Greek."

"It's not Hispanic," the dark man says.

"It's not Greek," the light man says.

I cock my head. "Could have fooled me."

The dark man jerks his head again, and it almost looks like he's seizing, the cords in his neck tightening. "Feathers," he says as his head stops moving. "Have you seen any... feathers?"

Carefully, I push my backpack farther under the counter with my foot. "Like bird feathers?"

"There's all kinds of feathers around here," Rosie snaps, though even she sounds somewhat confused. "We live in a forest. Birds live in trees. There's bound to be feathers all over the ground."

The light man shakes his head once, from side to side. It's not fluid, but staccato, as if the joints in his neck are partially frozen. "This is not... a bird feather. It's big. It's bigger. It's—"

"Blue," his counterpart finishes. "Everything about it is blue."

"No blue feathers, no green feathers, no feathers the size of a house," I say. "Fellas, I haven't seen your man, and if you aren't going to tell me your names and if you aren't going to buy something, I suggest you say sayonara and walk through the door."

They narrow their black eyes at the same time. I meet their gazes coolly, even though I've curled my hands into fists behind the counter and I'm digging my nails into my palms hard enough to draw blood. They glance at each other again, and this time I'm sure I see the strange eye twitch, and I wonder if they're communicating. I wonder if they're from On High. I wonder if they're angels.

But they're making my skin crawl, and all I want is for them to leave. I clear my throat and their eyes stop twitching. They look at me again. "I hope," the dark man says, "that you are telling us the truth, Benjamin Green. About Calliel. About feathers." He curls his lip, the closest thing to a human expression I'd seen since they'd walked in. It's a monstrous thing. "And scratches."

They turn as one and walk out of the station and continue out of sight down Poplar Street.

Rosie lets out a breath she's been holding. She turns to look at me. "Benji, what the hell is going on?"

"These are some strange days," I mutter, unsure of what else to say.

THE Strange Men (which is how they were referred to throughout the town, like you could hear the capitalization of each word) apparently stopped intruding on people after leaving the store. The doc and Worley were able to contact enough people to spread the word to others, and nobody answered any questions from the Strange Men. I consider the people they would have spoken to, knowing some are less skilled as actors than others. I worry that the Strange Men will run into Griggs or any of his deputies, but by the grace of God (a phrase that I can't use anymore without basking in irony) they never come into contact. Griggs and the Strange Men are people I do not want meeting.

So members of the town rally behind us, and I wait for a snake in the grass to show his face and hiss little secrets, but it doesn't happen. After leaving the station, the Strange Men disappear.

By five that afternoon, the phone lines began to buzz with more whispers that fan the gossip wildfire. Most are rational, or so I'm told. Most just wonder what Cal has done to attract the attention of the Strange Men. Most believe Cal to be some dashing bank robber, or an international jewel thief. Okay, most don't *actually* believe that; that theory comes directly to me from one Matilda Bajko, a kooky old bat who sighs when she says Cal's name as she explains breathlessly in my ear over the phone about how she believes he's on the run from Interpol. I don't have the heart to tell her that I don't think Cal even knows what Interpol is. Let alone how to steal anything.

But there are those who whisper different things. A strange light in the sky? they say. A meteor no one had seen? they conspire. Men in black suits coming out of nowhere and leaving just as mysteriously? Why, it's obvious! How could they have not seen it before! *Aliens* have landed in Roseland! But why are they asking about Cal? This stumped the conspirators until Gerald Roche, a retired banker and admitted sci-fi enthusiast, decided Cal had seen something he wasn't supposed to see and was on the run and the government was trying to hunt him down.

Regardless, everyone agrees, it's exciting. It's mysterious. It feels like *secrets* and if there is one thing a small town always has, it's secrets.

Strange days, indeed.

I RESIST the urge to drive straight home after I close the shop to see if Cal is there waiting for me. Ever since the Strange Men left the store, my phone has been ringing off the hook. It isn't until dusk that Mom starts calling me, but I let it go to voice mail, which I ignore. Her questions are going to be harder to dodge. I know she's going to be waiting up for me no matter how late I drive in, but there's something gnawing at the edge of my brain, something that has been there ever since this morning when Nina mentioned my father by name.

I need to see him, to be near him even if he's just mostly bones.

So instead of continuing straight toward home, and instead of turning right to mile marker seventy-seven and the river beyond, I turn left, heading toward a lost hill that never was. Autopilot takes over, like I'm being directed to this place by something that I can no longer find the strength to believe in.

It is here, now, that I fall back to my darkest hour.

this is the hour we collide

IT RAINED the day my father died. The kind of rain that starts early, and the clouds are so heavy you know the cloud cover is going to stick around all day. The kind of day you wake up only to want to pull the covers over your head and sink back into sleep.

The alarm went off early, predawn light entering the room. I looked out the window and saw through the rain that my dad's truck was already gone. I was surprised at that. It seemed too early for him to go meet up with his friends already, but since I didn't know what they were doing in Eugene, I guess I didn't give it much thought. He would be back, he'd told me, at some point that afternoon.

I opened the store that morning, knowing it would be quiet unless the rain let up. That was okay with me—I still had history and algebra to catch up on. I started the coffee machine. I put the pastries in the display cases. I turned on the lights.

And it continued to rain.

Abe came in and shot the breeze with me for an hour. He showed me how to find the value of X when I only knew Y. He drank a cup of coffee and then headed out. The rain hurt his joints, he said. The cold too. Such an oddly cold day for May. He was going to go home and use a heating pad on his knees. I smiled and waved to him as he left.

Rosie brought me soup around eleven. Chicken noodle, freshly made. She smiled and then made the mad dash back to the diner.

Around one, I heard the wail of sirens in the far-off distance.

It was two when a deputy's car pulled into the station. It sat outside in one of the three parking spaces for a moment. I could see the deputy moving around inside. Dominguez, I think it was, talking into the CB. Eventually, he backed out, his lights started to spin, and he took off.

It was raining harder at three that afternoon, like a wall of water.

Then it was four. And then 4:17 happened. I will remember that exact time for the rest of my life. It was 4:17 when my mom pulled into the station. The lights from her SUV filled the store. They switched off, and for a moment the afterimage danced along my vision. Then my eyes cleared, and I saw my mother through the rain, still sitting in the SUV. I couldn't make out her face clearly through the rain sluicing down the windshield. I sat there and waited. *Maybe she's on the phone,* I thought. She'd gotten a hands-free headset she seemed to be in love with. I couldn't see clearly to know if her lips were moving or not. So I waited.

And waited. Five minutes. Then ten. I became worried at 4:27. At 4:29, the car door opened slowly. As if it wasn't raining. As if it was a beautiful day and she had all the time in the world. As if nothing else mattered.

Her foot came out first and touched the pavement of the parking lot. She let it rest there for a moment, and I saw her press down on it, as if testing her leg to make sure it could hold her. Her other foot came down. She reached up to grab the top of the door and used it to pull herself up. I thought she was sick. I thought she was drunk. I thought I should go to her. I needed to help her. She was my mother and she was obviously not well. Something was wrong.

But I couldn't move. Something stopped me. I don't know what it was, but try as I might, I could not move.

She took another tentative step forward, and then closed the door behind her. Her head was bowed, her blonde hair hanging wet around her face, almost like a veil. She took another step and almost stumbled, her right leg seeming to buckle. She caught herself on the side of the car before she fell.

And still I could not move. Still it rained.

The florescent lights buzzed overhead. One began to flicker, snapping on and off rapidly. The tips of my fingers tingled at my sides. My head ached. My heart was sore. It hurt because I was watching my mother falter in the rain and I could do nothing to stop it. As she took another step toward me, I was sure something awful was coming. She took another step.

I could lock the door, I thought. *I could beat her there and lock the door. Keep her out of here. Keep her from bringing in the rain and the clouds. I'm dry here. I'm warm. Sure, the light above looks like it's dying, and the buzzing noise is driving me insane, but I'm dry in here. I'm safe. She's my mother. I love her. I love her completely, but she's going to bring the rain inside.*

She reached the door, and for one moment, one single heartbeat, her eyes met mine and I took a step back. The skin around her eyes was swollen, her cheeks puffy. The whites of her eyes were bloodshot in vibrant red lines. Her lips trembled. I saw all of this in one second. A second, really. Just one moment for me to see it all.

She opened the door.

The bell rang overhead.

A blast of air, wet and moist and smelling like deep earth, rolled over me like a wave.

"Benji," she said, her voice raw and cracked.

"Mom? What's wrong?"

She shook her head. Took in a great gasping breath.

Impossible, I heard my father whisper in my head. *Improbable.*

I couldn't move. "What?" I said. "What? Oh, no. What? Oh, please just tell me what."

Her eyes welled. "He's…. Oh, my God."

Choke your hands up on the bat, son. It's the only way to get a good swing in. Not that high, a little lower. There you go. All right. Incoming, you ready?

Pain in my stomach, sharp and burning. I wrapped my arms around myself, clutching as I bent over and gagged. A low moan escaped me. "Ah," I said. "Ah. Ah."

"He's gone, Benji."

Heard another one today, Benji. It's bad. You ready? Did you hear about the guy that went to a zoo that had no animals except for a dog? It was a Shiatzu!

"Oh my God, Big Eddie is *gone*," my mother said.

Hand me the 5/8 wrench, Benji. We'll see if we can get this son of a bitch started. Motherfucker ain't gonna get away from us, no sir. This bastard is ours.

"I don't know how it—oh, *Christ*," she cried.

C'mon, son! You're better than this. How could you get a C in English class? It is your first language, after all. I'm kidding! Ha, ha! Don't give me that look, just do better, for Christ's sake.

"This isn't real. This isn't real," she said, taking another stumbling step.

I will always look you in the eye. I've raised you to be honest and kind. I've raised you to be brave and strong. If you can become the man I think you'll be, then you and me will always be eye to eye. You get me?

"My heart—oh, how my heart *hurts*," she moaned as she gripped the countertop.

And you know what my father told me? He told me I wouldn't amount to anything. He told me I would come crawling back. That I wouldn't be able to stand on my own two feet. He said it's what I deserved for getting your mom pregnant when we were so young. But you know what? I never crawled back. I amounted to something, though it might not be much. I am standing tall. And you know what else? I've still got your mom. And you, my son. I've still got you. And damn if that isn't the only thing I could ever want.

"You shut your mouth," I said hoarsely.

My mother recoiled as if I'd slapped her, her eyes wide. She recovered and started to move toward me again. I knew I should have taken her in my arms then, held her close, protected her with all I had, but she'd brought the rain and I couldn't seem to find the rationality in all my horror.

"Back off," I hissed at her through gritted teeth. My eyes were burning, my stomach sick. "You're lying. Why are you lying? Why would you say that to me?"

"No," she moaned. "No, baby, I'm not. There was an accident, his truck went off the—"

I wanted to go to her, to hug her. Protect her. But she had brought in the rain and I couldn't bring myself to console her. "You're lying!" I shouted.

"Benji, you need to listen to me!" she cried. "You need to hear me! He's—"

"No," I snarled at her. "He's not dead. He's not dead! *I* would know if he was! *I* would know because I would *feel* it! He wouldn't do that to me! He wouldn't *dare*!" I stepped away from her so she couldn't touch me, so I wouldn't feel her skin against mine. It burned. It hurt. It felt like betrayal, heavy and real. *This isn't truth!* I screamed in my head. *This isn't truth! She lies. She lies with her fucking mouth!*

"There was an accident," she said tearfully, moving around the counter. "The truck rolled down an embankment. Out near seventy-seven."

"No. You lie. Stop it. Please, oh please, just stop." *He can't be dead because I would feel it. I would know. There would be a light extinguished within me and it would be dark, it would all be dark and I would* know. *He's my fucking* father. *He's not supposed to leave me. Not now. Not yet. Not ever. We had a deal. We had a deal that he was going to stay alive forever because he's my dad. He's Big Eddie. Nothing happens to Big Eddie. Nothing.*

She came around the side, her face wet. "The truck went into the river," she said, her voice breaking on the last word. "They don't know yet how long he was in there. In the river."

She was cornering me, and I growled at her, teeth bared, panic bubbling to the surface. She was trapping me, trapping me with her lies, her stupid fucking *lies*.

"Don't come any closer," I warned her in a low voice. "Dad's in Eugene with his friends. He's with his friends and hanging out." Then something hit me. It was afternoon. Dad had told me he'd be back by the afternoon. He'd be at the house. Mom just got confused. She got confused with her lies. He'd be at the house. He was at home.

"He's at home," I said brightly, even as my heart shattered and my mind broke. "It's afternoon and he's at home." I ignored the tears falling on my face, the way my nose ran. I ignored the way I sounded hysterical, the way hiccups interrupted my words. "He went home because he told me he'd come home in the afternoon."

She stood a couple of feet away from me and reached out a hand before thinking better of it and pulling it back. "No," she croaked. "No, baby. No. Big Eddie's gone. Sweetheart, oh. Oh my God. How... I don't know...." She started crying again and slumped against the counter. She'd be okay, I knew as I pulled my keys from a pocket. Even if she was a liar, she'd be okay because Dad was at home and I'd go get him. I'd go get him and bring him back to the store and she'd see. She'd see him standing so fucking *big* and so fucking *tall* he'd block out the darkened sky, and as she stood in his shadow, her tears would dry and she'd smile such a beautiful smile and she'd tell me she's sorry. She'd be so damn *sorry* for all the lies she'd just told. She'd see. I'd show her if it was the last thing I did.

"I'll show you," I told her. "I'll show you."

She cried out after me as I hopped over the counter and ran out into the rain. I tore around back to where the Ford—

she'll purr, benji, and you'll know love because she's so cherry

—was parked. I threw open the door and my cherry baby roared to life. "We need to find Dad," I told the Ford. "Take me home so we can find Dad." The tires squealed as I slammed on the gas, quickly righting the truck as the rear began to fishtail onto Poplar Street.

Even as I gunned the engine, I was pulling my cell phone from the console on the dash. *Don't you dare be talking and driving at the same time*, Big Eddie whispered in my head. *If I catch you, you'll lose the phone. We clear?*

I hesitated for a moment, but then realized he would forgive me. He would see the fear in my eyes and he would forgive me. And it was just a phone. So what if it was taken away. That'd be fine. I'd give up the phone. Right then, I would have given up *anything*.

I fumbled through the contacts list, barely keeping my eyes on the road. Then *BIG EDDIE* was highlighted. I put the phone to my ear. His voice immediately came on the line, and I cried out such a call of relief that I almost didn't hear his words. And it took me a moment to process them.

"*You've reached Big Eddie's phone. Sorry I missed your call. Leave me a message and I'll get back to you when I can.*"

"Dad?" I choked out, even as I heard a beep in my ear. "Is that you? Hello?"

Nothing.

I hung up. And called again.

Immediate. "*You've reached Big Eddie's phone. Sorry I missed your call. Leave me a message and I'll get back to you when I can.*"

And again. And again. And again. Immediate message each time. The phone never rang.

I almost missed the turn to Big House. It was raining even harder by the time the Ford's tires left asphalt for the gravel driveway. Mud slung up in arcs behind me. Rocks flew. I slammed on the brakes in front of Big House, almost skidding into the porch. I couldn't see his truck, but that didn't mean anything. It was afternoon. He said he'd be back. Maybe the truck broke down on the way home and he had to have it towed to a shop. Maybe he'd had a few too many beers hanging out with his friends and he'd had to hitch a ride home. Mom would be pissed that he'd left the truck all the way in Eugene, but that was okay. I could drive him there to get it tomorrow. I smiled, thinking that we could make it a mini road trip. Maybe take a couple of fishing poles with us and stop off near the bridge on the way back. It would be just the two of us. Just the two of us and nothing else would matter.

I stepped out into the rain, leaving the Ford's door open behind me. Days later, I'd have to reupholster the door since it would sit open for another six hours, and the material became bloated and reeked of mold. I'd do it with a grim expression on my face, cursing myself when it wasn't looking right, berating myself that Big Eddie would have done it right the first time. Big Eddie would have made it look spectacular right away. But that was still days away.

I bounded up the steps and threw open the door. The house was almost quiet, the only sound water falling on the roof. "Dad," I tried to call out, but it came out as a croak. I cleared my throat and took another step into Big House.

And with that second step, with that small movement that meant nothing, came the first cold realization that my mother had not been lying. She had not been making it up. It was a tiny part, a tiny voice screaming from the depths. I pushed it away, but it had done enough damage, even in a split second. "Dad?" I said again. It was a little louder.

Another step into Big House, and I wanted to scream. "Dad?" I said, raising my voice. "You here?"

Upstairs. He can't hear me because he's upstairs in the shower or in his bedroom or he's just playing a game and trying to trick me. He and Mom came up with this stupid trick, this awful *trick, and pretty soon, he's going to jump out and yell* surprise! *Surprise and weren't you just so* scared? *Weren't you just freaked out over nothing? Just a joke, son. It was just a joke. It was just a joke and I'll never leave you. I'll never leave you, I promise.*

I ran up the stairs, ignoring how the rain falling on the roof sounded like the roar of a river.

He wasn't in the bedroom or the bathroom. He wasn't in my room or the spare room. He wasn't in the closets. He wasn't in the attic. I went room to room, whispering his name, saying his name, finally *bellowing* his name, demanding that he come out from wherever he was hiding, that he show himself and end this joke, end this whole fucking thing. I was tired, I screamed at him. I was so tired of this game and I wanted it to be over.

No reply came.

I slumped against the wall near the stairs and slid down, wrapping my arms around my knees. I sat there, shivering, for I don't know how long. Finally, I pulled out my phone again and called my father for the last time.

"You've reached Big Eddie's phone. Sorry I missed your call. Leave me a message and I'll get back to you when I can."

The howl that tore from me then echoed throughout the house.

"YOU'VE reached Big Eddie's phone," I say now, sitting in the Ford at the gates of Lost Hill Memorial Cemetery. "Sorry I missed your call. Leave me a message and I'll get back to you when I can."

I open the door to the Ford and step out into the dark. There's a chill in the air, but I've forgotten my coat at home or back at the store. I don't know. It doesn't matter.

I hop over the security chain stretched out across the road. The cemetery closes at nightfall, but I've been here after dark many times over the past five years. It's better for me to be able to come here without anyone else around. There's nothing more awkward than standing above a loved one's remains and having someone mourning two headstones down. Do you acknowledge them? Do you ignore the tears on their face? Or do you just exchange a knowing look that says, "I know. I know what you're going through."

But you don't. Not really. Everyone grieves differently. No one handles the loss of a loved one the same. Some put on a brave face for others, keeping everything internal. Others let it all out at once and shatter, only to pick up the pieces just as quickly as they came apart. Still others don't grieve at all, implying they are incapable of emotion.

Then there are the ones like me, where grief is a badge we wear, where it's hard to let go because we don't want to. We probably wouldn't know how even if we wanted to. There's unanswered questions, unresolved feelings. There is anger that this person could even conceive of leaving us behind. We are the furious ones, the ones that scream at the injustice and the pain. We are the ones who obsess and slowly lose rational thought, knowing it is happening but unable to find a way to care. We are the ones who drown.

I pass the Old Yard, those graves time is erasing, the names on the stones all but illegible. These people are forgotten. These people don't have fresh flowers on the grass, no one who actively mourns them. Their mourners are likely dead themselves by now, on their way to being disremembered. How would it feel to live a full life and have no one remember it, to have no one remember the extraordinary things you accomplished, even if it was just waking up every day and finding the courage to get out of bed?

I see her, then. Even in the dark, even in the distance. She means something different to me now, with her stone wings and outstretched hands. She means so much more. She beckons me without moving, she calls for me without making a sound, even though in my head I can hear the flutter of wings and I see the color blue. I push it away before it can become something more, focusing on the stone angel getting closer. Her face is kind, but also sad, as if she knows what has happened to me, and what she must do. She hasn't moved since I first laid eyes on her, always watching. Always guarding.

This last thought causes an ache in my chest.

And now, for the first time in weeks, I stand before my father.

Fifteen words:

EDWARD BENJAMIN GREEN

"BIG EDDIE"

BELOVED HUSBAND AND FATHER

MAY 27 1960—MAY 31 2007

"Hey, Dad," I say softly. "Sorry it's been awhile."

When I first started visiting him, I felt foolish talking to him out loud. *He can't hear you*, I had chided myself. *He's not really there and you're just sounding like a nut job.* But I pushed on, and eventually it became easier, and I could even hear what I thought would be his replies, said in that gruff voice of his, buried deep in my mind. These days, there are times that I have to struggle to remember his voice just right. It seems to take longer and longer to find the cadence, to get the timbre just right. But eventually it comes to me and it's like he never left, and he's standing next to me, saying all the things I want to hear.

But it feels different tonight. Something feels… closer. Just out of reach.

I scan the rest of the boneyard, but it's empty, the nearly full moon chasing away some of the shadows attempting to creep in. The hairs stand up on the back of my neck. I tell myself I'm just imagining things, there's nothing here with me. I turn back to my father, the guardian angel still reaching for me, her palms up. Not able to stop myself, I reach out and touch her palm, the stone cool against my fingers. I raise my eyes to her face, and she's watching me with gray eyes, her lips slightly parted. For a moment, I think she'll speak. But, of course, she's made of stone. She's not real.

I let out a deep breath. "It's been kind of crazy these last few weeks. I don't... I don't know if I'm doing the right thing here, Dad. I thought I was. I thought... God, I don't know what I thought. Did you send him here? Calliel? I don't know why I think that, but there's a part of me that thinks you did. If you did, then I'm sorry. I'm sorry for messing things up. I'm sorry for making him go away. I'm sorry I couldn't figure it out in my head. Dad... I'm drowning here, okay?" My voice cracks, but I can't seem to stop. I have to get this out. "I can't seem to keep my head above water anymore. Things are just snowballing and I don't know how to stop it. Five years. Five years I waited for something to happen, and now that it's all at once, I... I need help, Dad. Please. I need help so bad, and I promise, oh how I *promise* you, that if you send him back, I'll do everything I can to make it right. I'll do everything I can to help him like you asked me to. I'll do it for you. And I'll do it for him."

I wipe my eyes with the back of my hand. "Fuck, do I miss you. There's times that I find myself thinking something and I'll turn around to tell you, and it hits me that you're gone. It hits me all over again, because I could've sworn you were just here. Like you were standing right next to me just a second ago. Why can't you be? Why did you have to go? Where were you going that day? You lied to me. I know you did. You weren't going to see any friends. What did you do? What did you see?"

A sob rips my chest and I try to choke it back down. "I'm so angry at you. I'm so fucking mad. You bastard. You fucking asshole. Why'd you have to go? Why did you have to leave me behind? You promised me. You promised me that you'd always be there. I'm your fucking *son,* and you promised me! *You fucking promised!*"

My eyes are bleary and my knees feel weak. I reach out to steady myself and grab onto the stone angel's hands. She holds me up as my body trembles. It hurts to stand here. It hurts to be here. Even after all the time that has passed, it still hurts. Everything about this place is—

blue

—pain and I just want it to stop. I just want it to be over. I just want to raise my head up and wake from this nightmare that I can no longer tell is real or not. There has to be an ending. This has to finish before it's too late.

Footsteps, from behind me.

I whirl around, the angel Calliel's name dying unspoken on my lips.

Standing ten feet away are the Strange Men.

I take an inadvertent step away, and the angel's stone hands jab my back. The Strange Men cock their heads at me at the same time, mirror images of each other, light and dark. I don't know if I should be frightened yet, but I'm well on my way. I try to keep it from my face.

"Hello," I say evenly.

"Benjamin," the dark man says. "Benji. Benjamin Green."

"Out here?" the light man asks, quirking his head at the other. "It seems… unwise."

"Why are you here?" the dark man asks. "What is it you hope to find?"

My heart is jumping in my chest, and my palms feel clammy. "I was just coming to see my father," I say.

"Father?" the dark man asks. "Father."

"Ah, the father," the light man breathes reverently. "His… name?"

"Green. Edward," the dark man says, his eyes twitching back and forth rapidly. "Edward Benjamin Green."

"Transposed," the light man responds. "One is the other and the other is one. Big Eddie? From the sign?"

"Yes," the dark man agrees. "The sign."

"Crossed?"

The dark man's eyes twitch again. "No," he says, sounding confused. "He… hasn't. He's…. paradox. Contradiction. How…?"

The light-skinned man reaches out a white hand and touches the dark man on his shoulder, a caressing slide of his fingers. "It doesn't matter. Not now. Later. Now is blue. Now is Calliel."

The dark man shakes his head quickly, as if trying to clear his thoughts. "Yes. Calliel."

They look at me again. The angel's hands are still pressed against my back.

The dark man says. "The angel Calliel. Where is he?"

"I told you," I say, my voice high-pitched. "I don't know who you're talking about."

"You're lying," the light man says. And then he smiles at me, and it's such a terrible thing that my stomach twists and my skin crawls. There's no humanity in it, just a wide grin under the dead, black eyes of a shark. "The scratches? Wings, we should think."

"What… scratches?" I say faintly.

"The angel?" the dark man asks. "Where is he?"

"I don't know any angel!"

"Lies," the light man says.

"Deceit," the dark man says almost regretfully.

They take a step toward me at the same time, and then another. And then another. "We can make you," the dark man promises. "We can make you tell us things. So many little things."

I take a step back and glance down as something falls. A vase. Flowers spilled.

The light man continues to grin at me. "Things... you wouldn't normally share. Things your heart keeps hidden. It will hurt. The angel. Where is he? The angel Calliel."

"He has broken law," the dark man says as they take another step. "He has disrupted order. The design. He is not belief. He has fallen from faith. His job was one single thing, and he broke. He broke from what he was."

"Make him call out?" the light skin man asks. "I think he will scream and the angel will come. Make him scream? He can... scream."

I feel like screaming. But I can't.

They are five feet away. The light man stretches out his arms in front of him, his bone-white fingers waggling at me, like he's saying *mine, give me mine, mine.*

"He'll come," the dark man says. "Scratches. On the ceiling. This boy is protected."

"How—"

I bring my foot up and stomp on the vase. It shatters. The noise causes the Strange Men to take a step back. I reach down quickly and grab a large shard, the end wicked sharp. I point it at the Strange Men. "Come on, then, you assholes," I snap at them. "You want to fuck with me? You want to fuck with my town? Come on, then!" By the end, I'm shouting.

A flutter of wings from overhead.

"He's here," the dark man says as he looks skyward.

"Expected," the light man says. "Make Benjamin scream? Maybe no time after. He should scream for his lies. He lies."

A snarl turning into a roar. Then, as if he had fallen again from the sky, Calliel appears in front of me, his dark-blue wings spread wide, thirty feet from tip to tip. The ground around us shakes as he lands between the Strange Men and me, crouching down, his head bowed. He's still wearing the jeans I'd seen him in last, but they are dirty and torn, revealing swatches of white skin that are almost luminous.

For the first time, a flicker of fear crosses the Strange Men's faces as they take a step back. Whatever hold they had on me is released, and I fall to my knees behind Cal, almost unable to believe he is here.

"Benji," he growls without rising, his head still bowed. Nothing in the world has ever sounded better than my name on his lips. "Are you okay?"

I want to tell him yes, I am okay. Now that he is here, I'll always be okay. And as long as he stays, everything will be wonderful and he'll never have to ask me that question again. But all I say is, "I think so."

He nods, the red stubble across his head almost glowing in the moonlight. His wings quiver and I smell earth. The smell is a palpable thing and it catches in my throat. "Stay behind me. Whatever happens, you stay behind me."

"Cal, I…."

"I know," his voice is still deep and rough. "There is much I have to tell you. But first…." He rises to his feet, towering far above me. He's magnificent, stretched so high he looks like he could reach up and touch the sky. His skin appears to be twitching, and he glances back at me just once. His eyes are almost completely black, his jaw set, and I realize he's *furious*, so much so that he's *shaking* with it. But even as those eyes fall on me, I understand it's not at me, none of his fury is directed toward me. His rage is meant for the Strange Men, and it takes my breath away. They've come to this place. They've threatened his town and threatened *me*. He's so far in his anger that it's making him quake. I nod at him, letting him know I understand. I move behind the stone angel, peering out around her wings.

He turns back to the Strange Men.

"Leave," he says coldly. "You are not welcome here. This is my town. I have not called for your assistance."

"It appears you misunderstand our intentions," the dark man says, cocking his head to the right.

"We are not here to assist you," the light man says, cocking his head to the left.

"Angels do not belong on the earthly plane," the dark man says, taking a step toward us.

"You have broken angelic law," the light man says. "You have defied God."

"Do not presume to know the words of my Father," Calliel says, his wings shuddering. "Michael does not speak for God, no matter what he says."

Michael?

"Michael sees all," the dark man snaps, anger showing on his smooth face for the first time. "He is a vessel, put in place to speak the wisdom of God. He is one of the Firsts. You know this, Calliel. And you know the consequences for disobeying him."

"Guardians such as yourself are not meant to become corporeal," the light man says, a sneer on his lips. "You are to assist your charges when the threads dictate."

"And a thread has arisen," Cal growls. The hairs on the back of my neck stand on end at the fury in his voice. "A thread has arisen for one of my charges. I followed that thread and it led me here. To see you threatening one of my own. So again, I find myself in a position of knowing what my Father has asked of me. You may leave now. Go back to Michael and tell him I still perform my duties as a Guardian. Tell him to come down himself instead of sending his minions."

The Strange Men look stunned. "You know that that is not possible," the dark man hisses.

"You know what could happen to him," the light man barks. "You know what is happening to you even as you stand here."

"Why you have chosen to take this risk is beyond comprehension," the dark man says, taking another step forward.

"How you have survived this long is a quandary." The light man takes a matching step. "Michael will want answers."

Cal forms his hands into fists at his side. "Last warning, men of nothing. Leave now. Threaten not my charges. I will not ask again."

"He's weaker now," the dark man says, a cold smile on his face. "Even he knows it."

"Yes," the light man says. "He is. This will end now as we were instructed. We cannot go back to Michael empty-handed."

"So be it," Cal says, bowing his head. "Father, forgive me for what I must do. I pray for you to have faith in me as I do in you. The thread is bright. Benjamin Edward Green is mine, and I will do what I must to protect him."

I am allowed a moment, an infinitesimal space in time where his words reach me and burn through me like fire. My mind is slowly catching up with my eyes, his sudden appearance after the absence of days that felt like years melting away like a bad memory. *He came for me*, I think, in this moment.

But that is all I am allowed. As soon as the echoes of his words die out, the faces of the Strange Men twist into something clearly not human. They retain their shapes, their colors of light and dark, but it's the way their mouths open wide, into gaping snarls that confirm they are no more human than Cal is. The roars that pour from their mouths are like a low screech, and they cause my eyes to water. I clap my hands over my ears to try and block the horrible noise. They hurl themselves at Calliel, hands outstretched, their fingers looking impossibly long, stretched out into points, like claws.

Cal moves before I can cry out a warning. Almost faster than my eyes can follow, he spreads his wings again, raising them up and then slamming them down toward the ground. He's launched into the air, even as the concussive blast of air from the downswing of his wings strikes me in the face, smelling of grass and earth. Blue lights flash and trail behind him, like a comet's tail.

The Strange Men land where he stood only moments before, screeching louder, glaring upward. I follow their gazes and see Cal thirty feet above them, the blue lights arcing their way around him, the stars a halo behind his head, his wings moving up and down lazily. The moon peeks out from behind the clouds like it wants to light up this creature in its sky and show the world something it has never seen before. I cannot make out his face, but I can see the anger emanating from him. He is breathtaking.

And then he crosses his arms over his chest as his wings fold to his sides. He falls backward. Above the angry calls of the Strange Men, I can hear the wind rustling over his wings as he plummets toward the earth. I only have a moment to be alarmed, to think maybe he is falling again, that something is wrong, that he's going to crash into the ground, and the Strange Men will fall on him with their terrible claws, their stretched faces.

But that is not what happens at all.

He's ten feet above the ground, falling headfirst, the Strange Men's arms outstretched as if they will catch him, when his wings snap open. Air immediately pushes against the feathers, slowing his descent. He folds them again as he twists his body. The Strange Men shout incoherently as he rockets between them, reaching, but grabbing only empty air, the blue lights flowing around them. The rush of air left in his wake knocks them off balance, and they stumble as they attempt to stay upright.

Even as he passes between them, he's spinning again, until he faces the Strange Men, his wings unfurling, causing him to come to an immediate stop in midair, his wings pumping around him. He catches both of the Strange Men by their necks as they fall into him. He raises them both off the ground, digging his fingers into their flesh. The Strange Men kick their legs, flailing and trying to scratch at his arms.

The expression on Cal's face is pure fury. A low growl rumbles out of him, his chest heaving. The Strange Men start to choke and gasp for air. I wonder what will happen if he continues to squeeze, if his hands will tear into their skin. Do they have blood? Will it pour over his fingers? He's called them men of nothing, but surely they live if they are struggling to breathe.

"I gave you warning," Calliel says coldly. "I gave you an opportunity to leave Roseland, to leave him alone. You ignored my warnings. You chose to attack what is mine. I will now rid this place of you."

"You know… what Michael… will do," the dark man gasps.

"You have… broken law," the light man gurgles. "You cannot believe… that you can stay here."

"You have forsaken your Father," the dark man spits out.

"You have only made this worse," the light man warns. "They will come for you in greater numbers."

Something crosses Calliel's face, and his expression falters. I want to call out to him, to say his name, to tell him to set them down, that he is not the judge and jury, not the executioner. But my words barely break a whisper; my throat closes in disbelief. Cal's eyes harden again and the snarl returns.

"This is *my* town. These are *my* people. Benji is *mine*. Let them come. You won't be here to witness it."

"The black," the Strange Men choke out as one.

"Sin," the dark man says.

"Vile," the light man says.

"Be gone," Cal says.

"No," I whisper.

The Strange Men begin to shriek again, their cries loud, echoing over the cemetery. Cal's blue lights begin to gather and swirl behind him, slowly at first, but then in an ever-widening vortex. There's no sound, but it's not silent. It's as if there's an *absence* of sound, as if it's being sucked toward the maelstrom. I can see through the center of the spinning blue halo, the headstones behind it flashing in the light. But then the center of the halo explodes outward, and a black void fills the circle. It looks like a large dark eye: a spinning blue cornea, a great black pupil.

Cal spins on his heels, his wings flaring out behind him, bringing the Strange Men around with him. As he whirls, he releases them, first the light man, then the dark man. The light man is the first to reach the dark eye, and he hits the black center… and disappears, his entire suit falling to the ground. The dark man follows, his suit fluttering down to the ground as he enters the black. As soon as they're gone, the swirling black hole explodes in a soundless flash that burns my eyes.

And then it's over.

He stands facing away from me, as if watching the empty space where the hole had been. His wings fold back against him again, and I can see he's trembling, clenching and unclenching his hands.

"Cal?" I manage to croak out.

He turns. The anger has left his face, replaced by despair. Horror. Anguish. "Benji?" he whispers, sounding broken. He falls to his knees, his wings shaking behind him.

I should run to him, I know. I should run and comfort him and make him okay. Make everything okay. But it's hard to move my feet. I'm weighed down by the last words I said to him, how I forced him away. How I made him leave. This isn't on him. None of this is on him. It's me. Everything about this is me. And again, he's come when I've called for him. He's come when I didn't deserve it. He's come to bring light to my world, to save my life and keep me from drowning. Dear God, how could I deserve this? How could he even be here with me?

I take a step toward him, hearing his ragged breath. It seems like I take days to reach him, hours stretched out where I'm sure I'll be struck down by the might of his Father, sure I've failed whatever test has been put before me.

But it doesn't happen.

I stand before Calliel. His head is bowed.

"Benji," he breathes. He doesn't look at me. "Are you okay?"

"Yeah," I choke out. I reach out and cup his face.

He leans forward, pressing his forehead against mine. Even in the dark, I can see the glitter of his eyes. "Your thread. I saw your thread, and I was scared. It was so bright."

"I'm sorry. I shouldn't have… I d-didn't mean…."

"I know," he says, and I almost believe he does. I feel his breath on my lips. "I know. I thought… no. I was scared. I didn't know what else to do. Benji. I'm sorry."

"I thought you were gone," I say weakly. "I thought you'd left me too."

He widens his eyes and pulls back, bringing his hand to the back of my head, pushing me into him as he kisses my forehead. "No," he says in obvious distress. "I will not leave you again. I will always be with you. I'm sorry. I'm sorry. Please believe me."

"You can't say that! You don't know what will happen! This is on me. This is all my fault, and I—"

"Never," he says. He brushes my tears away with his thumbs. "Never again. You are my—"

"Benji?" a voice calls out, cracking.

"No," I whisper.

Cal spreads his wings quickly as he rears back, the blue bright against the night sky.

I turn my head.

Standing next to the stone angel who guards the small patch where my father sleeps is my mother. And she has seen the angel Calliel for what he really is.

part iii: trust

The man at the end of his life sat on the river's edge.
The River Crosser sat next to him, waiting for another passenger.
"I can't go across yet," the man said, picking at a blade of grass.
"What happens if my son needs me and I am not here?"
The River Crosser didn't answer immediately, just sat, watching the man.
Finally, the River Crosser stood up straight and stretched. He looked out at the river.
"You know," he said with a frown, "everyone will always need something." He
sighed. "But you have to trust they'll know how to take care of themselves."

the voice of god

MY MOTHER had received a message from Rosie, she told us, her voice wavering. She'd been in the next county over, delivering some baked goods to a women's shelter. She'd stayed a bit later than she planned, talking with some of the women, making plans to assist them with a fundraiser happening in the fall. She hadn't even realized she'd left the phone in her car. She hadn't gotten the message until dusk, as she was driving home.

Strange Men, Rosie said in the message, were asking questions about Big Eddie. My mother needed to find me, to make sure I was okay, that nothing had happened to me. The store was already closed when she'd arrived. She drove to Little House, and I wasn't there. She was worried about me, she said, though she couldn't really explain why. Just a feeling she had when I didn't answer my phone when she called. She didn't know who these Strange Men were, or why they had been asking about Big Eddie. Why now, all of a sudden?

She thought about driving to mile marker seventy-seven, but she knew she'd kick herself if she got all the way out there and I wasn't there. She wasn't sure there was time for that, especially if she was right. She knew Cal was gone. The Strange Men could only have made this situation worse. She decided to go to the cemetery first, be it intuition, be it knowing how I am, she didn't know. She'd cried out in relief when she saw my truck. She parked next to it and hopped the chain.

And then?

Blue lights. Impossibilities. A light and dark man attacking me. Wings spreading and soaring into the sky. Cal. She wasn't seeing what she was actually seeing, was she? It wasn't possible. The world didn't work in mysterious ways. It was only black. It was only white.

"IT'S not possible," she says now as I hand her a cup of coffee in Little House. She shakes, worried (of all things to worry about) that she'll scald herself if she keeps shuddering. "Things like this don't happen. Not here. Not anywhere."

"They do," Cal reassures her from his place near the kitchen doorway. His wings had faded again even before we left the cemetery. "People just don't know how to look close enough. Amazing things happen all the time. Little threads connect you all. It's really quite beautiful."

I groan inwardly as my mother's eyes bulge. It's probably not the best time for one of his esoteric meanderings, and I tell him so. His eyes are warm as he smiles at me. I don't know how much of that is for me and how much of it's because I let him drive the Ford back as I drove my mother home, unsure if she was going into shock. I was relieved when we pulled past Big House that Nina wasn't waiting on the porch, nor did the lights seem to be on inside. I didn't think I was ready for Christie and Mary to be in on this. Not yet.

"How long have you known?" my mother suddenly asks.

"About Cal?"

"Yes."

I glance at him. He's watching me with such awe that my heart skips a few beats. I don't know where we stand and I'm trying my best to keep from flushing, but I don't know how long I can last. It's only now that I truly realize I didn't think he'd come back. "Since I found him," I admit.

"And where was this?" She sounds like she's on the verge of hysterics.

I think about lying, but that would just make things worse. "Mile marker seventy-seven."

Her face goes white, and she grips the cup so tightly I'm afraid it will shatter. "Benji," she whispers. "The meteor? That light?"

I nod.

"You know this isn't…."

"Isn't what?"

She looks unsure as she glances between the two of us. "You said he was an angel. You said he was the guardian angel of Roseland. Of us. Of you."

I nod again, waiting.

"Things like this don't happen, Benji. Not here. Not in the real world." She almost looks like she doesn't believe her own words.

"You saw the same thing I did," I tell her quietly. "You saw his wings. You saw the Strange Men. You saw it with your own eyes."

"I know what I saw!" she snaps at me, slamming down the mug on the counter. "I'm looking for a goddamn explanation! Why here? Why now? Who were those men? Where did they go? What does he want with us! With you!" By the time she finishes, she's shouting.

I flinch, not knowing how to handle the anger in her eyes. I open my mouth to say something, *anything*, to make her calm down, to make her see what I see. Her anger is only giving fire to my own, and I can't lose it here. Not now. Not yet. Fighting will solve nothing—there's too much more to learn.

But before a word can fall from my lips, Cal takes three big, quick strides over to my mother. She gasps and tries to shrink away, but he's too fast for her. I am alarmed (*please don't send my mother into the black!* my mind shrieks) and I'm about to step forward when he reaches his hands up and frames her face. She struggles to move away, but he's holding her tight. Her movements weaken until she stares up at him, tears streaming down her face. She gasps into his touch.

"Lola Green," he says, his voice rough but kind. "I have watched you for many, many years. A little girl who liked to cause mischief with her sisters. A young woman who cared more for her family than almost anyone I've seen. A woman who grew and loved with such ferocity that it was like watching a whirlwind. I watched your heart shatter, though it was done in secret because you wanted to protect your son. I watched you attempt to fix yourself, away from anyone who could see inside because you believed that it was the only way your son would survive. You don't know if you've done right by Benji because he's not the same person he was when his father was here. You don't know what else to do. You don't know if you are strong enough. I assure you that you are."

She begins to weep openly, raising her hands to grip his arms. There's a faint buzzing in my ears, like everything around me is vibrating, humming with an electrical current. I see tiny blue flashes, but they are too small to be important.

"You are strong," Cal says, brushing his thumbs under her eyes. "Stronger than you could ever know. And you are not alone, not like you think. Benji is with you. Your sisters are with you. I am with you. And God, my Father? He is *always* with you." As he says this last, I hear the first waver in his voice. His breath catches on his words like he is having trouble speaking.

Like he doesn't believe himself.

But my mother notices none of this.

"Who are you?" she asks quietly through her tears.

"I am Calliel," he tells her with a small smile. "I am the guardian angel to Roseland and its people. And I am with you."

"This... isn't...," she tries again, fighting against what she sees in front of her.

He shakes his head. "It is, Lola Green. It is what it is. I promise you."

And then her eyes shift, and something else rises behind her sorrow, her disbelief. "Guardian?" she asks, her voice low. My heart sinks—I know where she's going with this.

"Mom—" I say, starting forward.

"Where were you when my husband died?" she grinds out. "Where were you when Big Eddie sat trapped upside down in his truck? Where were you when the water filled his lungs? You say you are an angel. Where were you then?"

"I don't know," he whispers, dropping his hands and taking a step back. "I don't know. I can't remember. I wish...."

"It's not his fault," I say, though I don't know how much I believe that. "He can't remember much since I called him here. Certain pieces have been taken from him."

"Get them back!" she growls. "You get them back and you tell me why you let him die!"

He looks confused, almost scared. "I didn't... I didn't know how to...."

"That's enough," I tell her. "This isn't going to solve anything. Mom, you have to believe me when I say I've asked the same questions. I've wanted the same answers, but it can't be forced. It just can't."

She turns on me. "How could you keep this from me? How could you even think that was okay? Benji, you could have been *killed* tonight!"

"I didn't say anything because of this right here," I retort. "I didn't say anything because I was scared you'd have this reaction. Mom, he's...." He's what? What is he to me? I don't know how to finish that sentence. I don't know if I want to. My head is starting to hurt and I'm exhausted. I'm losing the ability to process any of this.

But he's here, I tell myself. *If I'm being honest, that's the only thing I care about. He's here. I'm angry, yes, and I'm freaking the fuck out, but he's here. He came back. He came back.*

"I care about him," I finally say, knowing it sounds weak. "He's my friend. I don't... he's my friend, okay? And he saved me tonight. I just...."

Mom doesn't look convinced, though I don't know why I think she should be. But she also looks worn, and heartbroken, much older than when I saw her earlier today. And maybe the real reason why I haven't said anything to her yet is not because of this reaction, or because of what our future might hold. Maybe the real reason is because I don't want old wounds to be ripped open for her, like they have been for me. I don't want her scars to be split wide-open. Yes, he is my friend (*let's not go any further than that right now,* I tell myself), but he is also a reminder of what we've lost. And it's worse to know there are questions he can't answer right now. Whether he's being truthful about the convenient memory loss or not. Thinking of him as a liar feels wrong.

"Mom, just... just give us time," I beg.

"Time?" she says incredulously. "*Time*? Time for what?"

"To figure out what's going on here. There's so much we don't know, so much that I'm still trying to figure out."

She shakes her head. "Benji, you have to see how ridiculous this is, right? Do you hear yourself? Do you hear *him*?"

"Time," I repeat. "That's all I'm asking for."

"I won't hurt him," Cal says seriously. "I can't hurt him."

"What do you think you did when you left?" she says as she scowls at him. "You disappeared for days like it was nothing. I don't know why or what happened, but don't you *dare* say you won't hurt him when you already have. This is my son, so don't you *dare*."

His face falls as he takes a step back. "Didn't mean to," he says quietly. "I thought leaving for a bit would be easier on him. I didn't mean to hurt him. I would never do that. I...." He shakes his head but won't look at me.

"Mom, that's enough for tonight. I'm exhausted, and I need to speak to Cal. Alone."

"Benji, you can't possibly think this is a good idea! You *saw* what he did to those men!"

Into the black.

"They weren't men," Cal mutters. "They were husks. Shells. They have no souls. Minions that do nothing more than Michael's bidding. They are abominations, and I do not know why Father permits them."

She stares at him, unable to speak.

"Mom, you can't tell anyone about him." I grab her arm to get her attention. She looks like she's going to protest, but I cut her off. "You can't. If this gets out to the wrong person, it's not going to end well. We have to protect him until we figure out what's going on."

"Griggs," she says suddenly, as if she's just remembered. "Griggs has been asking questions about him. About Cal. No one is saying anything to him, but he's asking."

"All the more reason to keep this quiet. Mom, you know as well as I do that Griggs won't let this go. We can't give him any more reason to look at us. We can't. I already think he—" I cut myself off before I finish.

"You think he what?" she asks me.

I already think he murdered Big Eddie. I think he was the one who ran him off the road. I think he's hiding something out in the woods, and I think Dad knew about it. I think Griggs knew he knew. I think he ran him off the road and stood there in the rain and watched him drown.

I think he killed Big Eddie and I am going to kill him myself.

"I think he'd make this worse than it already is," I say, averting my eyes. "We can't take the chance of him finding out anything. Not until we know more."

"Benji—" she starts again.

"Mom, just do me this favor, okay? Please don't say a word. Not to the Trio, not to anyone. I need time to figure this out. I'm asking you for time."

"How long do you think something like this can stay quiet?" she asks. "Everyone in town knows him. You let him walk around and show his face and get to know people like he was one of us. How long do you think it's going to take before people start asking questions? If they haven't already? How long, Benji?"

"As long as I can," I tell her sharply. "I never ask you for anything. You know that. Not *ever*. But I'm asking you for this one thing. No. I'm not asking you. I'm *begging* you. Please."

She looks dazed. "I have so many questions," she says, but it's more to herself than to me. "So many…." She looks back up at Cal as her eyes harden. He still looks miserable as she steps up to him and pokes him in the chest with her finger. "I don't know who you are, or what you are," she says as she trembles. "I don't know why you're here. But I *do* know this: if any harm comes to my son, there will be no place in Heaven or on Earth where you could hide that I wouldn't find you. If you hurt him, I will *break* you. Do you understand me?"

He looks like he's about to speak but thinks better of it, nodding instead.

My mother reaches up and cups his face much like he did to her earlier. She pulls him down and whispers harshly in his ear. I can't make out her words, but his eyes go wide as he looks over to me. She pulls back to look him in the eye. "Do you promise me?"

There's no hesitation. "I promise," he says, and chills roll down my spine.

She watches him for a moment before she pulls his head down and kisses his forehead softly, and it makes my heart ache because I don't know if he's ever felt something like that from his Father. She sniffs as she lets him go. Cal looks bemused as she turns away from him. "I'll send one of the Trio to the store tomorrow," she tells me, "or I'll go in. I don't want you in town until I've had some time to think."

"Mom, I don't—"

"I brought you into this world," she snaps at me. "It's my job to make sure nothing takes you out of it. You're right when you said you've never asked me for anything before. But the first time you *do* ask me for something it's to keep a secret about an *angel* that fell from the *sky*. So, yes, you will do this *one* thing for me. Are we clear?"

I sigh. "Crystal."

She grabs me in a rough hug, to my surprise. She smells of lilacs, a scent she's had for as long as I can remember. "Do you care for him?" she whispers in my ear, and I can feel her tears against my neck.

I can feel his eyes on me when I answer. "Impossibly," I tell her. "Improbably."

She gasps and shudders against me because she knows those words. Then she's gone, the front door to Little House opening and then closing.

WHEN a person goes through something incredible (say, like a graveyard attack by Strange Men only to be saved by a man with wings), it's as if the body's immediate reaction after the adrenaline fades should be to shut down, to sleep, to recharge. I feel my body doing just that, my knees buckling, my mouth going slack, even as I stand there in the kitchen. Cal takes a step toward me, his eyes hooded. I shake my head at him and turn and walk out of the kitchen and down the hall to my room, where I shut the door behind me. There's guilt when I see him, and it hurts. I lie on my back on the bed and try to think of ways to fix this.

There's a shuffle of feet down the hall. I hold my breath. Shadows cross under the door and pause. I watch to see if the doorknob turns in the dark, if the door will open and he'll stand before me, staring at me with those dark eyes and that red hair. He'll open his mouth and beg me, plead for me to let him in, and I will say—

The shadows shift, turning away. I think he's about to leave and I rise from the bed to chase after him, but then I hear a low grunt and a weight pressed against the door. The shadows underneath move again. I realize he has slumped against the door and is sitting outside.

Waiting. Guarding.

My thoughts are selfish, even if I don't want them to be. *What about* me? *What about* us? *Why did* you *leave? What did* I *do?*

You. Me. I. Us.

The shadows move, then settle.

No, I tell myself. *I can't be thinking of him like that. Not anymore. I've barely started and already he has control over me. Already he has control over my heart. I don't know how to reconcile the nine days I did have him versus the five days I didn't. I don't know what I'm doing. I can't do this. I can't.*

Why not? a voice whispers back.

My feet are on the floor. I'm standing. I'm walking toward the door.

The floor flickers beneath me, and for a moment, it's a raging river. Then it's gone.

Wake up.

The river splashes water up to my chest.

It's time to wake up.

I get caught in the current.

It's time to wake up and be true, son. It's time to open your eyes and see, maybe for the first time. I don't know how much longer I can do this, how much longer I can hold on. But I promise not to let go until I am sure you are safe. Wake up, Benji. Wake up and be true.

I reach the door and gasp for breath, pressing my palms against the wood.

Something shifts outside the door. "Benji?" a worried voice says.

"No," I manage to say. "Just… wait."

"But…."

"Cal… *wait.*"

He sighs but I can feel him settle against the door again, his weight pushing it against my hands. I take another breath, letting my head rest upon the wood. For a moment, it's like I can feel him there, just on the other side. There's a heat against my skin, a bright burst. It's so warm I almost have to pull away for fear of burning, but it subsides, only giving residual pulses. *It's his fear*, I think, fighting against the lump in my throat. *It's his anger, his sorrow. It's whatever causes him to find the black, the tide he rises against. It's there because of me.*

I turn and slump against the door, sliding until my ass reaches the floor. He's mere inches away but there's a wall between us, one that is more substantial than the door. I need to tear it down. I need to break through, but I don't know how.

You know, my father whispers. *Oh, Benji. You know. You built it, so you can destroy it.*

"Benji," Cal says through the door.

"Yeah?"

"I'm sorry. You know, for…."

I bow my forehead into my hands. "Yeah. Didn't think I'd see you again. Thought you'd left."

His reply is muffled and quiet. "That's not what I wanted you to think. I'm sor—"

"No. It's not your fault. It should be me apologizing to you. Again."

He's confused. "But you didn't do—"

"Yes, I did. I did everything. I pushed, Cal. I pushed and pushed because I thought that knowing what I needed to know mattered more than you not being able to remember. I shouldn't have done that. There's no excuse."

Quiet, for a time. Then, "You had your reasons. I don't blame you. I can't."

"Why do you do that?"

"What?"

"You justify my being an asshole. You do it all the time."

He chuckles and there's a bump against the door, like he is laying his head against it. "It's because I see the good in you. It's bright, you know. Like the sunrise. Like the sun rising on my face. I watched the sunrise every morning while I was gone. It reminded me of you."

"Where'd you go?" I choke out.

He sighs again. "The woods. I wandered for a bit. I watched for the threads, but I couldn't see any. Not the whole time I was gone. I was worried about it, wondering if they were hidden from me. But I don't think they were."

"Nothing bad happened while you were gone. Not really."

"Oh. That's good. I hoped."

"Cal?"

"Yes, Benji?"

"Why did you go?"

"I didn't mean to worry you."

"No, that's not the—Look, that's in the past. It's done. You're here. I'm here."

"Are you?" There's a rustling against the door, like he's rubbing his hand against it.

"Yeah. I am."

"I was getting scared."

"You? Scared? I didn't think you were scared of anything."

He laughs. "There are a lot of things I'm scared of, Benji."

I wait for him to elaborate, but he doesn't. "Why were you scared this time?"

There's a pause, and for a moment, I think he won't answer. I chide myself again for pushing, but then he speaks. "I was scared... I was scared because I could feel your anger. You were mad at me, and it scared me. I don't think I've ever felt such anger before. Not since I've known you."

He means longer than two weeks, and we both know it. "Cal—"

"Hush, Benji. Please let me speak." The recrimination in his voice is soft.

I wait.

"I was scared, and that in turn made me angry. I told myself that you were being a child, that you didn't understand at all what it meant to be lost. I hated myself for thinking it. It was petty. I didn't think I would ever know what pettiness felt like, and jealousy. I shouldn't have felt that way."

"Why did you?"

"Because of your father."

"Big Eddie? I don't understand."

"Benji, do you know who my father is?"

"God?"

"For lack of a better word, yes. The one you know as God is my Father. Do you know the last time I got to see my Father?"

Never met him. I'm pretty far down on the totem pole.

"You haven't," I say, feeling like my chest's being crushed. "You never met him."

"Right. I've never met the one who created me. I just know he did because that is what I am supposed to know. I was created and I do what I'm told. Or at least I did."

"So you were jealous?"

"Yes. As much I hate to say it, as much as it tears me apart, yes. I was jealous of you because you had what I never could. I was jealous of him because he had you. I've seen many people in my lifetime, Benji. So many people, even in a little place such as this. But I can tell you that there has never been such a man as your father."

"I know," I say, because I can't say anything else lest my voice would break.

"You do, don't you?" he says, sounding surprised. "You do know. You know what you had; you know what he was."

"The greatest man in the world," I say.

He laughs. "In the eyes of many, you speak truth."

"I miss him."

"And you will. Every day for the rest of your life, you will miss him."

"Like you do? With your dad? Your Father?"

"Yes. But please don't think I'm blaming you or Big Eddie. For anything. That is not my intent."

"Don't you get to talk to him, though? Your dad." I swallow. "God? Or whatever?"

"I thought so. I guess. I don't know. There are times I don't know if I ever did. If I've ever really known him. Not like I thought I did."

"But... isn't he always there for you? You are one of his."

His voice grows harder. "I am. Or so I think. I can't remember the last time I heard him, though. It's lost in the fog. There's still so much that I can't remember. It burns, Benji. It's like a fire in my head and I can't put it out. It makes me angry. I shouldn't be angry."

"To be angry is to be human," I say, gooseflesh prickling up my arms.

You know that that is not possible, the dark man whispers. *Why you have chosen to take this risk is beyond comprehension.*

You know what is happening to you even as you stand here, the light man croons.

Cal ignores me. "So I left, because my anger was growing. My ire. And I couldn't handle it, not when it was… not when it was directed towards you. I left, because I needed to find my thoughts. I left because I needed to find a way to *not* be. I left to speak with Father. For days. For all those days in the trees, I waited. I prayed. I screamed. I asked him why. I asked him why he had forsaken me. I demanded an answer. I demanded to know why this was happening to me, why I had been tested again and again and again. It wasn't fair. It wasn't right. Who was he to do this to me? I've given him everything. I've done everything he's ever asked of me. I've done all that I can. I've made mistakes, yes, but every living thing does. But what was it that I'd done wrong that caused him to ignore me? I was his son and he'd abandoned me, cast me aside as if I was nothing. I was alone in a place where no one knew who I was. At least when I was On High, I was alone because I was supposed to be. I'm tired of it, Benji. I'm tired of being alone."

"You're not alone," I say, my voice cracking. "You've got me. Right?"

"While I was ranting, while I was raving about being alone, about being left behind, screaming that it wasn't fair, that I'd given *everything*, you know what happened, Benji?"

"What happened?" I ask, sure he's going to tell me God answered him. My own anger is growing, but not at the angel on the other side of my door. No, my anger is growing because of God, that bastard God who I am sure is the one who has taken everything from me and Calliel. He's the one who took my father; he's the one who caused Calliel to doubt himself. He's the one who has caused me to doubt myself, to drown in a river I am no longer sure I can keep my head above. It was him, and he finally answered his son who was screaming his name.

But that's not the answer I receive.

I hear Cal take a deep breath. "You happened. It was you, Benji."

"I don't think… I don't understand."

"Your thread. I saw your thread for the first time in five days, and it lit up the sky so brightly I thought the sun was rising. I thought it was the sunrise, but it was you. It's always been you."

"And you came for me," I say, realization dawning. "You came for me because you got your answer. God answered you."

"Yes," he says. I can hear the quiet smile in his voice. "When I was at my darkest, when I was sure I'd be torn apart, your thread exploded for all the world to see. But then I realized it was only for *me* to see. *I* was the only one who could see it, and it meant he was listening to me. It's not always going to be with words. I won't always hear his voice in my head, and I don't know if I ever really have. But he spoke to me, just the same. He showed me the way, and it led to you. I don't think I've ever moved as fast as I did then."

I chuckle, wiping my eyes. "You were very fast."

"Wasn't I?" he says, sounding pleased.

"They didn't stand a chance."

"Michael's husks," I hear him growl through the door. "They are nothing compared to me. I don't know why he thought they could do anything. They are abominations. I don't know why they are allowed to exist. Soulless creatures who do not serve anyone but him."

"Will they come again? The Strange Men?"

"I don't know," he sighs. "Maybe, after a time. Not right away. He'll have seen what I am capable of. And I'm sure he's got much more to worry about than just me."

"Are you… getting sick?" I ask, the blood roaring in my ears. "They said you were weaker. They said you shouldn't stay here."

"Lies," he says firmly. "Just words. I am fine. I am strong."

"You sent them away. You sent them into the black."

"I know," he says, sounding pained. "They… they were threatening you and I couldn't stop myself. I couldn't see you hurt."

"You are not the judge," I remind him, allowing my words to harden. "You are not the jury. You are not the executioner." *And I cannot judge you. I can't. Not when….*

"I know." Barely a mumble.

"You do not decide fate."

"I know."

"What did my mother whisper to you?"

I don't think he's going to answer. But then: "She told me I have to protect you. That you've been alone for so long you may not remember how to live. She wants me to show you how."

"And you promised her that?" I ask, heart sore.

"Yes. Always."

"Cal…."

I hear him shift on the other side of the door, rising up until I'm sure he's standing above me. I wait.

Finally: "Benji?"

"Yeah?"

He's hesitant, almost shy, his words like a staccato beat. "Can you open the door now? I'm sorry if you're still mad at me. I just don't want to be alone anymore. Okay? Please?"

I close my eyes. So many things are still unsaid between us, but I no longer have the heart to bring them out. For all that I have suffered, it's nothing compared to his grief. I had my father. For sixteen years, I knew joy. I knew complete happiness. I saw the sunrise every day because I saw the man who created me every day. I knew the weight of his arms on my shoulder, the rumble of his voice, the sound of his laughter. I knew love because I was loved. I was my father's son.

No. I *am* my father's son. My father would not have allowed another to wallow in anguish, to drown himself in a river. My father would not have allowed despair if he could have helped it. My father was the greatest man who ever lived, even with all his faults. He would know what to do. He would know what was in my heart.

"You gonna leave again?" I ask him gruffly, opening my eyes.

"Only if you make me," he whispers. "Please don't make me."

My heart breaks and I jump to my feet, flinging the door open. He's standing so massively tall, the shadows from the dark dancing across his face. He's breathing heavily, and the glitter in his eyes knocks the breath from my chest. The red stubble across his face looks wonderfully rough. He looks almost feral, like he's poised to attack, but still he waits.

But I can no longer deny him, or deny myself. He spreads his arms as I leap at him. He catches me deftly, crushing me into his chest. The scent of him invades me, threatening to tear me apart. His lips find mine as he lifts me up. I wrap my legs around his waist as my tongue meets his, tangling as he takes a lurching first step. I want to push into him further, until he can feel my thunderous heart breaking against my chest, until he can see that my sorrow is not so different than his. *We are the same*, I think as he grips the back of my neck with one gigantic hand, holding me steady so he can kiss my lips, my cheeks, the tip of my nose.

"You are not alone," I whisper hoarsely against his face, moving my lips across to kiss his closed eyes. "You are with me."

"I know," he says, his voice cracking. He buries his face into my neck then, latching his teeth onto the skin, and swirls his tongue over. He walks further, carrying me against him, until he pushes me back. I land on the bed and he looms above me, so big he blocks out everything else. Only he exists; he's everything. It feels critical, this moment, like we've reached a precipice and we either have to jump or fall back the way we came. I don't want to fall anymore. Not now. Not again.

I reach up and put my arms around his neck, and that's all the permission he needs. He falls against me, so heavy I almost can't breathe. He reaches one hand down and lifts up my shirt, tucking the cotton up under my chin. He rubs his beard against my flesh, leaving trails that burn. He bites gently at my stomach, soothing the sting from his teeth with his tongue.

It's only later, with his mouth on me in ways I never expected, that I can truly feel his need. I am necessary to him. I understand that now, and the realization threatens to crush me more than he ever could. But it's a weight I will carry gladly. Even as I tell him he is not alone, that I am with him, I can see it's the same in reverse. There's a bright light rising from deep within me, like the morning sun breaking over the mountains. It warms me from the inside out, even as he slips a wet finger into me. I call out his name, my muscles trembling, pleasure exploding.

When he enters me again, it's with a careful motion, pressing one hand down against my chest as he watches my face, hooking my leg above his shoulder with his other hand. He leans down, kissing me as he pushes in until his hips are pressed against me. I rock my head back, and he trails his tongue down my neck.

"Faster," I whisper. "More."

He growls against my neck but then he begins to snap his hips against me, slapping his balls against my ass. He takes me in hand, my cock like iron against his calloused hand. It only takes a few strokes before I'm spilling over, spunk on his hand and my chest. He grunts above me and I'm filled with great heat as his shoulders tremble. The muscles of his chest constrict, the cords in his neck stand out. He's still shaking when he drops down onto my chest.

I cradle his head against me, rubbing my fingers through his hair, feeling him still move within me. He's pulling me back together, piece by piece. The shapes may not fit the way they used to, but there is a pattern there. A design. Slowly but surely I am being put back together. I'm not whole yet, not completely, but I am getting there.

He sighs contentedly, his breath warm on my skin. He turns his head and places a gentle kiss to the place where my heart beats. The action is one of such singular beauty that I'm annihilated. If this is what he can give me, then I will take it all.

And I will give it back just the same.

adrift

THAT night, I'm chest-deep in the river again. The rain falls overhead, causing the water around me to splash up in tiny droplets. Occasionally feathers impede my progress, forcing me back. Sometimes the river mud sucks up around my ankles, pulling me down. River water pours into my mouth, choking me, but I break the surface.

There is the metallic screech of the upside down truck as it scrapes against an unseen rock on the riverbed. The sound makes me grind my teeth. I take another step as I look over my shoulder. A dark figure stands on the side of the road, watching. I can't make out who it is, can't see a vehicle stopped on the road. The angle is wrong, the rain too heavy.

A large wave hits the side of my head and I'm submerged again. For a moment, I stay there. The sounds are muffled underwater, the raindrops a soothing, drumming sound above me. I have enough air. I'm not choking. I'm not drowning. I'm alive.

I open my eyes.

Silt and grit sting. I squint and make out the faint outline of the truck ahead. I bring my arms up in front of me and kick off the river bottom, taking a slow, lunging leap toward the truck.

The front left side is smashed from its impact with the boulder near the river's edge. There's a metallic groan up the driver's side of the vehicle, starting at the fender, going across the door and to the rear of the truck. It could be from the boulder as well, though—

it's from whoever ran him off the road

—I can't be sure. The red of the truck is like a bright beacon that calls to me. I take another lunging step. Do I need air? I can't remember the last time I took a breath. I can't remember how long I've been hiding in the river. It doesn't matter. I feel okay. I don't feel like I'm dying. I'm not drowning. I'm fine.

I'm fine until I see the driver's window is broken. I'm fine until a flash of white floats out of it. I'm fine until I realize it's an arm. I'm fine until I see it's an arm and it—

is my dad oh god that is my father

—floats up and down gently, the fingers extending in the current like it's waving me over, beckoning me to the truck. The skin is white, so white, much whiter than my father ever was. It's—

dead he's dead it's all dead

—enough to make me open my mouth. I inhale to scream, but river water pours in and I begin to choke. I kick for the surface, but it's too late. I'm stuck under the surface, stuck in the mud and silt and current, and I can't move. I can't *breathe*, and I am *drowning* in this river and I—

A strong arm wraps around my chest and pulls me away.

I awake as the bed shifts, pulling me from the dream. It's still dark, far too soon for us to head to the roof to watch the sunrise. He is moving quietly, as if to avoid waking me. He pulls on his jeans over his naked form, his skin illuminated by dim blue flashes that begin to swirl around him. A chill strikes me that has nothing to do with the sudden loss of warmth next to me.

"Where are you going?" I ask, trying to keep the fear out of my voice.

He stiffens for a moment, then turns to me, the top button of his jeans still undone, the auburn fur on his stomach disappearing into the denim. He reaches down and grabs me by the back of the neck, pulling me up to kiss me deeply. I wrap my arms around him, trying to pull him back down into the bed, to cover us both deep under the comforter where we can hide until sunrise.

But he won't come, he won't follow me down. He breaks the kiss and presses his forehead against mine. "A thread calls," he says roughly. "I must find it."

"You're going to come back?" I ask, hating the way I sound, unsure and weak.

Calliel smiles at me so brightly I have to kiss him again. "Yes," he says. "I will come back. And then we can watch the sun come up, and I will have some green marshmallows while you tell me I should eat other things because the marshmallows aren't good for me."

"Promise?"

"Promise." The blue lights began to flash brighter, and I can see the faint outline of wings. "They come easier now," he tells me. "I think I might be able to call them without seeing threads first."

I'm relieved, because I can tell myself it means he isn't getting weaker, like the Strange Men said. Wings mean strength. Wings mean health. Wings mean vitality. He is an angel. He is not weakening.

He slides his shirt over his head and gives me one last look before he is out the bedroom and down the hall, then the door closes on Little House with a thud.

I consider following him, but I don't. I try to sleep again, but I can't. I'm still awake when he returns deep in the night. The hunger he comes at me with then is something wicked and bright. I don't ask him where he went, if he has saved anyone or merely been a presence for someone who needed him. It doesn't matter. He has returned and he wants me. That desire is evident on his face. It's enough.

CAL'S return spreads quickly through Roseland. The first day is relatively quiet, given that I'm not at the store. We walk up to Big House early that morning, shortly after coming down off the roof. Cal wraps an arm around my shoulder as we walk, and I relish the feel of him against me. He is chattering away, telling me about a squirrel he saw in the forest during his self-imposed exile. It seemed to follow him over the course of the five days. He is clearly excited about the animal, and I can't help but grin at him as he imitates the sound it made, a high-pitched squeak that he performs by sucking in his cheeks and sticking out his lips. It's not a sound a big guy like him should be able to make.

We are barely on the porch of Big House when the door flies open and Nina barrels out, knocking me out of the way in her rush to tackle Cal. He laughs as he picks her up, spinning her in a circle, her legs kicking out as they whirl. Under his laughter, I can hear her saying, "Blue, Blue, Blue," over and over again. He finally sets her down, brushing the tears from her face.

"I am happy to see you, little one," he says with a smile.

She smiles sweetly for a moment… then punches him in the arm. Nina is a lot stronger than she looks, and I wince at the meaty thud. Cal grunts, though I think more from surprise than pain. He stares down at her, eyes wide. "What was that for?"

"Leaving," she says with a scowl. "You going to do that again?"

A low blush rises up the sides of his neck and into his cheeks, reddening the skin and making his facial hair appear even brighter. "No."

She watches him for a moment, trying to figure out if he is telling her the truth. She finally sniffs once and looks him up and down. "Good," she says. "People missed you here, Benji especially. I was sad. We were all sad. If you do that again, I am going to be very angry with you. This is your home now, you know. You can't just leave your home."

It's my turn to flush. I've never really thought about that. About where this is going, what he and I could mean to each other in the future. Would he stay? *Could* he stay? The Strange Men whisper in my head, saying it isn't possible, that he is getting weaker. I shove them away when he glances at me with a low smile before looking back at my little aunt. "I promise I won't do it again," he says with complete seriousness.

"Did you find what you were looking for?" she asks with curiosity.

He hesitates for a moment. "I think so, though not in the way I thought."

"Is that okay, then?"

"It is," he says simply. He looks at me again and my face feels like it's on fire.

She grabs him by the arm and pulls him toward the house. He reaches out and snags my hand, pulling me with him.

MOM is gone. Turns out she opened the store herself that morning instead of asking Mary or Christie. I should be surprised at this, but I'm not. We each have our own ways of dealing with things. My mother and I don't know how to articulate our feelings very well. After Big Eddie died, there would be times that days would go by before we would see one another, each of us sequestered in separate parts of the house, or in separate parts of Roseland. The Trio tried to get us together, to eat meals, to watch TV, to have conversations neither of us felt like having. It was a good effort, but none of them could really understand the depths of our heartache. We were points of a triangle: her, me, Big Eddie. It had been the three of us. But then that triangle had been shattered, leaving us to drift aimlessly.

I know people think that she, as my mother, should have been the one to direct me, to point me toward the future. *She should be offering guidance,* I'm sure they said. *Yes, she lost her husband but he lost his* father. *There's a difference.* Maybe there was. Maybe there is. I lost my best friend on that day, but my mother also lost the only man she'd ever loved, the man who had been by her side since they were kids. Her first, her only. We didn't have him to hold us together. Even though the Trio tried, it wasn't the same. If we ever passed by each other in those weeks and months that followed, there was usually only a shared glance, a matching look of pain etched across our faces. That was how we grieved. That was how we dealt with the inevitability of the unknown.

Eventually we got better, though not all the way. She recovered more quickly than I did. And more completely. I am ashamed to admit there were some dark days where I resented her for her ability to move on. Every smile was like a slap to my father's memory, every laugh an affront to the loss of my father. How dare she be happy, I thought. How dare she act like everything is right as rain and nothing will ever bother her again. The Trio was instrumental in breaking her out of her bitter shell. Christie told my mother, *You can sleep now, finally. We're going to stay here as long as you need us. You sleep and let us carry you for a while.* I remember thinking how hollow the words sounded, how smug I thought her voice was.

But still, I let them try their consoling ways on me, only because I knew it made them feel better. For years following his death, there were false confessions about my well-being, fabricated details about how I was feeling. *I'm fine,* I told them. *Time heals all wounds,* I said as I smiled, a bitter imitation of my mother. *He wouldn't want me to be mourning him like this. Big Eddie would want me to live.*

And all I wanted was for Big Eddie to be alive. To be here, with me and my mom. To make the triangle complete again so we wouldn't have to drift, so we wouldn't be lost within ourselves. Sometimes, I thought we grieved only because we didn't know what else to do. We'd never find a way out of the black hole we'd created for ourselves. After a time, it became normal, safe. No one could expect much from you if you were grieving. You could slide through life without making a splash because you didn't care. It didn't matter who saw you or what they said. It didn't matter what you looked like, if you were able to get yourself out of bed the next morning, even if it was raining outside. My mom took me to a specialist once down in Eugene, maybe fourteen months after Big Eddie died. He poked and prodded and eventually told us I was suffering from depression. I had laughed a genuine laugh at his diagnosis, the first laugh since I could remember through that hazy fog. *Of course I'm depressed,* I told the doctor, wiping the tears from my eyes that I wasn't sure had come from the laughter. *That was probably the easiest diagnosis you've ever had to give.*

The doctor wanted me on antidepressants. He wanted me to talk to someone. *Your mother is recovering,* he told me quietly. *Your aunts have made sure she is not letting herself drown. Benji, it's so easy to drown and you could become a danger to yourself.*

Poor word choice there, Doc, I'd said sarcastically. *Maybe read the file next time before you open your fucking mouth.*

He'd looked alarmed, but I was already storming out of the room.

Needless to say, I didn't take the drugs. I didn't talk to anyone. I ignored friends and family. People stopped calling me, asking me to hang out. My senior year of high school was a dream I can barely remember.

I lived day by day, allowing my grief to drift out into the open.

There were days I went to mile marker seventy-seven and sat in the Ford, poring over the police reports, the photographs, trying to recreate the accident, but missing so much information it was impossible. Other days I sat silently under the stone angel for hours, staring at the fifteen words that meant nothing, that gave no measure of the man buried underneath. I was obsessed with his death and the questions I did not have answers to. The stone angel offered me nothing.

It was on one of these days, the harder days, that I came home, planning on heading up to my room to look at the scene photographs again, suddenly sure I had missed something, sure that I was going to find an answer that had eluded me and the police and anyone else who had investigated my father's death. I was going to have proof positive that my father had been murdered, that he'd been run off the road and left there to die, to drown in the river. I was practically vibrating as I opened the door, ignoring a strange sensation that felt like a hand on my shoulder, a breath on my neck. It was nothing. Just my imagination.

Voices, in the kitchen. Mary and my mother. They had not heard me enter. I heard my name. I thought about ignoring it. I needed to get upstairs, to finally discover the truth.

But I crept toward the kitchen instead. I heard Mary: *You lost your husband, but he lost his father, the only one he will ever have.*

My mother murmured something in return, her voice a whisper.

Mary: *I know you can see it, hon. Big Eddie tied all of you together, but he's gone. He's not coming back. You can't allow your son to follow him, because that's what's happening. He's lost weight; he barely says a single word to anyone. The school called again and left a message. He cut class. They're talking about expulsion, Lola. Expelling him. Not graduating. He's got to get his grades up and he's got to start going back to class, otherwise he'll be held back. And then what about college?*

A sigh.

I left quietly.

The next day, I went to class.

I came home and did homework.

I offered fake smiles. False laughter.

I came downstairs for dinner, ignoring the looks of surprise.

Smells good, I said. Brightly.

After a time: *Benji, can I talk to you a moment?*

Can it wait, Mom? I'm kind of behind on homework and need to get caught up. I flash her a smile, quiet and earnest.

Oh? Homework? Sure, Benji. It can wait.

Thanks.

Benji?

Yeah?

I think... I think everything is going to be all right.

Of course you do, I thought. Of course you do, you bitch. How dare you forget him like he's nothing. How dare you. *Sure, Mom. Whatever you say.* I gave her another smile as she left the room.

And for the next few months, I focused on what needed to be done not to draw attention to myself. I buckled down. I worked hard. The police reports, the coroner's reports, the photos, the little chunk of metal that supposedly came from his truck, twisted and black—all stayed locked up, secreted away. They would have my undivided attention later. I would give them all the time they needed once the focus was no longer on me.

But the longer they stayed hidden, the harder it was to find the courage to look at them again. Maybe I was seeing things that weren't there. Maybe there was no evidence to suggest anything happened other than what the investigators said. Maybe my father was going to Eugene to meet with friends. Maybe he lost control of the truck (a deer? slick roads? distracted?). Maybe he crashed down the embankment, flipped his truck, and drowned just like they said. Maybe that's all it was.

Adrift. My mother and I were adrift, occasionally colliding and bouncing away. The wounds scabbed over but never healed, just waiting to be torn open again. That's the thing about grief: the longer it festers, the harder it is to cleanse.

So I'm not surprised that my mother isn't there the morning after Cal returns. She's seen something that has altered her perception of the way the world works and needs time to work it out on her own. It helps me that she had the exact same reaction I did when Cal first revealed himself: shock, denial, then anger. She and I are more alike than I like to admit, and I would do well to remember that.

Mary rejoices at seeing Cal again, much like her twin. Christie seems more subdued and gives a less warm reception, but Cal still has her smiling by the end of breakfast, charming her completely. If my mother has said anything to either of them, they don't show it on their faces. I like to think that they wouldn't be able to hide the shock of something so life-altering from me, especially given they are blood relations. I watch closely for any telltale sign, any flicker of fear or amazement based on anything other than the conversation at hand.

There's nothing.

Cal and I spend the rest of the day in bed. I don't hear my phone ring later that night, my mother leaving a message in a flat voice that she wants me to open the store tomorrow, but that Cal should stay at Little House. *Like hell*, I think when I listen to the message. Cal's running his big hands up my thighs, cradling my balls. *Like fucking hell.* I toss the phone to the floor as he leans down and swallows me whole. Fast learner, he is.

The second day, Roseland rejoices at Cal's return.

It doesn't take long for word to spread that the big guy is back. What starts off as a quiet morning soon leads to the bell above the door ringing steadily. I begin to recognize the looks that people give when they walk in: a brief smile for me, almost as a courtesy, their gazes darting until they find who they are looking for. Their eyes light up, and they step forward, hand outstretched if they are male, arms wide open for a hug if they are female. "It's good to see you," becomes the mantra of the day. "Glad to have you back. You sticking around this time?" Cal glances at me every time before he answers, as if seeking my approval, as if I am the one making the decision for him. And every time I nod. "Sure am," he says. "Benji's going to let me drive the Ford. It's so cherry, you know?"

They know.

Rosie comes to steal him away later in the afternoon, taking him back to the diner, wanting to show him the green-clover marshmallow cupcakes she made just for him. His eyes go slightly dreamy at the thought (not an "I don't know if I'm going to like that" uttered) and she glances at me, as if asking my permission. I shove down the slight panic, rolling my eyes and muttering that she's going to be responsible when he's destroyed the town due to his sugar high. She laughs and has started pulling him away, the other ten people in the store waiting to follow them out, when Cal stops. And turns. With a determined look in his eye. I know what that look means. I have about four seconds to make up my mind on whether or not to stop him before he's on me, leaning across the counter, hooking his hand around my neck, pressing his lips firmly against mine. The world goes white around us as he nibbles on my bottom lip, briefly touching his tongue to mine. He pulls away and presses his forehead against me. "Okay, Benji?" he asks quietly, kissing my cheek. "I'll be back. I promise."

"Sure," I manage to say. "Have fun."

He pulls away and turns toward Rosie, who has the biggest shit-eating grin on her face. "Looks like someone has been holding out on me," she says, eyeing me over his shoulder. "Cal, it appears you owe me a story or two."

"I know a lot of stories," he assures her as I groan, already wondering what the hell he's going to tell her. Or them, as the rest of the people begin to follow as well, like they're his little groupies. For the most part, they smile at me, reaching out to pat my hand as they walk by, ignoring the furious blush on my face. "How lovely for you, dear," Eloise Watkins says, she of the Friday Virginia Slims. "He does have quite the ass. And that red hair…." She sighs and follows him out the door.

"Good for you!" Doc Heward says cheerfully. "It's about time."

"About time?" I call after him. "He hasn't been here that long!"

"Bah!" I heard him call back through the door, following the rest up to Rosie's.

"Son of a bitch," I mutter.

That bastard knew *exactly* what he was doing when he kissed me in front of everyone. I'm fine with being out, but that's different from everyone knowing my business. Granted, I expect half the town assumed we were already fucking the first day they met him, so I don't suppose it's anything too bad. Well, not until the gossip wildfire reaches my mother and she finds out my… well, whatever he is to me… kissed me in the middle of the store in front of half the business owners on Poplar Street. That should make for a lovely time at the next meeting of the Roseland Chamber of Commerce. Hysterical.

The bell rings overhead and I roll my eyes without looking up from going over the delivery invoices. "If you're looking for Cal, the party's moved up to Rosie's."

"Cal?" a man says. I look up, not immediately recognizing his voice. I'm instantly wary of the stranger standing before me. He's a lot older than me, probably in his forties. He's on the losing side of fat, his middle thick, his arms like slabs of concrete in the gray collared shirt. He's balding on top, his dark hair thinning in little wisps. His eyes are small, and he almost reminds me of a fish, the way his lips pucker as if he's bitten into a lemon. His face is doughy and pale.

"Can I help you?" I say. He doesn't seem like one of the Strange Men, but given the last few days, I don't want to take any chances.

"Oh, I'm sure you can," he says as he walks to the counter and places his meaty hands flat down on top of it. "You said something about Cal?" he asks, watching me closely.

His voice is familiar to me, though I can't quite place it. I rack my brain as I say, "Uh, sure. He's up at the diner with most of the rest of the town."

"Is that a fact?" he says, sounding amused. "So old Cal Blue came back, did he?"

"I'm sorry, do you know him?" I feel cold.

"Not personally, though I've heard a lot about him," Fish Eyes says, a small smile on his face. "Seems a lot of people around here are talking about him."

I school my face so it's blank when I shrug. "He's all right."

Fish Eyes laughs. "I'm sure he is. And you must be Benji, right?"

"Yes."

"And you run the station here, right?"

"Yes."

He nods. "Big Eddie's Gas and Convenience. Quite the mouthful."

"Can I help you with something?" I want him to leave. I wonder briefly if my thread is showing, if Cal is racing toward the store. I hope not. The moments when threads show during the day, I've had to calm him so his wings aren't visible. I don't know what would happen if they exploded out of him in the middle of Rosie's Diner. Probably not the best thing to happen. I will myself to calm.

"I'm sure you probably could," Fish Eyes says. "Tell me, Benji. What does a guy your age get up to in a small town like this?"

"Mostly work," I say with a false smile. I can almost place his voice, but the answer dances away. "I own the store, so I don't have time for much else."

"Well, as long as you're staying out of trouble, then you should be okay," Fish Eyes says. "Would hate to think anything would happen to you. Or Cal. Good old Cal Blue, right? That his name?"

"You ask a lot of questions, mister."

He laughs like that's the funniest thing he's heard. "I am a curious man," he agrees, wiping his eyes. "I like to know everything I can, if you catch my drift."

"Can't say that I do," I say, trying to sound bored. *Stay away, Cal. Stay away.*

He looks behind me. "Why don't you give me a pack of them Marlboro 100s and we can call ourselves square."

I turn, an idea forming in my head. I reach up and grab the smokes. "Got your ID on you?"

He looks taken aback. "I'm flattered, Benji, but I think I'm a bit above eighteen."

"Federal law requires me to swipe a driver's license through the reader every time I sell cigarettes. Don't want to get dinged by the state. They do random tests." I shrug like it is out of my hands. "For all I know, you could be an agent doing an inspection. Haven't had one in a while."

"Do I look like a government agent to you?"

"You look like a lot of things to me. Got that ID so I can ring you up?"

He narrows his eyes as he reaches into his back pocket for his wallet. He opens it and slides an Oregon driver's license across the counter. I snap it up, trying to look at ease. I turn to the ID reader behind me and slide it through. I glance down at the screen on the reader. *VERIFIED*, it says. *JACK TRAYNOR DOB 11/14/1959.*

Traynor.

Where have I heard—

No. Oh fuck.

The gunman: *All I wanted was a fucking hit, man! Traynor told me I could get it, that fucking bastard!*

Then—

Mayor Walken: *You seem to forget, Traynor, that you are operating in* my *town, with* my *permission, which makes me* your *boss.*

Then—

The smoker: *I say we just take them out now. Kill the fucking faggot before he goes any further with this.*

He's here, I think. *He's here and he knows I was there that night. He knows I was listening.*

For each thought I have, each voice that goes through my head, another second ticks by. I can hear them counting off in my head and it's *one* and it's *two* and it's *three...* until I realize that I'm still staring at the reader which is shouting: *TRAYNOR TRAYNOR TRAYNOR.*

"There a problem?" I hear him ask, an edge to his words.

"No," I say, sounding remarkably calm. "No problem. It just didn't read it. Shouldn't be but another moment." I swipe it again. The screen lights up brighter than it ever has before, saying *TRAYNOR,* shrieking *TRAYNOR.* It's trying to tell me what I already know. *Get it together, Benji,* I tell myself. *Focus. Get it together and fucking do your job. He's waiting for you to fuck up. He's waiting for the look on your face. Do your fucking job.*

I plaster a smile on my face, the skin feeling tight. I turn back to Traynor, who is watching me with a scowl. I hand him back his ID, which he snatches out of my hand. I ring up the smokes. "That'll be $7.86," I tell him evenly.

He hands me a ten. "You know, you look a little nervous."

Fuck. Calm. Calm. No threads. Cal, stay away. "Just tired," I assure him as I make his change. "Been a rough couple of weeks."

"Is that right?" he says, holding out his hand for the change, hooking his fingers up. I can't help but think how much like a bear trap it looks.

I nod and drop the dollars and coins into his hand. And just like that, the trap closes, his fingers encircling my wrist, vise tight. I know he can feel my pulse, the blood rushing in erratic beats of my heart. My hand is clammy and my breath lodges in my throat. It's like the world has gone silent around us, as if we're stuck in a vacuum. I don't know if I could call out even if I tried. *No, Cal. Stay away. Stay away.*

Traynor has a shrewd look on his face, as if he can see inside my head and knows every single damn thing I'm thinking. There's so many weird things going on in this town that I banish Cal from my thoughts just in case Traynor *can* see inside. *These are some strange days,* I think frantically. I'm expecting his eyes to start twitching back and forth and his head to cock to the side, like he's a bird stalking its prey.

"You okay, there, Benji?" he asks, deceptively soft. "You getting sick?"

"Might be the flu," I say weakly, the first thought in my head. "Been going around town. May head on home when the shift change gets here in a few minutes." There's no one coming in, but he doesn't know that. At least I don't think he does.

If he's worried about my words, he doesn't give a reaction. He grinds his fingers into my wrist and I bite back the whimper that threatens to rise. "You know," he says, "faggots can find themselves in a world of hurt if they don't mind their own business."

"I don't know what you're talking about."

"Sure you don't," he says, squeezing my wrist again. "But you look like you need a reminder, just in case."

Anger is rising and I do nothing to stop it. I try to jerk my hand away, but he outweighs me by a good seventy pounds, and his hand is a steel trap. "Get the fuck out of my store before I call the cops," I growl at him.

He laughs. "The cops? You want to get the sheriff in here, boy? Well, that might be the best idea you've had in your short, short life."

The bell rings overhead as the front door opens. Traynor stiffens and immediately drops my wrist, leaning back on his heels. He doesn't turn away from me.

"Everything okay in here, Benji?" *Fuck.*

"Everything's fine, Abe. Just selling this gentleman his smokes. He was just on his way out."

Traynor sneers at me. "That's right. Just got my smokes. Hey, Benji?"

I say nothing, pulling my hands into fists at my sides.

"Remember what we talked about, okay? I would hate to see something happen to someone so young. Seems to me there's been enough death in this place." He smiles as he says this last, and it's all I can do to keep from launching myself over the counter and ripping his fucking face off with my bare hands. I want to cause him pain. I want him to hurt.

He snorts and brushes past Abe none too gently and walks out the door, the bell ringing overhead. He gets into an old Mazda and waves at me as he backs out onto Poplar and drives away.

"What in the hell was that about?" Abe asks, rushing over to me. "You okay, boy?"

"I'm fine," I mutter. I try to hide my wrist, but it's too late. He grabs it and pulls it up to his face. The ache is deeper than the red marks, easily seen as fingerprints. It'll bruise later, mottling my skin into deep blues and greens.

"You're not fine," he snaps at me. "Who was that man?"

"Just some guy," I sigh. "Friends with the sheriff."

Abe's jaw drops. "Benji, you've stepped into some shit here. You've got to watch yourself before something happens."

"I know," I say, withdrawing my hand. "I may need to call that—"

The bell rings again. "Abe!" Cal crows.

"Shit," I mumble, trying to catch Abe's eyes, to tell him to keep his fool mouth shut. He either doesn't see or he ignores me.

"Cal," he says tightly. "It's good to have you back, but you seem to be doing a piss-poor job at this whole guardian-angel thing."

"I can handle myself," I snap at Abe. "I've been doing just fine for years without him here."

"Fine?" Abe says, arching an eyebrow at me. "That's what you call it? *Fine?*"

"What's going on?" Cal asks, his voice low and dangerous.

"Some guy was just in here and he attacked Benji!"

"Abe," I groan. "He didn't *attack*—"

Cal's in front of me even before I can finish my sentence. He towers over me, irritation flashing in his dark eyes, his upper lip twitching. "Show me," he says.

Try as I might, I can't refuse him. I hold out my wrist again, and his touch is gentle as he rubs his fingers on the darkening skin. I try rolling my wrist in his hands, and while it hurts, it doesn't seem like anything is sprained.

"Who did this to you?" he says, his voice vibrating with fury.

"It doesn't—"

"No games!" he barks. "Tell me."

"Traynor," I say, looking away.

"Traynor?" Abe says, sounding surprised. "Wasn't that... Arthur Davis said that name. That was *him*?"

"Who is Arthur Davis?" Cal says with a scowl. "He is not one of mine. He is hidden from me. Traynor is too. You asked me about him once."

"Shit," I mutter again.

"Arthur Davis was the guy with the gun that you scared to kingdom come," Abe says.

"I will find him," Cal promises. "I will find this Traynor. He will not bother you again."

"No," I say sharply, and he flinches. "You are not to do anything like that again. You promised me."

"He *hurt* you." Now it looks like his anger is directed at me. "Why didn't I see your thread if you were being hurt?"

That's a question I can't answer, though part of me wonders if I kept it from him by merely wishing it so. This isn't information I think needs to be shared, if true. That would mean that God... crap, I can't even begin to think of it. "I'm fine now," I reassure him. "Abe came in and rescued me." This is supposed to be a joke, but it comes out flat.

But to Cal, it's serious. He turns to my old friend. "Thank you," he says somberly. "Thank you for doing what I could not."

Abe shrugs. "Don't need to worry about that. I saw you up with those people at Rosie's and figured Benji could use some company." He raises his hand to cut Cal off as he tries to interrupt, guilt pouring off him. "Didn't mean a thing by that. You might have been watching Benji for a long time, but you aren't the only one who cares what happens to him. People are just a mite glad you are back, and I'm one of them. I don't expect you to leave again anytime soon, we clear?"

Cal nods, bowing his head. He entwines his fingers into mine and grips me tightly. I squeeze back to let him know that everything is okay, even though it's so far from okay it's mind-boggling.

"What are you going to do about this, Benji?" Abe asks. "This is getting to be bigger than all of us."

"I may need to make a call," I admit.

"To who?"

I avert my eyes. "That FBI agent. Corwin. This might be the wildfire he was talking about."

"Government men," Abe mutters. "We'll see what he's capable of, I guess."

"I don't know why you just don't let me handle this," Cal mutters. He keeps his hand in mine, tightening his grip. He looks worried and guilty.

"Hey," I chide softly. "None of that. I know what you're capable of, but Abe's right. This might be getting bigger than we are. You've still got my back, right?"

He looks at me incredulously. "You're not leaving my side again."

I roll my eyes. "You've got a job to do, Cal. And so do I. But we'll figure something out, okay?"

"Government men," he grumbles. I don't even think he knows what that means. Abe starts to chuckle and I follow suit. Somehow it's not as hard to laugh as I thought it would be.

the life and death of joshua corwin

I WOULD learn later that Agent Joshua Corwin was a family man, much to my surprise. He had a wife and three adorable girls, nine, and thirteen, and fifteen years old. He and his wife Rebecca had been married for twenty years. They'd been high school sweethearts who married upon graduation. They'd gone to college together at the University of Oregon, Rebecca electing to pursue a degree in journalism, Corwin going into criminal justice.

Shortly before graduating college, Corwin was recruited into the FBI. His plan had been to become a police officer for a few years before applying to the academy, but they came knocking years early with an offer he could not turn down. After training at Quantico and passing with flying colors, he was assigned to the field office in El Paso, focusing on narcotics coming across the border from Mexico. Rebecca worked as an on-air reporter for the local ABC affiliate.

He and his wife were twenty-three when their first daughter, Alex, was born.

They were twenty-five when their second daughter, Jennifer, was born.

They were twenty-seven when the world went insane on September 11. All other assignments were put on hold as tons of steel fell in a cloud of dust so thick it looked like the deepest fog. By then, Rebecca had worked her way up to a weekend anchor desk with hopes of going to weeknight anchor as soon as that old fossil Bill Macklin decided to retire. But 9/11 gave them different priorities, much like it did the rest of the world. They made the decision that Rebecca would stay home with the girls, while Corwin, like so many others, was reassigned to work on a terrorism task force. It was a completely different animal than he was used to, but like the rest of the country, he felt an absurdly ridiculous charge of patriotism in the years that followed.

Eventually, missing the work he used to do, he put in a request to go back onto a drug task force, and when a spot opened up back in their home state of Oregon, he jumped at the chance and dragged his family back to the Northwest, including their new addition, their youngest daughter Lily.

I would learn later that Corwin was a big softie when it came to his daughters, his little girls. He doted on them, giving them whatever they wanted. They were all daddy's girls, through and through. He was never harsh, never cross. He could be stern, but only when they were in the wrong. They loved him; they thought him the greatest man who ever lived. And for all they knew, maybe he was.

His marriage was strong and deep. Friends would say they'd never seen a couple so devoted to each other as Joshua and Rebecca. They acted like they were still eighteen, so young, so in love. They were strong together, playing off each other's strengths until they had created a formidable team. He worshipped the ground his wife walked on.

Life was good for Agent Joshua Corwin and his family. He had a good job. He had a great family. He had the life he'd always wanted to have. It was wonderful. Everything was just wonderful.

He couldn't possibly ask for anything more.

Those are the things I learned about him after I killed him.

OF COURSE, I knew nothing of Corwin's life when I first called him, the day after Traynor visited the store. I was solely focused on not sounding like a complete idiot when I called him, especially when I realized just how thin my story sounded. It didn't help that Cal paced in front of me, scowling, muttering to himself that he just couldn't *believe* I thought he couldn't protect me. Didn't I know he was an *angel*? I reassured him that I knew that and more, pressing a kiss against his lips which he returned with a desperate edge. It bothered him immensely that Traynor had gotten in and out without him knowing. It bothered him that he did not know who Traynor was. It bothered him that he was still cut off from his memories.

But I think what bothered him the most was the fact that he had been surrounded by adoring people while I was getting harassed. I never said anything to him about this, and while he didn't articulate it in so many words, I could see any anger he directed at himself. People came into the store the next day to see him again, but he was less forthcoming than he'd been the day before. He flat-out refused to leave with any of them. A thread arose at some point that morning, and I could see the conflicted look in his eyes as he glanced between me and the door. Rosie had walked in at that moment, much to his relief. He must have thought she carried her shotgun everywhere, because he felt at least a slight comfort leaving her there with me, even though she didn't have it on her. She'd been puzzled, but I just shook my head, telling her Cal was being Cal, and he worried a little too much.

She didn't leave until he returned.

"CORWIN," a gruff voice says into the phone.

"Agent Corwin?" I ask. "Joshua Corwin?"

"Yes."

"My name is Benji Green."

"Yes?"

"You gave me your card a few weeks ago. In Roseland? You asked about my father, Big Eddie? I'm sorry. Edward Green. It was at the gas station."

He gives me a brisk, "Hold on." I hear him cover the phone, then a muffled voice speaking to someone else. I can't make out any of the words until, "And can you shut the door on your way out please? Thank you." There's another pause. "Mr. Green?"

"Uh, yeah. You can call me Benji. If that's okay."

"And what can I do for you, Benji?"

I'm at a loss of where to begin. I want to ask questions immediately, demand an explanation, but my mouth feels dry, and I don't know if I'm entitled to these answers. The silence begins to drag on until Cal comes up behind me and wraps his arms around me, pulling me into his chest. He reaches a big hand under my shirt and rubs my stomach in slow, soothing circles. He leans down and kisses the top of my head. "You got this," he murmurs. "If you have to talk to him, then talk."

"Benji?" Corwin asks, his voice sharper.

"Sorry," I mumble. "I'm... nervous. About calling you."

"Did something happen?"

"I don't know. I think so. I think many things happened. I think things are *going* to happen."

"Gossip, huh?" He sounds amused.

"Like wildfire."

"Griggs?"

"Yeah. And the mayor."

"Walken," he growls. "Why am I not surprised?"

"And Traynor."

Silence. It feels thick. Then: "Did you say Traynor? As in Jack Traynor?"

This can't be good. "Yes."

A sharp intake of breath. "Oh, Jesus Christ, kid. Have you seen him? How do you—No. That can wait. Listen to me. You stay away from Jack Traynor, you hear me? That man is a fucking sociopath. Do you understand? You do *nothing* with Traynor. You say *nothing* to Traynor. I'm serious, Benji."

My hands feel clammy. I glance down at the marks circling my wrist, the red having faded into blues and purples and greens. "He's here. In Roseland," I say faintly.

Corwin swears. "We were told he was back East. What the hell is he doing in Roseland?" The question seems to be rhetorical, so I don't answer. I don't *know* the answer, regardless. "Listen, Benji," Corwin says brusquely. "I need to meet with you. Get some information. This isn't going to be strictly on the record. For now. But if Traynor is involved, this just became a whole new ball game. When can you meet?"

I try to backpedal. "Uh. Look. Maybe this wasn't such a good idea. If he's as bad as you say, it may not be good for me to be seen talking to you, you know? What if he comes after my family? My mom? The Trio?" I tilt my head back to look at the man behind me, making sure he understands what I'm trying to say. He smiles softly at me and kisses my forehead.

"You want to know something, Benji?" Corwin asks, his voice going softer.

No, I don't feel that I do. But there's something in his voice that I can't deny. "What?"

"A man called me five years ago. Told me he thought something was going on in his town. Thought he should alert the authorities outside of the sheriff's office. Wouldn't tell me his name. Said he had a family to think about. That he had a son."

"No," I whisper.

"When can you meet?"

"I have a store to run," I hedge.

"Get someone else to watch it. This is important."

"I...."

"Benji, your father was trying to do what's right. Now it's up to you."

"Fuck," I say, closing my eyes.

I ASK Mom to watch the store, telling her I need a day off again. She averts her eyes from Cal standing right next to me. She says I seem to be taking quite a bit of time off lately. I remind her that out of the last three years, any time off I took was because she forced me to. She huffs a bit at that then acquiesces. She doesn't know Abe will be paying her a visit at the store to let her know he also knows about Cal, and to try and talk her down from whatever ledge she seems to be standing on. It's an ambush, I know, but I don't know how else to go about it. It's starting to feel like I'm juggling too many things at once, and soon everything will come crashing down.

I feel absurd heading to the next town over, like I'm some kind of spy on my way to a covert drop. The whole thing is made a tad bit more ridiculous when Cal tells me in a very serious voice that he's been watching TV in the back office at the store and that anytime spies get together, they wear sunglasses. He asks if I'll buy him a pair of sunglasses because he still doesn't have any money. The flush that rises up his neck while he says this is enough to melt the ice that has surrounded my heart since hanging up the phone with Corwin. I take him out and buy him sunglasses. He makes me buy a pair for myself as well, the same as his. We look like idiots.

Cal drives because I don't think I can focus enough. Though I do admit to going out of my way to get that damn beaming smile he gives me when he's tickled to no end. Driving the Ford inspires it. Green clover marshmallows do too. And I seem to be mashed up in there as well, because there are times he'll look at me and that smile just comes out of nowhere, curving his lips as his eyes grow bright and warm, threatening to knock me on my ass. I thought about asking him to stay in Roseland, but even as the words came out of my mouth, he began to growl at me like some kind of feral cat and I left it alone.

We are quiet most of the way into Oakland, a small town about halfway between Roseland and Eugene. This leads us down the Old Forest Highway before hitting I-10, directly past mile marker seventy-seven. This, of course, causes my pulse to quicken as my heart begins to race. Before we round that last curve, Cal pulls me across the bench seat until I'm nestled up against him with his arm wrapped around my shoulders, my face in his neck. I shake for a time, breathing him in, and when I open my eyes again, we are already on the main highway, sunglasses and all.

"BENJI?" a rough voice says. I turn in the booth I sit in at the local diner, almost knocking over the cup of coffee I have yet to touch.

Corwin stands next to the booth, his suit slightly wrinkled, his dark hair windblown and all over the place. He looks like I remember, disheveled but still with an air of authority around him. He slides off his mirror shades and I see his eyes are a chocolate brown, but they still look slightly cold. "Agent," I allow.

He narrows his eyes as he glances over at Cal. "Who is this?"

Cal stands, his stance tense. He is bigger than Corwin, both height-wise and around. "I'm with Benji. He's mine. You will not hurt him."

Corwin doesn't look intimidated in the slightest. "I'm not here to hurt him," he says, keeping his voice even. "I'm pretty sure you can stand down, big guy, before you hurt yourself."

I groan and pull on Cal's hand, forcing him to slide into the booth next to me. He crowds me up against the wall of the diner. I take in a deep breath and smell earth. It calms me, at least a bit. He takes my hand and I clutch at him, pulling our joined hands down to my lap so Corwin can't see. I'm not worried about Corwin's opinion of us, but we're in a place that is not our home. I don't want people to turn hostile.

Corwin sits across the table, folds his glasses, then puts them in a pocket in his suit jacket. He cracks his knuckles and glances between the two of us before focusing on me. "I was glad to get your call, kid. Didn't think anything would come of it."

"Why did you stop in Roseland that day?" I ask, curious.

A strange look comes over Corwin's face. It almost looks like he's embarrassed. He cracks his knuckles again and sighs. "You know what? I don't know if I can answer that."

My eyes widen as I lean forward. "Like, it's top secret or something?" I almost consider looking around to see if there are any spies listening in. I still have my sunglasses in my pocket. Should I put them back on?

He laughs. "No, kid. Not anything like that. It just sounds… weird." He pauses as a waitress comes over and sets another cup of coffee on the table. He lifts the cup and drinks it black.

Cal makes a face. "I don't see how you guys can drink that. I told Benji I wouldn't like it and I didn't. It's gross." He scowls as he takes a drink of his juice as if to prove his point.

"It puts hair on your chest," Corwin tells him.

"Already got it," Cal says proudly, and I have to grab his shirt before he pulls it up to show Corwin just how much hair he has. Corwin looks at the two of us like we're the oddest things he's laid his eyes on. *If only he knew what weird really is,* I think. *Hell, he's the FBI. They probably know everything about angels already. And aliens.*

"Why was it weird?" I ask Corwin as Cal grabs my hand again.

Corwin has to drag his eyes away from Cal. *Another one under his spell*, I think. "Huh?" Corwin says.

"Why was it weird?"

He blushes again. "It sounds a little crazy."

"I know crazy, trust me."

Cal grins at me.

Corwin watches me for a moment then says, "For some reason, I believe that. I, uh… okay. Look. I don't believe in ghosts. I don't believe in psychics or mystics or anything weird like that."

"There goes my whole notion of the *X-Files*," I mutter.

He ignores me. "But I *do* believe that people can have hunches, or feelings… you know, that something is… off. I don't think it's any kind of sixth sense or anything like that. To be in my line of work, though, you almost *have* to have it. It's saved me a few times, whether or not I could admit it at the time." He looks at me defiantly, like he expects me to make fun of him. I keep my face passive.

He continues: "I was digging through some old case files, trying to clear off my desk. It's this whole new initiative going through the Bureau right now: out with the old and in with the new. Cases are being labeled with a priority level so the higher-ups can figure out how the distribution should work. Cases that are considered dead or cold are obviously given a lower priority than the rest."

"What does this have to do with me?" I ask. "Or my father?"

He glares at me. "I'm getting to that, okay? Look, this isn't easy for me to tell you, because obviously you don't know what was going on. So just listen."

I nod, gripping Cal's hand tightly.

"Everything is digital these days," Corwin says, "but even five years ago we still had a shitload of paper files. And my desk was buried in them. I had a pile that I considered my "dead" pile, and I planned on taking those all at once to be put into storage. I wasn't planning on going through them at all. They were dead. They weren't coming back to life. So… shit."

"What?"

He takes a large sip of coffee and starts wringing his hands. "I was working late one night. I had to stay late because we were planning on going on vacation soon. Me, the wife. The kids. It'd been so long since we'd done anything, and I was feeling a bit guilty. So I was working late, trying to get all this shit done so I could take a week off work without thinking of the pile of paperwork waiting for me when I got back. It was going on ten o'clock. I was the only one left in the office, aside from the cleaning crew. I know this. I *know* I was the only one left. I was almost done. I was ready to go home, so I picked up the last stack and put it in the cart. There were probably a hundred other files in there. I got up and started pushing it toward the elevator and…." He stops, looking embarrassed again. "I can't really explain it, okay? I'd gone maybe three steps and it was like… it was like a hand dropped on my shoulder. Out of nowhere."

"Out of the blue?" I ask, my hands like ice. I force myself to keep looking at Corwin. I want to turn and look at Cal, to see the look on his face, to start the questions all over again, to ask what he knew, when he knew it, and why he did what he did. This is not coincidence. This is no longer about what's impossible or improbable.

There is a pattern, I think. *Shapes. A design.*

"Yeah," Corwin mutters. "Out of the blue. I don't mind admitting it scared the shit out of me. I spun around, jerking the cart with me, but there was no one there. I told myself I was just tired. That I was imagining things. But you know what? I remember. I remember in that split second feeling *fingers* curling around my shoulder. I *know* what I felt. It was *there.* But no one was behind me." He looks at me nervously. "I know how this sounds, okay? I know what it sounds like. But I'm not crazy. I'm not."

I shake my head, feeling numb. "I don't think you are. At all." I hazard a glance at Cal, but his face was impassive. I know he feels my gaze on him, but he's studiously avoiding it. I try to pull my hand away from his because I feel there's untruth mixed in with all the rest of him, but he refuses to let me go.

Corwin doesn't seem to notice any of this, only looks relieved at my assurances. "It's just strange to say it out loud," he admits.

"These are some strange days," Cal says, and I have trouble swallowing. It feels like my throat has closed.

"Yeah," Corwin says. "But I'm not done. When I saw no one was there, my heart just jumped into my throat. I'd never felt like that before. It was like a small electric current running through my body and I felt… more alive. Like there was something *more* about me. Something I had never thought of before, and it felt *important.* I'm not explaining this very well."

I'm confused, but I just nod.

"The point is, I spun around and the entire cart got knocked over. Literally *thousands* of pages from *hundreds* of files fell to the floor and scattered everywhere. It would take weeks to put everything back together. But out of all those files that spilled, out of all the pages on the floor, there was still one in the cart, still one thin file intact, not a single page spilled. I hadn't come across it when clearing out my desk. It must have gotten lost in the shuffle. I hadn't even thought about it in years."

The waitress comes back, refilling the coffee and Cal's juice. She asks if we want anything to eat and we say no. She stands above us, and I see her glance at Cal's hand entwined in mine in my lap. She rolls her eyes and walks away.

"What was in the file, Corwin?" I ask, not sure if I want the answer.

He looks down at his hands. "Part of my job is to track trends, data analysis involving drug shipments. In early 2006, I began to notice what seemed to be an increase in the distribution and use of methamphetamines. There'd always been concern in Oregon about meth usage, given how much of the area is rural, but it spiked drastically, like either multiple labs and dealers had popped up out of nowhere, or there was a massive new operation that was manufacturing and distributing meth."

"I don't understand," I say quietly, feeling sick to my stomach, "I've never heard of anything like that around here."

"Well, you probably wouldn't, would you?" he counters. "Most organized meth labs aren't exactly out in the open for everyone to see. This wouldn't have been because of one man making meth out of his bathtub. The point is, I began to track where it was coming from, as that was my job. But I came up with nothing, just a bunch of dead ends. There were never reports of anyone buying the massive quantities of chemicals I would expect for the size of the operation I felt was happening. No large shipments of fertilizer aside from the usual to farms in the surrounding counties, all of which have to carry permits to lawfully order. Even my usual contacts couldn't tell me if there was a new major player out there.

"You have to understand that all I had to support me was a bunch of random statistics that might have just been a fluke. Meth manufacturing can be a relatively cheap process when done right, and the use of meth was on the rise, so it was easier to turn a profit. For every number I had showing the spike, you could have found the same thing happening all over the country. I didn't have any evidence. Nothing concrete, anyway."

"Then how'd you find anything?" I ask.

He sighs. "I had a buddy in the DEA who owed me a favor. His reach goes further than mine, and I had him put out a couple of feelers to see if he could get a nibble where I couldn't. He ran into someone who gave him someone else's name. Turned out to be a hard-core drug user, but one who still seemed to be in his right mind, for the most part. We call 'em twitchers, because of the little seizures they seem to have, the shakes. He pointed us south. Turns out I'd been looking too far north. Portland, Tigard, hell, all of Multnomah County. I even spread my dragnet as far as the coast, places like Tillamook and Seafare. But he told us south. And that's when I got a phone call. One of those quirky twists of fate. Luck, pure and simple. Early 2007, it was. Somehow landed on my desk. Maybe someone heard of my project, maybe they just tried to pass the buck off, I don't know. But I picked up the phone and on the other end was a man who refused to give me his name. Deep voice, though. Sounded like he'd be a big guy." He watches me directly as he says this last, anticipating my reaction.

I feel the blood drain from my face as I draw in a sharp intake of breath. "Dad."

Corwin nods. "I think so. I really do. Like I said, no name, wouldn't give me his phone number, wouldn't tell me where he was from or how he knew what he knew. Told me he was worried about what would happen to his family if he was found out. He had a son, he told me. Sounded real proud when he said it too." I close my eyes. "Said he didn't want to take the risk, but wanted to let me know he had reasons to suspect the good sheriff of Douglas County might not be as clean as he'd led others to believe. Seems said sheriff was actually quite the opposite of clean. And maybe others were involved as well. He didn't have a whole lot to go on, but he wanted me to send the cavalry out here with guns blazing."

A tear slips down my cheek. That sounds just like Big Eddie. "But you didn't, did you," I say bitterly. "You didn't do a damn thing." Cal puts his arm around my shoulder and pulls me into him. I don't care if someone has a fucking problem with it in the diner. I take comfort from his heat and the low growl coming from his throat, directed at the man across from us.

"You have to understand, Benji," Corwin said, looking miserable, "there wasn't a whole lot I could do, at least not right then. Regardless of the small town it was in, sheriff is still an elected position, and then the mayor's name was dropped as potentially being involved? It would have been a bureaucratic nightmare to accuse them without any evidence. My superiors would have laughed me out of their offices, and no judge would have granted me a warrant. It was all speculative. All I had were flow charts and the voice on the phone of a man I didn't know. Hell, I had one of our geeks in the computer lab run satellite searches over the Umpqua National Forest and couldn't find a damn thing that stuck out. If they *were* doing anything, it'd have to be well hidden."

"They were talking about moving," I say suddenly, flashes of conversation running through my head. "They said things were getting too close."

"Who?" he says excitedly.

"Walken. Griggs. Traynor. A couple of others."

"How do you know this?"

I hesitate, only because Cal doesn't know the full story here either. But I've already opened my mouth, so I spill the rest of the story about the night I stood under the sheriff's window. I get to the part about Walken threatening Traynor, and Corwin lets out a low whistle. "That guy's got some balls if he tries to bully Traynor. That is not a man I would want to fuck with."

"Tell me about it," I grumble. Corwin arches an eyebrow at me and I show him my arm, the bruises still identifiable as fingers wrapped around my wrist. Cal lets out another growl as Corwin touches my hand gingerly. Corwin pulls out his phone and says, "May I?" I nod and he snaps some photos, first one side and then the other.

"You didn't tell me any of this," Cal says through gritted teeth. "Why couldn't I see it? The thread? What is going on here?"

"What?" Corwin asks, bewildered.

I panic for a moment and shake my head at Corwin. "We'll talk about this later," I say to Cal.

"Planning on it," he snaps at me.

"You think my father was murdered too, don't you?" I ask Corwin. It feels odd, this certainty I feel. Having validation, after so long wondering on my own, is surreal.

He sits back against the booth and drums his fingers on the table with one hand, looking at the photo of my wrist on his phone with the other. "I talked to him three more times," he finally says, "over a period of two months. Tried to trace the number each time he called, but he was smart. The numbers were for disposable cell phones. Couldn't even ping them on any cell tower. He was quick with the phone calls."

"I looked at his cell phone records after he died," I say, wondering just how I missed all of this, how I could have been so blind. My father must have gone to great lengths to keep this hidden from us. I can't help but feel anger toward him, that he could have kept this to himself, that he was making secret phone calls to the FBI without saying a damn thing about it. "The one for the store phone too. Never found anything that wasn't supposed to be there. He made sure of that."

"Hey," Corwin says with alarm. "That's not why I'm here, Benji. I'm not trying to dig at old wounds or say anything disparaging against your father. What he did was a brave thing, contacting us like he did. He didn't have to. He could have kept on going with his life and not said a word. He spoke up."

"And he died," I snap. "He fucking *died* for it. What the fuck does that do for me?"

Corwin looks sympathetic when he says, "Sometimes we have to risk everything for the chance to do one thing right. I'd like to think your father knew that."

"It was you, wasn't it?"

His eyes widen. "What?"

"You convinced him to meet with you," I say coldly. "That's where he was going that morning. Not to see any friends. He was going to meet with you. He didn't want to. He told you he didn't. But you made him go anyway."

Corwin flinches as if I've raised my hand to him. "The last time he called, I told him it was important for my case that he come in and meet me face to face. I told him that unless he was a material witness, nothing he'd told me would mean a damn thing. I couldn't find enough proof to support the claims. I'd tried to convince him the other times he'd called, but... I pushed him this time. Hard." Corwin looks away. "I told him to think about his son. Did he want his son to grow up in a place where he could be exposed to this bullshit? What if they found out he was speaking to me? Wouldn't that put his family in danger?"

"You used us against him? What the fuck is wrong with you?"

"You have to understand," Corwin pleads. "I thought I was about to lose this case. I had a witness who wouldn't even give me his name, and a bunch of loose information that wasn't connecting. I couldn't find a damn thing about Walken *or* Griggs to support this. No evidence of money laundering, no embezzlement. The town books were in order. Hell, Roseland was audited in 2005 and passed with flying colors. There was *nothing*."

"What I understand," I grind out, "is that you killed my father."

Corwin closes his eyes. "He finally relented. We set up a meeting. I offered to meet him halfway, but he wanted to come to Eugene. Said he wanted to get as far away as he could before he would meet me. We were supposed to meet at a park.

Still wouldn't tell me his name. Told me he was a big guy. That he'd be wearing a John Deere hat."

"Oh, God," I whisper.

I GAVE him that hat when I was eight years old. I'd been so proud of myself for saving up money, doing extra chores and not telling anyone why. I wanted it to be a surprise. I'd convinced my mom to take me to the store to buy it, telling her she needed to wait in the car because I wanted to do it on my own. I'd gone in and told the clerk I needed the largest size because my father had the biggest head ever. I'd counted out the crumpled dollars carefully, adding coins when I ran out of paper. The clerk had wrapped the hat (so *green* it was, the words JOHN DEERE in bright yellow, like the sun) in tissue paper before putting it into a brown paper bag. I marched out of that store, feeling high and mighty for thinking of this all on my own. He would love it, I knew. He would think it was the greatest thing in the world.

But that quickly gave way to nerves a day later: Father's Day, the reason I thought to buy it for him to begin with. I cursed myself as I nervously handed him the paper sack, wondering why I hadn't saved a bit more money to get wrapping paper. He would hate it, I knew. It was such a dumb present. It was awful. Even as my mother murmured to him that this was all from me, that I'd thought of this all on my own, I felt my face burn. He lifted the tissue paper off as if he was unwrapping the greatest gift in the world. There was such reverence in his eyes, such excitement that I almost couldn't bear the thought of disappointment taking over, a crushing look that would show how much I had failed. But it never came. He lifted the hat out of the paper, brushing his fingers along the brim gently. His eyes went back and forth as he read over the two words there. His voice was a little rougher than usual when he spoke. "You got this all on your own for me?" he asked, touching the hat again. I nodded at him, unable to speak. "Well, isn't that... just something," he said. "Isn't that just fine. Why, it might be the finest hat I own. You know what we have to do to it, Benji?"

"Crack the brim," I said, finding my voice, feeling very warm.

"That's right." And with that, he took the brim between his two big hands and started to mold it in a semicircle, shaping the green. After, he put it on his head, and it fit just right without him having to undo the snaps on the back. "Very handsome," my mother said with a smile.

He turned back to me and said, "Well?"

"Looks good, Dad," I said. But inside, I was screaming with joy, knowing I'd done something right in his eyes. And only a moment later I found myself being pulled upward into a hug that seemed to go on for days.

"Thanks, Benji," he said, kissing my forehead. "It's the best present I ever got."

He wore it almost every day.

"I GAVE him that hat," I mutter to Corwin. "Years ago. It was found floating in the cab of the truck when he was pulled out of the river. Have it back at the house with some other things." Things that were his, things that I keep away from everyone else. The hat, given to me by an officer whose name I couldn't remember. A shell casing. A photo of him and me, sitting side by side up in the mountains on a dirt road on a hunting trip when I was four or five, him feeding me a piece of jerky. A yellowed note that says, *Benji, make sure you rake the leaves today after school. Just get around Little House and I'll help you with the rest this weekend. Love, Pops.* Things that would have meant absolutely nothing to anyone else, but meant everything to me.

"He was a great man," Cal whispers in my ear. "You know this."

Corwin nods at my words, looking slightly ill. "I waited," he says. "I waited at the park for hours. No one ever showed. I wondered if he'd gotten scared and flaked on me. It never crossed my mind that something happened to him. I just thought he'd worked himself up too much to actually show. It's happened before. So many times.

"I went back to Eugene and never heard from the guy again. Eventually, it was made clear by the Agent in Charge that my time would be better spent on projects of merit rather than ones that had nothing to support them. I was told in no uncertain terms to drop it, that obviously it was going nowhere, and I had a witness who no longer wanted to play ball." He smiles sadly at me. "I saw the news story about your father. About his accident. I figured it was him. The timing was a bit off, though. We were supposed to meet at two, and he'd apparently crashed in the early morning. It would have been too early for him to leave to meet me. But then they showed a video of him speaking at a Chamber of Commerce meeting, and that voice... I knew it was him."

"Why didn't you do anything then?" I ask, wiping my eyes.

"It all comes down to proof, Benji. There was no proof of foul play. The official police report listed it as a single-vehicle accident. There was no evidence of a second vehicle involved. Nothing on the coroner's report to suggest foul play. The timing wasn't right. The Old Forest Highway ends at I-10, yeah, but even if he was going to I-10, who's to say he was driving to Eugene?"

"I know. I've read all the reports. I've thought of all these scenarios. Probably many more times than you ever have."

He nods, like he expected that. "Then you should know there's nothing there. It was officially ruled as a single-vehicle accident possibly precipitated by speed and the road conditions due to the rain. The report was signed off by Griggs."

I eye him carefully. "But you don't believe it, do you? Not now. You think something happened."

"Yes," Corwin says, and I sigh. "I think somehow, someone found out your father was speaking to me and decided to make sure it wouldn't happen again. I think your dad was run off the road and left in the river to drown. I came here a few weeks ago because of that dead file. I was told it was done. I almost *believed* it was done. But...." He shook his head. "There was *something* there, I know it. It can't just all be coincidence. It just can't."

"What do you want me to do?" I ask, suddenly unsure about all of this. It's one thing to be on the phone with the man, and it's another to hear confirmation of what I've long suspected. Now that it's at hand, I feel small and weak. Uncertain and indecisive.

"Nothing," Corwin says, a stern edge to his voice. "Especially now that Traynor is involved. Benji, the things that man has done would curdle your stomach. It's best to keep your distance, as much and as far as you can. I'm going to be sniffing around town a bit. This is officially off the record, at least for the moment. The wife thinks I'm out of town on some work training, and work thinks I'm on vacation. I'm going to take a few days and just look around and see what I can see. Griggs is in on this, I'm sure of it. Walken too. If what your father told me is correct, they could be supplying methamphetamines up and down the West Coast."

"Arthur Davis," I say, his name coming out of nowhere. "You might want to check into Arthur Davis."

He opens his phone and types something into it. "Why him?"

I tell him the story of the attempted robbery, how Arthur dropped Traynor's name and how the attempted robbery ended in the gunman's supposed suicide. By the time I finish, Corwin is shaking his head, his jaw set. "Jesus," he says. "I mean it, Benji. You need to keep your fucking distance. These people are animals. You need to keep yourself safe. If anything comes from this, we have bias intimidation of a witness and assault and battery against Traynor. Don't suppose you called the cops after he left."

I roll my eyes. "I'm sure Griggs would have loved to take that report."

Cal growls at him again. "You don't need to worry about him. It is not your job. It is *my* job. And I am more than ready to do what is asked of me."

Corwin stares at him. "You're an odd duck, you know that?"

"I am not a duck at all," Cal snarls. "You just do your job and let me do mine. Benji belongs to me and no one will take him from me."

"Hush," I tell him lightly. "Nothing is going to happen to me. And besides, I can take care of myself. I have for a long time." Cal looks at me like that is the stupidest thing I've ever said.

"You guys been together a long time?" Corwin asks bluntly.

"Yes," Cal says at the same time I say, "A few days."

Corwin stares.

"Long story," I say as I flush.

He nods. "I'll be in touch, Benji. Just keep doing what you are doing, and don't let anyone know yet that you spoke to me. If you see me around Roseland, act like you don't know me. If the shit starts to hit the fan, you call me. That number I gave you is a separate private number. Most people don't know I have it, not even my wife." I arch my eyebrow at him, and he rolls his eyes. "Not like that. I deal with some shady people sometimes with what I do, and I don't want to bring my work home with me. And sometimes, like now, I don't want to bring things into my work. Not yet. We clear?"

I nod. He stands up from the booth, dropping a twenty on the table. He starts to walk away but pauses at the edge of the booth. He doesn't look down at us. "I'm sorry about your dad," he finally says. "I... I always wanted to say that. You know, how sorry I am. What he tried to do was a very brave thing. You have every right to hate me, but the only thing I've ever wanted was to help people and to put the bad guys away. I like to think that maybe your... Big Eddie was like that too."

I nod again, blinded by tears.

He leaves. That is the last time I see him alive.

I'M NOT the one who physically killed Agent Joshua Corwin, though it might as well have been me. It is my fault just the same. Had I not called him, he might not have found a reason to come back to Roseland. He might have escaped the pattern, even if it seems to have been calling to him. Who's to say he wouldn't have been freed from it? Had I not involved him, he might be with his family instead of lying in a morgue a hundred miles away in the coastal town of Bandon, his bloated body having washed up on a rocky beach four days after we met in the grimy diner.

The *what ifs* haunt me almost as much as my own memories do. I lost my father to something I still don't quite understand. He was taken from me, yes, and even if I believe more and more that his death was not an accident, a small part of me still questions whether it could be true. What I can't question is the fact that I helped to take Corwin away from his family. His daughters will not have their father because of me. His wife will not have a husband because of me.

I don't know much about Corwin's last hours. I didn't see him around Roseland in the days that followed our meeting. All I know is that Abe came in, his hands shaking slightly as he grabbed a newspaper off the stack near the front door. He flipped the paper over and showed me the story in the bottom right-hand corner with the headline: *Body in Bandon Identified as FBI Agent.* Even as those words blurred and my head started to pound, I read on, and Cal came up behind me and wrapped his big arms around me, holding me close. Agent Corwin had been found facedown on a beach outside Bandon, Oregon, by an older gentleman out for his morning walk. He told police he first thought it was a large sack washed ashore, and that he was going to pick it up and throw it away. He hated litter on the beaches, he said. But when he'd gotten closer, he'd seen white hands, which went to arms and a torso, the face down and turned away. The older gentleman said he froze for a moment, that he could not believe what he was seeing. That he hadn't seen a dead body since he'd fought in World War II, and that he realized not enough time had passed between the last time and now. Not having his cell phone on him, he stumbled back and headed for the nearest set of stairs, where he flagged a passing motorist who called the police.

Since Corwin was found naked, he had no form of identification. All of his teeth had been pulled from his head. His fingers had been cut off, as were his toes. An obvious attempt to keep him from being identified quickly. I haven't been able to work up the courage to find out if these atrocious things were done before or after he was killed. I don't think my sanity could take knowing.

A sketch of his face had been plastered all over the coastal news, and word quickly spread of the John Doe. I heard vague talk of this dead man but didn't make the connection. Why would I? Even before the FBI could be called in to help with the investigation, one of Corwin's colleagues saw the sketch. There was no question as to the John Doe's identity. Agent Joshua Corwin had been murdered, they said. Shot through the back of his head. Based upon the angle of the bullet wound, he would have most likely been on his knees at the time. Hearing that only made the news worse.

Did he beg? Did he plead for his life? Did he tell the shooter he had a family waiting for him, he didn't want to die, he just wanted to go home? Did he cry out his daughters' names? Did he whisper that he loved his wife?

Did he pray?

That's the one that gets me the most, especially as I watch my own angel as he cups my face, as he brushes the tears from my cheeks, never recoiling from the anger in my eyes. Did Joshua Corwin pray for release? Did he ask God to save him? If he did, why was the prayer not answered? Where was Corwin's guardian angel? Where was the guardian angel of Bandon? Why was Corwin's thread not seen? I'd met the man. I saw his strength. His thread would have been as bright as the sun.

These are questions Calliel can't answer. Or maybe he won't, I don't know. He says he still can't remember a lot of what happened before he fell from On High. I want desperately to believe him. I think part of me even *does* believe him.

"God has a plan," he says quietly, later that night. He's curled around me as I shake in the dark. He strokes my back gently. "I know it may not seem like it at times, and it's hard to understand and it always seems unfair, but my Father has a plan, Benji. I've seen it in the shapes. In the patterns. The design. This is nothing you did. This is not your fault. If anything, it's my Father's. And I think I can truly understand anger now. I hurt for you, Benji. Oh, how I hurt for you. I don't want you to be sad. I don't want you to cry. You've done so much of that, and I don't want to see it anymore. I'd do anything not to see it anymore. I'd do anything if I could just see you smile at me. I understand anger, yes. I'm angry at what I've seen in the shapes. That damn pattern. That bastard design. But most of all, I am angry with my Father for hurting you. I don't want you to hurt anymore. I don't want you to hurt ever again. I would take all of it from you if I could. You are mine, and I would take it all."

His words soothe me, even if they cause my chest to hitch.

I think about going to the funeral, but in the end I don't, unsure if it's my place. I don't know if I could stand to see the grief-stricken faces of his family. I don't know if I would be welcome, even if I would be unknown. I don't know if I'm already being watched somehow. It doesn't seem possible that an agent with the Bureau could have driven out to a diner to meet with me without leaving some kind of trail behind. Thoughts of phones pinging off cell towers and recorded conversations bounce around my mind. I don't know how possible it is or if I've seen too many movies. At the very least, I expect the FBI to question me. I *did* call Corwin at his office one time. Surely they will check the call log. Surely they will wonder why he was so far away from home when he died.

The media began to speculate, helping to spread rumors like wildfire. After all, a big thing *did* happen in a small town. A mystery occurred, one that had no answers, so of *course* there was speculation. It was discovered (leaked?) that Corwin worked on a drug task force. Surely that was related somehow? He'd gotten caught up in something related to his work and had paid the ultimate price. Maybe, some thought, he'd been dirty and had been double-crossed. Maybe he was undercover and had been found out. The FBI didn't release much information, aside from saying they believed someone out there had to know what happened. Anyone with *any* information was urged to step forward. The FBI didn't take kindly to their own agents getting gunned down. They had some leads, though they declined to reveal what those leads were.

Corwin's funeral was held on a bright sunny day in Eugene. Abe didn't want me to go, the fear in his eyes palpable. Cal didn't want me to go, the anger in his eyes like fire. We didn't tell my mother. Much went unsaid, though I am sure we all thought it. Traynor. Or Walken. Or Griggs. Or one of their people. Someone had forced Corwin to his knees, stripped him of his clothing and shot him through the back of his head. Did he say anything about me to his killers before he died? Did he tell them I was the one who had called him? Did he tell them what he knew? Did they force it out of him?

Again, so many questions with no answers. I didn't go to the funeral. I didn't show my face. I didn't *step forward* as they had asked. It wasn't out of fear for myself, not completely. It was out of fear for my family. If I'd shown up to Corwin's funeral and someone was watching to see who would go, then I ran the risk of endangering everyone I loved. I couldn't take that chance. I had to protect my family.

Roseland was in the claws of the men who ran it. I could feel the grip tightening around us, and soon there would be no way to struggle for release. There was something coming on the horizon. It felt like things were building, though I couldn't say to what point that might be. All I knew was that I was stuck in that grip. I couldn't get out, not anymore. I thought about struggling, but I refused to pull anyone into it with me.

This was the life and death of Joshua Corwin. He lived until I killed him.

these flickering lights

I AM in the river, chest-deep. Shadow of a figure up on the road, hidden by rain. Flashes of crosses and feathers. The current is rough against my skin.

"Benji." My name is uttered. It's as loud as I've heard it. Is it the river? Is it my father? Is it a guardian angel who I—

need can't live without must have love love oh god i love

—know will wrap a strong arm around me and pull me from this place? I don't know. I don't care. Whatever the whisper is, it says my name like a caress and I lower my head beneath the surface of the river because that's where it is, that's what it wants. Who am I to fight it? Who am I to deny it?

The sound of the rain thundering down from above is muffled underneath the surface. I open my eyes and prepare for the sting. It comes, but not as painful as it was before. The world appears a quixotic blue—

blue i shall call you blue because all i have is blue

—and I think about how nice it seems, how soft and wonderful and muted. I don't know why I never thought of it this way before. It's safer down here, floating in the deep blue dark, and I think how wonderful it feels just to float. I could float here for the rest of my—

A sharp sound, metal moving against rock.

It grates against my ears and I grit my teeth. But it dislodges something inside me as well, and I no longer want to float in the blue. The river is trying to hold me here, trying to make me forget. *Breathe*, it whispers in my ear. *Open up your mouth and take a deep breath and you will be fine. It's all blue, you know. Everything down here is blue.*

The sound is louder. I see a faint shape outlined ahead.

The truck.

I push forward, twisting through the river. The red truck comes into sharper focus, the cab upside down and pressed against the bed of the river. Its tail end is at an angle and breaches the surface.

I move closer and see the driver's window is busted out. It must have happened in the impact. It must have been—

A flash of white.

It's an arm, I think wildly in the river. *It's an arm. It's Big Eddie. It's my father. The last time I saw my father was in the morgue when he was dead and white and not my father. He was so fucking* white *and the man in scrubs said it was because he had been underwater for a long time, that it was the river's fault he looked the way he did. This is the river. This is my father. This is—*

I'm closer now. My father holds something in his hand that drifts gently up and down. It's too hazy for me to see it, so I move closer. I don't want to see my father's face, I don't want to see any more of his body trapped here underneath the river, but I must get closer. My chest is starting to burn, and all I *really* want to do is take a great gasping breath, so *all* the blue fills my lungs and *all* the river is within me. It's so fucking dangerous, this thinking, and part of me is *screaming* to stop, just *screaming* for me to kick to the surface, to pray and pray and *pray* for the angel to pull me away. But I can't. I won't. Not when I am so close and can see—

An arm wraps around my chest and pulls me away.

But not before I see the great blue feather in my father's hand.

Rising up.

Rising down.

THIS was the last time I saw my father's face.

"Are you sure, Benji?" my mother asked, her voice hollow. "I don't know if you should do this."

"Let one of us handle it," my Aunt Mary said, tears leaking from her eyes. She'd been this way since she, Nina, and Christie arrived hours before. "You shouldn't have to see this. It's not fair. I don't want you to hurt anymore."

"It's morbid is what it is," my Aunt Christie said, glancing around, narrowing her eyes. "Why does anyone even *have* to do it?"

"Benji, Benji, Benji," my Aunt Nina said, petting my hair and kissing my cheek. "You are strong and brave. Big Eddie always thought so. You know that? He always thought so. All the time he did."

I must stand, I thought. *I must stand and be true.*

"I just don't get it," Christie said, sounding upset. "Why do you have to go in there?" She wrung her hands, cracking the knuckles.

"His wallet was lost in the river," I said, my voice rough. "His wallet is gone, and even though it's his truck, they still need a family member to identify him."

"Griggs knows him," Mary muttered. "*He* should have been able to do it just fine. Don't know why he needs to involve *us*."

"Benji," my mother said, biting her bottom lip. More tears welled in her eyes. "Maybe they're right. Maybe you shouldn't see—"

I shook my head and said, "No. No, I will do this. This is my father. He would do the same for me, so I will do what needs to be done."

A knock on the conference room door. We fell silent as the door opened. Doc Heward, on call because the county coroner was out of the state at the moment, stuck his head in, eyes somber and gentle. "Everything okay in here?" he asked kindly.

"You tell 'em, Doc," Christie insisted. "You tell 'em that Benji doesn't need to go in there. You've known Big Eddie since he was a tyke. You can tell if it wasn't him. Please don't make Benji do this."

He looked miserable. "I'm afraid I can't do that," he said, darting his gaze to me before looking away. "It's the law, Christie."

"*Fuck* the law!" she snarled, looking wild-eyed. "*Fuck* the law!"

Mary recoiled and Nina covered her mouth to keep from snorting at her sister using a bad word. My mother shook her head, tears falling from her eyes. None of them knew I'd already talked to the doc. None of them knew he told me he would be more than willing to identify Big Eddie for me, that it *was* Big Eddie in there, he already knew. He'd fudge the paperwork a bit. No boy, he said, should have to see his father in such a way, especially a boy like me and a father like Big Eddie. Let him help in what little way he could. Let him take some of the pain away so I could remember Big Eddie the last time I'd seen him, that smile on his face, the stubble on his head. Let him do this for me, please. By the time he'd finished begging me, there were tears in his eyes.

But not in mine. No, thank you, I'd said. No, thank you. I will do my job. I will see to my father the way I am supposed to. You shouldn't try and stop me.

He'd hung his head.

"*Fuck* the law!" Christie repeated. "Griggs said—" She stopped herself and shook her head. I didn't care right then to know what Griggs had said. All that mattered was seeing to my father.

Old Doc Heward said in a small voice, "Benji, are you ready?"

No. No, I wasn't ready. No, I didn't want to do this. I didn't want to stand. I didn't want it to be true. All I wanted to do was find a dark corner and curl up until I was as small as I could make myself and just stay there until the world passed me by. I'd put myself in this position but could only now fully realize what I was about to do. Some small, tiny part of me still believed this to be a nightmare I couldn't seem to wake up from. That part of me was sure that any moment now, my screams would be heard, and a rough but gentle hand would shake me awake and I'd open my eyes. I'd open my eyes and find myself staring into green like so many fireworks blasting across a black sky. He'd have a tight frown on his face, lines around his eyes as he squinted at me. "Benji," he'd say, his voice a deep and worried rumble. "Benji, it's okay. Wake up. You need to wake up because it was all a dream. Dreams can't hurt you because they aren't real. None of this is real and you need to *wake up*."

"Yes," I whispered aloud. "Yes. I think so, yes."

I'd always heard the first step is the hardest, and once you take that first step, all the ones that follow are infinitely easier by comparison. I contemplated that first step for what felt like ages, but in the end, my right foot lifted slightly off the floor and the step was taken. Then another. And another. It did not become easier.

Doc Heward held the door open for me, his eyes filled with so much pain for me. I made it through the doorway and into the long, cold gray hallway. The door closed behind me, but not before I heard my mother gasp and shatter again, the quiet murmurs of the Trio, the only family I had left in the world.

Doc started to speak, but I couldn't hear his words because I was so far away. I was so far away and I almost couldn't tell which was the dream and which was real life. I heard my father's voice in my head, like so many memories rising at once, the cacophony so brilliantly loud that it caused my—

eyes to water as my father said, "I got a guy, Benji. I've got a guy who can get us a V8 cheap for the Ford. He tried to swindle me a bit, but I reminded him we don't do that kind of thing here and he

"—told me he understood and gave me a fair price," I whispered aloud.

"What was that, Benji?" The Doc asked kindly.

I shook my head. "You think you can give me a moment?" I asked. "I'll meet you down the hall. I just need a moment."

He nodded sympathetically and moved slowly down the hall, pressing his hand up against the wall as if he couldn't support himself.

This was getting more real by the second, and I almost couldn't catch my breath. My vision narrowed as I took another step, and bile rose at the back of my throat. "It's not real," I said. "It's not—

going to be easy, but I think we can swing it," my father said with a laugh. "Look, I know I said this was going to be just an office, but think about it, Benji. What if... what if we could just build a whole other house? It won't be as big as ours but just... what if? If we really buckled down and agreed to do this thing, it could

—be yours one day," I said as I took another step. "It could be yours one day, if you wanted to stay here, that is. I know there's a big wide world out there, but sometimes... sometimes, you just want to come home, you know?"

I did know. Oh God, how I knew.

I followed Doc's silent advice and pressed my hands against the wall to help support my weight. The concrete was cool underneath my hand, and didn't the hallway seem longer somehow? Didn't it just seem like the longest hallway ever to have been built? It went on for miles, it seemed. I didn't know if I could make it. I didn't know if I could travel that great distance, realizing more and more what waited for me at the end. "I've always thought," I started then paused. I slid my fingers over the stone, rough against my skin and it—

was so funny to see Big Eddie dressed in drag that Halloween, getting ready for the Roseland Chamber of Commerce's big party. He came down the stairs in the ugliest dress I'd ever seen, plaid with greens and blues and oranges and red. I burst out laughing as he tried to squeeze his gigantic feet into what had to be the biggest pair of high heels in existence. My mother collapsed against a wall, holding her sides, tears on her cheeks as she laughed so big. Big Eddie glared at the both of us and said, "What's so flipping funny? I'm going to show the town how much I support my son. My big old gay son, because he is my son. If he is gay, then I want to show I've got his back. I've always—

—got his back," I said as a tear slid down my cheek. "Even if I look like a big old tranny, the people here are gonna know that my son isn't going to take shit from any of them."

Memories like knives. Memories like ghosts.

I was haunted all the way down that hallway. I felt stabbed repeatedly as I heard his voice in my head again and again. I couldn't stop the memories, no matter how much I wanted to. I hated myself for all the good I remembered, because I wanted to let my anger consume me so I could focus on all the bad. I wanted to scream and shout at him, to let him hear my fury. To let him hear my fury and wake the fuck up, to stop playing this dangerous game that was breaking me apart.

I was six when he picked me up and threw me over his shoulder and tickled my sides.

Another step.

I was... I don't know. I was some age somewhere when he looked at me and smiled for no reason at all. He reached over and ruffled my hair and said, "You're going to be a good man, you know that?"

Another step and I *didn't* know that, not anymore.

He sat on the patio beside me at Little House as we watched the sun go down. After a quarter-hour silence, he said, "Sure is a great night." Then he grunted that sound that meant he was happy. I could only nod.

Another step, and I opened my eyes to see I was almost at the end of the endless hall. The doc waited for me near a door that looked like black iron. He had his hand on the handle, and he didn't know I saw him wipe his other hand across his eyes and take a shuddering breath.

It was almost real.

I heard my father singing quietly to himself as he sanded a piece of wood that would become the trellis up the side of Little House. It was something I'd heard him sing many times before. An old Seven of Spades song. "Float," it was called. Some bluesy riff from the forties. Covered by many others through the years, but the Seven of Spades one was always his favorite. It was the song he sang when he was content and lost in his own little world. He—

I stopped. This couldn't be real.

"Sometimes I float along the river," I sang quietly to myself, my voice cracking. "For to its surface I am bound."

I took another step.

"And sometimes stones done fill my pockets, oh Lord," Big Eddie hummed. *"And it's into this river I drown."*

"Are you sure about this?" Doc Heward asked me with a worried look, as if he could hear my father singing off-key in my head.

No. "Yes."

"Benji, this doesn't need to happen. I've told you I can—"

"Open the door, Doc."

He watched me for a moment. I don't know what he saw, but it must have been enough. He heaved a great sigh and opened the door. It squeaked on its hinges, the sound low and grating. I ground my teeth together. It went on forever.

Finally he walked through the door. I followed him down a shorter hallway until we came to a second door. This one had a small window about head height, and was a pale green. The doc paused again and turned to look at me. I almost screamed.

"We'll go through the door," he said quietly. "In the upper-right corner, there is a TV. When you are ready, I'll turn the TV on, and on the screen, you'll see a video of the room next door. I'll ask the ME's assistant to show you a face. You say yes or no and that'll be it. We'll be done. You can leave. You can go back to your family and let them hold you. That's what you will need, and you have to let it happen. Do you understand?"

I was distracted by a low buzzing noise. I looked up. The fluorescent light overhead was flickering. The electrical buzz was soft but steady. I stared at the light as it went out then back on. Out then back on.

"Benji?" Doc said, sharper.

I looked back at him and nodded tightly. The light continued to sputter.

He opened the green door. It made no sound. I was led to a windowless room. It was colder than the hallway, much colder. A small desk was against the far wall, battered and littered with papers and pens. Pencils and a handful of paper clips scattered near the edge. A stapler and a half empty cup of coffee. The swivel chair next to the desk was blue and worn. There was another door on the opposite side of the room. It was closed.

In the right-hand corner above me was a TV. The screen was black, and I could see myself in the reflection, eyes blown out, mouth slack. The light in the room flickered here too. I disappeared on and off the black screen with the flashing light. The doc muttered to himself, something about the wiring in the old building. He said nothing about the charge in the air that I was sure he felt. How could he not?

He turned to me again and opened his mouth, but I stopped him. "Doc," I growled at him. "If you ask me if I'm sure one more time, I'm going to get angry."

His shoulders sagged as he exhaled. "I've known you since you were born," he said finally. "I've known your father since he was even younger than you are now. I can tell you the ache I have in my chest, but it won't even compare to what I know you are feeling." He looked away. "I hurt," he said. "Because he was my friend, I hurt. But you? Benji, he was your *father*. I can't even…." He couldn't finish.

"Show me," I said. "Show me."

He pulled out his phone and dialed a number. "Eric? The family is ready. Okay. Okay." He closed the phone and slid it back in his pocket. "Deep breath, okay?"

I nodded.

He reached up to switch on the TV and I thought *no, no, no*, because it *wasn't* real, *none* of this was real. I thought I felt the brush of a hand on my shoulder, but that was impossible because my back was against the wall. There could be no one there.

But even as I screamed at the doc in my head, I said nothing aloud, because I needed proof. I needed proof in this nightmare. Tangible, verifiable proof that I could see with my own eyes, so I wouldn't have to hear the words I still considered untrue. It was necessary, I told myself. It was the only way.

Doc touched the button on the front of the TV, and there was an electrical snap. A small shower of sparks fell from the back of the TV to the floor, hissing as they hit the cold concrete. The doc jerked his hand away and stared dumbfounded at the TV. A smell of burning plastic permeated the room. "Goddamn wiring," he muttered. "Told them a thousand times to get this fixed. Not in the budget, my ass." His phone rang. "Yeah? No, the TV shorted and damn near shocked me! The what? The camera went out?" He frowned. "That's not hooked up to any of the wiring, is it? That's odd. How the hell.... No. Just give me a moment." He snapped the phone shut and reached up carefully toward the TV again, which had already stopped smoking. He tapped the power button quickly, as if thinking he would still be shocked. Nothing happened. He pressed the button and held it down. Nothing.

"Benji, I'm sorry. I don't know what the hell happened. Looks like the monitor is dead. This building has had the same wiring since the fifties. I guess there was a surge somewhere."

And now I would never know if my father was truly gone. This was my only chance to see and it had been taken from me. I would have to take it from the words of others that he was gone, and there would always *be that little voice in my head that said 'what if?' What if they were all lying? What if this whole thing was one big hoax? Big Eddie wouldn't leave me. He told me he wouldn't. He told me he'd be back in the afternoon. He promised.*

"Open the door," I said.

Doc's eyes widened. "What?"

"The TV won't work. Your camera doesn't work. Open the door. I want to see for myself."

He shook his head. "I don't think—"

"I'm not asking you to think," I snarled at him. I immediately felt guilty at the way he recoiled, but it did nothing to stop me. "Open the door, Doc."

"Your father wouldn't want this," he said. "He wouldn't want this for you."

My eyes started to burn. "If he's gone, what does it matter?" I said hoarsely. "What does it matter what he would have wanted?"

"It will *always* matter," the doc argued.

I shook my head. "You have to have this for your reports. I have to have this for my sanity. Open the door."

He hesitated, and for a moment I thought he was going to refuse. I thought I was going to have to push my way past him and bust through the door myself. I would be careful—Doc was getting older and I didn't want to hurt him. But not even he would stand in my way. The sinking feeling I'd had in my stomach for the past two days was swiftly turning into a black hole, and I had to stop it or let it consume me completely. I didn't know which option was safer. I wasn't sure if it mattered.

Doc closed his eyes and his lips moved as he muttered to himself, and it took me a minute to realize what he was doing. Out of all the things he could have done, the fact that he seemed to be praying was the most unexpected. I felt sick at my anger, but it did nothing to quell it. I let him have his moment, let him say whatever he wanted to whomever he was saying it to. The buzzing of the lights grew louder, like a hive of angry wasps.

Doc finished his prayer and opened his eyes again. There was still doubt there, but it was resigned. He knew I would not back away from this. Not now. He didn't even ask me if I was sure again. I almost wished he had.

He turned to the windowless green door that had started to take on a menacing shape. *Maybe they were telling the truth*, I thought nervously, starting to fall into the black hole. *Maybe this is real life. Maybe I'm not asleep.*

He opened the door and stuck his head in. I heard the murmur of conversation. I couldn't make out the words. There were protestations from the unseen Eric, but the tone in Doc's voice silenced him. I heard footsteps, and then a young man who seemed oddly colorless came through the door, pushing past the Doc. He moved with an economic grace, no step wasted, almost like he was floating. Eric wouldn't meet my eyes as he flitted by me and out the other door, shutting it behind him.

"It's cold in here," the doc told me kindly. "I have a jacket if you think you'll need it."

"Why is it cold?" I asked, suddenly unsure.

"To… preserve the body."

"Like a freezer?"

"Yes."

That didn't sit right with me, the thought that my father could be cold. What if he didn't want to be cold? What if he wanted to be warm? It wasn't fair. If *he* couldn't be warm, then I wouldn't either. "I don't want a coat," I said roughly.

"Okay, Benji. Okay. Do you want me to be in there with you?"

I thought I did. I thought I wouldn't want to be alone, even more so than I already felt. The black hole was opening wider and I was starting to collapse in on myself. I didn't want to be alone. But I heard myself say, "No. I'll go by myself."

He nodded, as if he'd expected this. "Then you need to understand something, Benji. I need you to listen and listen good. Are you listening?"

"Yes."

"That may be your father in there. But it's not *really*. It may look like him, but it's *not* him, okay? Your father is in a better place, a warmer place, a *happier* place, so whatever you see in there is not who he is anymore." His voice started to waver. "You should pull the sheet from his head, and take just a moment to be sure. You might want to stay longer, but I am begging you not to. I don't think I could stand it. Just take a peek and then come out, and I'll help you remember who he was. I'll help you remember everything he was to you. He's not what's lying in there. That body is not all he was. Do you understand?"

That's what they say to prepare you, I thought. *That's what they say when it's going to be bad. It's going to be bad.*

"Yes," I said.

"I wish you'd change your mind."

"I won't."

Unbelievably, he smiled as he shook his head. "Stubborn. Just like him."

And then he held open the door.

A wave of cold air washed over me, carrying with it a sharp medicinal smell, like antiseptic. My arms prickled, the thin long-sleeved shirt I wore doing nothing to keep the cool air out. I felt dizzy when I inhaled, but I swept away the vertigo, forcing my vision to clear, forcing myself to take the next steps until I was through the doorway into what was essentially a freezer.

"Close the door," I said, trying to keep my teeth from chattering.

For once, Doc did not argue and did as I asked.

I turned away from the door. In the center of the room stood a metal table. On this table was a great white sheet. And under this great white sheet was the form of a man. I could see the points of the feet, facing away from each other at a slight angle. Following the sheet I could see the gentle press of a stomach. Further, a slight peak of the nose.

I tried to breathe through my mouth because the cold air in the room was becoming harder to take, the medicinal smell like waves crashing over me again and again and again. My tongue stuck to the roof of my mouth. *Get it done!* I cried to myself. *Get it done and get out!*

I took a step.

I ignored the way the lights above began to flicker.

It's just bad wiring, I told myself.

I took another step and gagged on the smell.

It's how they keep things clean.

I shivered with the next step, my teeth starting to chatter.

It's how they keep things preserved.

Another step, and I knew it would just take one more.

I was almost there, so I took it. I took the last step.

The lights buzzed loudly.

Before I could stop myself, before I could turn and run from the room screaming that it was a *lie*, this was all a *lie*, and please, *please*, let me just wake *up*, I raised my hands to grip the sheet near its edge. I focused on what was so clearly the point of a nose and thought, *Big Eddie never had that big of a nose. A mistake! There's been a mistake and he's alive! He's alive, he's alive, he's alive.* My father was alive. He was not under the sheet. His nose was not that big. He was somewhere safe and soon would come out of hiding and take me in his arms, and I would feel my back crack as he hugged me tightly.

With this certainty, I pulled back the sheet.

And moaned.

It was too much at once. Big Eddie Green was lying there, in this cold room, on this cold table, under this cold sheet that felt scratchy in my hands. I thought I could refuse to believe it at first, that my mind in a last-ditch effort to save itself wouldn't let me see what was actually there. But it did.

His skin was starkly white, much whiter than it had ever been in life. I was distracted by splashes of color, though, like paint on a canvas. The area around his closed eyes was violet, like a mask made of bruises. A bloodless red cut zigzagged across his forehead, starting from his left eyebrow and rising up to his right temple. A navy blue knot of flesh rose from the left side of his head, as if he'd struck it on impact. His parted lips, a pale pink. The hint of white teeth underneath. That dark stubble on his head. On his face.

Only then did I become aware of a low sound in the room, almost like a strangled cry, a gasp of air. I looked around wildly. No one was there. I was alone. And only then did I realize the sound was coming from me as I let it out again. A hand had seized my lungs and my throat had closed. I couldn't breathe. I couldn't pull in air. I was suffocating next to a Big Eddie whose face was covered in *impossible* colors, in such an *improbable* shape. Bile tried to rise, but my throat was too constricted for it to get any farther.

It's a lie, I tried, one last time. *He said he'd come home in the afternoon. It's a lie. It's a lie.*

I thought the life I have now would not be possible. Your mom. You. None of this seemed like it could be real. Like it could be mine. It seemed impossible.

I opened my mouth to admit the truth to myself.

Instead, I screamed.

I had to be sedated then and for the days that followed. I was told later my screams could be heard throughout the building, and I didn't stop until Old Doc Heward injected something into my arm. The world fell into a hazy mix of violet, like bruising. Red, like cuts. Blue, like knots. For want of my father, I was lost.

A WEEK after Cal returns, we sit on the roof, in the dark. Waiting. Watching.

So much to say, so many things to ask, but for the moment I don't care. I don't care about any of it. For the moment, all I care about is the way I fit against his chest like we were made for each other, two separate pieces interlocking to be made whole. All I care about are his arms around me like I'm the most precious thing in the world to him. For all I know, maybe I am.

That's all I care about. Until I open my mouth. "The dreams are getting worse," I say as the sky begins to lighten in the east.

Cal pulls me in tighter. "I know," he says gruffly. "Don't you think I know?"

"You saw it the last time, didn't you."

"Saw what?" he asks, but he knows.

I wait.

"Yes," he sighs. "Yes, I saw it."

"Why would my father have a feather in his hand? One of yours?"

I can feel his frustration mounting, but not at me. Not yet. "I don't know," he says. "I wish I did. I'm praying every chance I get. I'm begging, I'm threatening, I'm *demanding* an answer. I can't remember, and I need to know why. My Father is testing me, and I don't know why. I don't know what I'm supposed to do." He's vibrating by the time he's finished, his anger spilling over.

"You guard," I say as I burrow myself further into his embrace.

I feel his tension ease slightly. "What?" he whispers.

"You guard," I say again, letting my lips brush against the hollow of his throat. "You come here and you do what you are supposed to do. You guard. You stand and be true." Those last words hurt.

"There haven't been any threads in a few days," he says. "I don't know what that means." He's right. It's been almost a week since Corwin was buried, and not once has Cal been called away, not once has a thread made itself known to him.

"Maybe they hired someone else to take over for Roseland," I try to tease, but it falls flat.

He shakes his head. "It doesn't work like that, Benji. There's protocol, procedure. At the very least, I would have expected Michael by now."

"Or more of the Strange Men," I mutter, shuddering at the thought. I was sure they were going to descend on the town in droves after Dark Man and Light Man were sent into the black, but there's been nothing. It's been quiet, aside from Corwin.

"It's like I've been cut off," Cal says. "Like I'm alone here. I've done something, and I can't remember what it is. I don't know what I did." He sounds so forlorn that I can't help but twist in his arms and kiss him soundly. He huffs his surprise, but he lets me in, my tongue touching his. He kneads at my back almost desperately, and I can feel his breath, hot and harsh against me.

"It may be a test," I say, pulling back, allowing my lips to brush his cheeks. "And you may be cut off, but you are never alone. Even if the majority of the town hadn't already fallen at your feet, you'd still have me." I kiss him again, hoping he can feel how true my words are.

He smiles weakly at me as I run my fingers over his cheeks. "You say that now," he says. "But Benji, I had something to do with your father's death. You can't deny that. Not anymore."

I ignore the dark twinge in my chest. "Dreams are just that," I manage to say. "Dreams."

"Except when they're not," he replies.

He's right, of course. I'm at the river almost nightly now, sometimes able to get close enough to see the feather in my father's hand before Cal pulls me away. There are times when I feel like he allows me to linger, like he wants to see what else there is under the river's surface, but he remembers his duty and pulls me away. I'm on the brink of something; a precipice. The edge of everything.

"Something's coming, isn't it?" I ask him, making sure I can see his eyes.

He hesitates, but then: "Yes. Yes, I think so. I think this whole thing has been a beginning and that the end is coming. This is my test. I think this is my test."

Chills, like ice, spread down my spine. "Do you remember anything? Anything at all?"

He tries to pull away, but I don't let him. I press my forehead against his, making sure I'm as close as I can get to him. "Little things," he says finally. "Like flashes of light. Pieces that don't quite fit. I can see the threads as I used to see them when I was On High. I remember praying, but I can't remember what for. I remember Nina talking with me before I fell, but I can't remember what she said. I remember the surprise I felt at her hearing me, but knowing it was because I was close."

"Close to what?" I ask, trying not to let him see how my heart is aching.

"To you, Benji," he says, bringing a big hand to the back of my head, holding me tight. "It may be pieces, but it's you. It all comes back to you. You are in my pattern. My shape. My design. Even through everything, it all comes back to you."

"Well, then, whatever it is," I tell him fiercely, "whatever is coming, we'll face it together, okay? I don't care what it is, Cal. I don't care how long it takes. We'll do it together."

He smiles sadly at me. "I really hope that's true, Benji. I do. I really hope so, because I don't know anything else right now. I don't know anything else but you. I can see the others in this town, and I care for them because I must. They are mine to protect. But it's you. You are the one I want."

I straddle his lap and take his head in my hands and pull him to my chest. He rests against me, my chin on his head as he clutches at my back. He shakes against me, and I let him because *if* there is something coming, he's going to need strength. I would gladly give him all of my own to help him stand.

Eventually he calms and props his hands against the roof. I turn and lie with my back against his chest as we wait for the sun. "Should we warn them?" I ask finally. "The town?

"About what?" he says.

"I don't know. We don't even know if anything will happen."

"No, we don't."

"But it will."

"Yes. I think so."

"Cal?"

"Yes?"

"I have to find out what happened to my father."

He stiffens underneath me. "I know," he says quietly. "But you must stay away from the river, Benji. Please. I know I can't explain much, and I know it may not make sense, but you must hear me. Please. Stay away from the river."

"It's Griggs," I tell him, certain. "It's Griggs, and Walken. It's Traynor. It's whoever they were calling the 'boss'. It's them, I know it. They killed my father. They killed Corwin. They killed Arthur Davis."

"And they'll kill you," he snaps, suddenly angry. "We must wait. We must wait until whatever comes shows its face. After that, I promise you I will do everything I can to help you. But we have to wait, Benji. Promise me."

"We won't have much time. They said they were moving everything on the day of the festival. Jump Into Summer Fest is only a few weeks away. I have to—"

"Promise me!" he snarls in my ear, slamming his fist down on the roof.

"I promise," I whisper, though it feels like a lie, to placate. To soothe.

And then a sharp intake of breath.

"What?" I ask. "What's wrong?"

"Damn," he mutters. He tries to hide whatever is wrong, but I can see he's favoring the hand he's just hit against the roof. I pull on his arm to show me, and my fingers feel slick. He sighs but doesn't resist. The sun chooses that moment to peek over the Cascades and the first rays of sunlight on a new day catch upon my life, now so unreal.

Embedded into the side of his hand is a small carpenter's nail, undoubtedly forgotten at one point on the roof. It's jammed into his hand almost to the nail head, his skin puckered around it. But it's not the nail itself that catches my eye; it's the dark-red blood welling around it.

I lift my hand in front of my face, staring at his blood on my skin. "That's not...." I breathe. "You got *shot*. I saw you get *shot* and—"

he is weaker

"—nothing was wrong with you!"

He winces as he pulls the short nail out of his hand. I pull my shirt off over my head, the morning air cool against my body. I wrap his hand with my shirt to stop the flow of blood.

"It's what the Strange Men said, isn't it?" I demand. "They said someone like you couldn't stay here. What happens if you do?"

He looks away, but not before I can see it in his eyes. He knows. This isn't a hidden thing, lost in whatever his Father took from him before he fell. He knows this.

"Calliel! You better fucking answer me on this! I deserve some goddamn answers after everything I've been through, after everything we've done. If you even remotely care about me at all, you will tell—"

"I'm becoming human," he says quietly as the sunlight catches his red hair. It reminds me of blood, and I almost cry out. He looks like he is covered in blood. "Father put it in place to avoid angels becoming corporeal. The longer I stay, the more human I become. And if I stay...." He watches the horizon.

"Cal?" I ask, already knowing the answer but needing to hear him say it. "What happens if you stay?"

He turns and kisses me deeply. I can feel the desperation behind it as he pushes into me. He's clawing at my back, trying to get as much of me as he can. I pull away only because I don't know what's wrong. He grabs my neck and jerks me close again. When he speaks, his voice is a rasp in my ear. I tremble. "If I stay... if I stay, the moment I become human, I will die. My soul will not be allowed to ascend. I'll fall into the black and be lost forever."

The sun continues to rise.

a knock at the door

HE'S DYING.

Ever since that night on the roof, weeks before, I haven't been able to think of much else besides blood dripping down Cal's wrist, the nail jutting from his skin, the curiosity on his face as he felt physical pain for what had to be the first time. Even pressed against me, his lips near my ear as he told me what would happen if he stayed, he seemed to be more worried about me than himself.

"You have to go back," I choked out. I wanted nothing less in the world, but it seemed to be the only way.

"No," he said, his dark eyes flashing. "I will not leave you."

"But—"

"Enough, Benji."

But it wasn't enough. It would never be enough. How could it be? I was angry that he could be so selfish as to allow me to watch him to die, knowing everything I had been through. I had nowhere near recovered from the loss of my father and he was expecting me to go through that again? The bastard. How dare he? I was drowning in a fucking river that he was still attempting to save me from, and he was telling me he was going to push me back in and hold me under. My father's death had nearly destroyed me. Cal's death would finish me.

This, of course, led to the question of how Calliel, after such a short amount of time, could mean as much to me as Big Eddie did. That was the question I didn't know if I wanted answers to. It's easier to ignore what's in your heart if you pretend it won't hurt you in the end. But even I knew that was a lie I used to placate myself.

I watched for signs of Cal weakening, of humanity springing forth and leaving his angelic side behind. I stayed awake long into those nights, lying against his chest, listening to his heart beat against my ear, his chest rising and falling with every breath he took. Aside from the nail in his hand and the blood from it, there was nothing else. He looked the same; he sounded the same. He tasted the same.

In those weeks leading up to the festival, no threads called to him, no reasons to leave my side. Again I wondered if it was because he was already more human than angel and had been cut off from God, or if he had been replaced by a new angel who was watching over Roseland. I listened for gossip to spread like wildfire, but heard nothing unusual. There were other rumors, of course. Rumors about me that I overheard at the diner. Rumors I overheard while shopping at Clark's on my day off, Cal at my side, dropping box after box of Lucky Charms into the basket ("I think I am just going to take all the green clovers out of each box and put them into one box so I can have a box of just green clovers.") These rumors were accompanied by furtive glances at us. No one seemed quite sure how we had met. Sometimes these questions were asked to others, sometimes they were asked, almost shyly, to me. He was just passing through town, I told them. He decided to stay a while ("Not so much passing as falling," Cal would tell me later, a grin on his face).

Most spoke of the fact that Cal lived with me and that each of us was rarely seen without the other. It's good for Benji, they said. He's been such a loner ever since Big Eddie passed, God rest his soul. It's nice to see him smile again. So they shacked up quickly. When you know, you know.

But I *didn't* know. I didn't know at all.

People loved him, though. If he left the store without me, he'd be mobbed almost instantly by people who just *happened* to be walking by the station. Cal! they'd exclaim. What a surprise to see you! What are you up to? Oh, well I don't mind walking with you since I was heading that direction anyway! Then they'd wave at me through the glass almost as an afterthought, and I'd roll my eyes as Cal turned back to me with a grin, the worry not quite leaving his eyes. If he did leave my side, it was only for a few moments, and only because I practically shoved him out the door. He'd take off on whatever errand I'd sent him on, almost at a jog, his companions struggling to keep up with his long strides.

"I wish you wouldn't make me leave you," he said with a scowl one night, very late. "I don't like to take my eyes off you. Not when we don't know what's out there."

I snorted as I rolled off him and onto my back. "That's life," I told him quietly. "You never know what is out there. You just have to hope and trust that you'll see the other person again."

He must have heard something in my voice betray me. A slight tremor, a rhythm to my words that belied the teasing lilt I tried to make him hear. Before I knew what was happening, he was atop me, crushing me into the mattress, teasing his tongue over my skin. There was always need with him, but this was somehow more. He held me as if I was something precious, something extraordinary, as if I was his guardian angel instead of him being mine. He spread my legs with his knee, and I saw blue, everything I saw was *blue*. He took me that night with such abandon that I cried out incoherently as he rammed into me, unable to form words, much less thought. Blue lights shot across my vision, though whether from him or in my head I didn't know.

I AWAKE early the morning after, shortly before he rises to wake me for the sunrise, heat radiating from him as he presses against my back, draping his arm over my waist. I turn over, my face against his. He chuffs quietly in his sleep, gives a light snore, then falls silent. First, I wonder if he dreams as I reach up to smooth the lines from his brow. And, second, I try to remember what it's like to sleep alone. I can't. These are the only thoughts I have until he opens his eyes right before dawn and smiles a sleepy grin at me. There is something there, in his eyes, a deep warmth far beyond anything I've seen in him before. I think I know its name, though I can't bring myself to say the words. It's as if in me he'd seen the greatest thing in his long life.

A life he is ending by being here with me, I thought as he pulled me to him.

Not everyone was kind, though. I didn't miss the scowls of Griggs as he drove by us on the street. Walken would nod coolly as he entered his office on the other side of Poplar. They knew, somehow, that I knew. *What* I was supposed to know didn't matter, just that I *knew*. I knew about Arthur Davis. I knew about Joshua Corwin. I knew about my father. These were men who killed to maintain their secrets. I didn't know which one of them pulled the trigger at Corwin's head, or hung Arthur by his neck, or ran my father off the road. I didn't know if the specific person mattered. Not even if it was Traynor, who'd disappeared. They were all complicit, and I would bury them alive if I got the chance.

Cal knows of my anger, though he says little of it. Sometimes I think he has plans all his own, though I don't know what they could be. I suppose I should be worried about what he will do. Or about my soul. But I don't think I am.

No FBI agents have knocked on my door asking after Corwin.

No Strange Men have wandered into town.

It makes me nervous.

It doesn't help that the dreams are getting louder and louder. Standing by the roaring river, the rain pounding down from the sky. The metallic shriek of Big Eddie's truck crashing down the embankment. Crosses. Feathers, both on the surface of the river and in my father's dead hand. A darkened figure up on the road. My name called, my body submerged. I've never really thought about *sounds* in a dream before, but as the dream progresses, each time an inch or two closer to the window, the world around me is *shrieking,* enough so that it feels like my head will split and save me the trouble of drowning. I don't know if the further I am getting in my dream has to do with Cal becoming more human. All I know is I have to get into the truck.

It also doesn't help that I've started having the dreams while I am awake. Conversations get interrupted because the river has rushed in and engulfed me. I swim as fast as I can (thinking *inhale, try, breathe, drown*), but the truck's only an inch closer each time. I'll snap from the waking dream, laughing it off if I'm talking to a customer or my family. If it's Cal, it doesn't matter because he already knows. He's the one who pulls me away.

But I'm getting closer each time. I have to see my father's face.

"I DON'T know if this is such a good idea," I mutter, sitting on the edge of the bed. "As a matter of fact, this sounds like an *awful* idea."

Cal is standing in front of the mirror, his face scrunched up as he stares at his reflection, trying like hell to tie his tie. For all that he can do, for all that he is, it's the tiniest of things that trip him up the most. The most human of things. Like tying a tie that I'm still unclear about why he decided to wear. (Where it has come from inspires a whole other set of questions I don't want to bother with; the slacks and dress shirt he wears are tailored perfectly, as if they've been made for him. Someone has obviously been sneaking around.)

I sigh and walk over to him, knock his hands away and untangle the knot he's somehow gotten his finger stuck in. "We can just stay in," I mutter.

"Your mother invited us," he says, checking himself out in the mirror again.

"Vanity," I scold him.

"It would be rude not to go. Do you like this tie?"

"It's okay, I guess. I don't know why you want to wear a tie."

"Oh."

"She also invited Abe."

"Yes. Good. I like Abe."

"And the Trio."

"Nina. Ah, little one. She is so special."

"And Mary and Christie," I remind him. "Who don't know you sprout wings like a butterfly."

He stops looking at his reflection to scowl at me. "I'm *not* a butterfly. I am big. Impressive, even. Suzie Goodman told me I was the most impressive specimen of man she'd ever had the pleasure of seeing."

I roll my eyes as I finish his tie. "And why were you talking to Suzie Goodman?" I ask, ignoring the flash of jealousy that I want no part of. I know as well as Cal does that he'd never do anything with her. He just likes to get a rise out of me. It doesn't bother me in the slightest, though I do cinch his tie more tightly than I need to.

"I was reading on the computer that you have to keep your man interested, so it's always good to make sure he knows others are."

I frown at him. "Angels are not allowed to go on the Internet."

He winces. "Probably a good idea. That place has so much *porn*."

I don't want to know. Okay, I do. "Let's just get through this so we can come back to Little House."

Cal kisses me gently before walking out of our room. "Sure thing," he calls over his shoulder. "I did learn some things on the Internet that I want to try on you. It's not *all* bad."

I stare after him as his laughter floats back to me.

IT'S a warm spring evening, the Jump Into Summer Festival now only a week away. Mom has invited Cal and me up for dinner at Big House with the rest of the family. She and I have kept our distance from each other since that night in the cemetery weeks before. It wasn't anything unusual for us, at least at first. Even though we live right next to each other, there's been times since I moved into Little House that we have gone months without seeing each other. We leave notes here and there. Maybe a text message or two. A voice mail if it's really important.

But now I have a life preserver of sorts, someone who is trying to keep me afloat. He has his hand curled in mine as we walk up the hill toward Big House, the sun already starting to set. A sweet breeze that smells like the trees washes over us, and for a moment, a brief second, I'm able to forget about everything that has happened, and everything that could still happen. For a moment, I'm walking up the driveway to Big House with my boyfriend to have dinner with people I care about. For a moment, I'm twenty-one years old and don't know what true pain feels like. I am young and alive and ready to face anything the world throws at me. I don't have a goddamn care in the world. Nothing can touch me. Nothing can hurt us. As long as I have this man by my side, as long as I can look the four women and one man who wait for us in Big House straight in the eye and tell them everything I'm feeling, then nothing else matters. It's a lovely thought, deceptive though it might be.

Nina waits for us on the porch. She stands as we approach her, looking almost shy. "Do you like my new dress?" she asks, twirling around. "It was blue so I thought of Blue." And it is, a dark-blue sundress that reminds me of his wings. It has little ruffles on the shoulders and white flowers sewn into the fabric. "Mary helped me pick it out."

Cal lets go of my hand and stands in front of Nina, then bends over until they are face to face. "It's the prettiest dress in the world," he tells her seriously. "And you look very beautiful, little one. But then you always have."

She giggles as she blushes, throwing her arms around his neck and kissing his cheek. I should have known she would be perceptive to the changes in him, that she could see things no one else would. She stiffens against him and her eyes go wide. "How?" she whispers as she stares at me. "What did you do?"

Wow. It sure is bright today.

The stars?

Oh, no.

The moon?

Bless the moon, but no. What did you do today?

I was at work, Nina. You know that. At the store.

No, Benji. What did you do?

I wait, feeling uneasy.

She pulls from his embrace and looks up at him. I can't see his face, but his posture is tense. "Things are different," Nina says as she squints, as if trying to physically see just what she felt. For all I know, maybe she can.

"It's not a bad thing," I hear Cal say in a low voice.

"But you hurt," she says, her lip quivering. "You ache in the haze of your mind. The pieces are shattered and you're trying to put them back together. Why do you want to remember so bad? Aren't you happy here? Can't you just live for now instead of then?" Her gaze flickers over to me as she says this last, and I have to look away.

"Because," he whispers as his shoulders slump, "I have to know what happened. I have to know what I did. I have to find out what I can do to make things right. This is my test, I think."

I start forward, wanting to wrap myself around him, to take him away from here back to the moment where nothing could touch us and none of this stuff mattered. But I stop as Nina speaks again. "If you did do something wrong, could you forgive yourself?"

"I am more worried about others forgiving me."

"Your Father?"

He sighs. "Among others." The intent of his words isn't lost on me.

"We make mistakes," Nina says kindly. "It's a part of who we are."

Cal starts to tense again. "I am not one of you," he says bitterly.

"You are more of who we are than what you used to be," I say, finding my voice. "If you won't go back, then we'll find some way to fix this, I promise you." I say this fiercely, as if I can make him believe with words alone. There's much I feel I have to say to him, but I can't find the right words.

"Sure, Benji," he says, smiling weakly at me. He looks like he doesn't believe me in the slightest, but he holds out his hand to me anyway. I don't hesitate.

"Remember what you're here for, Blue," Nina says, looking at our joined hands. "If this is a test, I think you may be doing it right."

"Cross your heart?" Cal asks.

She doesn't hesitate and my heart skips a beat. "Hope to die."

"Stick a thousand needles in your eye," I finish.

"Thank you, little one," he says, holding out his other hand. She laughs quietly to herself and takes it, her hands so little in his.

"I like your tie," I hear her whisper as we walk up the stairs. "Very handsome."

"I bought it for Benji," he whispers back. "I made some money from Benji working at the store and wanted to look nice for him."

I stumble on the last step, and he looks at me funny. "You okay?"

I nod. "Nina?" I ask, without taking my eyes off him. "Can you give us a minute?"

She giggles again, and I hear the door creak as it opens and then closes after her.

And then I kiss him with everything I have. "You look so fucking hot in that tie," I pant at him as our lips separate. "Sorry I didn't say that earlier."

He flushes and looks shy again. "It's really okay?"

"Better than okay. Thank you. You don't need a tie to impress me, but thank you."

The smile he gives me then is brilliant, and that warmth I saw earlier in his eyes blossoms like fire. I think I know what it means. I think I know what it says.

I have to find a way to fix this, I think frantically as I kiss him again. *This can't be an ending. This must be the beginning.*

"Cal, where in California are you from?" Christie asks, causing me to choke on a piece of bread.

We're all sitting around the large dining room table, Abe on my left, and Cal to my right. Nina and Mary sit across from us. My mother and Christie sit at the ends of the table. I give serious thought to telling Christie to shut her fucking face, but I don't think that would quell the innocent question I took to be overtly suspicious. *She's family,* I remind myself. *She's not like everyone else.*

I jump in. "Redding."

"San Diego," my mother says at the same time.

"Sacramento," Abe says at the same time.

Everyone stares at us.

"He traveled a lot," I say hastily as Cal watches me. "He never stayed in one place for too long. Kind of his thing."

"I moved around a lot," Cal repeats as I resist the urge to kick him under the table. "Always moving. Kind of my thing. Lola, would you happen to have any green clover marshmallows? I think I would like some."

My mother smiles weakly I as stifle a groan. "Sorry, Cal. Fresh out. I'm sure Benji has some back at Little House when we're finished."

"Rosie told me you had a thing for those," Mary says, eyes sparkling. "I found that to be so dear."

"Rosie is a good person," Cal says as he chases a carrot around his plate with a spoon. "She carries that shotgun around with her everywhere and made me cupcakes. I like people like that."

"Do you?" Christie asks, amused. "It seems to me shotguns are a scary thing."

"I'm not really scared of much," Cal says. He glances at me and smiles. This look is not missed by anyone at the table.

"Good to know," Christie says. "Do you have family back in California, Cal?"

Dammit. He speaks before I can stop him. "I have a Father," he says quietly. "And many brothers."

Not quite a lie.

"Big family?"

"You could say that."

I start to sweat.

"Are you the oldest?"

He shakes his head. "Youngest."

Oh, that's right. He's only a couple of hundred years old.

"What about your mother?"

"Jesus, Christie," I snap. "What's with the third degree?"

She looks surprised. "I just wanted to get to know your friend better. Seems everyone in town just adores him, and I wanted to see what all the fuss is about. Besides, if he's going to date *my* nephew, I think I have a right to know him better!"

"Dating? We're... we're not—" I sputter. "We're just... shit."

"Language," Nina scolds me.

"We're dating," Cal tells the whole table quite loudly.

Abe and Nina grin. My mom looks stressed. Mary looks confused. Christie looks triumphant. I look embarrassed, I'm sure. And Cal? Cal looks pretty damned pleased with himself.

"I guess," I mumble. "Let's just drop it, okay?"

Dinner resumes, conversations veering here and there. Sometimes I speak up, other times I listen. I try to include Cal, steering the conversation away from any dangerous topics. My mom had asked me before why we just didn't tell Mary and Christie about Cal since they were the only ones here who didn't know, but I'd asked her to keep it under wraps for now. Mary, though I love her, isn't known for her discretion, and I didn't need Cal's coming-out angel party to include the whole damned town. In my head I saw the swarms of media that would descend on Roseland, cameras flashing, reporters shouting. Then scientists would come and whisk him away to some secret underground testing facility where they would experiment on him, trying to find some way to hold him hostage and try to ransom him off to God. It was an awful thought, but one I believed to be entirely plausible. I put the kibosh on that idea as soon as it'd come from her mouth.

Dating, I think, barely able to restrain the eye roll. The concept behind it is so completely ludicrous I can't even grasp it. One does not *date* a guardian angel, even if one is having sex with a guardian angel. Even if one has developed... *feelings* for said angel that defy logic or explanation. At the very least, I don't deserve someone like him, to be sure. One can't get smaller than being a small-town boy from a place like Roseland. I run the town's only gas station, which still bears the name of my dead father. I have no prospects for the future. I am drowning in my own grief. I am selfishly motivated and desperate for answers I don't know how to get.

But even then, even with these thoughts, even with the conversations around us, something happens. Abe is talking about the caves in the back hills again, most likely filled to the brim with gold nuggets the size of ponies. Christie listens with rapt attention, her eyes glittering with excitement. Mary and Mother are discussing the upcoming festival, and what they'll need in order to prepare all the pies that have been ordered. Nina sits counting the peas on her plate with a look of pure concentration on her face, her tongue peeking out between her teeth as she moves each one from one side of the plate to another. This is my family, and the noise around me is soothing in a way it hasn't been in quite a long time. That's mostly my doing, I know, given my self-imposed exile in the Land of Sorrow. But hearing the overlapping voices and laughter, seeing the bright eyes and smiles, does more for me than I ever thought it could.

The strangely joyous moment is only confirmed when through it all, the noise, the laughter, the brightness of the room, I feel a hand on mine underneath the table. I turn my hand palm up and long fingers brush along the skin, causing the hairs on my arm to stand on end. I'm electrified as Cal brushes the tips of my fingers with his own. This is nothing erotic, though my dick thinks it's a fine idea. The touch is not meant to be about sex. It is *touch*, feelings conveyed through a simple action that mean more to me than any words. He slides his fingers between my own, engulfing me as we blend together. I can feel him watching me out of the corner of my eye, and I think to turn, but realize I don't have control of my emotions. It's too much. It's all too much, and I think about getting up and leaving the table. But he knows, like he always does, and squeezes my hand tightly, letting me know that he isn't going to let go, no matter how hard I fight against it. Only he knows at that moment what is running through my head. Only he knows.

Eventually, I calm. Eventually, I stop listening to the little voices in my head telling me it won't matter in the long run; I will lose everything and be alone again. Eventually it feels like blessed silence.

The only thing missing is my father. His presence doesn't loom over the table as much as it has in the past when the remaining family came together those few times after he drowned. Then, it was like a large unspeakable thing had fallen over us all, threatening to bury us with its weight. It is still crushing. Devastating. Still painful, yes. Still there, yes. But it's almost muted somehow, like seen through a fog. The warm hand in mine squeezes again and the fog shifts, only to come into sharper focus, and I recognize it for what it is.

It's in my mother's laugh, a sound as big as I can ever remember. It's in the way Nina blushes when Cal winks at her. It's the way Mary leans over and brushes a lock of hair out of Christie's face. It's in the way Abe drops a hand on my shoulder and tells me he thought he heard a rumbling noise in his old Honda and wants to bring it in next week for me to check it out.

We are moving on. We are letting go. I am realizing that some things might be more important than my own selfish desires for answers I might never find. It burns, this feeling. It hurts. It claws at me, but it's undeniable. Cal glances at me again, those dark eyes sparkling, and it's like a hammer to my chest.

But then that feeling is taken away only a short time later.

We're clearing the table when my mother comes out from the kitchen, wringing her hands. I wonder at it, having noticed her pointed looks at Cal that got more and more obvious over the past hour. I don't know what she's up to, and I have a feeling I don't *want* to know. She's planning something, her nervous hands doing little to detract from the determined look in her eyes.

"Cal?" she says, and the noise in the room stops. I can hear Mary and Christie chattering in the kitchen while they start the dishes, but the rest of us are quiet, waiting. "May I speak with you? Alone?"

I narrow my eyes and before I know what I'm doing, I take a step to stand in front of him, as if to protect him. It must look ridiculous, given how much bigger he is than me, but at the moment, I don't know what she wants and I'm not going to take the chance.

"Why?" I ask before Cal can speak.

She glances at me before looking back at Cal. When she speaks, it's to him. "There's something I need to say to you. Something that I need you to hear."

"Lola," Abe says. "Maybe we could just—"

"It's okay, Abe," Cal says lightly. "She has the right."

"The rest can go," I say with a scowl. "That's fine. But if you think I'm going to go too, you better try again."

"Alone," my mother repeats.

A knock at the door, light but strong.

We all turn to look.

"Now who could that be?" my mother says to herself, starting for the door.

Something is off. I didn't hear a car come up the driveway, much less see headlights. Cal has begun to growl, his hands turning to fists at his sides. Thoughts of the Strange Men start running through my head. Thoughts of Traynor standing at the door, a cigarette dangling from his lips. Something is wrong.

I brush past him and put my hand on my mother's shoulder. "I'll see who it is," I say. "Why don't you just hang back?"

She starts to object, but Cal's growling grows louder as he sidesteps us and heads for the door. I rush after him. "Who is it? A thread?" I mutter once I catch up to him.

He shakes his head. "No thread. It's *him*." For the first time since I've known him, I hear fear in his voice, underneath the growling, buried in the bravado.

This can't be good.

I reach the door first, much to Cal's dismay. Already I can hear the others following us down the hallway. "You don't open that door, Benji," he snarls at me. "You get behind me and you let me deal with this. I am a guardian and I will guard. Do it now and don't make me ask you again."

I obey, instantly. I can't ignore the fury on his face, the way his eyes look like they have turned to oil, liquid and black. Had this occurred only a few short days ago, I'm sure blue lights would have been flashing all around him, forming the outline of his wings. But as it is, there is only a charge in the air, like static, palpable and thick. I don't want him to open the door.

The knock comes again.

"Don't open the door," I whisper. "Please."

"Benji," my mother asks from behind me. "Who is it?"

Cal kisses my forehead and opens the door.

A man stands there, a man unlike any man I've ever seen before. The sun has set long before, the sky behind him like a deep bruise. The light from inside the house bleeds out onto the porch. The shadows from the darkening night seem to crawl over his shoulders.

He is an imposing figure, all sharp angles and planes. His black hair is short, nary a strand out of place. The goatee around his thick lips is perfectly trimmed. His throat is exposed, showing olive skin that disappears into an opened button-down white shirt that looks crisp. He wears a black dress coat that appears tailored to fit his strong body, buttoned once in the front. He's not bigger than Cal, more lithe and long, but he radiates authority. He is devastatingly handsome, but in a cold, manufactured way.

"Calliel," he says, his voice whiskey smooth. "How lovely to see you again, brother."

"Michael," Cal says quietly in greeting.

Michael.

Cal's voice, a memory: *I can't tell the future. I can't speak to God's plan. I don't think anyone can, even the higher-ups, the archangels, though sometimes I wonder what exactly Michael knows....*

The Strange Men: *This will end now as we were instructed. We cannot go back to Michael empty-handed.*

Cal: *Minions that do nothing more than Michael's bidding. They are abominations, and I do not know why Father permits them.*

I feel eyes on me and pull myself out of the memories. The archangel Michael is looking at me with undisguised curiosity, cocking his head to the right, and for a moment I expect his eyes to twitch back and forth like his Strange Men. "You must be Benjamin Edward Green," he says to me. His voice is kind, and that makes his smile all the more terrible. "It's nice to meet you, Benji. You've certainly made quite the impression, from what I understand."

"Don't you talk to him," Cal snaps, pulling me behind him. I press my forehead against his back, smelling earth, the charge in the air increasing. "This does not concern him."

"Doesn't it?" Michael asks. "It seems to me it most certainly *does* involve him. You made that perfectly obvious once you made the decision to come here."

"I... I don't...." Cal sounds upset. Uncertain. I move around him again and stand by his side. This time he doesn't stop me. I take his hand in mine.

Michael laughs in disbelief. "You don't *remember*?" He shakes his head. "Father certainly does enjoy his games, doesn't he?" And before I can shout out a warning, Michael flashes out his hand, pressing his palm against Cal's chest, right above his heart. Cal stiffens as if electrocuted, his hand gripping mine so tightly I think my bones will break. There's a dull flash in Michael's eyes, a light that is only there for a moment before falling away. He pulls his hand back and Cal shudders, bowing his head. "Father does enjoy his games," Michael repeats quietly, the laughter gone from his voice. "The parts are there, I see, but they've been shattered. The shapes aren't making sense. It's jumbled. Like a knot."

"Can you return them to me?" Cal asks, his head still bowed. "The memories?"

"No," Michael says. "I was not the one who took them from you. This is a test, Calliel. He is testing your faith, it would seem." Michael snorts derisively. "He's been silent on the matter. To me. To the others. No one really seems to know what he's up to."

"Benji?" my mother asks shrilly. "Who is this?"

Michael peers over Cal's head. "I am a friend," he says. "I have not seen Calliel in quite some time, and I decided to check in on him."

"Are you one of them?" Abe asks, his voice hard.

"He is," Nina whispers. "So many lights. White. So much white around him. He's so bright."

"He's a... an *angel*?" my mother says lowly.

"Someone's been talking." Michael sounds amused.

"What do you want?" I ask, trying to sound stronger then I feel.

Michael looks at me, and I feel like quaking where I stand, but I don't break the gaze. It is startling to realize that he isn't blinking. My skin crawls. "What I want," he says slowly, "is to make sure everything is in order. That all things are in their natural place."

"What do you mean?"

"He means me," Cal whispers.

Michael nods. "This whole... *thing* you've got here. This is disorder. This is chaos. I don't know what Father has planned for you, but he hasn't stopped me from being here. There are rules, Calliel, as you well know. You are not allowed on the earthly plane. You watch. You protect. You guard. You do *not* reveal yourself. It is within us all to do so, of course, but we are not meant to have free will. Father placed the ability to become corporeal to test us. To give the *illusion* of free will so that we may be tested."

"It's not his fault," I snap. "It was mine. I prayed for him and he came. I pulled him down. I did this, not him. You leave him alone."

"Oh, Benjamin," Michael says. "While I am sure it's a perfectly lovely thought, it's not a correct one. A human cannot just pull down an angel from the sky. Not by praying for it. Prayer doesn't work like that." He frowns. "No, this appears to be all on Calliel. I can see the how of it, but I can't yet figure out why. What does Father hope to achieve?"

"It doesn't matter," Abe said, stepping forward. "He's not going anywhere with you. He stays here. Where he belongs."

Michael blinks. "Hasn't he told you?" he asks, scanning each of our faces. He looks at me last, and I know his words even before he speaks them. "If he stays here, it will kill him." Nina gasps and covers her face. "He is not human. He is an angel.

Angels are not meant to stay on this plane of existence. If he dies here, his soul will become nothing."

"I'm fine," Cal growls. "I don't feel any different."

Michael looks at him sympathetically. "Now that's not even remotely truthful, Calliel. You and I both know that. I think Benjamin does too, by the look of it." I look away before Cal can see in me whatever Michael did.

"I'm fine," Cal says again, more forcefully.

"Be that as it may, I would prefer if you returned to On High with me now," Michael says, taking a step back. "It would allow us to avoid any further... unpleasantries down the line. We'll return, speak to Father, and get this whole mess sorted out, and then maybe, just *maybe*, you can return to your job. How this town hasn't burned to the ground without a guardian is beyond me."

"I can still see the threads," Cal says hoarsely, which causes Michael's cool façade to slip, for just a moment, surprise seeping in. "I am still able to see them."

"That's... not possible," Michael says, visibly trying to compose himself. "You aren't even...."

"It's true," I say. "He saw my thread after your Strange Men came and attacked me. He saved me from them. They wanted to hurt me."

"That was an unfortunate mistake," Michael allows. "I'd been called away and let the... Strange Men, as you call them, have free rein in locating Calliel. The more human he became, the harder it was for us. That mistake was mine, and I apologize."

"Benji could have been killed and you *apologize*?" Cal snarls. "Michael, those things are dangerous! I still can't understand why Father allows their existence!"

"Much like I don't understand how Father allows yours," Michael retorts. "And the only reason I was away to begin with was to try and placate the roar your falling has caused. You have put On High into disarray and others are demanding answers."

"You know I have no answers to give, even if I wanted to."

"Yes, yes," Michael says, waving his hand in dismissal. "I will demand an answer from Father, one way or another. These games of his are getting tiresome, no matter what he hopes to learn about the humans. We have other things to worry about, you know. Will you return with me now? Save your friends here from further heartache?"

"No," Nina says, stepping forward. "Blue stays here. He won't leave with you."

"That's right," Abe rumbles, moving to stand on the other side of Cal. "I know a bully when I see one. He isn't going anywhere. You'll have to go through me. I'm a lot sprier then I look."

My mother comes to stand beside me, putting one hand on my shoulder and the other on Cal's. "Cal belongs with us," she grinds out. "I'll be damned if I'll let you take him away." I might have doubted my mother, but how could I have doubted her heart?

I move in front of Cal again, blocking his massive body with my skinny one. Michael, who wears an expression of amusement, looks down at me. "And will you threaten me too?" he asks, a small smile on his face. "You are all nothing if not protective of the ones you care about." He bends down until his face is level with mine. His eyes are so deep, they appear infinite. For all I know, they are. "You should remember, Benjamin Edward Green, that things are not always what they seem. But I believe you shall learn that in due time. I believe you shall learn all things." Whether his words are a threat or not doesn't matter. They still chill me to the bone.

He stands again. "This is not finished, Calliel," he says sharply. "Either you will die here or you will return. Make your choice quickly, for I fear you don't have much time."

"Why are you guys all at the door?" I hear Christie call out from down the hall. "Is there something out there?"

"Something comes, to be sure," Michael says, glancing over his shoulder.

Headlights, starting up the driveway.

"Who is that?" Mary asks as she came up behind us, pointing at Michael.

"A friend," Cal snaps. He is getting riled up, and I can tell it has more to do with the oncoming car than the archangel standing in front of us.

"Who is this?" Michael asks with a frown. "I do not have eyes in this little place. The threads. I can't see them."

"What threads is he talking about?" Christie asks. "Why is everyone standing in the doorway? Move! I want to see!"

Cal begins to growl, and I know who it is even before I see the decal on the side, the lights on top of the car.

Griggs.

old bones

"A WELCOMING party?" Griggs asks with a sardonic nod of his head as he steps out of the cruiser. "How wonderful."

"Sheriff?" Christie asks, her voice going cold. "What are you doing here? None of us called you out here."

He shrugs easily, averting his eyes. "Thought I'd stop by and check things out for myself."

"Check what out, George?" my mother asks.

Griggs ignores her and looks up at Michael. "Haven't seen you around before, friend."

"I don't suppose you have," Michael says slowly. "I'm not exactly from around here."

"Could tell by your clothes. Pretty fancy."

"How kind of you, Sheriff."

"Got a name?"

"I do."

"Well?"

"Well, what?"

Griggs's mouth stretches to a thin line. "What is your name, friend?"

"Michael."

"Got a last name, Michael?"

"Oh, I'm sure I do, but none I feel at this very moment needs to be shared with you." He pauses, considering. "Friend."

The sheriff's eyes narrow. "You friends with Cal Blue here?"

They glance at each other. "You could say that," Michael allows. "More like... business associates."

"Oh? And what line of business would that be?"

"Security." No hesitation. It would have been funny had it not been between a high-ranking angel and a man I'm pretty sure is a sadist.

Griggs arches an eyebrow. "Security? And what are you supposed to be guarding?"

Michael laughs. "Now *that's* an amusing question."

"Wasn't meant to be funny," Griggs says with a frown.

"It was," Michael assures him.

"Cal Blue?"

"Yes?" Cal says. His lips are almost twisted into a sneer.

"There's no one in the state of California named Calliel Blue. Trust me on that; I looked."

"That doesn't mean a thing, Sheriff," Abe says. "You should know that better than anyone. I assume that to be elected into your position you have at least *some* knowledge of the law. Well, not that I voted for you, anyway."

"I wasn't talking to you, old-timer," Griggs says coldly. "You'll know if I am. You can trust me on that."

I am angry. "You got a problem, Sheriff? Ever since Cal came to town, you've had a bug up your ass about him. What the fuck do you want?"

"Benji!" my mother snaps.

Griggs smiles but it never reaches his eyes. "What do I want?" he asks. "What *I* want is to know why your little boyfriend here is lying about who he is. I want to know how he came to be in Roseland out of the blue. My problem, Benji, is I want to know who the *fuck* he is."

"I don't see how that concerns you," Michael says, cocking his head. He seems curious about the sheriff.

"That's because it doesn't," I say, unsure if I should be agreeing with him. "Cal hasn't done a damn thing wrong. As a matter of fact, he's probably done more right for this town than you ever have."

"Might be a good idea for you to shut your mouth, kid," the sheriff growls.

I take a step toward him. "And why is that, Griggs?" I say, keeping my voice hushed so the others on the porch can't hear me. "Am I going to have an accident? End up in the river? Get a bullet in the back of my head?" He's good. He doesn't even flinch. "I know what you've done. And one way or another, I swear on all that I have that I will make you suffer."

His eyes glitter as he twitches his lips. "Boy, you have no idea the unholy mess you are walking into."

"I think I know plenty," I tell him. "You will pay and *everyone* will know what you've done."

He laughs loudly, raising his voice. "Threatening an officer of the law? Benji, I expected you to be smarter than that. But then, the apple never did fall far from the tree, now did it?" Cal grabs my arm before I can launch myself at the bastard who dared to insult my father. I want to tear him to pieces and split his bones while he screams for me to stop.

"That's... *enough*," my mother says, her voice quaking. She comes down the steps, surprising us all with the ferocity in her voice. She pushes past me, almost knocking me over. Cal grabs me as I stumble and pulls me against him, putting his arm across my chest protectively. I am very aware of Michael watching us closely.

"Lola," Griggs warns, "this is none of your concern. You stay out of this."

"I am *done* with you," she snarls at him. "Unless you have probable cause to be on my property, I suggest you leave. The less you do for this family, the better."

He glances over my mother's shoulder at the rest of the family standing there, as if looking for something. He must not find what he's looking for, because he takes a step back toward his patrol car. "I will find out what you're hiding," he says to Cal. "I know it's something, and as long as you are in my town, I won't stop until I find it out."

"Now *that's* an interesting use of taxpayer money," Abe says. "I wonder what the town would think of such things, Sheriff? You know, the people who elected you? Maybe you should ask *them* what they think about Cal here before you misappropriate your department's time and energy. It'd be interesting to see how quickly one could gather enough signatures to petition for a recall election for a sheriff using bias and intimidation to get what he wants, wouldn't you say? Especially in front of so many witnesses."

The scowl on the sheriff's face deepens. The hatred in his eyes is plain as he looks at each of us in turn, but never more than when he glares at Cal and me. I stand firm, not diverting my gaze, attempting to show I will not be cowed by this man. Not now. Not at my home. He points his finger at me. "You *will*—"

"Enough," Christie interrupts in a hard voice. "It's time for you to get back into your car, George. This has gone on long enough. We'll be in touch if we require your services any further."

"So that's how it's going to be," Griggs says. "After all I've done for your family over the years. Who knew it would have come to this?" His petulance is almost laughable, but I can't rein in an angry desire to attack him.

Griggs turns to move back to his car, but is stopped when Michael says his name. I'd almost forgotten the archangel was even there. He walks over to the sheriff, his long legs making quick work of the distance between them. He moves with such fluid grace it almost seems like he's floating. If you didn't know what he was, you'd have thought he might have been a dancer at one point in his life. If you *did* know what he was, you could almost imagine his wings carrying him over.

He has several inches on Griggs as he stands before him, and for a moment the sheriff's perpetual sneer falters as he looks into the angel's eyes. I don't know what he sees, and I don't know if I want to. If everything I've heard about the angel hierarchy is correct, then Michael is almost the top of the top, just under Metatron, the one Cal said had disappeared long ago. That alone is enough to intimidate.

"What do you want?" Griggs asks. "You better take a step back."

"I try not to involve myself in little things," Michael says softly, though his voice still carries back to where we stand. "There are matters of greater consequence that always seem to demand my full attention. However, the fact that I am here should be enough to convey the importance of the situation." He glances back at Cal as he says this last before returning his attention to the sheriff. "Since I *am* here, I must admit to being a bit curious about you. We are not meant to interfere, much as we sometimes want to. Our Father has dictated as such. But even still...."

Michael flashes his hand up and presses his palm flat against Griggs's chest. The sheriff's head falls back and his mouth opens in a yawning gape, but no sound comes out. The cords in his neck stand out as his hands twitch lightly at his sides. It's over in a matter of seconds, and the sheriff gasps as Michael frowns and takes a step back from him. "Ah, Sheriff," Michael says as he shakes his head. "If you only knew.... No matter. Leave this place. I have no desire to look upon your face any longer."

Griggs looks confused and angry but obeys almost immediately. We stand watch as he starts the car and the headlights come on. I can see him watching Michael through the windshield before he turns the car and peels out down the driveway, the engine a fading roar.

"What in the hell is going on?" Christie snaps. "Who is that man?"

"He *is* kind of scary," Mary says. "Did you see the look on George's face? I thought he was going to piss himself, to be honest."

"Bad word," Nina intones quietly.

"Calliel," Michael says, still facing the way the sheriff has gone. "To me, please." His tone leaves no room for argument.

But that doesn't stop me from trying. I grab Cal's arm as he starts toward Michael. Cal pauses for a moment, then looks back and shakes his head, his eyes resolute. "I must go, Benji."

"You're leaving?" I ask, hating the way I sound.

His eyes widen and he pulls me into him. "No," he says harshly in my ear. "No, I am not leaving you. I will never leave you. I need to find out what he needs, and then we can go home, okay?"

I clutch at him.

"We'll go home," he whispers, kissing my forehead.

"Now, Calliel," Michael says.

"Okay," I mumble and let him go. He holds his head up high and squares his shoulders as he crosses over to Michael. As much as I strain to listen, I can't hear a thing beyond the murmur of deep voices. A hand falls on my shoulder and I feel a breath on my neck. I almost cringe until I realize it's my mother. She wraps her arm around my shoulders, and soon we are surrounded by the rest of our family, Nina leaning against me on my other side, Mary and Christie at my back, Abe standing next to my mother, a hand on her shoulder.

From what I can see in the dark, Michael does most of the talking, though his words seem to be few. He does not punctuate anything with movement, keeping his hands folded behind him as if he stands at parade rest. Cal stands next to him, head bowed. One might think it was a defeated pose, but I can see that Cal is merely listening to Michael's voice.

"This turned out to be a weird night," Christie mutters.

"I enjoyed myself," Nina says with a smile. "So many people!"

"Certainly unexpected," Mary agrees. "Security, huh? At least they *look* the part. All that man flesh. Michael, is it? Don't suppose he's a queen like Cal?"

"He's not your type," my mother sighs as Abe snorts. "Trust me."

"You need to be careful of Griggs," Abe says. "I've told you that before, Benji. But he's got his eye on you, and he might have…." He trails off, seeming hesitant to say the rest.

And I realize this is a moment, an opportunity for someone to say aloud what I had thought and what I am sure the others had thought about my father. I could tell them all I know, but I don't, simply because I want to distance the danger from my family as much as possible. I can't bear the thought of one of them getting hurt because of me. Corwin's death has weighed heavily on my mind, dragging my guilt to the forefront for all to see, even if they don't know what they're looking at. I would not survive if I caused the death of another person, especially one of the people standing near me. My conscience would not allow it. But here? Now? There is this *moment* where it seems like we have stepped to the edge of a precipice and all held our breaths, waiting for one person to have the courage to finish Abe's sentence. It needs to be me. It needs to be me because I have had the thoughts every day. It needs to be me because I am my father's son and I will not rest until I am sure *he* can rest.

"And he might have been the one who killed Big Eddie," I say.

Michael stops speaking and looks out into the dark again. Cal turns neatly on his heel and comes back to me, stopping a few feet from where we stand huddled as if trying to protect each other from a gathering storm. He watches us for a moment, but I can't make out the expression on his face. Is he resigned? Defiant? I don't know.

He holds out his hand to me.

I don't hesitate and step from my family and grab the rough familiarity of his hand. "Michael would speak with you, if you'd allow it," he tells me quietly as he pulls me against his chest. "He says he has words for only you to hear."

"What did he tell you?" I all but demand, sure that he is forcing Cal to return to On High.

"Nothing I didn't already know," Cal says. "That I am wrong for being here, that it is killing me. That he'll return to collect me when the time is right. That he's sure Father is testing me, though he doesn't know how." He sighs as he rubs my back. "He's seen the knot in my head, how the pieces are all tangled and not making sense. He saw something in Griggs, but he will not tell me what."

"Why not?"

Cal chuckles ruefully. "Michael's always been a stickler for the rules. Since he is sure this is a test, he does not want to interfere."

"But he *is* interfering," I remind him. "He's trying to make you leave."

"He's conflicted," Cal says. "He doesn't understand what Father wants, and only knows what he's been told in the past. It's confusing him. He's frustrated."

"He can go fuck himself," I hiss angrily. "Tell him to go away and leave us alone. Or better yet, I'll do it myself. He wants to talk to me, right? I'll make him go away and never come back."

I can't help but notice the way Cal quirks his lips at the sides, like he's trying to stay serious but can't help but be amused by the tiny human in front of him who wants to go kick an archangel's ass clear across the county. I try to scowl at him, but don't succeed.

"And then he'll leave?" I ask. "Without you?"

Cal nods eventually, though it looks forced.

"Then you get the rest of them inside," I tell him. "I'll go talk to the big, bad Michael and see what the hell he wants."

"I'm not leaving you alone with him," he snaps. "You can forget that right now."

I can't help the grin that follows. I stand on my tiptoes and brush his lips with mine. "I can take care of myself," I say, as if I'm not talking about an angel of God. "Please. Just do as I ask."

Cal rolls his eyes, an action I think again is so unbefitting an angel, so *human*, and my breath catches in my chest. Something warm lights itself at the base of my spine and roars up me until all I can hear is a deep-pitched buzz in my ears. I feel alive and powerful. Even more, I feel awake, truly and completely *awake,* for the first time in years. I will do anything for this man (*for that is what he is becoming,* I think) in front of me. I will do anything to save him.

I walk away from him before he can see this in my eyes.

Michael hasn't moved, and I come to stand beside him, leaving enough distance between us so we are not touching. If he wants to do his weird hand chest zap mojo thing, he can reach out easily, but I don't think his request to speak to me is about that. I glance behind me to see Cal ushering everyone inside, over the protests of my mother. The others go inside Big House, but she refuses, sitting herself down on the patio defiantly, watching Michael and me with a guarded expression. Cal does what I thought he would and sits in the wicker chair beside her. They do not speak.

"What do you want from me?" I ask the angel.

"Walk with me," he says and turns toward Little House. I think to hesitate, to say we need to stay in the light, but then I think better of it. I glance back at Big House and see Cal standing again near the porch steps, his big arms crossed over his chest. I shake my head once at him, and he nods but doesn't move to sit. I can feel his gaze on me as I turn to follow Michael.

My steps are slow, the pace set by Michael. He seems to enjoy looking around in the dark, staring up at the stars, reaching out to brush his fingers along the trunk of a large tree, his fingers coming away with sap that oozes like black oil. He brings his hand to his face and inhales the scent. It hurts my heart to see, though I can't say why.

"I was not the first angel," he says as he rubs the pitch against his slacks, "but I was one of the Firsts. Do you understand?"

"Yeah. I think so. Metatron was first, right?"

Michael stops and squats on his heels, rubbing his fingers along the grass. "Yes. I must admit to being surprised that you know that name."

"Cal mentioned it once. Said no one had seen him for a long time."

"Longer than you could possibly imagine," Michael says, picking a pinecone off the ground and rolling it in his hands. "But that is beside the point. When I was much younger than I am now, I felt I had to compete with my brothers for my Father's affections. I was one of the Firsts, which meant I had brothers to compete with, or so I thought. Things were much different then. We were young. Cocky. We thought we could do it all, or at least my brothers and I did. Father was strict in his rules, and we acted out as much as possible, specifically because a time came when it appeared he loved his humans more than he loved us. That was not the case, of course, but we were his sons and we worshipped the ground he walked on, so it was easy to get jealous. Metatron above everyone else, though. There's something about being the actual first. In essence, he was the *only* because he was the first. Gabriel, David, Raphael, and I couldn't help but feel inferior to Metatron, who seemed to have Father's favor above the rest of ours, seemed to have his ear more than the rest of us. But then Metatron was gone."

"Where did he go?" I can't help but ask. I am unsure what this has to do with me, but it seems important that I listen. "Did he fall?"

"It would seem so," Michael says as he stands. "No one really knows for sure how or why, and Father would not say. If I had to guess, I would say he was cast out."

I feel cold. "Is that what happened to Cal?" I whisper.

Michael looks at me sharply. "No. And please don't misinterpret what I am saying as that. No, Calliel is… something else entirely. He is no longer part of a design, the pattern. Something has shifted and I don't know what it is. I don't know what my Father has planned for Calliel, or why he is testing him like he is. I was not being facetious when I said that Father likes his games. He does, as I am sure the history of humanity could tell you. But he is not cruel, at least not intentionally. He believes all beings should have to prove themselves. I don't know why he's picked Cal. Or you." He pauses. "Or your father, it would seem."

Nausea rolls over me in waves. "I don't understand."

"Nor do I," Michael admits as we resume our slow pace toward Little House. "Fathers are mysterious creatures, are they not? We may not always understand their motives, or even agree with the choices they make, but we love them just the same for all that they are."

"My father…," I start but the lump in my throat stops me from finishing.

"Was the greatest man in the world?" Michael says kindly. It's like he can read my thoughts. For all I know, he can.

I nod.

"Most sons think that. I could say the same about my own, but the comparison isn't fair for either of us. I do not know this Big Eddie, and you don't know my Father. Not in the way I do."

"Does your father love you?" I ask.

Michael smiles. "Oh yes. I should think so."

"Does he love Cal? And me?"

"Yes, child. He does."

We reach Little House, and I can't help but notice the way Michael reaches out and strokes the wooden railing on the porch, a loving caress. This only fuels my anger. It seems wrong for him to touch what my father made, though I don't know why.

"Then why must we suffer? Why does he hurt us every single day? Why did he let Calliel fall and take his memories? Why is he allowing it to *kill* him while he stays here? Why did he allow my father to die? Why does he have to take everything I love if he's supposed to love me?" My words are harsh by the end

Michael doesn't flinch. "You can't know," he says quietly, "how much you truly love something until it's gone."

"That's not fair," I say as I tremble.

"No one said it would be. He tests you, Benji, and he tests Calliel for a supremely simple reason. You are tested because if you aren't, how could you know what you believe in?"

I can't do it. I can't get into a philosophical debate with an archangel, knowing how ridiculous it is and how unprepared I am. Not to mention I'm too angry to listen to what his words actually mean. I go in a different direction. "You touched the sheriff. Just like you touched Cal."

"Yes."

"Do you know what happened to my father?"

"Bits and pieces."

"Tell me."

He sighs. "Benji, how are you supposed to know love if the answers are given to you?"

I hate his backward questions. "I *know* what love is," I snarl at him.

"No," he says. "You know only *grief* now. There is a difference, though I don't expect you to understand what it is, at least not yet. You have all but *buried* yourself in it, so how could you? How can you love if you don't even know yourself anymore?"

"That's not fair," I croak out.

"Do you love Calliel?" he asks.

I freeze, unable to answer, unable to process the question. Any part of it.

"And yet he loves you," Michael says. "I could see it the moment he opened the door. Maybe because it was so unexpected, or because it was so bright, I don't know. But it almost knocked me flat."

"He... he doesn't... he *can't*...."

"And you don't see it," Michael says, as if I'd agreed with him. "Because some part of you is already grieving for him. You think him lost, and so you are burying yourself in preparation."

"You said... you said he would die."

"Did I?" Michael asks, testing the porch step with his foot. "Not even I can know what my Father has planned. True, it *is* killing him to stay on this plane of existence, but it is up to God, as you call him, to decide Calliel's fate."

"Then why do you want to bring him back? Why are you here? Why did you send the Strange Men after him?"

"Because there is an order to things, even if you can't see it in all the chaos. There is a balance, and Calliel has broken that balance."

"But if it was God that did it, then wouldn't you think he has a reason?"

Michael almost looks embarrassed. "I am a sort of stickler for the rules. Comes with being one of the oldest. And Father has not spoken to me yet regarding this, so I must follow protocol until I hear otherwise. But...." He stopped, staring up at Little House.

"But what?"

"This house has some old bones. Good, but old. You must be very proud of it."

"This is the house my father built."

He arches an eyebrow at me. "I expect you helped, though. I can feel you in every part of it. There *is* love here. Old love. New love. You've just forgotten what it feels like."

"I...."

"I like you, Benji. That surprises me. I can see why Calliel loves you as he does. Such a little thing, this place seems to be, but it too surprises me." He turns to face me. "There are other... *levels*... of existence. Other planes. Worlds you couldn't possibly imagine exist. There may even be an infinite number of them. I don't think even Father knows for sure. Once he started creating, I don't think he knew how to stop. And within these infinite levels, there is one that sets itself apart from the rest. On this level, there are people who can do the most beautiful things with earth and water, fire and wind. They can manipulate the elements like it's so much magic. It's a beautiful sight to behold. But... there is a darkness coming. One we don't know yet how to stop, no matter how much we wish we could. And we must stop it, before it finally spills over onto the other levels. It is too important to ignore. Metatron...." He sighs and shakes his head.

"What does that have to do with me?" I ask harshly, unable to fully comprehend his words.

"That's just it," Michael says. "I don't think it has *anything* to do with you... at least it shouldn't. But then why is my Father so focused on this plane, this corner of the universe, this planet, this country, this place? Why is he doing what he's doing?"

I say the only thing I can think of: "God works in mysterious ways."

Michael stares wide-eyed at me for a moment before he bursts out laughing, using Little House to prop himself up as bends over, clutching his stomach. I can't find the humor in it, but I start to laugh along with him because if I don't laugh, I'm sure I'll lose it completely. So we laugh. We laugh until we can laugh no more. And when we finish, I know our conversation is almost over.

Michael stands before me and drops his hands on my shoulders. He isn't laughing any longer. "I believe there will come a time, Benji, very soon, that I'll return to give you a choice. You must think hard on the choice you will make, because I don't know if it can be reversed once it has been made. I might have been a bit premature when I said Calliel has broken the design. He might have just made it different. For some reason my Father has allowed me to come here, and I think I have become part of this test, whether I asked to be or not."

"Test of what?" I ask, unable to look away.

"Faith, Benji," he says, like it is the most obvious thing in the world. "It always comes down to faith. To do what you must, you must *believe*. Father has tested one's faith for as long as I can remember. It's kind of his thing, in case you haven't heard the stories. But I may need to speed things up a bit. As I've said, my focus and *his* focus need to be elsewhere."

"I thought you were a stickler for the rules," I say without thinking.

He laughs again. "Maybe some part of me wants to see how this plays out too. It's certainly a first in all of my existence. Who wouldn't want to be a part of history?"

Somehow, I don't think I want to know just how long his existence has been.

"I will send one of the Strange Men, as you call them," he says, squeezing my shoulders. "They will not be here for you, or for Calliel. Think of it as a… a gift. Once you catch sight of the Strange Man, you will know I have assisted you and that you should follow. You may get the answers you desire, but remember this: sometimes the past is better left alone. Do you understand?"

My heart pounds in my chest. "Yes."

He lets me go and steps back. "I have enjoyed our conversation, Benjamin Green. I think maybe you have taught me some things. I hope you will continue to surprise me." He turns and starts walking toward the forest behind Little House.

"Wait," I call out before I can stop myself.

He stops but doesn't turn.

"What did you tell Calliel? Just now?"

He looks up at the stars again and I follow his gaze. They look so brilliantly blue against the night sky I think them like ice. "I told him that even though I would return for him, I could understand why he did what he did. I told him he was very lucky to have found one such as you, even if it can only be for a moment. I'll see you soon, Benji." Even as he speaks the last words, white lights begin to flash around him. They become almost too brilliant to look at. I cover my eyes with my hands, squinting through my fingertips. I can make out the vague outline of massive wings, much larger than Calliel's. They stretch out wide, glowing in the dark until they snap around Michael, cocooning him. The light explodes outward, and by the time the burned afterimage fades from my eyes, Michael is gone and I can hear footsteps racing down the driveway.

Cal crashes into me, grips me tight, and runs his hands over me to make sure all my parts are still attached. Once he is satisfied I am in one piece, he cups my face in his big hands and kisses me, pressing my lips against my teeth. "Are you all right?" he asks hoarsely, brushing his lips over mine again and again. *"Are you all right?"*

I stare at him, seeing my reflection in the black of his eyes.

And yet he loves you....

"I'm okay," I whisper, though that is so far from the truth it's extraordinary.

"What did he want?" he asks me. "What did Michael ask of you?"

I kiss him again, needing to feel his strength. I hope he has enough to give for what is to come.

"Benji! What did he want!"

I shudder in his hands. "To let us know we don't have much time," I whisper. "I think the end is about to begin."

part iv: the river

The man past the end of his life stood at the edge of the river.
The River Crosser was long gone, having warned him he would not come back.
The man had said he understood this, and that he couldn't leave. Not yet.
"You may always be lost, then," the River Crosser had cautioned before he departed.
Alone, the man stared long at his reflection, which had again appeared in the water.
He saw many things flash by about his own life, both the good and the bad.
He saw that he had not taken his life for granted, and that he had been kind.
But above all else, what he saw the most was love.
And it gave him strength.
So he stood, his shoulders squared, his head held tall.
He breathed in the air around him as twilight began to fall.
And at the sounds from above of great wings taking flight,
he cried out for the river to hear, his voice booming through the darkening night:
"If it takes all I have and if it means I will never be found,
then so be it! For my family, for my *son*, into this river I drown!"

michael's sign

ALL over town, the flyers read:

THE ROSELAND CHAMBER OF COMMERCE
PROUDLY PRESENTS
The 52nd ANNUAL
JUMP INTO SUMMER FESTIVAL
MAY 19, 2012
MUSIC~FOOD~CRAFTS~GAMES
LOCAL BAND THE WAYWARD BOYS AT 6PM!
PREPARE TO JUMP INTO SUMMER!!!

THE morning of the festival dawns cloudy and gray, with a promise of rain later in the afternoon that could put a damper on the festivities. A buzz spreads through town, like it does every festival, but it's muted compared to years past. *What if it rains?* some in the town are asking. *What are we going to do if it rains?* They try to think back to other festivals, if there was a time when a spring rainstorm had fallen on the day of. No one can seem to remember any rainouts. Mid-May is usually a drier time, full of sunshine and blossoming flowers and bees buzzing lazily.

Of course, weather contingencies have been in place for years, just in case. Mayor Walken goes on the local AM radio station morning show (*Terry In The Mornings!*) to reassure Roselandians that the show will go on regardless. Why, he spoke to Pastor Thomas Landeros of Our Mother of Sorrows just this morning, and the pastor assured him the church would be opened up and the pews cleared out of the way so people could set up their tables for the food and crafts. As planned, the festival will take place at the end of Poplar Street opposite the gas station, in front of said church, as it has for the past twenty years. It will be just like God is there with us, he says in that politician's voice of his, earnest and soothing. And the Shriner's Grange is only a short walk down a stone path from the church. Any overflow can be set up in there, and The Wayward Boys will be able to play their brand of bluegrass folksy twang inside as well. It'll be fine, he says. We'll pray that the rain stays away, at least until Sunday. If it doesn't, the emergency plan has always been to gather at the church anyway, as it's set up on a hill, higher than the rest of the town. Surely safe from any flood waters, should they come.

And *should* they come, he says, Roseland will be ready. Heavy bags filled with sand have already been pulled from the town's storage in case they're needed to block the river. He knows, he says with certainty in his voice, that everyone will be willing to lend a hand, should it come down to it. After all, Roseland is the greatest little town in the world, and its people always want to help out their neighbors. It's times like these that we remember just how wonderful Roseland really is. With that, he signs off and *Terry In The Morning* switches over to sports and weren't the Trail Blazers just *so* close to getting into the NBA Finals this year? Interim Coach Canales certainly rocked this season *out!*

Abe turns off the tiny radio I'd pulled out from the back office. "The greatest little town in the world?" he says. "Walken sure knows how to spin it, doesn't he?"

I shrug as I look out the front of the store. The gray clouds are thick, looking as if they're stacked on top of each other, growing darker as they rise in the sky. The wind is starting to pick up, and an errant festival flyer blows down the center of Poplar Street. Peals of thunder echo down the mountains, but the sound is faint and doesn't seem to be getting any closer or louder. Not yet. We'll be closing the store at noon (as is tradition—Big Eddie was a big fan of the festival and often sat on the planning committee) and then heading over to help my mom finish setting up her table and bring in all her pies and cakes. She and the Trio are still up at Big House, churning out last-minute cookies and cupcakes in a furious cloud of flour and panic.

It seems oddly domestic and normal, especially given what we now know about the way the world works. It's been just under a week since Michael knocked on the door and Griggs stopped by for one of his unannounced-threats-disguised-as-a-concerned-visit. I've been watching for Michael's sign, but nothing out of the ordinary has happened since he disappeared in a burst of feathers and a flash of light. I glossed over Michael's warning when Cal asked what he told me, only because I think I'm protecting him, at least in the best way I know how. I'm no closer to solving anything, whether it be Big Eddie's death, what exactly Griggs, Walken, and Traynor are doing (or even who their boss supposedly is), or where they're doing it.

A few days ago, I left a grumbling Cal at the store with Abe under the pretense of needing to run over to the next town to visit a friend of mine. I'd really headed past mile marker seventy-seven and crossed the bridge further down the highway and then doubled back, returning to the spot where he'd crashed from On High. It hit me that what I'd heard that night at Griggs's house, through the anger in their words, had an undercurrent to it. Not quite fear, but nervousness, especially Traynor. *This whole thing has bad mojo written all over it. First the guy dying in the river. Then that fucking meteor thing falling right near there. Jesus, Griggs! It's like the universe is telling you to get the fuck out, and you're saying we need to* wait?

I parked and hiked through the woods, making sure to keep an eye out on the time. Cal would be expecting me back shortly. He was pissed I'd left without him, and if I was late, I was sure he'd come looking for me. I still didn't understand *how* I could block him from seeing the pulse of my thread, but it seemed it was possible. I'd prayed for him to come that night with the Strange Men, and he said my thread had lit up like the sun in the sky. I'd prayed for him *not* to see it, to stay away, when Traynor had come into the station, and he hadn't seen my thread.

So with simple thoughts such as *stay away, Cal* and *I am okay, Cal* and (ridiculously) *I am invisible*, I returned to where he'd fallen. The blowback was still evident, burnt trees lying on their sides, the crater in the middle of the clearing still blackened.

If you knew what you were looking for, you could see the outline of wings in the crater, only instead of charred earth, they were made up of different types of blue flowers, ones that I had never seen before in all my years growing up in the woods. They stretched out along the crater, their design a bit fuzzy but obvious to me. I stared, dumbfounded, before plucking one, and heard the stem snap with a moist crack. I brought it to my nose, and it smelled of earth.

Stay away, Cal. Stay away.

I left the crater and went up the hill, deeper into the forest, looking for any signs of a structure, *anything* that would potentially show some kind of drug lab operating in the trees around Roseland. The air smelled fresh, not acrid. No trash littered the forest. No conveniently high hippie wandered toward me, telling me he'd just bought the most righteous shit from a sheriff, a mayor, and a scary-looking man who smoked.

Michael. You said you'd give me a sign, so... give me a sign.

The only response was the birds in the trees.

So I left.

Cal noticed nothing out of the ordinary when I returned.

I look at him now and find him watching me, like he's asked me a question I didn't hear. "Sorry?" I say with a smile that feels fake. All I can seem to focus on is how much more pale I think he looks. I don't know if it's my eyes playing tricks on me, if I'm overreacting, but all I can hear in my head is that he's *dying*, that staying here is *killing* him, that God thinks this is just some test, some goddamn game. It's up to *him*, Michael had said. Only God can change his fate.

And you better, I think as Cal returns the smile, showing teeth. *You just better change his fate or I'll hunt you down and find you myself. I don't care if you're his Father or if you are God. You take him from me and I will do my best to take everything from you.*

They seem empty, these thoughts. I'm sure God is used to being threatened.

"What'd you say?" I ask him, trying to keep my voice even.

He walks toward me slowly, as if he's stalking me. He might very well be doing just that. I want to look away, sure he can see right inside my head and know what I'm thinking, but I don't. Even if he is becoming more like the rest of us, there is still something unfathomable about his eyes, something not quite human, a certain awareness, almost alien in its intensity. I know if he asks me to tell him everything I am thinking right at this moment, I'll tell him. I'll give him all my secrets and ask for nothing in return. I'll do anything for him because I lo—

Oh.

Oh *shit*.

"You okay?" he asks me as he stands in front of me. I look up at him, and for a moment I allow myself to imagine his wings behind him, blue and beautiful, the feathers like silk, whispering as they rustle against each other. Blue lights shoot everywhere and the feathers (like the one in my desk at home that is *mine*) rise as he stretches his wings. The feathers (like the one in my father's dead, floating hand, because that one is *his*) rise to block out the overhead lights. But that's not real, because they aren't there, they aren't in front of me. I don't know if he can even pull out his wings anymore. No further threads have called for him, and where once that might have made him restless, nervous that he hadn't been called, now he seems almost at peace. There is still strength there, exuding from him, a reservoir I don't think has even been tapped, but it's not the same as when he first arrived.

For some reason, he's happy.

"I'm good," I manage to say. "You okay?"

He grins. "I'm awesome."

I should have never taught him that word.

The bell rings overhead.

"Oh, thank God you're here, Rosie," Abe drawls. "Gives me someone to talk to so these two can continue to gaze into each other's eyes."

Cal and I both flush at the same time, but it doesn't stop him from leaning down and kissing me sweetly on the lips. I sigh to myself and wonder if it matters anymore, all the things I tend to think are important. Maybe all that matters is right here in front of me. Maybe that's the thing I should be focused on. All the rest will still be here weeks from now, but Cal might not.

He pulls away and watches me for a moment. Then, much to my dismay, he says with a knowing smile: "You're looking at me differently."

Shit.

"I...." Have no idea what to say.

He shakes his head and kisses me again before stepping away.

Rosie is grinning at him like he's the greatest thing she's ever seen (to be fair, Rosie's lived in Roseland all her life, so he just might be). "I am so very glad you decided to come to town," she tells him without so much as a look at me. I don't know if she's saying this on my behalf or for her own nefarious purpose. I almost tell her to back off my angelic boyfriend but I think the reference would be lost on her, so I resign myself to the fact that I'll be stuck in Cal's shadow for the rest of the time I know him. This splits my train of thought two ways, the first of which is thinking there's no place I'd rather be than in his shadow; the second is wondering just how long I will know him.

You can't take him from me. You just can't. He's here for me, not for you. If you really are his Father, then you should love him enough to let him go.

Much like I love my father *too* much to let him go.

Dammit.

"Heard about that storm?" Rosie asks. "Or should I say storms?"

I nod. "Radio."

"Sounds like a doozy! Haven't had one of them probably since…." Her voice trails off as she realizes her faux pas.

But it's not like I can blame her. It's been almost five years. People are still sad, yes, and everyone knows the hole that Big Eddie left in our lives, but I seem to be the only one still fixated on it, the only one still drowning. I almost allow myself to feel anger about their perceived callousness, how quickly they were able to toss him aside like he was nothing, but that's not the case. *I'm* the one with the problem. *I'm* the one people are tiptoeing around like I'm made of so much glass that even a whisper could see me break.

"It's okay," I tell her kindly, even though my voice sounds rougher than I want it to. "You can say it. Hasn't been a doozy of a storm since the day Big Eddie died." And it had been too. What started out as a light sprinkle had eventually turned into a torrential downpour right before Big Eddie had been pulled from the truck. They'd had to move fast given how quickly the river could change from docile to manic. Looking back, I thought the sky itself was weeping openly at the loss of such a man from this earth. I thought Heaven cried for having to take him away from me, and God was begging for my forgiveness. I decided quite readily that if it was true and Big Eddie was gone, I didn't give a damn if God felt sorry. I didn't care if he was contrite and if he made the world cry for me and my father.

"It's fine," I say again to Rosie. "I'm not going to break. I'm okay. I think. No, I *know*." Maybe I'm getting there.

Rosie glances at Cal before smiling sadly at me. "He was a good man, Benji. You know that; I don't need to tell you again. I don't think you could find a single person in this town to say anything against him." *Pretty words, but I have a feeling there's a few who'd disagree with you.* "But I'm sure glad to hear you say that, and I'm thrilled to see you smile the way you have been lately. And I think we know who we have to thank for that."

Cal flushes again, but even *I* can see the pleased smile on his face that he tries to hide with a bow of his head. I refrain from rolling my eyes, but not by much. It is easier than sinking into the twinge in my chest, especially since now I know that it could have a name, should I choose to give it one. It's easy, almost too easy.

"Shouldn't you be down getting your food truck set up?" Abe asks Rosie.

"Getting there," Rosie says. "I've got some heavy lifting that needs doing and was hoping a certain big man would come help me."

I say nothing, waiting for Cal to make the decision on his own. It takes a moment, and many emotions appear to cross his face. While it might be indecipherable to Abe and Rosie, I've been around him enough to catch it all—his hesitation, his annoyance (however brief), his fear (even more fleeting). He knows what today is, what the conversation I overheard at the sheriff's house means for today. In those few short seconds, he goes to war with himself, and I don't know which part of him will come out the victor.

Abe decides for him. "Go on, Cal," he says, not knowing Cal's internal conflict. Or maybe he does. If anyone else could know, it'd be him. "I'll stay behind here with Benji and close up the store, and we'll head down to the festival in another hour or so."

Cal looks to me. "It'll be good," I say. "Rosie could use the help and I'll be there before you know it."

He crowds against me again, placing his hands on my neck, stroking the skin under my ears with his thumbs. His touch is familiar, warm and urgent. "You'll be down right after noon?" he asks me. Or tells me. I don't know.

I nod. "Sure will, and we'll have some fun. And then maybe I can get Christie or Mary to come open the store in the morning tomorrow so you and I can sleep in."

"After the sunrise?"

"After the sunrise."

"You promise?"

"Yeah, Cal."

He looks dubious. He kisses me again and steps back. "There's something I want to talk to you about tonight," he says. "Something important. Just us two, okay?"

I tell myself I don't know what it could be, but the heat of his gaze makes me a liar. "Sure," I say, turning before he can see anything else on my face.

He walks around the counter and stands beside Rosie, who grins up at him. "I'll take care of you, and make sure you get delivered safe and sound back to Benji. Deal?"

"Safe and sound," he echoes, looking out the windows, undoubtedly searching for threads. He must see none, because he looks back at me. *Calm, Cal. I'm safe and fine. We're okay.* He nods as if he hears.

Rosie puts her arm through his and starts to pull him toward the door. "Oh, before I forget," she says, her hand against the glass. "Those storms coming in? Supposed to be real bad, from what I understand. You may want to consider putting up some plywood against the windows."

"You think the storms will be that strong?" Abe asks.

She shrugs. "Couldn't hurt. Having Dougie do the same up at the diner. I don't think we'll be seeing any out-of-towners this year. Probably would get stuck here if they tried. Roads are supposed to close all over the place."

"No way in or out?" Abe says with a frown. "I don't know why they just don't postpone the festival until next weekend. It's not like it'll do anything for the economy if no one shows."

"I thought the same thing," she agrees. "But you know Walken. A stickler for tradition, that one. Third Saturday in May, just as it's always been. Eh. The town's seen worse, and I'm sure the weather reports are being overblown as it is. We'll survive."

Cal looks agitated and is about to open his mouth—to say what, I don't know. "We'll see you down there," I reassure him. "Maybe I'll even close up a bit early. Probably won't be too many others coming into the station."

The bell rings overhead as Rosie pulls him out the door before he can protest. She says something that makes him chuckle softly, a sound I can hear before the doors shut and they disappear down Poplar Street.

Abe huffs out a laugh before staring at me pointedly.

"What?" I say.

"Boy, if you don't know, then I don't know what to tell you," he says with a smirk. "I just wonder what Cal wants to tell you tonight." He starts walking back toward the office, most likely to pick up the old half-finished crossword book he's been working on since 2006. "I just hope you'll say the right thing back."

I gape after him.

IT HAPPENS sixteen minutes later.

Only a couple of people come into the store after Cal and Rosie leave, grabbing a few last-minute necessities. Soda. Ice. Potato chips. It's twenty past eleven, and I think I'll close up the store. Abe is bent over the counter, trying to figure out what twenty-six down is with a clue for an eight-letter word that means *a certain angel.* He has the first letter *G* and the last letter *N. No wonder he's been working on this book for six years,* I think with a shake of my head as I walk toward the front door, getting ready to switch over the sign to "Closed." "Hey," I call over my shoulder. "Let's head down and—"

A Strange Man stands across Poplar Street, watching me.

He's different than Dark Man and Light Man were. He's completely bald and his white skin is luminous in the weak sunlight that appears from behind a drifting cloud. His face is smooth, and for a moment he reminds me of Nina with her sweetly cherubic face. But the Strange Man is nothing sweet. Although I can't quite place if he actually looks menacing or if it's just the memory of his counterparts that comes roaring to the forefront of my mind. He's dressed in the same dark suit and skinny tie over a white shirt. He looks to be a bit taller than I am, and even with the distance between us I can see his eyes look flat and black, like they're dead.

He's flickering in and out of view, like he's a malfunctioning projection. For a split second he disappears, and then he's there again, on and off, on and off, just like the lights were in the freezer that stored my father's body so long ago. I don't know why my mind makes this connection, but it does and my skin feels instantly clammy. For a moment, I wonder if the Strange Man will suddenly flicker out of existence, only to reappear right next to me, his fingers turning to claws, his face stretching into a horrible shape.

But he doesn't. He continues to flicker in and out and cocks his head, watching me.

Once you catch sight of the Strange Men, Michael whispers in my head, his voice a memory, *you will know I have assisted you and that you should follow.*

Michael's sign.

"Abe," I say, not turning around. "I have to run home for a minute. Do you mind closing the store?"

Silence from behind me. Then he says, "Why do you have to go home?"

The Strange Man holds his hand out in my direction as if silently asking me to take it in mine. "Need to get some plywood to board up the windows just in case." It's easy, this lie.

Footsteps approach from behind me. "What are you looking at?" Abe's voice is hard, as if he doesn't believe a single word coming out of my mouth.

Out of the corner of my eye, I see him follow my gaze across the street to where the Strange Man stands, having not yet moved from the same spot. His eyes do not widen. He doesn't gasp; he does not start to tremble. He looks confused and darts his gaze up and down Poplar Street. He can't see the Strange Man.

"Why are you so pale?" he asks me quietly.

"Worried about the storm," I say. "Don't want anything to happen to the store."

"And that's all?"

"Yes."

He grabs me by the shoulders and forces me to turn and face him. "You're lying," he snaps at me. "What is it? What do you see, boy?"

I close my eyes and take a deep breath. "Nothing," I say. "I told you, I just need to go get some plywood."

"There's some in the back," he says, giving me a little shake.

"Not enough."

"It's Michael, isn't it? It's that bastard Michael. What did he say to you? What did he ask you to do? What did he promise you?"

He told me he would help me find the truth. And I can't tell you because I need to keep you safe. This is not your fight. This is not Cal's fight. This is mine. Stay away, Cal. Stay away.

I open my eyes. "This has nothing to do with Michael, Abe. I'm asking you to trust me on this. I'll be back before you know it."

"At least tell Cal! Have him go with you!"

"*No,*" I say, startled at the anger in my voice. Abe flinches. "Leave him out of this."

"Then I'm coming with you."

"Abe...."

He shakes his head angrily. "You can't lie for shit, boy. You aren't going back to your house. You see something out there, and by God you aren't going wherever you think you're going without me attached to your ass."

"Abe, just listen to me for a second."

"No, *you* listen. The day your daddy died, I got down on my knees and I prayed. I prayed for his soul to rest in peace. I prayed for you and your mom to receive strength. And I made a promise. Do you know what I promised, Benji?"

I don't know, but my heart already hurts.

"I promised him," he says roughly, "that I would do my *damnedest* to watch out for you, to make sure that nothing happened to you. I've let you grieve and I've grieved along with you. I like to think that you are my own because you *are* my own. It'll be a cold day in hell before I let you walk out that door without me, you can bet your ass on that." He stops, glaring at me defiantly.

"I can't risk you getting hurt," I say weakly.

He nods. "And I can't risk you going off on your own. Not when I can go with you. No arguments."

Shit. "Strange Man, across the street."

Now his eyes widen. *Now* he gasps. He looks over again, out the windows. "There's nothing there," he says, sounding confused.

"Oh, he's there. You can trust me on that. Michael told me he would send him."

"To do what?"

I look back at the Strange Man, who cocks his head again, so like a bird. He's flickering even more now, as if my indecision is causing his existence to wane. Michael said he would send me a sign, but he didn't say for how long.

"To do *what*?" Abe asks again, giving me another shake.

"To show me the truth," I whisper as the bald man frowns.

Abe sighs. "And Cal? He needs to know, Benji. He needs to know, because if he doesn't and something happens to you, it's going to destroy him."

"No. I can't risk him. I can't take the chance. He's becoming human, and I can't take the chance." *Stay away, Cal. Stay away. Calm. Hush.*

"Human?" he says as he bows his head. "Oh, Benji... he's becoming human?"

"I can't risk him," I say again. Because I can't. I won't. Once this is done, I will find a way for him to survive and stay with me forever. I will find a way to keep him with me at Little House and the world—be it Griggs or be it angels from On High—will never bother us again. We'll live out the rest of our days as everything passes us by.

"He'll find you. The threads. He'll see."

"Abe."

"What?"

"The Colt .38 Super. In the office lockbox. Get it and the ammo. Quickly. If you're going, we need to move. I don't know how much longer Michael will allow the Strange Man to stay."

He doesn't move.

"Abe. *Now.*"

He hurries to the back office.

Stay away, Cal, I think. *I can't let you get hurt. Stay away.*

The Strange Man begins to smile.

a thousand needles in your eye

WE DRIVE down Poplar Street in the Ford, away from the festival. As we pass the diner, Dougie opens the front door, having finished boarding up the windows. He sees us and waves as we drive past him, a questioning look on his face. He's obviously headed toward the festival, and I hope he gets distracted and doesn't run into Cal to ask where Abe and I are going.

I don't know where we're going. As soon as we hopped into the Ford, the Strange Man disappeared, only to reappear farther down Poplar Street, headed toward home. Or Lost Hill Memorial. Or the Old Forest Highway, which would lead to mile marker seventy-seven. I follow him, and when we get within twenty yards, he vanishes and then returns, farther down the roadway again. Every time he reappears, it looks as if his smile gets a little bit bigger.

"Don't know how much time we'll have now," Abe says as he waves at Dougie. "Cal's going to find out one way or another. You sure about this, Benji?"

Stay away, Cal. "Yes."

We reach the intersection as the Strange Man disappears again. I stop at the stop sign, waiting to see what direction he'll lead us, though I know in my heart where it will be. The cloudy sky has taken on the peculiar orangish-reddish hue of an approaching summer storm. I can see rain falling far off in the distance, probably over in the next county. The rearview mirror shows rain falling on the mountains behind us as well.

"Odd storm," Abe mutters, as if he can hear my thoughts. "Falling all around Roseland but it doesn't look like it's getting any closer."

"Maybe we prayed the rain away."

We look at each other and chuckle quietly, trying not to let our laughter turn into full-blown hysterics. The world has taken on an impossible (improbable) hue, and I barely recognize it anymore. I try to catch my breath, and Abe continues to huff out his laughter next to me, a high-pitched sound like he's almost crying.

I wipe my eyes and pretend the tears are from laughing too hard as I look all three directions we can take. Nothing. Should I go left and head to the stone angel where my father rests? I don't know what going there would solve. There's nothing there I haven't already seen. I don't think there are any clues or mysteries buried with my father.

What about straight ahead? Big House and the house my father built await me there. Could my father have put something inside? Secreted away some journal or evidence that would explain everything completely? My father could have written out a final note to me, telling me he was sorry, he never meant for any of this to happen.

But, of course, that's not how life works. Life is not a series of hopes and dreams cobbled together to make the shapes fit into the pattern, into a design. No, it doesn't work like that at all. The Strange Man appears off to our right, heading toward the Old Forest Highway, toward mile marker seventy-seven, where so many things came to an end and so many things had their beginning.

I'm not surprised.

I turn right and follow the bald Strange Man, who disappears and then flickers back farther down the highway. I almost choke when I see him raise a single hand and waggle his fingers at me like he's waving before he vanishes again.

Abe is staring at me out of the corner of his eyes, a determined look on his face, as if he expects me to stop the Ford and tell him to get out. I consider it, to a point, wondering how I can justify needing to protect Cal but be perfectly willing to put Abe, an old man, right in the middle of harm's way.

"Don't you even think about it," he growls at me. "I have the gun." He shakes it in my direction, his finger near the trigger.

"You wouldn't shoot me," I say, hoping that's true.

"If it meant saving your sorry ass, boy, I wouldn't bet against it."

I EXPECT the Strange Man to stop or even disappear completely as we approach mile marker seventy-seven, so I'm surprised when he continues to disappear and reappear farther down the road, past the mile-marker sign. I slow and think about stopping completely (to do what, I don't know), but the Strange Man beckons me again, this time almost frantically. He glances over his shoulder as if looking for something and then turns and waves to me again. A visible tremor goes through him, and he grimaces as if in pain. His movements become more staccato, his flickering more rapid. With a sideways glance at the river below where my father drowned, I press down on the gas and continue up the road, which rises up a hill into the Cascades.

"Where's he taking us?" Abe asks. "Do you know?"

"No," I say, watching as the Strange Man appears again, this time with his mouth wide open like he's screaming as he bends over, holding his stomach. "Something's wrong with him, though. It's like he's in pain."

"Didn't Cal say they didn't have souls?" Abe asks, squinting ahead as if that'll bring the Strange Man into view. "I didn't think they could feel anything."

I shudder at the memory of fear in their eyes and voices when Cal had opened the black hole back at Lone Hill Memorial. "They can feel things," I say quietly as the Strange Man's mouth stretches wide again before he disappears.

We round an almost blind corner. The Strange Man stands just before the Oakwood Bridge, a steel monstrosity that crosses over the Umpqua River churning angrily some fifty feet below in the gorge. The bridge itself is one lane each way, and a hundred feet long. Cement walkways line either side of the bridge for tourists to stop and take photos, blocked off by metal girders. The roadway is blacktopped, a dotted yellow line running down the center.

The Strange Man is now in the center of the bridge, jerking his arms at his sides. He looks as if he's having a seizure, still upright but shaking violently, snapping his head back and forth. His white skin has started to redden, as if he's heating from the inside. He rocks his head back, opens his mouth wide, and a little tendril of smoke rises from his throat into the air.

Any remnants of the sun have disappeared behind the approaching clouds. Even inside the cab of the truck, the air from outside feels electric, like the storm is ready to break open at any moment and plummet toward the ground. It feels more like dusk than midafternoon. I flip on the headlights and the Strange Man is illuminated briefly before he disappears in an intense flash.

And reappears, stock still, on the other side of the bridge.

He waves. And smiles.

Headlights are coming down the mountain road behind him. They hit him briefly and he is cast in shadow before he disappears. We approach the bridge at the same time. It's another truck.

"Someone coming in for the festival?" Abe asks.

"Maybe." I frown. The truck approaching seems to be a newer model, its headlights a bright blue LED. I can see a bar of the same LED lights across the top of the cab. A metal grill guard wraps around the front. The truck looks black. The windows are tinted, and given that, and the distance between us, and the lights in my eyes, I'm unable to see anyone in the cab.

Suddenly, everything feels wrong as we drive onto the bridge

I look down at the speedometer in the Ford. Thirty-five miles an hour. I glance in the rearview mirror. No one behind us. The Strange Man has not reappeared. *It's all wrong. Cal, it's all wrong.*

Everything goes to hell when the light bar across the top of the approaching truck abruptly flashes on and the truck shoots forward. We're already a quarter of the way across the bridge and I can't go left or right. I have a moment to decide whether to hit the brakes and try to reverse or to plow forward. I press down on the gas. The Ford gives a loud roar and I think about my dad, how he was so proud to find that V8 engine, how he hadn't let the guy screw him over with the price, because that's not how we do it around here. The Ford sounds like it's alive, and it is angry. Big Eddie would have loved that sound.

"Oh my Jesus," Abe breathes, beginning to brace himself for impact as the black truck crosses halfway over the center line, barreling down the road.

"Trust me," I say through gritted teeth as I move over to meet it head-on.

As the trucks race toward each other, an eerie calm befalls me, belying the sweat that drips down my back. I can't hear the wind outside or the scream of the engines. I can't even hear Abe shouting next to me anymore. All I can see is the light, and it is so *blue*, everything is *blue*, and I think of Cal and everything I should have said. I think of everything I should have confessed to him. I open my mind as widely as possible and think *Cal*. I say *Cal*. I scream *Cal*.

I jerk the wheel to the right at the last possible second. It's almost a good plan. It almost works. Everything tells me it should work. But physics is an impossible thing.

The Ford whines as we swerve to the right, the tires squealing along the roadway. The front corners of the vehicles miss colliding by inches. There's a brief moment when everything around me slows down and I look into the driver's window of the black truck and see the vague outline of a person. They seem to be looking at me as we flash by each other, and then they are gone.

Even as I look ahead to correct our path, there's a jarring impact on the driver's side truck bed. The steering wheel jerks in my hands, causing my palms to burn as I struggle to hold on. The bed of the Ford begins to fishtail to the right, toward the cement divider that separates the road from the walkway. This all only takes a second or two, but it goes on forever in my head. *The black truck,* I think. *Must have hit the back. Won't be able to buff that ou—*

The right side of the Ford smashes against the divider, and Abe cries out as he is slammed into the door. There's a moment when all motion seems to stop, but then the world tilts as the truck flips up and over the divider with a metallic shriek. The windshield shatters. I'm upside down in a haze of sparkling glass before I even know what's happening. The world tries to right itself as the truck barrel-rolls into the metal girder. The seat belt snaps harshly against my hips, but all I can see is *stars* and all I can feel is *heat* and all I can see is *blue* because sparks have showered in through the broken windshield, pouring onto my face, like a—

cross your heart hope to die stick a

—thousand needles in my eye.

There's a sickening sense of vertigo as the metal girder splits at the weight and impact of the Ford. The truck starts to slide to the right and catches on something. There's another pause before I hear another metallic moan and the truck slides again, and the back window implodes in on us as the truck begins to tip at a precarious angle.

Then it's almost quiet aside from the ticking of the engine. A tinkling of glass.

I'm confused. I don't know what has happened. I think of angels and wings and rivers. There's a cross too, a cross I hate because it's always covered in feathers and I can't make it stop. I want to sleep. It would be so easy to just sleep. Maybe I should. This is probably just a dream. I dream big. I dream in color. Like my father. Big Eddie is my father. He sleeps under a stone angel in a place with no hills. *Sleep*, the stone angel whispers. *It's okay just to sleep. You'll feel so much better if you do. I'll hold your hand and protect you from everything while you sleep. It is what I was made for. It won't just be for fifteen words that mean nothing. Those fifteen words don't mean a thing. Just sleep.*

I do. I want to. I do. I will. I am falling—

My face feels wet but the moisture is dripping *up* my face. The sensation makes my skin crawl. I open my eyes. I'm upside down, my back resting against the bench seat, held in place by the lap belt. The view out the front of the truck doesn't make sense. It's all broken glass and crumbled cement. The sky where it shouldn't be. Everything opposite. There's a roaring noise in my head and my left eye begins to burn as a bit of blood drips into it. I open my mouth to say, "Hello?" but no sound comes out, just a weak rush of air. Nothing hurts yet, and I wonder at it. I'm bleeding, but there's no pain. Maybe I'm not hurt that bad. Maybe it's not my blood.

My hands are pressed against the roof of the cab. I try to ease myself down, but the seat belt is still latched and it holds me at the waist. I lift my hands from the roof and swing gently in the truck, upside down. The effect is instant. The truck begins to groan and starts rocking slowly, seesawing up and down. Up and down. I quickly reach up and press my hands against the roof again and hold my breath for as long as I can. Eventually the truck stops moving, but not before I feel the truck slide just a *little* bit farther down.

I lick my lips, trying to get them wet. I taste copper. I work my salivary glands, trying to get enough spit in my mouth to swallow. My throat is too dry. It burns. I'm parched. I would do anything for a drink of water. Anything.

There's movement to my left. Or maybe it's my right. I don't know which way is up, so I am pretty sure left and right don't matter anymore. There's a man lying against the roof of the truck, almost against the back, where the window used to be. Two black bands hang down around him. Seat belt. Seat belt is broken. There's cement where the back windshield used to be, jutting into the cab. Maybe it's…

"Abe?" I croak out. Is that Abe? He was in the Ford with me. Before….

He groans and shifts. The truck shifts with him, beginning to rock again.

I don't—

Oh Jesus.

It makes sense. It all makes sense, and it's enough to cause bile to rise. The back of my throat tastes acidic, and I have to fight to keep from vomiting as my stomach clenches and spasms against the clinch of the lap belt. It's so crystal clear, and I wish it wasn't because now all I can hear is the shift of the truck and the distant call of the river below.

The truck has flipped. We're upside down. The bed of the truck has fallen off the side of the bridge and hangs over the river. The rear of the cab has caught on the edge of the bridge, stuck against the cement. It's the only reason we haven't slid off and plummeted to the river below.

Abe groans again and starts to push himself up. He collapses with a gasp of pain, and it's only then can I see a shiny knob of bone sticking out of his arm.

The truck rocks further. Up and down. Up and down.

"Abe," I whisper. "You gotta stay still. Don't move. Please. Just stay there."

"Benji?" He stares at me with bleary eyes. "What… where? My arm hurts, boy."

"I know," I say, my voice cracking. "Just don't move."

CAL! THREAD! SEE MY FUCKING THREAD!

"Where are we? What happened?"

"Truck flipped," I grind out. "I'm stuck."

"Oh. God, it hurts. Let me help you—"

"No!" I shout as he sits up. There's a groan of metal against stone and the truck moves a couple of inches, the back of the cab sliding along the pavement. "Stay there! Bridge! We're on the bridge!"

He freezes, his eyes wide. His vision seems to clear and he looks at our surroundings, and I can see the moment it hits him how precarious our situation is. His face goes even whiter. "Shit," he breathes. "Boy, we've got to get you down from there."

"No. No, the whole thing is going to go over. You gotta climb out, Abe. Get help. I can't... I can't move."

He's incredulous. "I'm not going to leave you in here!"

"Go," I snap at him hoarsely. "Don't you be fucking stupid. Don't you dare!"

He looks up at me miserably. "Phone," he groans. "Where's your phone?"

"I dunno. It was on the seat before we got hit." My hands are starting to hurt, pressing up against the ceiling. My strength is slowly ebbing. I don't know how much longer I can hold myself here.

The wind begins to howl. The truck slips farther.

It won't be much longer now.

He raises his head carefully, looking around. "Don't see it."

Oh God, hear me now. Please. Please send him. I'm sorry for everything I've done. I'm sorry I've kept secrets from him. I need him. If not for me, then at least for my friend. Abe needs your help. He needs it more than I do. Please, oh please, help him.

There's no response, but isn't that the way of things? The decision gnaws at my insides, but I don't care. I can't. This man is my friend. He is my family. I won't let him fall.

"Fuck it!" I snarl at him. "You listen to me. You listening, old man?" He nods, not meeting my eyes. "When you move, you gotta move fast, okay? It's going to hurt like hell, but you gotta roll out. Roll over until you feel the cement on your back. Once you do, you keep fucking rolling, you hear me?"

"But the truck," he whispers. "You...."

Blood drips from my face to the roof. I know where it's coming from now. It feels like my shoulder has been sliced open. The blood is steady, not gushing.

"It doesn't matter," I tell him. "It's either one or both of us, and I'll be damned if I'm going to let you go down with me. You listen to me, okay? You have to go get help. You can't let them get away with this. It's Griggs. It's Walken. It's Traynor. And whoever their boss is. They have killed, Abe. They've killed so many people, and you have to stop them. I can't. Not anymore. You have to—"

Footsteps, crunching glass.

"Hello in the truck!" a voice calls out. Not Cal, but familiar.

"Oh, thank God!" Abe cries out. "Help! Benji's stuck! The whole damn thing's about to go over!"

"Is that so?" a voice drawls, the footsteps getting closer.

"No," I whisper. "No. Not like this."

Jack Traynor crouches under the hood of the Ford, cocking his head to peer in at us. The smile he gives is one of such terrible beauty that I want to scream and fight and rip him to shreds. He reaches up and presses against the truck, and it rocks even further, and he laughs quietly. "You bastard," I whisper. "Oh, you fucking bastard. You did it, didn't you?"

He misunderstands me. "Yeah, thought you guys would go over a lot more quickly. Still a pretty crazy flip you did. Kind of exciting to watch."

"My father," I snarl at him. "You did it!"

He's taken aback a moment, the surprise on his face almost comical. He glances down at Abe, who is glaring up at him. "Ah, son," he says, as he rocks the truck again. "That was before my time, though I do admit to copying the move a little bit. Works better than you'd think. By the time this old beater falls, there won't be many people left for anyone to figure out a single thing. I wonder if it'll explode? Like in the movies." He looks wistful. "But no. No, it wasn't me who done in your dad. Had I been around, I would have done it gladly, but I can't take credit. Seems to me that you just couldn't keep to your own business, could you? Like father, so much like son."

"I'll fucking kill you!"

He smiles again. "No. No, I don't think you will. Should have just left the grown-ups alone, Benji. This whole thing could have been avoided had you just minded your own business. If it's any consolation, it will be quick. I'm sure of it." He says this last as if he's being kind, and a shudder tears through me.

Abe moves then, quicker than I could ever imagine, given his age and injuries. I see a flash of silver in Abe's hand before the gunfire erupts inside the cab, the noise deafening in the enclosed space. A spray of blood erupts from Traynor's right side and he howls as he falls backward, out of sight. Abe's hand is shaking as he raises the gun again, but it's too much for him and it falls to the floor, bouncing out of his reach. He tries to move, but the truck has started to sway again alarmingly.

Traynor curses loudly, and there's a reverberating bang that shakes the truck. "You assholes!" he shouts, and the bang happens again. "You faggots! Oh, fuck, I'm going to *kill* you!" His foot flashes up in my vision, and he gives a vicious kick to the hood of the truck. It rocks up... up... *up*... and then I'm sure it's going to fall with one more kick that doesn't come.

"What the fuck is that?" I hear Traynor say hoarsely over the groan of metal.

Then, above all else, I hear it—the beating of wings.

Cal.

An answering roar comes from above. It is filled with such extraordinary fury that it shreds my heart. I try to call out to him, but I can't find any words, less and less making sense in the garbled mess in my mind. Instead, I scream out to him and let all my anger and fear pour out of me. Only one thought repeats over and over: *He came. He came.*

He came.

He answers my cry with another furious shout and the beat of wings grows louder even as the truck creaks and tips dangerously. The blood continues to drip down my side and face and another wave of nausea rolls over me. My vision narrows and shadows start to dance across my eyes, unconsciousness trying to pull me under, clawing at me, dragging me down. Not thinking, I snap my head back and forth, trying to keep myself awake. Blood sprays in tiny droplets over the ceiling of the cab, which rocks even further. Traynor cries out again, but there is terror in his voice now, not just pain. Abe clutches his arm and gasps as the truck tips up again, causing him to roll further into the cab. The truck tips up again, and it reaches an apex, so much farther up than it was before. I know this is it, this is the moment when the truck will slip off the edge and I will fall into the river, and I will drown just like my father did.

Some part of me recognizes that your life is supposed to flash before your eyes at the moment of your death. Time is supposed to be slow so you remember every little detail about your life in a series of memories—still photos that burst across your mind like a comet in the dark. You see the good. You see the bad. You see the people you've hurt, the people you've loved. Memory explodes like a star and it rushes over you in an overwhelming wave that blocks out all other senses.

This does not happen to me. I do not see my past.

I see my future.

The wings beat again, and a whistling sound cracks through the air, signifying a heavy descent. Traynor screams and kicks his leg up into the air again, but whether a reflex of fear or to kick the truck again, I don't know. Before his foot can make contact with the truck, there's a flash of brilliant blue and the cab shakes as the ground rolls beneath it when the angel Calliel lands on the bridge. He snaps his hand out and grabs Traynor by the ankle before he can connect with the truck again. Traynor's scream is choked off. Cal snarls at him and pulls on his leg, whipping him around and hurtling him in the other direction. I can see Traynor's face for a split second, and his eyes are blown out, his mouth twisted open so wide that he reminds me of the Strange Men. He makes no sound as he flies out of my line of sight, only leaving a brief arc of blood from the wound on his side. I hear him crash down on the other side of the bridge, and I feel a brief moment of remorse that he didn't go over the edge.

But the thought disappears as the truck starts to slide off the edge of the bridge. The grating of metal against the cement behind me is so loud I have no choice but to bring my hands to my ears in an attempt to block it out. The seat belt pulls against my hips as I swing back and forth. I close my eyes. *This is it. So close. This is it.*

But it's not.

The truck shakes as something slams into the top of it. It's jarring, the shockwaves cause my teeth to chatter, and then the truck stops moving. I open my eyes and see Cal standing at the front of the truck, his lower body straining, his wings starting to flicker in and out around him like the bald Strange Man.

"You have to get out!" he yells. "I can't hold it."

"Abe, go!"

He looks scared. "What about—"

"*Go!*"

He does, with one last glance at me. Even though he must be in astonishing pain, his face hardens and he pulls his broken arm up to his chest and moves carefully but quickly through the broken glass, banging his head on the dash and muttering to himself. He makes a play for the gun and snags it around the barrel before he gets clear and rolls out onto the pavement. He turns and holds out his hand.

Fuck, this is going to hurt. But I hear Cal grunting, see him getting pulled closer to the edge as the truck slides. I look back behind me and enough of the rear of the cab has cleared the cement that I can see the river below, rushing so far underneath me it seems a frightening distance. I turn back to Cal in time to see his wings disappear completely.

"Benji!" Abe cries as the truck slides further over the edge.

Knowing there's not much time left, I curl myself up toward the floor of the cab so when the seat belt comes undone, I'll land on my back instead of my neck. The muscles in my stomach howl and burn, and my fingers fumble with the latch. More blood gets in my eye. I can't see. My fingers feel numb as they skitter off on the belt. *I'm going to die here. I don't want to die. I don't want to die. Please just let me—*

I find the latch. I pull the metal tab up and the seat belt releases instantly. Before I can even brace myself, I crash down onto the roof of the cab, the air knocked out of me, slamming my head against the roof. There are stars everywhere for a moment, and they are so fucking *blue* that I just want to follow them into the dark. I almost do, but then I hear him say, "Benji, don't go," and I can't. I can't leave him here alone. Not after all he's done for me. Not after all he's done to get to me. I can't. I won't.

Forcing the stars away, I roll over, glass cutting into my arms as I crawl forward. The truck shifts again, and Cal and Abe both cry out. Abe leans in closer, reaching out his hand for mine. I raise my hand toward his and his fingers graze against mine and—

The truck slips even farther. I glance back and see the cab is caught on the very lip of the bridge. Only another few inches and it will fall. It starts to slide again. "*Benji!*" Cal shouts, the terror in his voice rocking me to my core. I turn back to Abe and push up with my hands and feet, launching myself toward his outstretched hand. We snap wrist to wrist, our skin slick with blood, but his grip is strong and he pulls as my feet scrabble for purchase, slipping against glass and debris. Cal cries out again as the Ford tilts upward and begins to fall off the bridge. The edge of the windowsill clips my left ankle, causing searing pain to shoot through my leg, and then the truck is gone and I'm partially on top of Abe, both of us gasping for air.

Only a few seconds later, there's a crash, a splash of water, and even though it's distant and muffled by the wind, it still grates against my ears.

Then I'm lifted up off the ground and cradled against a broad chest. Cal has fallen to his knees near the edge of the bridge, pulling me tightly against him. He brushes a big, calloused hand against my face, wiping away the dirt and blood and tears. "Are you okay?" he asks me roughly. I can feel him shaking against me. "Oh, please tell me you're okay. Please, Benji."

I reach up to touch his face. "You came," I whisper.

He turns his head to kiss my palm, his stubble scraping against my flesh. "Saw your thread," he says. "Saw Abe's too, but your thread was like the sky exploded. So bright. So blue. I was scared." His voice cracks, but he pushes on. "Didn't think I'd get to you in time." He kisses my hand again, an action so tender I start to shake right along with him.

"I called for you," I breathe. "And you heard me."

"Yes," he says simply.

I tear my eyes away from his. "Abe?"

"I'll be fine, boy," he says. "Takes more than a car crash, a broken arm, and nearly falling off a five-story bridge to keep me down."

I allow myself to chuckle.

Then:

A groan, from the other side of the bridge. Cal begins to growl, his eyes going completely dark, tightening his grip on me. Jack Traynor groans again, unaware of the man holding me in his arms, the man who is still not quite yet a man. A man who has blue lights starting to flash around him, weak but there nonetheless. Cal's jaw twitches as he grinds his teeth. His nostrils are flaring. A vein sticks out on his forehead. He's staring at me, but I don't know if he's really seeing me. I see the faint outlines of his wings as he lowers me back to the ground next to Abe.

"No," I tell him weakly. "You can't." I try to lift myself up to stop him, to grab on to his arm and pull him back to me, to stop him from leaving, but I am so damned tired, and I can't find the strength to move. He touches my face again. "You can't do this," I repeat.

"I will do what I must," he says, his voice a horrifying thing, deep and so unlike the Cal I've known. Gone is the warmth. Gone is the sweetness. This is an angel, vengeful and powerful.

He stands above me, the blue swirling lights growing brighter. His wings begin to flicker in and out. Feathers brush my face. They smell of earth. He takes a step away from me and starts crossing the road. I know Traynor is awake when he starts to scream. The wind picks up, carrying his cries. Each footstep Cal takes makes a resounding boom in the air.

I roll to my side. *No*, I think. *Can't let him do this. Can't let him kill. He'll be damned. He's not meant to harm. He's meant to protect. Oh God, I hurt. I hurt so bad.* "Cal," I call out in a croak. "Don't do this. Please don't do this." I push myself up to my hands and knees.

Calliel doesn't look at me. He's advancing on Traynor, who is trying to scramble away from him, pressing himself up against the concrete divider. He tries to push himself up with his legs to get on the other side of the divider, but he cries out and grabs his side. His shirt is soaked with blood, his eyes wide in fear. He's able to prop himself partway up, leaving a bloody smear on the concrete behind him.

"Abe, we have to…." I glance down at my old friend, but his eyes are unfocused, in shock. Dazed. Confused. I need to get him help. I need help. Cal needs help. *Oh God, Michael, whoever, please hear my prayer. Please let Cal hear me. Let him listen.*

"You," Cal says, his voice like thunder, "tried to take from me what is rightfully mine. You dared to touch my wards. My Abraham Dufree. My Benjamin Green." My name from his lips sounds like an earthquake. "Your heart is filled with malice and hate. You are a blight on the skin of this world, and I will do it a favor by removing you from it. I *am* the judge. I *am* the jury. And on this day, I will be *your* executioner."

"No," I moan. "Cal. You can't do this." *Get up, Benji. Get up. Get up.*

Traynor cries out again when Calliel reaches him. Cal bends over and wraps his right hand around Traynor's neck and lifts him into the air. Traynor starts to choke, kicking out his legs, battering them against Cal's sides and thighs, trying to break Cal's grip on him, beating against his arm. The blue lights blaze again brightly, Cal's wings appearing, disappearing, reappearing in rapid succession.

I sit back on my knees. I'm still dazed. I force my mind to clear. I zero in on the hand around Traynor's throat, drops of my blood dripping down his hand and onto Traynor's skin. I force myself to my feet, trying to keep weight off my ankle. "Cal!" I scream. "Don't! Don't do this. You're more than this!"

But he doesn't hear me. The lights are starting to swirl in a circle off to his right, little blue flashes breaking off from his body and wings and starting to spin in a vortex. Cal takes a giant step over the divider, dragging Traynor along with him. Traynor kicks and punches Cal viciously, but the angel does not lessen his grip. Traynor only stops when the black hole takes shape next to him, and then he freezes, a strangled cry coming from his lips.

Cal lifts Traynor up and over the railing until he is hanging in empty space, the river below him flowing wildly. Traynor starts to flail again, his legs kicking nothing but air as he tries to get back onto the railing.

"No!" I shout. Stronger, louder. I've hobbled halfway across the road, trying to keep off my sore ankle. "Cal! Look at me. You turn and look at me, goddammit!"

"You have a choice," Cal snarls, "which is better than you ever tried to give mine. You may die now in this river and suffer the wrath of hell, or you may go into the black. Make your choice, human, before I make it for you."

Traynor's eyes are bulging from their sockets. I don't know if he can even answer, given the stranglehold Cal has on him.

"Calliel!" I shout. "Look at me!"

"No answer?" Cal roars, shaking Traynor violently. "Then I will decide for you! You have been tried and found guilty of your sins. The punishment is the black. You are not worthy of the soul you carry, and within the darkness you will have it ripped from you and you will be *nothing*."

Forgetting my ankle, I run the last few steps as Cal begins to twist, bringing Traynor up and over the railing again to send him into the black hole that is swiftly spinning, the blue lights surrounding it almost too bright to look at. I vault over the divider, standing between Traynor and the black just as Cal begins to thrust him toward it. Traynor smashes into me, knocking me backward, and I'm falling. I'm falling, and I can feel blackness against my skin. I can feel its caress. It tells me it's okay, I can follow it into the dark and it will care for me. It will touch me. It will *love* me. I'll float forever, just like I was on a river. Doesn't that sound nice? Doesn't that sound lovely? No more worries, the black croons. No more cares. No more—

wake up, benji

—wondering about what could have been or what would be. It will give me truth, it promises. I will have all I desire, all that I've ever asked for, here in the dark. I just have to say yes. I open my mouth and I think maybe I *will* say yes, because I'm tired, and it's so much easier to—

wake up, son

—close my eyes because the *blue* is fading, it's going away, it's become nothing, and how can I be sure it was even really there to begin with? How do I know this isn't all just some dream? Angels can't be real. I don't love him because he doesn't exist. And even if he *is* real, he would never love one such as me. I've never known love because I've never—

it's time for you to stand

—had family to care for me. Everything is *black*, all I have is *black*, all I know is *black* and black is despair and anguish and grief and I've let it *bury* me. I've let it *bury* me until it's all I can feel, it's all I can breathe. It's—

time for you to stand and be true wake wake wake

—too much, it's too late, it's not going to matter. I've lost. I'm here in the dark and nothing else will matter because it's—

Blue. There is so much blue.

And then the black is gone, and I take a deep gasping breath and my body hurts again. My face feels tacky with blood. I open my eyes. Traynor is on the ground, trying to crawl away. Cal stands before me, looking horrified, holding onto my arm with one strong hand. The blue lights are gone. His wings are gone. The black hole is gone.

"You almost went through," he says hoarsely. "You almost went into the black."

"You are *not* the executioner," I tell him harshly, my skin prickling at the thoughts the black put in my mind. "Do you hear me?"

"But he—"

"I don't give a fuck!" I shout at him. "You do not kill!"

"I must protect," he whispers, looking down at his hand on my arm. "I am a guardian."

"And you did that," I say, trying to keep the memory of his black eyes at bay. Regardless of what he's becoming, there was nothing human about them.

He gives me an uncertain smile and takes a step toward me.

Jack Traynor rises behind him. It's a swift movement for a man shot in the side. He pulls a wicked knife from a sheath in his right boot. His face is twisted into an angry snarl, sweat and blood drenching his skin. I have no time to shout as he raises the knife above his head. I have no time to move as he brings it down toward the back of Cal's neck, the blade gleaming dully. I can do nothing as I look on.

Except there's a loud bang, and the side of Traynor's skull seems to part, his furious expression melting. He jerks to the right and flips over the railing, disappearing from sight. The knife clatters to the ground. The sound of the gunshot echoes down the valley before it too is gone. Then there's only the sound of the wind and the river below.

"Bastard," Abe says, lowering the gun. "You guys okay?" He looks so tired.

I nod, unable to speak. Cal is looking down at the knife on the ground, the knife that should be buried in his spine. He touches it with his boot and then kicks it off the edge of the bridge.

"Think maybe we need to see Doc Heward," Abe mutters. "Maybe even head on in to the hospital." He points down the road toward town. Traynor's truck is parked on the road. "Think he left the keys in there?"

"Maybe," I say, almost disbelieving what has just happened. "You shot him!"

"Yeah."

"In the head!"

"Yeah."

"Holy fuck!"

Abe rolls his eyes. "Wasn't going to let him get the drop on Cal, all right?"

"But...."

"You're welcome, Benji."

I nod, unsure how to ask when my best friend learned to shoot like a gunslinger.

Then, a sound above the river.

A car is coming up the road, from town. Headlights shine through the trees that shake in the wind. "Cal, who is it?"

He shakes his head as he frowns. "Can't tell. Can't see a thread. Benji, it's... different now. I don't feel the same. Something has... changed."

He's almost human.

I touch his hand. "Can you see mine?"

The frown disappears. "So blue," he sighs. "Like it was made for me. Yes. It's still there. I think it will always be."

Oh God.

He helps me over the divider, and we stand next to Abe. He's starting to turn a little gray, and I'm worried. Hopefully whoever is in the car has a phone, because I don't know where mine is. Probably with the Ford in the river. The car winds up the road, goes around that last corner, and slows when the driver sees the black truck on the side of the road. Not a car, though. An SUV that looks familiar....

"Oh thank Christ," I breathe.

"Who is it?" Abe asks.

"My Aunt Christie." I raise my hand and wave at her, and she speeds up, heading toward us, flashing her lights. "She'll have her phone. We can call Doc Heward and see if he can get a helicopter to take Abe to the hospital."

"No need to make that big of a fuss," Abe sniffs, though he sways when he says it. I put my arm around my friend, and he sags slightly against me, putting his head on my shoulder. I kiss his wrinkled forehead, and he huffs quietly to himself. I can tell he's pleased.

Christie screeches to a halt in front of us and flies out of the front seat, leaving the door open. "What the hell is going on?" she asks, her face white. "Oh my Jesus, are you okay?" She rushes over to us and cups my face. "What happened?"

"There was an accident," I say.

Abe snorts from his place on my shoulder. "That's one way to look at it."

Christie looks confused. "What happened?" she repeats.

"A man named Jack Traynor tried to kill us," Abe says. "Would have, too, if it hadn't been for Cal, here."

She glances up at Cal then looks around. "Where is this Traynor?"

"Dead," I say with contempt. "Bottom of the river. That's his truck right over there. How'd you know we were up here?"

"Dougie," she says, distracted. "He saw you guys tearing off down the street, wanted to know where you were headed in such a hurry."

I nod. "We gotta get some help for Abe. He's got a broken arm."

"And Benji's cut up pretty bad," Abe says. "Don't let him tell you otherwise." He shakes against me. "Take this," he mutters, shoving the gun at Christie. "I don't want to see it again." She widens her eyes, but wraps her hands around the grip and holds it at her side.

"What about you?" she asks Cal. "Why aren't you hurt?"

"Just got lucky, I guess," he says with a shrug.

She frowns. "You came up with Benji and Abe? Dougie said he didn't see you in the Ford."

"He was there," I say, sounding snappish. "Christie, we need to get going. Can you call Doc Heward? We need a Life Flight waiting for us when we get back into town. If he can't get one because of the storm, then you'll need to drive us over to Glide to the hospital." She nods and goes back to her SUV.

My gaze follows Cal as he walks back over to the space where the Ford fell through. He stands near the edge of the bridge, looking down into the water. His shoulders slump, and it's odd that I already know what he's thinking. Abe turns with me as I move to face him.

"It's not your fault," I say, that twinge in my chest so fucking loud and strong I think my heart is going to burst. *Holy fuck. I really do love him. Shit.*

He shakes his head miserably. "If only I'd gotten here sooner…."

"You got here in plenty of time," I say with a snort. "*We're* okay."

"But the truck!" he says as he turns back to us. "It was so *cherry.*" He sounds so forlorn I almost laugh at the absurdity of it.

"The *truck?*" I say, trying to scowl. "*That's* what you're worried about? You sure know how to make a guy feel appreciated."

A small smile forms on his face.

Love, I think again in unfathomable wonder as it starts to rain.

The first bullet strikes him high in the chest, near his right shoulder. A look of confusion dawns on his face as he takes a step back. The red blossoms quickly against his white T-shirt, and I think of roses.

I hear the unmistakable cock of a hunting rifle expelling a shell.

The second bullet clips the side of his head, really no more than a graze, but the blood that arcs from it is plentiful as his head rocks back. He takes another step back, his heels skittering along the edge of the bridge.

The rifle is cocked again.

The third and final bullet is a gut punch, and I can hear him exhale heavily, his hands going to his stomach, blood spilling out over his fingers. He looks at me, and I can see the surprise on his face underneath all that pain. He's never looked more human. No blue lights. No wings.

It feels like he teeters on the edge of the bridge forever. The blood from his head wound drips down his face and into his stubble, and it looks like he's wearing a mask of smeared red. It feels like forever we stand there.

But forever does not occur, no matter how hard I wish it so.

His gaze meets mine, and under the pain, under the shock and anguish, I see something just for me, something Michael first mentioned what seems like years ago. Out of everything I see and feel—my brain scrambling to process the horror before me, my feet finally starting to move, the hoarse scream that tears from my throat—what I see in him shatters everything I've known.

Love. He loves me back.

But I'm not quick enough.

He closes his eyes and turns his face to the sky. Thunder rumbles in the distance.

He trembles once. Takes a breath.

And slips off the edge of the bridge.

There's no sound as he falls. No shout. No cry. No groan. Nothing. One moment he's there, and the next he's not. I trip over the rubble from the crumbled divider and fall forward, sliding on rock and dust. I almost sail right over the edge. I catch myself on a rebar, the steel tearing the flesh of my palm. My head hangs over the edge of the bridge. I force my eyes open.

There's nothing but the river below, moving as it always has.

"No," I say. "That's not...."

I will always be with you, he'd said to me once.

"No." Something begins to rise within me, a terrible anger. "No." It rolls over me in waves, and I can't stay afloat. "No." Rage and fury, amassing as one.

Nothing comes up from the river below. It's raining harder now.

I lift myself up from the ground. There's a roaring in my ears.

I turn.

Sheriff George Griggs stands beside an open rear door on Christie's SUV, a rifle in his hands, pointed at me. He must have been hiding in the back. He moves carefully around the door, then closes it behind him with a gentle *thunk*. He sees me watching him and winks. He cocks the rifle again.

"No," Christie says. "Not him. Not yet."

"You sure about that, boss?" Griggs asks her, smiling at me. "One shot and he's down. Wanted the big guy to feel his."

Boss?

"Not until we find out who else he's told. What else he knows. No more loose ends. Not now. We can't take the risk. I already had to get rid of Dougie."

Griggs snorts. "Dougie was a fucking dumbass, anyways."

Christie frowns. "He was just in the wrong place at the wrong time."

Boss. No. No.

"You bitch," I mutter. "Oh, you fucking *bitch*."

"I don't expect you to understand, Benji," she says almost regretfully. "Some things happen just because they have to."

I charge at her. A crack of gunfire and a divot appears in the pavement two feet in front of me. I stop.

"Not so fast, Benji," Griggs says. "She might be the boss, but if you take one more fucking step, the next bullet is going into Abe's head. His old brains will be all over the ground before you can even think your next thought."

I gag, clutching at my stomach. My vision narrows as my blood boils. My eyes feel lazy as they shift out of focus.

And it is here, in this moment, in this impossible (*improbable,* my father whispers, *it's all so improbable*) moment, that I fall to my knees. The ground beneath me is solid, but that roaring in my ears is like swiftly moving water, and I lay my hands against the pavement. They get wet and the ground rolls beneath me. The rain splashes fat drops onto my skin. I try to clear my head, but it's a losing battle and I can't breathe, I can't move. And as darkness clouds my vision, I am overtaken by a river.

And it is into this river I drown.

look away

I AM at the river. It's raining. I stand on the road. It's the same. It's all the same.

Except it's not. The rain is falling harder than it ever has before. Lightning flashes overhead. Thunder cracks like—

gunfire oh my god shot he's shot he's shot and

—God is angry, rolling through the hills, causing the trees to shudder down to their roots. This is different. Things are not the same.

I slide down the embankment. I can feel the mud on my clothes. On my skin. Could I feel that before? I'm drenched. Did I get this wet before? I don't know. I can't remember. This may be the first time. It may be the last time. I don't—

The world lights up an electric blue as lightning touches down on the other side of the river. Then there is a cross, a white cross, bigger than any I've seen before. It stretches to the sky and screams *HERE LIES BIG EDDIE! BIG MOTHERFUCKING EDDIE LIES HERE BECAUSE HE'S* DEAD, *HE'S NOTHING BUT* BONES *AND* DUST *AND HE WILL* NEVER *BE ANYTHING MORE EVER AGAIN!*

"Help me," I tell the rain, the river. I turn my face toward the sky and water falls on my tongue. It tastes like earth. "Help me. I'm haunted."

Another flash of blue (Blue?) light and the cross is gone, but the ground, the river, the earth, the entire *world,* is covered in large feathers. They're a deep blue, almost black, but they are all covered with splashes of blood and the red is so *bright* it stings my eyes and I cry out because I know—

he's gone dead shot dead fell bitch whore

—what it means, I know the red is truth and the blue feathers will be nothing more than memory. Even as I think this, the feathers begin to melt, leaving behind droplets of blood that mix with the rain and reflect the menacing sky above.

Things change further. There's a whine of an engine up on the road. I turn, but I can't see the road from my position. There's a crash of metal against metal, a breaking of glass, and it sounds so familiar that mile marker seventy-seven disappears around me and I'm—

stuck upside down in the Ford and am I still in there? Is this all just a dream? I hit my head, maybe. Maybe nothing that followed is real and we're still in the truck and that's why I can hear the crashing in the dream because it just happened to me and Cal is still okay. He's still fine and I can stop him from dying. I can stop him from getting shot and leaving me. I can end this now. I

—look up as there is an even greater collision, and a red truck flies over the embankment, almost all the way to the river. It smashes into the ground and clips a boulder. The truck flips and lands in the middle of the river, its back end angled up toward the sky. Lightning arcs again, and the rain falls. Brakes squeal from up on the road and a shadowy figure appears, staring down at the truck in the water. I can't make out who it is. I can't tell if it's a man or a woman. They stand in the rain, barely moving until they reach into their coat and pull out a small object. It lights up and is put to the figure's ear. The voice is garbled, as if coming from underwater, and I still can't tell the sex of the voice. It says, "It's done. He never made it out of the county."

I'm in the river. The water is cold. I'm drenched. My teeth chatter uncontrollably. The truck groans against the current. I look back. The dark figure is gone. Time has passed, though I don't know how much. I don't know if it matters. I take another step, and the river mud sticks to my feet, sucking them down. A thought runs through my head—

cal's gone he won't be able to pull me out of the river

—but it hurts too much to think, so I push it away as I submerge myself under the water.

The silt and grit feel harsh against my open eyes. The truck is vaguely outlined in the river. I push up from the riverbed and kick harshly. I'm propelled toward the truck. I expect to see my father's—

dead

—arm hanging out the blown-out window, but the window is empty. There is no blue feather. I swim closer. The current is strong.

Just float, the river whispers. *You could stay here and float forever.*

But I can't. Not yet. I have to see my father's face.

I get closer. I touch the truck. Do I need to go up for air? My lungs don't hurt. My chest doesn't burn. I'm not choking. I'm okay.

You don't need to go up for air, the river says. *Just open your mouth and inhale down here. It's easy to breathe underwater. All it takes is that one... first... breath.*

It's trying to trick me. It's trying to mess with my head. I can't let it.

I pull myself along the edge of the truck. I swim as close to the riverbed as I can to look inside through the busted window on the door. I reach the door and grab it, anchoring myself to the truck. I'm pressed against the river bottom and the weeds tickle my stomach, the rocks scrape against my skin. I look inside the truck.

It's pitch black. Like darkness has fallen inside the cab and nowhere else.

But don't I hear voices? Yes. Yes, I do. They are muffled. I can't make them out. I need to hear them, because the cadence, the *timbre*, to the voices sounds familiar. It causes me to ache because I know who they are now.

I close my eyes, and pull myself into the truck underneath the river.

Into the black.

This is what I hear in the dark:

"Am I already dead?" my father asks.

A response, strong and kind. "Almost. You're almost there." Cal. The angel Calliel.

"*Dad!*" I try to scream.

He doesn't hear me. "Will it hurt?" There's fear in his voice.

Calliel doesn't hesitate. "No, Edward, Big Eddie that was. It will be like going to sleep."

"What if I don't want to sleep?"

"There is an order to things. A design. A pattern."

"*Fuck* your design!" Big Eddie cries. "I don't want to go!"

"I know," Calliel says, his voice shaking. Something's wrong. "And I wish it wasn't this way. But I was given a test. I had no choice. I'm sorry."

"Why?"

"Because my Father wants me to prove my faith in him." His voice cracks.

"I'm a father too," Big Eddie whispers. "Do you know my son?"

"I know. Benji. He's… wonderful." Cal sighs.

"He's the greatest thing to happen to me. You can't take me from him. You just can't. He is my *son*. There's so much more I have to teach him!"

"It is not up to me. I can't…."

"You could," my father argues. "If you really wanted to. You could."

"It's not the way of things, Big Eddie."

"Why?" my father asks, his voice getting weaker. "Why must we suffer? Why must we hurt?" His words are like an echo, and I think *Michael*.

There's a pause. Then, "How else can you truly have faith?" Cal doesn't sound like he believes his own words. They sound like recitation. "How else could we know how to love unless it's gone?"

"Can you save me?"

"No. Not in the way you're thinking."

"He'll ask questions. He's my son. He's smart. He won't let this go. He could get hurt. He could *die*."

"I know," Cal says roughly. "I don't want that to happen, either."

"You have to protect him. If you are who you say you are, if you're a guardian angel, if you've been watching us all this time, then I'm asking you. No, I'm *begging* you. Do your duty. Guard him. Protect him with everything you can. Never take your eyes off him and let no harm come to him. Do you promise me?"

Hesitation. "Big Eddie, I—"

"*Promise me!*" Big Eddie roars in the dark. "*You fucking promise me! This is my son! You fucking promise me!*"

A beat of time. I float in the black water. Then a whisper: "I promise."

"I won't cross," Big Eddie swears. "Not yet. Not while there's still a chance he could get hurt. He'll need me."

"You *can't* wait," Calliel says, sounding horrified. "You have to cross, Edward! If you don't, you might be stuck in limbo forever."

"I don't care. As long as my son is safe, my *family* is safe, I don't care."

I hear the defeat in Cal's voice. "There may come a time when you *will* care, Big Eddie, and I don't know if there will be time to save you."

My father's quiet as he says, "It doesn't matter, angel. I still have a job to do, and so do you, now. You promised me."

"Yes," Calliel whispers. "I know. I...."

"What?"

"I've watched you. For a long time. You, while you were young. You and your son. Benji. You know he believes the sun sets and rises with you, right? That you hung the moon and the stars for all the world to see?"

My father sobs quietly. "I know. I know. Don't you think I know that? Ah, God. I can't leave him. I just can't. How can God want this? How could he think this was ever right?"

"I promise," Cal says, his voice stronger, "that I will do everything I can for Benji. I promise you he will know peace again. It will take time, but one day, he'll look to the sky and the sun will rise above the horizon and warm his face. He will know peace. I promise you."

"Why? Why would you do this? Why did you promise me?"

"Because I love him," the angel Calliel says. "As I love you. You are all mine to cherish. And I have cherished you for so long. All of you."

"Angel?"

"Yes, Big Eddie?"

"I'm tired." And he is. I can hear it. It's like knives embedded in my skin.

"It's time to sleep, Edward Benjamin Green. If you will not cross, you will need your strength. I can't say what will happen to you, but if you stand, if you can stand and be true, then there may be hope for us all."

"I'm...." He sighs.

"What?"

"I'm scared. Will you... will you stay with me? Until the end?"

"Until the very end. You've led a beautiful life filled with love and honor. Remember that, as it will warm you like fire and help keep the river away."

"Will you tell him? Will you tell Benji I love him?"

A shuddering breath. "He knows. Oh, Edward, how he knows. But yes. Of course, yes. I will remind him every day. It may just be a touch, but he'll know."

Silence. Then:

"Your feathers. They're...."

"Yes."

"They are so... blue... and...." His voice trails off and doesn't return.

"Good night, Big Eddie," Cal says with a catch in his voice. "I will not forget my promise. Sleep and go with the grace of my Father. May you find peace, old friend."

And in this dark, in this river, I open my mouth to scream. Water floods in and down my throat and I can't breathe, I can't take a breath, and I'm drowning, drowning, and I—

I OPEN my eyes.

And groan as pain washes over me in rolling waves. My entire body aches like I'm covered in bruises from head to toe. My face is sticky and my ankle is on fire. My limbs are screaming at me. I try to stretch them out, but I can't move very far, and my shoulder feels like it's been sliced open. And a smell. Holy shit, that *smell*, like cat piss and ammonia all mixed into one. It stings my nostrils, burns my eyes. I cough as I try to take a breath around the gag in my mouth. The cough burns my chest. Sprung rib? What the hell? What the fuck is going—

Something wet drips on my forehead. I open my eyes again.

It's dark, though there must be a light somewhere because it's not pitch black. I'm lying on my side on a floor. It feels like rough carpet beneath me. My clothes are soaked to the skin, my hair wet and plastered against my forehead. I try to push myself up, but my arms are restrained behind my back. My legs are tied together. I wiggle my fingers and feel hard, thick plastic. It takes me a moment to realize what it is.

Zip ties. The sheriff's department made a big deal about them when they arrived, saying they were less chafing than metal handcuffs and easier to put on whoever was being arrested. The backs of my hands are pressed together, fingers pointed out. My hands feel like they're going numb.

Griggs.

Boss, he called her.

Christie.

Everything hits at once. I cry out against the gag in my mouth, banging my head on the floor, trying to make myself sleep again, trying to knock the thoughts out of my head. Cal's eyes on mine, the surprise, the horror. The pain. The love. Oh, *God*, so much love there, and how could I have never seen it before? How could I not have realized?

And then he fell….

Griggs. I'm going to kill him. I'm going to rip his bones from his body, and once it's done, I'll go to the river and float away. I ache with the thought of it.

A muffled voice growls at my right.

My eyes are adjusting to the weak light emanating from somewhere. It's not so much a room I'm in as it's a shack. The walls and ceiling are dilapidated and leaking water. Rain thunders down on the roof, and a peel of thunder rumbles through the air, causing the shack to quiver on its foundations.

There's a small camping lantern set on a card table pressed up against the far corner of the room. Two dark light bulbs swing overhead. Piled against the wall near the table are a dozen black trash bags, stuffed full, straining the plastic. One has split open and lies on the floor, spilling out its contents. Empty antifreeze bottles. Empty brake fluid containers. Plastic bottles with holes cut through the top.

If what your father told me is correct, Corwin whispers in my head, *then they could be supplying methamphetamines up and down the West Coast.*

But this looks small-time. Dirty bathtub bullshit in this dirty fucking shack. It smells awful in here, the stench almost making me gag, a mixture of fumes from the discarded bottles. If they are making meth in here, it couldn't have been a lot, not the size Corwin was talking about. What the fuck did my dad know?

Another muffled growl.

I crane my head to the left.

Abe has his back against the wall, his arms tied behind him, a sharp jut of bone sticking out of his forearm, tearing his flesh. He's completely gray, sweat pouring off his skin. The cloth wrapped around his mouth and neck looks soaked. Our gazes lock, and his eyes are filled with such relief I can see him trying to smile around the gag. The smile falters as a tremor rolls through him, and he tilts his head back against the wall, his face twisting into a grimace against the pain.

I cry out around the gag, my anger almost overwhelming. How could they want to hurt him? All he wants to do is live out the remainder of his days in this goddamned fucked-up little town. All he wants is to make up problems with his car so he can come and sit and chat with me all day. All he wants is to one day close his eyes, only to open them and see his beloved Estelle looking back at him. He never wanted this. He never asked for this. It's my fault as much as it is theirs.

The archangel Michael warned me—*you may get the answers you desire. But remember this: sometimes the past is better left alone.*

But I didn't leave it alone. I couldn't.

I kick my feet and hop/roll over to Abe. By the time I reach him, my wrists are rubbed raw from the cuffs and my whole body is a bundle of exposed nerves, but it doesn't matter. If we're going to die in this fucking pit, then we'll face them together.

I rest my head on his outstretched legs for a moment to gather my strength and he makes a soothing sound at the back of his throat, as if he's trying to calm me. A sob bursts from my throat, and it's all I can do to keep from curling up in a ball and waiting for the end. Abe makes the noise again and twitches his leg a little bit. I know he's trying to let me know he's here with me, I'm not alone. He doesn't know that makes it worse. This is my fault.

I lift myself off his lap, jerking myself up despite the sharp flare of pain. I rest my back against the shack wall, brushing my shoulder against Abe's. I turn my head to look at him. He tries to smile again. I almost break, but not quite. Not yet.

I close my eyes and lean my head against the wall. Abe lays his head on my shoulder and we sit there, in the squalid dark, water dripping down on us, the storm raging outside. I try to turn my mind off, but I can't. I think of my mother and wonder if she knows of her sister's betrayal. What about the rest of the Trio? Nina, surely not, but what about Mary?

I think of Joshua Corwin, special agent with the FBI, now resting in the ground, a hole in the back of his head, his body ravaged to hide his identity.

I think of Estelle, a woman I barely remember but know I love, if only because she loved Abe with her whole heart.

I think of Rosie, sitting in her diner, a mischievous smile on her face.

Doc Heward in his office, squeezing a stress ball with the name of an anti-inflammatory medication on the side.

Jimmy Lotem, from the hardware store, and his poor mother with cancer.

Eloise Watkins and her long Friday cigarettes.

Pastor Thomas Landeros, his hand on my back as a coffin is lowered to the ground.

A stone angel, silent but always watching.

The archangel Michael, his secretive smile, his Strange Men.

Big Eddie. Big Motherfucking Eddie. My father. The man I will worship for the rest of my life, no matter how short that might be.

Abraham Dufree, my best friend. The way the skin around his eyes crinkles deeply when he smiles and laughs.

And Calliel. I think of the guardian angel Calliel. His dark eyes. His bright smile. His red hair. The freckles on his nose and shoulders. The way he held me. The way he kissed me. The way he loved me. The sunrises. The dreams he saved me from, even if he was just trying to save me from the truth. The way he protected me. The way he guarded me. The blue lights. His massive wings.

I take in a deep breath and wonder, like my father, if the end will hurt. It's almost comforting to know even my father had fears, that he wasn't perfect. He might have been the tallest, he might have been the fastest, and he might have been the greatest man alive, but he was still a man.

The door to the shack suddenly bangs open, letting in a cool blast of air that knocks back the stink of the room. There's another flash of lightning, followed by a quick rolling blast of thunder. The storm has to be on top of us now.

Griggs is first into the room, his sheriff's uniform soaked, even with the heavy coat he wears. He sees us staring at him, and he smiles, opening his coat to reveal the hunting rifle. He walks farther into the shack.

And then she follows him in. My aunt. Christie, one-third of the Trio. My mother's sister. The *boss*. Her eyes are flat, her mouth a thin line, water dripping down her face, smearing her makeup, making her appear ghoulish. She catches me looking at her and reaches up to wipe her eyes. Her mascara smears, and it looks like she's now wearing a black mask that trails down her cheeks. "Both awake, I see," she says.

"We need to do this now and get it done and over with," Griggs snaps. "Teddy and Horatio will be back with the truck in a couple hours. We need to finish packing up the rest of the site before they return."

"We have some time, George," my aunt says. "I doubt they'll be able to return in this storm as it is. I told them to call when they were heading back, but I also told them to stay and start setting up the new site if it looks to be too much to travel in this storm. Of all the days for it to rain." She sighs, showing just how inconvenient this weather is for her.

Griggs snorts. "Fucking rain. You'd think God was out to get us."

I'm cold, and it has nothing to do with how wet I am.

Christie walks over to the table and turns the lantern up to its highest setting, chasing away some shadows and creating new ones. The light illuminates a switch on the wall. She flips it, and the two light bulbs overhead burst into life. The light is almost blinding. Stark. "You need to call in the bridge," she tells Griggs. "Let them know that a concerned citizen called you, saying that it looks like an accident has occurred. Your deputies will be too busy with the town to do anything about it now, but at least it'll look like the accident happened when the storm hit. It'll make things easier later, when they find the Ford."

"Yeah, yeah. I was already going to do it," the sheriff grumbles. "Don't need you fucking harping on my back. Christ."

"George," Christie snaps. "Shut your fucking mouth and do what I tell you without complaint. I'm getting sick of your attitude. I'd hate for you to be a situation that needed to be rectified."

I'm shocked when Griggs looks contrite—cowed, even. He mutters something under his breath, but then he nods and moves toward the door again, squeezing the radio on his shoulder. "Dispatch, come in." He lowers his voice, and I can't hear the rest of the conversation aside from an occasional screech of static.

Christie pulls out her cell phone and flips it open, presses the call button, and puts it to her ear. "Walken," she says after a moment. "They're here. No. No. Traynor's dead." She glances over at Abe and me. "I'm surprised, too, but he always was a little sociopath. We're better off in the long run without him. No. Yes. Cal Blue is dead. No one could survive that fall."

My anger rises again, as does my heartache. It's like poison traveling through my body, and I allow myself to settle in it. It feels like fire.

Christie turns and continues to talk on the phone. As soon as her back is turned, Abe raises his head off my shoulder and nudges me sharply. I look at him and his eyes are narrowed. He nods down at the space between us. I widen my eyes slightly and shrug. I don't know what he wants. He makes sure my gaze is on his, then very pointedly looks down between us. I glance back at Christie, who is arguing softly into the phone. Griggs is still preoccupied with the radio. I look down between us.

Clutched in his left hand is a pocketknife, the blade closed. Estelle's gift from so very, very long ago, somehow missed by Griggs and Christie.

I love you, my husband. Forever, Este.

I nod. Not much time.

I move as close to him as I can get, keeping my eyes on Griggs and Christie. They're still distracted. Abe grips one side of the knife, pointing the closed blade at me. I move my arms behind me toward him, ignoring the pain that snarls in my shoulder. My fingers brush against the metal. I extend my thumb and forefinger and—

Christie turns to look at us, frowning. I glare at her, staying still. She turns back to the phone, saying, "I don't *care* what you think—" and I grasp the blade between my fingers. My fingers are wet and the blade slips before I can get a good grip on it. I grab it again. Slip. My hands are starting to sweat, and we don't have fucking *time* for this and—

"She's *what*?" Christie snarls. "Fucking Lola! Dougie didn't talk to her before I got to him, did he? Shit. Fine, put her on the phone."

I stare at her, the knife all but forgotten. Perversely, she turns to me and brings her finger to her lips, winking at me as she shushes me.

"Lola!" she says into the phone. "I'm fine, love. Don't worry. No. No, I forgot something up at Big House and drove back to get it, and by the time I got here, it started raining cats and dogs!"

I shout against the gag, the sound muffled but still carrying in the small room. My aunt narrows her eyes and pulls my gun out of her coat pocket. She says, "Hold on a moment," into the phone and puts it against her shoulder as she takes five large steps over to where we sit against the wall. I only have a moment to brace myself, but it's not enough, and galaxies of stars explode across my vision as she smashes the gun against the side of my head. The pain is so overwhelming and bright I'm unable to make a sound. Through the haze, I hear Abe spitting around his own gag, trying to put himself in front of me. My vision clears momentarily, and she pushes Abe back against the wall, pressing the barrel of the Colt against his forehead. Her words, however, are for me.

"Make another sound," she hisses, "and I'll put a bullet in his head right now. We clear?"

I nod, feeling fresh blood trickle down my neck.

She puts the phone back to her ear. "Sorry, sister. No, it was just the TV, the volume got loud suddenly. Must have been from the storm. What?" She frowns down at me as she lowers the gun, taking a step back. "Benji? I haven't seen him. The station's closed? No, he's not here. Are you sure he's just not over in the Shriner's Grange? I can't see Little House clearly through the rain, but I don't think his truck is there. No. Abe and Cal too? I'm sure they're fine, honey. I'm sure of it. If they are all gone, then that must mean they're all together. They'll be okay." She smiles at me as she says, "Anyway, Cal is such a big guy. He won't let anything happen to them, I just know it."

Bitch, I say with my eyes. *I'll kill you. I'll fucking rip your head off.*

"Just stay in the church with the town until the storm passes, okay? I'll stay here at Big House where it's nice and dry. Call me when the rain lets up and I'll meet you. If they're not back by then, we can go looking together, but I promise you they're fine. Don't worry so much. Okay. Okay. Love you too." She sighs and disconnects the call. She stares down at her phone for a moment. She shakes her head and slips it back in her pocket.

She looks over at us and brushes her hands over her face. I'm pressed tightly against Abe and hope she can't see between us. Abe has pressed the edge of the pocketknife into my hand again, and I'm pulling at the blade with my fingers after having stretched them to the point of pain to dry them on my shirt. My head is pounding but I'm trying to push through it to focus on the knife.

Griggs comes back. "Done," he says. "Called it in. They'll check it when the storm lets up. According to the weather report, the front slowed and now it's just sitting over Roseland. They don't expect it to clear up for hours. We have time before anyone finds the truck."

Christie looks moderately relieved. "All that remain are a few loose ends," she says. "This day can't be over soon enough."

He shrugs at her, and I see something in his eyes that turns my stomach. It's almost like adoration. It's cemented when he leans over and kisses her on the lips. She starts at this, as if it's unexpected. She pulls away, but not before I see the small smile on her face. She steps away from him and the smile melts away into a sharp look. Griggs doesn't look contrite in the slightest.

I pull on the blade of the knife, but the handle slips partially from Abe's grip. I look over at him, and his eyes are drooping, his head bobbing. I elbow him sharply and he snaps his head up, his pallor graying further. I don't know how much blood he's lost, or how much pain he's in, but given the fact that a bone is sticking out of his arm, I'm surprised he's stayed conscious this long. He turns to me, eyes slightly out of focus, but he nods and I feel him tighten his grip on the knife handle. I start to pull on the blade again, pinching it as tightly as I can, and it starts to open and this will work, this will work and—

Christie turns and walks over to us. We both freeze. She has a determined look on her face, a cold calculation in her eyes that I've never seen before. I think she's seen the knife and she's going to take it from us, but she reaches down instead and pulls the gag from my mouth, letting it rest around my neck. My jaw aches as I open and close it. I glare up at her as I run my tongue over the back of my teeth, trying to get the taste of dirt out of my mouth. Griggs pulls up a chair from the table and sets it behind her. She sits, crossing her legs, her shins only inches away from my face.

"Now," she says carefully, "we're going to have a talk, you and I. I will ask you questions, you will answer the specific questions, and that will be that. Are we clear?"

"Fuck you," I snarl at her, trying to grab the blade of the knife again.

She sighs as if she's dealing with a petulant child. "Benji, this can go very easy for the both of you. Or it can be very difficult. The choice is yours."

"Did you do it? Did you kill him?"

She looks taken aback. "You were there, Benji. Did it look like I had a rifle in my hand?" She frowns. "How hard did you hit your head?"

"My father!" I shout at her. "Did you kill my father!"

Something crosses her face then—a shadow, a stutter. Her eyes go wide and she purses her lips like she's trying to think up something to say, *anything* to say. Finally, "It was an accident, Benji. You know that. He lost control and went into the river."

I'm quaking. "You're lying."

"Am I?"

"Yes. I know you had something to do with it. You knew he was going to meet with Corwin. You knew he'd found you out, or at least about the drugs. You knew he was going to turn you in. Did he know? Did he know about you specifically?" The knife begins to open again.

She suddenly leans forward, grabbing my face in a single hand, squeezing my jaw harshly. She brings her face close to mine. I don't look away. "This," she says, a sneer on her lips, "is why you're here now, Benji. You don't know when to stop."

"And I won't stop. Not now. Not now, you fucking bitch."

"George," she snaps, not taking her eyes off of mine.

He steps forward without hesitation, and I have no time to brace myself against the butt of the rifle smashing into my stomach. The world grays around me and all the air is expelled from my body. My throat feels constricted, and I can't catch my breath. Vaguely, on the outskirts of my consciousness, I hear Abe yelling against his gag, but his protestations seem unimportant. I think I'm about to pass out, but then I'm finally able to suck in a thin breath that burns my lungs. My face is wet with rain water and sweat, and tears threaten to follow, but I won't allow them. I won't allow myself to show weakness. Not here. Not in front of them. I take in another breath, gasping in the air.

"This could be quite simple, Benji," my aunt says again. "I will ask the questions, you answer them. Then we see what happens from there."

"Fuck you."

She shakes her head. "So like Big Eddie. Stubborn until the very end. Who besides Special Agent Corwin did you talk to? You're not wearing a wire, I already checked. But that doesn't mean you haven't spoken to anyone else. Who else is there?"

Going from my father to Corwin to wires confuses me. "What?"

She speaks slowly as if I'm dumb. "Who besides Special Agent Corwin did you talk to?"

I think about lying. I think about telling her I spoke with the whole goddamned FBI and that they're about to bust in this place and take her down, but I don't want to take the risk. If they'll hit me, they'll hit Abe. I can't see him hurt any more than he already is. So I answer her truthfully. "No one," I mutter.

She stares at me for a moment. Then, "You're lying."

I'm insistent. "No, I'm not!"

"Who else have you told?"

"Nobody. Corwin was the only one I talked to!"

"George," she says.

The rifle slams into my stomach. I lean over and gag, a thin stream of spit hanging from my mouth. It feels like my eyes are bulging out of my head, and my body feels like a bundle of exposed nerves. I put my forehead against the ground and through the fireworks in my head, I think, *Please.* I pray, *please. Please God, Michael, whoever. Please. If not me, then please help Abe get out of here. Just make them stop. Please. Cal. Cal, please don't be dead, please see my thread. God, please. Dad. Oh, Dad, I'm sorry. I'm so sorry, but it* hurts. *Oh my God, I* hurt. *Please let it be quick. If not for me, then for Abe. If we go, let it be quick for him.*

The fireworks go off in my head again, all exploding in shades of such *blue* I almost cry out. The rain drips through the walls and down from the ceiling onto the burning skin of my neck and it's one drop, then two, then three, and I count all the way to seven before I stop. There's no answer. No one hears my prayer. No one is coming. We are alone. We've always been alone.

I sit back up with a groan.

"You know," my aunt says, "I'm rather upset that it's come to this, Benji." There is something akin to sadness in her voice, and for an impossible moment, I almost believe it. "When we started this little… endeavor, I never thought it would come to this. But I guess like all things, choices had to be made. To take on something such as this, you have to be prepared to make sacrifices."

"Why?" I gasp out, trying to buy more time, my aching hands scrabbling against the knife in Abe's grip.

"Why?" she repeats.

"Why this? Why all of this?"

She laughs. "Benji, this isn't going to be like some movie, where the villain gives a whole speech at the end about the hows and the whys. There's no extraordinary meaning behind any of this. It's simple really; I grew up poor. I didn't want to be poor anymore. Meth is cheap to manufacture, easy to distribute, easy to collect on."

I turn my head pointedly to look around the shack. "This? How can you make any money making it in here? It's not big enough!"

She glances around, almost fondly. "This is where we started," she says. "When we didn't know what we were doing. We had some junkie chemist in here who we'd promised all the crystal he could smoke if he showed us how to make it. He was a strange man, but good at what he did. Money was tight at first, but the more we made, the more we sold. We watched his process as closely as we could, figured out we didn't need the junkie anymore." She smiled sadly. "He overdosed in a shitty apartment outside of Bandon. All the crystal he could smoke and he smoked it all at once. Such a terrible tragedy."

The blade catches in my fingers again, but it slips. It isn't working. My hands are covered in sweat and blood and water. I can't get a good enough grip on it to pull it out. I don't think there's enough strength in my numb fingers to pull it out anyway. The zip ties are cutting into my flesh, cutting off the blood flow. I'm about to give up when I get another idea. Fuck, it's going to hurt, but it's the only option left.

"It still doesn't explain how you could make meth in this little space," I point out.

"Jesus, boy," Griggs snaps. "What the fuck is it to you?"

"Curiosity," I say, pinching the blade once more with two fingers. As soon as I feel it start to pull up, I slide, I curl my hand and fingers up toward my wrist, and slide the tip of the knife down through my knuckles to the webbing between the two fingers. It doesn't cut, not yet. I grit my teeth, gathering my resolve.

"Curiosity killed the cat," the sheriff singsongs.

"And satisfaction brought him back," I growl.

"Caves," my aunt says.

"What?"

"The cave system is quite extensive," she says. "Back up in the hills right behind this little shack. It's almost shocking how far they go into the mountains. How wide they get. How underground they are, perfect for hiding from any normal satellite imaging used by law enforcement. Little shafts that open up from the ground, perfect for ventilation. And since they're a part of the incorporated township, it means this area is not regulated by the Bureau of Land Management, and the caves have never been recognized as part of a national park. Which means the local government has control of the caves. It also helps when there's a certain member of the forestry service capable of being bought and told to look the other way. Especially when there are funds to do so, seeing as how a certain mayor likes to skim off the top and got caught by our illustrious sheriff here. Blackmail is a wonderful thing when used correctly, Benji. Don't let anyone tell you otherwise."

My head is spinning. But still my resolve is growing as the knife begins to cut into my flesh. One quick jerk upward, one solid movement. Yes, it's going to hurt as it slices into my hand, but it'll catch on the bone and the knife will snap open. I can do this. I can do this. Pain is nothing in the face of death. Cal felt pain. My father felt pain. I can feel pain. I can do this. It's not over. It's not over yet.

"So you blackmailed the mayor to be involved in this?" I say, gritting my teeth against the sting.

Christie rolls her eyes as the sheriff snorts. "He became a willing participant once he saw the financial aspect of it," she says. "That man has dollar signs for eyes."

"And you and Griggs? Why did you do this with him? When did you start all of this?"

She looks amused. "Benji, life doesn't provide all the little answers just because you ask for them. I would have thought you'd have learned that by now."

"What about—"

"Enough," she interrupts. "No more wasting time. Who else is there?"

Almost ready. I can do this. I can do this. Have to keep my face schooled. I cannot show anything, not even a grimace. Can't give myself away. "No one," I say. "You've killed everyone else."

"What did you tell Corwin?"

I look her in the eye. "That I knew Big Eddie had been murdered. That I knew he wasn't going to Eugene to meet with friends." *Do it. Just do it. The pain will only be for a second. It'll cut deep but you'll have a chance. Hit the bone and pull up.*

I steal a glance at Abe. He must see something in my eyes because he gives me an almost imperceptible nod. He tightens his grip on the knife.

"Who else?" she asks again.

"No one."

"Benji, I'm getting tired of this. Who else?"

I start to panic. "No one!" I say again. "What'd Corwin tell you?"

She looks at me coldly. "By the end? Everything. Traynor probably went a bit overboard with his fingers." She grimaces at the memory. "But he was pretty convincing that he hadn't told his superiors yet."

"And no one else has come to Roseland asking after him," I snap at her. "So there is no one else."

"George?"

"He's lying," Griggs snarls. "If he didn't say anything, that big fucker did."

Now. Now. Now. I brace myself for the pain and am about to jerk my arms up to open the knife when Christie says, "Maybe we need to go about this a different way. Get the old man." She stands and pushes her chair back

Abe starts to tremble. His hand slips and he drops the knife, the blade closing on the soft flesh between my fingers, cutting through and closing. It falls to the floor. I make a grab for it and close my hand around it just as Griggs grabs Abe by the collar and pulls him up. Abe cries out at the movement, the pain in his arm no doubt excruciating.

"You leave him alone," I cry, my voice cracking. "Don't you touch him!"

"Then tell us what we want to know."

"I told you! There's no one else!"

Griggs rips off Abe's gag and drops him on the ground on his stomach in front of me, his hands bound behind his back. Abe grunts at the impact and turns his cheek so he's facing me. There's a moment, as we watch each other, when a myriad of emotions flicker across his face. There is fear and anger. Pain and trepidation. But then they are all swept away as his eyes harden and his jaw sets. The Abe I see now is the Abe I know. The strong one, the one who has stood by my side and by my father's before me. He's….

No.

"Leave him alone!"

Christie hands Griggs my Colt. He sets down his rifle on the chair and pulls out the clip before pushing it back home. He then drops to his knees and presses the barrel against Abe's left temple.

The knife. I have to open the knife. The back of my hands are pressed together. I grip the knife between two fingers on my left hand and attempt to grab the blade by pinching it with the knuckles on my right hand.

"Who else?" Christie demands.

"No one," I grind out, the knife slipping again.

Griggs digs the gun into the side of Abe's head. "Who did you talk to?" he snaps.

"There's no one else!" I shout, holding the knife steady again.

"Look away," Abe says, his voice calm. "Look away, Benji."

"You hush," I say hoarsely. "Please. Please just let him go. There's no one else. I swear. I would tell you if there was. I swear." My knuckles catch the blade, and I pull. It doesn't open.

"You're lying," Christie says, taking a step back. "You want to watch him die in front of you?"

"Benji," Abe says. "Look away."

"Please. Oh, God, please. Please believe me. I wouldn't lie. I can't lie. Christie, you *know* me. Please. You don't want to do this. I'll do anything you want." I pull on the knife again, and it opens.

"Who else knows?" Griggs snarls. "The ATF? The DEA? Your mom? Nina? Mary?"

Christie's eyes grow dark at the mention of her sisters, but she doesn't stop him.

"No," I croak. "How could I tell them what I don't know? Take me instead. Please."

"Benji," Abe says softly. "Listen to me."

I look at him as my eyes start to burn.

"They won't believe you, no matter what you say," he says steadily. "It doesn't matter. Not anymore. They're too far gone to pull back now."

Michael! God! You fuckers! Help me!

"Don't hurt him," I whisper. "You just can't." I pull the knife all the way open and hold the handle between my fingers. I curl my hand up until I feel the blade poke against my wrist. I twist it until it touches the plastic of the zip tie.

"Benji, look away," Abe says. "Don't watch. Look away."

"Tell us what we want to know!" Griggs shouts, digging the gun into Abe's head again. "I'll kill him right now if you don't fucking tell us!"

"Please," I try again. "I didn't. I swear it. Please."

Christie sighs. "I think he's telling the truth."

"The fuck he is," Griggs snaps. "He's just like his fucking father."

"Benji," Abe says. "It'll be okay. You know why?"

I shake my head, tears falling on my cheeks. I turn the knife until the blade is flat against my wrist and slide it up between my skin and the plastic. I cut myself, and blood trickles down my wrist.

"It'll be okay, because I'll see *her* again. My life. My love. My Estelle. I love you, boy, but I'm tired. I think I have been for a while. I'm ready to go home. I know I promised you, but it'll be okay."

"No," I moan. "You can't leave. You can't leave me here alone."

"Last chance," Griggs says.

"You are *never* alone," Abe says. "Your father has always been with you. And you know Cal has always been with you. Always. When I see that boy of yours, I'll tell him you'll see him soon. And when you're ready, we'll be waiting with open arms."

"Who. Did. You. Tell," Griggs says quietly.

Nothing I can say to Griggs matters, so I say the only thing that *does* matter. "I love you, old man."

"I know," Abe says with a strong smile. "Look away, Benji. For me. Please. Close your eyes and look away."

The knife falls to the ground behind me. I look away as my chest heaves.

"George, wait," my aunt says, sounding unsure.

"No," Griggs says. "This ends now."

"I'm coming, Este," Abraham Dufree says with relief in his voice. "I'm coming home. I've missed you, Lord knows I have. Our Father, who art in heaven—"

"George, *don't*—"

"—hallowed be thy name—"

"I'm done fucking around!"

"—*thy kingdom come*—"

I squeeze my eyes shut and scream.

"—*THY WILL BE DONE*—"

The gunshot is flat in the shack. It does not echo above the rain.

memories like knives

ON THE third day after my father's death, I awoke from a difficult sleep. I felt groggy, my eyes gummy and stuck together. I groaned out loud. I was thirsty. My stomach rumbled. My mouth was sour. And then everything hit me at once.

He's gone.

The thought was like an explosion in the dark, and I gagged, just once, only then remembering being sedated three times in the last three days—each time I'd awoken, screaming. Ranting. Raving. I had tried to hurt my mother. She'd sat next to my bed the first day, and I'd opened my eyes and tried to launch myself at her, convinced everything that had happened was her fault. It wasn't intentional. It wasn't rational. I was lost under a wave of black, and I didn't know what I was doing. All I knew was that *she* had been the one to tell me; therefore *she* had been the one to make it so.

So when I opened my eyes on that third day, I tried to keep all my emotions in check. I didn't want to sleep again. I didn't want to float in the black. I wanted to feel the pain, I wanted it to burn. I wanted to feel grief squeezing tightly around my heart, because that was the only way I would know it was real. Being in the black was confusing. It was deceptive. It was easy. If I stayed there for too long, I'd never want to come back.

"Easy there," a voice said. That voice I knew.

I turned my head to the right. I was in my room at Big House. In my bed. My back was sore. I was sweaty. I needed a shower. I needed to stretch my arms and legs. I needed get out from under the comforter.

"You need to just breathe," Abe said, as if he could read my thoughts. He sat in a chair next to the bed, watching me with sad eyes. There was no one else in the room.

"Water," I croaked out. "Thirsty. Please."

He nodded and lifted himself up from the chair and moved out of sight. I heard the faucet in the bathroom a moment later. Only then did I allow a tear to fall from my eye. It tracked its way over the bridge of my nose and fell to the pillow. I thought, for a moment, about asking to be put back to sleep, for Doc Heward to come back and give me another injection so I could go back into the dark and float. I pushed this thought away as the fog from the drugs began to clear from my head. *Too easy*, I thought. *It'd be too easy.*

I saw a flash of blue out of the corner of my eye, bright and warm. I looked, but there was nothing there. I thought it an aftereffect of the sedative.

Abe came back and helped me sit up in my bed. He handed me the cup of water and then sat back in the chair with a sigh.

"Where is she?" I asked finally, the silence too loud.

He didn't have to ask who. "With the Trio," he said quietly. "Christie told me they're thinking about staying here. For a while, at least. To help with Lola. And you."

"I don't need to be taken care of," I snapped. "Neither does she. Not by them. I can do it. We don't need help."

His words were pointed, but kind. "Benji, you haven't been in a position to help anyone these last few days."

I said nothing. He was right, of course. I looked away. I hurt all over, a pain that seemed to be buried deep into my bones.

"Has the funeral happened yet?" I asked gruffly.

"Of course not. Lola would never do that without you. You have to be there."

"He's still...." I couldn't finish.

Abe knew what I was asking. "Yes. He's still at the morgue. They had... they had to make sure there was nothing wrong with Big Eddie. Do you understand?"

Yes. Yes, I did. They had to make sure there was nothing wrong with him so they cut him open and dug around on his insides. They desecrated the body of my father in search of the truth. Had it been Doc Heward? No, I thought not. It would have been the medical examiner, the one who'd been out of town on the day I saw my father in that freezer. I nodded at Abe and asked him what they found, because they *would* have found something. There *would* be something there, because the only way my father would leave me would be if he was forced to. This was not going to be something as cosmically simple as an accident. He didn't slide off the road because the pavement was wet. He didn't swerve to miss a deer. No. To rid this earth of my father would take something darker than that. A conspiracy to take him away. They would find something, because Big Eddie was too big to go out because of something as mundane as a car accident. He could not die because of something so artless.

"What did they find?" I asked Abe.

He shook his head. "They haven't said yet. It takes some time for the tests to be done. Tox screens, blood work. They'll want to make sure there were no drugs or alcohol in his system at the time of the accident."

Stop saying accident, you old bastard. It wasn't an accident. "Big Eddie wasn't like that," I said sharply. "He would never have been so stupid."

"I know, Benji. It's routine. They have to check. To make sure."

I have to go to Eugene. Meet up with some friends. I'll be back in the afternoon.

"He told me he'd come back," I mumbled as I started to shrink back in on myself. "He said he'd come back."

"I know he did, boy. Big Eddie was a man of his word too. I'm sure he would have come back just as soon as he could have."

We were silent, for a time. Then, "Did I hurt her?" I asked in a small voice.

Abe sighed and grabbed my hand. His old skin felt soft against mine. "No. Scared her, yes. But hurt her? No. You didn't touch her, though it wasn't for a lack of trying. Doc Heward is a lot quicker than he looks, I'll give him that."

There was no recrimination in his voice, but I still needed him to understand. "I wasn't... I didn't want to hurt her," I said. "She... she was the one... I just can't stop thinking that she took him from me."

"But she didn't," he said. "Lola had nothing to do with it. She's in just as much pain as you are, Benji, and she's going to need you as much as you need her."

He was right, of course, but still I was stubborn. "She has the Trio," I said bitterly.

"As do you, but it's not going to be the same. The Trio will love you and will hold you, but they can't ever understand completely what you and your mom are going through."

It hit me then, the grief, and I felt awful. "But you can, can't you. You know. You know as much as we do."

He looked down at his hands. "This is such a shitstorm," he said quietly.

I snorted. Truer words had never been spoken.

He didn't look up at me when he spoke. "I know it's going to be hard, boy. Lord knows I do. People will tell you pretty words about how Big Eddie is at peace now. That he's with God and all the glory of heaven is shining down on him. They'll say you should remember the good things about his life because it will help you find some measure of solace. Maybe they're right. Maybe that's the right way to go about it. Maybe that's exactly what you need to do. Think about how wonderful your father was, how much he loved you. How much you loved him. Maybe that can carry you through the darkest hour. Maybe it will be enough."

My breath hitched in my chest.

"But you know what? It may *not* be enough. You will be angry. You will be sad. You will think the world is crashing down around your ears and there is nothing you can do to stop it. After... after my wife died, I was lost. I was lost for such a long time. Estelle was *everything* to me, and I didn't know what to do without her. There were times I would forget she was dead and I would turn to tell her something, only to have to remember it all over again. And each time I had to remember, it was just as crushing as when she first died. People told me their pretty words, gave me their sympathy, but I didn't want to hear it. They didn't understand that she was *mine* and she was *gone*."

I began to weep.

"And then one day, Big Eddie came by and told me he just wanted to sit with me on the porch, and that if I wanted to talk, he'd be there. Otherwise, we could just sit. And that's what he did. Day after day. Always on his break from the store. Forty minutes. Every. Day. And we didn't talk, most of the time. We just sat and let the world go by, and I was okay with that.

"But eventually, I couldn't take the silence anymore and began to talk, and I told him everything I was scared of. I told him everything I missed about her. I told him she was the most wonderful woman to have ever existed and how every day in the time I knew her, I still couldn't believe she'd chosen me above everyone else. I didn't have money. I wasn't the most handsome. I wasn't the funniest, or the classiest. But she still chose me, and *I didn't know why*. And do you know what Big Eddie said, Benji? Do you know what he told me?"

I covered my face with my hands as I cried.

"He told me memories are like ghosts, that they will haunt you if you let them. He said it's okay to be haunted for a time, because it's the only way a person can grieve properly. 'But you can't let yourself drown in them, Abe,' he said. 'There is going to come a time when ghosts are all you're going to know, and it may be too difficult to find your way back.'"

Abe got up from the chair and put his hands on my shoulders. "So you grieve, Benji. Lord knows you're entitled to. How could you not? Big Eddie was the greatest man I've ever had the pleasure of knowing. I have no qualms in saying that he was like a son to me. Hell, he *was* my son. And I hurt because of that. I hurt because he was my son. And your mother hurts because she was his wife. This whole town *hurts*. But you? Benji, *you* hurt because you lost your *father*. Big Eddie might have meant much to all of us, but it's going to be hardest for you. He was more than just a father to you, I know. He was your friend. I don't think I've seen a boy love his daddy as much as you loved him, and the same was true in reverse. So if there is ever a doubt in your heart, you remember this: Big Eddie loved you. He loved you, boy, because you were his. So you grieve. You grieve and let the poison out, and you *remember* him. But you cannot forget that memories are like ghosts, and they will *drown* you if you let them. That's not what Big Eddie would have wanted from you. *For* you."

I grabbed at him blindly, feeling the bones under his thin frame. "You'll help me?" I gasped at him. "Please say you'll help me. I can't do this on my own."

He put his chin on my forehead and held me close. "You have my word," he said quietly. "I've got you, boy. I've got you."

THEY leave after he's shot Abe in the head, Christie almost looking horrified, Griggs snapping at her and waving the gun in my direction. The sound of the gun cut off my voice, and I find I can no longer speak, or even make a single noise. My breath whistles in my throat as Griggs snarls at Christie to let him go, that he was just doing what she was no longer capable of. Did she want them to go to jail? Did she want this whole operation to get completely fucked over? She doesn't have time to answer—her phone rings, a sharp sound completely out of place in the horror that is this shack.

"Hello? You're on your way *back*? How close are you? Shit. You should have just waited until after the goddamn storm had passed! It's too late now. Just get here as quickly as you can." She hangs up the phone and tells Griggs they need to finish in the caves. "Leave him here," she says without looking at me. "We'll deal with him later."

Griggs glances back at me and then follows her out into the storm, switching off the light as he goes. The naked bulbs overhead go out, and the only light that remains is from the lantern on the table near the door.

I slide from the wall and lie on the ground, as much on my back as my bound hands will allow.

I don't think I can process what has just happened. My old friend lies on the ground, mere feet from me. He's on his stomach, his head still turned, facing me. Eyes closed, mouth slack enough to show slightly yellowed teeth. Were it not for the circular wound on his temple dribbling a small amount of blood and the fact that his arms are still secured behind his back and his legs tied together, it'd look like he is just sleeping. An awkward position, to be sure, but he could just be sleeping.

Sleep sounds good right now. I wonder what would happen if I closed my eyes. I'm tired. I think I might be done. Cal's gone. Abe's gone. Big Eddie's long gone. Everything I touch gets taken from me. Everyone I love dies. It's only a matter of time for my mother. Mary. Nina. Christie, though she's not the same in my mind anymore. Everyone I love will be gone, and I'll still be here, in this shack in the middle of the forest during a black storm that will cause the river below to rage. Michael said we're all tested, that this is how we find our faith. How else could we know love unless it was taken from us? I know love. I don't need it to be taken from me to know it. I know faith. I don't need it to be tested in order to understand it. God and his games are beyond me now. I can't even find the desire to pray, not that it would be heard.

Memories like ghosts. Memories like knives.

But I'm tired. So very tired. I feel my strength leaving me, and I wonder if I'm going into shock. It wouldn't be surprising. Things have happened that are very shocking. I laugh quietly at this, my punch-drunk mind finding humor in the wordplay. The ceiling above me looks like it'll give way any minute. Maybe the river will rise all the way up past the banks until I'm submerged in its murky waters. It'd be so easy to drown. I don't want to see the ceiling anymore. I don't want to see Abe's sleeping face anymore. I just want to close my eyes.

So I do. It's dark. I tilt my face toward the ceiling.

My father sings: "Sometimes I float along the river—"

I sing: "For to its surface I am bound."

My father sings: "And there are times stones done fill my pockets, oh Lord—"

I sing: "And it's into this river I drown."

And as soon as I sing the last word, a drop of water falls from the ceiling and lands directly on my tongue. It slides to the back of my throat, leaving a trail of water in its—

wake up

—wake. It doesn't taste like rain. It doesn't taste like rust from sliding along the roof of the shack. It tastes like—

wake up wake up

—the river, like the river from my dreams, the river where my father drowned, the river where Cal's body lies. It tastes like sorrow and skin. Anger and bones. It tastes like everything I've ever wanted to say to those who are gone. It tastes like *I love you*. It tastes like *I miss you*. It tastes like *I am so angry you're gone.* It tastes like—

up benji wake up cal wake wake

—regret. It tastes like knowing you can never go home again.

But most of all, it tastes like strength.

"Wake up!" a voice shouts in the shack. It's deep, that voice. It's familiar. It's loud. It's angry. It's here with me, but I can't. I just can't. I don't want to wake up. I don't want to open my eyes. "Wake up!" my father roars, right next to my ear. It's unexpected, and I jerk awake, my eyes flashing open, sure I will see—

my dad father big motherfucking eddie

—someone standing above me, sure I am no longer alone and that memories, like ghosts, have risen, have become corporeal.

But he's not.

There's no one there.

I shift on the floor, frantically looking around for the owner of the voice, even though I know who it is. Even as I twist my head, a sharp pain cuts into my finger. I gasp at the suddenness of it, piercing through all my other aches in body and mind. I roll onto my stomach, away from the wall, trying to see what I cut myself on.

Estelle's gift to her husband lies on the ground against the wall.

"Wake up," I say. "I gotta wake up."

Yes, boy, Abe whispers in my mind. *You gotta wake up, because* sometimes, *all we want to do is to jump into that river and drown. It's easy. It's relief. It's the warm embrace of death. But it's also selfish. It's selfish and solves nothing, and that is not who you are. So you wake up.*

I don't want to die here. I can't die here. I have to tell people what I know. I have to tell the world what has happened. If not for my father, then for Cal, who only wanted to protect what was his. For Abe, who deserved more than to die on the dirty floor in a derelict shack in the middle of the woods. They deserve more, and only I can give that to them. Then I can sleep. Then I can float on the river's current and drift away.

Like ghosts, my father says.

Like knives.

I lie back on my side and count to three before I jerk myself up and onto my ass, using my legs as leverage against the floor. My ankle screams at me, but I ignore it. The pain is nothing. It's nothing compared to everything else.

Then I'm up and take a moment to catch my breath. The air inside the shack is stifling and hot, the little cracks in the walls not enough to ventilate the inside. Another splash of water lands on my head and trickles down my face. The rain thunders on the metal roof, and it sounds like a rushing river.

I press my back up against the wall and scrabble for the open pocketknife. My fingers brush the blade, and I follow it back until I reach the handle. I twist it up in my fingers until the blade is pointed up. My fingers are sticky with blood, sweat, and grime. I can't let it slip. Not now. I don't know how much time I have, but it can't be much.

I press the blade flat against my wrist and slide it up against my skin until it's under the plastic zip tie. It cuts into the already sliced flesh and I grit my teeth. This is nothing. The pain is negligible, I tell myself. I've been through worse. I'm going through worse. The searing of the knife into my flesh? This is nothing.

But the pain grows as I twist the knife, until the edge of the knife is pressed against my wrist, the sharper edge against the plastic of the zip tie. Blood drips down my fingers. I close my eyes and try to visualize my hands behind me. Instead of focusing on the damage I'm doing to my wrist, I focus on what I have to do to make this work. I grip the handle of the knife tightly with my knuckles.

A sound, above the rain. A low rumble. Lights roll up through the shack, flashing through the metal slats. The sound of tires on gravel. The harsh squeal of brakes.

A truck, a large one by the sound of it.

Not much time, I tell myself. *Not much time at all. You going to do this?*

I am.

I grip the knife as tightly as I can. Taking a deep breath, I lift my knuckles up and down, trying to press it as hard as I can into the plastic and away from my flesh, but it's not far enough. Each sawing motion nicks my wrist again and again, the point of the blade stabbing into my arm. Blood flows more heavily. I grit my teeth and press up again. The sting of tearing flesh causes my eyes to water. I don't even know if this is working. I don't even know if Estelle's gift is cutting into the plastic at all. Maybe the knife is too dull. Maybe the plastic is too strong. Maybe the only thing I'm doing is cutting my wrist. It's not going to work. It's not going to—

The zip tie gives a little. The sawing motion is becoming harder to do because the knife is cutting into the plastic. The pressure around my right wrist lessens slightly. It's working. I saw up again and tears stream down my face as my wrist is sliced again. More blood drops onto my fingers and gets onto the handle of the knife. The zip tie gives further. Blood flows onto my knuckles and the knife cuts deeper and I think it's about to—

The knife tumbles from my grip and lands on the floor. I reach for it and close my hands around the handle. Dirt from the floor mixes with the blood on my hands. I try to grip the knife, to twist it again, but I can't get a good hold on it. I drop it and try to rub my hands against the back of my jeans, the back of my shirt. I can't get them clean, not enough so I can hold onto the knife again.

The door to the shack rattles. I freeze, waiting for someone to open it. It doesn't. Just the wind. It's just the wind.

The zip tie has been cut, though not completely. I try pulling my wrists apart. The pain causes my vision to gray, but there is some give, the plastic seeming to stretch. I put my wrists back together. My hands are soaked in blood. I don't know how badly I've cut myself. Abe still sleeps in front of me, but he's not asleep. Not really. My vision tunnels again and I bang my head against the wall behind me, thunder covering up the rattling of the metal. I hit my head again. And again. And again. New pain shoots through the fog. I'm awake. I'm alive. I'm not asleep. I'm not in the river.

I close my eyes as my arms tremble. And knowing what will happen if this doesn't work, I take in a deep breath and jerk my arms apart as hard as I can, with all of the strength I have left. The strain against my arms is incredible, and the muscles burn and start to cramp. I tilt my head back until it hits the wall. I grit my teeth and pull harder, the zip ties cutting into my skin even further. My head feels like it will explode, like my eyes are bulging from the sockets. Just when I think I can't take the pressure any longer, I reach down deep within me and find the last reserves I have left and give just a little bit more.

The band around my right hand breaks.

I bring my hands to my lap, crying out softly at the tingling of blood circulating again through my arms, like a deep vibration. I hold my injured wrist to my chest and rock back and forth, hitting my head against the wall behind me. I think this might be a dream and it isn't the zip tie that has snapped, but my mind. This can't be real, that I'm still tied up and sitting in this dirty place.

I open my eyes.

I'm free from the tie, though the skin on my right forearm looks shredded. The blood isn't gushing as much as it's oozing, so I probably didn't cut as deep as it felt like. I grab the knife and use it to cut off a strip of my shirt. I tie the strip around my wrist carefully, slipping the ends through and into a knot. I pull one end with my teeth and the other with my good hand. The pain is excruciating, and my eyes water. The cloth is not enough to completely stanch the flow of blood, but it has to be enough. For now.

I cut the ties around my legs and then close the knife and put it in my pocket. I stand shakily, my legs and feet still slightly numb. I move slowly around Abe, not wanting to hurt him any further (*because he's sleeping*, I tell myself). I reach the door to the shack and peer through the cracks in the slats. It's still daylight out, though the light is very weak, hidden behind the black clouds. The rain is still pouring as hard as I've ever seen it. The fresh air through the slats is the best thing I've ever smelled. I inhale as deeply as I can, but it's too much and I start to cough. This hurts my chest, and I wonder if I've cracked a rib or two.

Once I stop coughing, I look through the slats again, but can't see anything. I can't quite remember where I heard the sound of the truck stopping. For all I know, I imagined it. I need to get out and get my bearings. Caves mean I'm north of the river and where Calliel landed, if they're the ones I'm thinking of. The caves have been closed off for as long as I can remember. No one has a need to go up there, or at least they never did before. There's nothing in them, no mineral deposits of any import (not since all the gold was mined), and no drawings on the stone walls from the Umpqua Indians who lived here centuries before. Nothing about them was supposed to be special, not anymore.

I have to get out of here. I have to get back to town.

Thunder cracks overhead. Lightning briefly illuminates the darkened sky.

Of course, I think. *Of course the storm won't let up. It's a test, remember? It's God's test, and he's going to flood the earth until we all float away. Once the surface is covered, the Strange Men will pull us down into the dark, and we'll find out what it truly means to love. What it truly means to have faith.*

I shake my head, trying to clear my mind of these odd thoughts. I feel woozy. I'm so tired. I could lie down next to Abe, maybe. Just for a little while. Just to sleep. Maybe it'll—

A hand on my shoulder.

A breath on the back of my neck.

A smell of the darkest earth.

I whirl around. There's no one there.

"I know," I mutter. "I know."

I take the knife back out of my pocket and open it. I press my hand against the door. "I'll come back for you," I tell Abe. "I won't leave you here, I promise. I'll come back for you and take you home, and the world will never bother us again."

He doesn't answer.

I pull the door open slowly. The blast of cold air is wonderful against my fevered skin. My face is instantly soaked and chilled. That clears more of the lingering fog in my head. The air feels clean and free. I almost want to take off running, but I don't think my ankle could take it. I'd get shot in the back, knowing my luck. The door opens to the forest stretched out in front of me, running down a steep hill. There is nothing down the hill or to my left. I look right and see a road. On this road is a large paneled moving truck, backed up to a rocky outcrop that rises from the forest floor. And by the rear of the truck stand three men.

I jerk my head back inside the shack. It looks like Griggs is one of them. The other two I don't recognize, but through the rain I can't be sure. I close the door again and go to the wall of the shack facing the truck. I shuffle some of the garbage bags filled with empty plastic bottles. The smell coming from the bags is almost overwhelming. I force myself back to reality and kick another bag out of my way. There's a large crack in this wall, near the floor. I slowly drop to my knees, ignoring how my whole body aches. I press my face up against the crack in the wall.

Griggs stands facing away from me, his sheriff's hat and uniform obvious, even through the heavy rain. The other two men are facing me, listening intently to something Griggs is saying. He's punctuating his words with his hands and eventually he points back toward the shack. The other two men peer around him with obvious interest. I freeze, feeling their eyes roam over me, and even though I'm sure they can't see me, it looks as if they are staring right at me. They turn back to Griggs, who taps his watch. One of the men shakes his head and says something Griggs obviously doesn't like. The sheriff grabs him by the collar of his coat and slams him into the side of the truck. Griggs pulls my Colt out of his coat pocket and presses it against the other man's head. The third man does nothing, standing with his arms crossed, occasionally glancing over at the shack.

The man pressed against the truck struggles in the sheriff's grip. Griggs snarls into his face and twists the gun into his temple, and it's all I can do—

look away, benji, look away

—to keep my anger from rising. I want to knock down the door and fly at Griggs, break him apart. I grind my teeth together and dig my fingernails into my palms to try and keep centered, to keep aware. The red sheen that threatens to fall over my eyes is held at bay, at least for now.

Griggs drops the man from the side of the truck and takes a step back. He waves the gun toward the rear of the truck. The other two men shake their heads but seem to do what he asks. They go to the back of the truck and open the large rear door. They pull down a long metal ramp and set it on the ground. Griggs says something else and disappears around the truck. The other two stand, leaning into each other. I'm too far away to see their lips moving, but they seem to be talking. They look back at the shack again and then follow the sheriff.

The truck. Unguarded. Headlights still on. The keys might still be in the ignition.

"I'll come back for you," I promise Abe as I stand. His face is turned away from me. I ignore the bloody hole in his head. "You won't stay here. I'll come back." My heart stutters in my chest, but I push it away.

I move to the door and open it slowly, poking my head out. No movement. I step out into the rain and am instantly soaked. I move along the outside of the shack until I reach the corner. Taking a deep breath, I turn and press my stomach against the wall and tilt my head around the corner.

The truck sits at the edge of the road. The headlights are still on. Farther up there's a dark hole in the side of the hill. The cave entrance. Lights have been strung up on the cave ceiling, leading deeper into the cave, but the entrance is empty. I gingerly put weight on my ankle, testing it out. The pain is there, and it burns, but it's not overpowering. I move around the corner of the shack, out into the open, and almost trip. There are four white propane tanks, the kind that hook up to barbeque grills, stacked against the wall. One starts to fall into the others, and I reach out and grab the top to keep the tanks from falling. The sound probably won't carry, but I can't take the chance. The top tank is heavy. It's full. I set it back up and look back at the cave entrance. Still empty.

Now. Do it now.

Shit.

Now!

I take off, running as quickly as I can, sort of hopping to keep as much weight as possible off my ankle. Rain slams into my face, the huge drops almost blinding me. The wind is strong. Thunder tears across the sky above. Forty feet. My chest hurts. Thirty feet. Abe and Cal are dead. Twenty feet. Please let the keys still be in the truck. Ten feet. The look on Cal's face before he fell off the bridge. Five feet. *Look away.*

I hit the passenger door almost running full tilt. I frantically scrabble for the door handle. It's wet and slides from my hand. I pull on it again. And again. The door doesn't open. It's locked. Without hesitating, I turn and run round the front of the truck, the headlights flashing in my eyes. I hit the driver's door and have started to pull on the handle when I hear the rumble of voices through the rain, coming from the cave entrance, which I have a clear view of. I see movement farther back in the cave. I'm almost frozen, until my father whispers *move, move, move.* I won't make it up the hill or back to the shack in time. I can't try and open the door. If it's locked, I'll get caught trying to open it. If it's open, they'll see the door. The voices get louder. I drop to the ground and roll under the truck.

My breathing is out of control, to the point of hyperventilating. A large rock digs into my back. The sound of footsteps and voices is deafening. The pulse in my neck feels like it's throbbing. Even though the rain is cold and the temperature has dropped, I start to sweat again. I stare up at the undercarriage of the truck, smelling metal and oil.

I can't make out what they're saying until they get closer to the truck and onto the metal ramp. Then their words reverberate through the truck.

"I always knew Griggs was fucking insane," a deep voice says.

The other voice is higher pitched. "Yeah, that's fucking hard-core, man. Even the boss seems a little freaked out."

"Ah, screw it," Low Voice says. "I'd rather a few people be dead than go to jail. I can't go back there."

"I dunno," High Pitch says, sounding nervous. "What kind of person do you have to be to consider putting a bullet into your own family? He's just a kid!"

"She's already done it once. Don't let the boss fool you. She's a cold bitch, trust me."

"What? What do you mean?"

There's a pause. Then, "Come here." I hear them move above me and down the ramp. I lift my head to see their feet walking around to the passenger side of the truck, near the door. The rear of the truck partially blocks them from being seen from inside the cave. "It was before your time, man," Low Voice says clearly. "That kid in there? His daddy apparently found out about this whole operation. Didn't know about the boss, but apparently knew about Griggs and Walken. She overheard him on the phone one day, talking with the FBI."

"Oh, shit," High Pitch breathes. "That guy… that Traynor…?"

"Man, fuck Traynor," Low Voice says. "The guy was a psychopath. But yeah. Apparently it was the same FBI guy. The kid called him in this time. His daddy did it before. Traynor wasn't around then, so she got Griggs to do it."

A chill runs down my spine.

"Do what?"

"Ran the guy off the road when he was going to meet up with the agent. Griggs ran the guy off the road, and he drowned in the river like a mile from here. Fucked-up thing was that it was her brother-in-law."

The red sheen falls over my eyes. I can't stop it. I curl my hands into fists at my side.

"Jesus Christ," High Pitch says. "This is some fucked-up shit, man. Why're we doing this again?"

"Money," Low Voice says. "It's all about the fucking money. But I'm not touching that kid, man. I'm telling you. I don't even want to be here when it happens. The little shit can die, I just don't want to see it."

"What if she tells us we have to go in there when we're done loading up?"

"We go. We close our eyes. But I'm not pulling the trigger. I can't do shit like that. But better him than us. Who the fuck is gonna miss him?"

"But... won't that make us, like, accomplices? Or whatever?"

"I dunno, man. I didn't go to law school. What the fuck you think I look like?"

"Fuck you. It's not like...." High Pitch trails off.

"What?" Low Voice asks.

"What's that on the door handle?"

The pair of feet nearest me turns to face the truck. "What the hell? It looks like blood. Are you bleeding or something?"

"I think I'd know if I was bleeding."

I close my eyes, feeling the tacky blood on my hands. I hadn't even thought of it. The rain hasn't washed it completely away. I wait for High Pitch and Low Voice to drop to their knees to look under the truck. They are quiet as if contemplating what they are looking at, and I slowly pull the small knife from my pocket. If they find me, I'll take someone's eye with me, that's for damn sure.

And just when I think I can't take it anymore, there's another voice.

"What are you two doing?" Griggs snarls from the mouth of the cave. "Get the fuck back to work!"

They hurry off back toward Griggs, and I lift my head, watching their feet. All three pairs turn back into the cave, Griggs snapping at both of them, though I can't hear what they're saying. I have to stop myself from getting up right now and running after Griggs, burying the knife in his neck over and over again until all of his blood is on the cave floor and I know he's dead. He killed my father on Christie's orders. I will see them both dead by my hands.

Wake up, my father says. *Wake up.*

I almost don't want to. I want to stay in this black-and-red haze and follow them into the cave and kill them before they kill me. I want to cause as much damage as possible before someone pulls a gun and shoots me through the head. They must suffer for what they've done.

It's a test, Cal whispers, that familiar rumble causing my heart to ache. *It's a test, Benji. You must not fall into the black. You can't go there.*

"Cal," I moan, closing my eyes. My hands start to shake. "Please, Cal. Come back. Don't be gone. Please come back."

I don't hear anything other than the rain.

Without thinking, I roll out from underneath the truck and stand. I pull on the handle, and the door opens. The inside of the cab is warm. The keys aren't in the ignition, nor on the seat. I flip down the sun visor. Nothing. They keys aren't here. Low Voice or High Pitch has them. This was a mistake. I can't use the truck. I've got to get the fuck out of here. Now. Now.

I close the door behind me as quietly as possible. I use my sleeve to wipe away the blood and grime my fingers left on the handle. I move around to the front of the truck, gripping the pocketknife in my hand. I'm about to cross back to the shack when I pause. If I'm going to make it, I can't use this old road. It'll be too easy for them to find me. The distance back to town is too great, the bridge too far away. I'll have to go through the woods to where Cal fell from the sky. Where my father died.

They can still beat me around in the truck, I think. *I won't be fast enough.*

I grip the knife in my hand and go back to the driver's side. The knife is sharp, well cared for. Abe said he could never let the blade become dull because it'd feel like he'd sullied his wife's memory. "Always keep it sharp," he'd told me quietly. "It helps me remember."

"Thank you, old man," I whisper out loud. I tighten my grip around the handle and stab the tire repeatedly. It takes a moment; the tire is thick. But eventually, after hitting the same place repeatedly, the knife goes through the rubber. I do the same thing in three other places, the air hissing steadily.

Low Voice and High Pitch return, carrying crates covered in blankets. I crouch down at the front of the truck and wait until they go back into the cave. Once they're out of sight, I do the same to the left tire. They won't go completely flat, not for some time, but it'll slow them down when they attempt to drive the truck. It has to be enough. For now.

I hobble back toward the shack, moving as fast as I can. I move past the propane tanks and press my back against the wall near the door, out of sight from the truck and the cave. Down the hill behind the shack, the woodland stretches out, intimidating, like the biggest forest I've ever seen. The river is about a mile away, maybe less. I don't know how much time I'll have before they come back to the shed to find me gone. If I'm not on the road, they'll know I'm in the woods. With my ankle slowing me down, it might be easier for them to catch up with me. I'm fucked either way. I should hole up somewhere nearby and wait for them to leave, but I don't know if there's anyone in the cave with them who I haven't seen yet. I don't know how many people are in on this. For all I know, Walken is already on his way up.

Distraction. I need a distraction.

What I need is for them to die.

The wind blows and metal rattles against metal. The propane tanks, stacked against the shack. Completely full. I don't have matches. I don't have a lighter. I don't have a gun to shoot them, though that might only happen in movies.

Something creaks inside the shack.

Abe is awake, I think, even though I know he's dead.

I open the door to the shack. Abe still lies on the floor, unmoving. The two old light bulbs overhead swing on their wires. Rain pounds the roof. There's no—

The light bulbs.

No fucking way could this work. It's nuts. I'll get myself killed. They'll never fall for it. I'll get caught before it could ever work.

But that doesn't stop me. I turn back and peer around the corner. No one is at the truck. I move back into the shack, flicking the light switch off. The bulbs hiss quietly as they darken, the only light left from the lantern. I take the pocketknife out of my pocket and use the handle to break the glass of the light bulb. The glass is hot. The filament is exposed. I crack it with the tip of the knife. I do the same to the other bulb.

Abe says nothing about my insanity.

I move back to the door and out into the rain. Movement around the truck. High Pitch. Low Voice. They head back into the caves.

I reach around the corner and grab a propane tank and haul it over to me. I push through the door into the shack and set the tank down in one corner, near the garbage bags. I do my best to ignore the words in bright red that says "Flammable" on one of the discarded bottles. My hands shake as I turn the propane canister so the nozzle faces into the stuffy room.

Not much time.

It takes me two minutes to bring in the three remaining tanks and put them each into a corner of the room, facing toward the center of the shack. Without a second thought, I twist the nozzle. Gas starts to hiss out quietly. I move to each canister, twisting each nozzle. They're all hissing by the time I'm finished. I'm dizzy, the room filling quickly with gas. I've kept the door shut as much as possible so the gas is trapped in the room.

"I'm not going to leave you in here," I tell Abe, trying to breathe shallowly. "I can't take you all the way with me. Not now. But I won't leave you in here."

He doesn't answer, but that's okay.

A single spark to light up the world, I think. *Flick the light switch. Electricity will try and connect through the filament. It'll spark. It'll spark, and all will burn.*

The gas is getting to my head.

I switch off the remaining light, the lantern. The shack goes almost completely dark.

I bend down near the floor and look through the crack toward the cave entrance and the truck. Griggs walks down the metal ramp, back into the cave. They haven't noticed the propane tanks are gone. I wait another moment, breathing in the fresh air, clearing my head. There's no one else in the truck.

"Time to go, Abe," I tell my old friend as I stand. I use the knife and cut his bonds. For a moment, his hands don't move, as if he's frozen with his arms strapped behind him. Then they fall slowly until they are resting at his sides, the fingers still pointed up toward the ceiling. I swallow past the lump in my throat because he isn't—

he is he is he is oh please he is

—sleeping. He's—

no no no no

—gone. He's gone, and I can't just leave him here. I can't leave him to burn with the rest of them. I can't let that happen to him. He promised me one day a long time ago, when I was lost in the dark, that he'd take care of me. Every day he's kept that promise. The least I can do is keep my promise to him.

I roll him over, slide my hands under his arms, and start to drag him toward the door. "I'm sorry," I tell him, tears streaming down my face. "I know you don't like to get dirty, but I can't carry you. I hurt my ankle and I'm sorry. Please don't be mad at me."

He doesn't say a word.

We reach the door and I set him down carefully, trying to ignore the way his head lolls to the side. The room is stifling now, the hissing sounding like a den of snakes. Water drips from the ceiling onto my sweat-slicked face. I open the door quickly and step through, then close it behind me. I look around the corner again. No one is there.

I turn back and open the door, moving as fast as I can. I grab Abe under his arms and pull as hard as I can. I drag him completely outside and then reach in to shut the shack door behind us. I take Abe's arms in my hands again and pull him away from the shack, away from the truck and cave. Away from his killer. Away from my Cal's killer. Away from the man who murdered my father. I pull with all my might, my ankle shrieking at me, the burning almost unbearable. I slide down the small embankment behind the shack and turn to pull Abe after me. He feels so much heavier now. Either that or I'm just tired. So tired.

I only get fifteen feet into the forest before I have to stop and rest. I lean up against a large tree trunk, trying to catch my breath. The walls I have built around my mind since I saw that first bullet strike Cal in the chest are starting to crumble. My hands are shaking. My mind is racing and I can't focus on a single thing. I just want to lie down and sleep, float away in the dark.

But even before I can hear my father, before Abe speaks in my head, before the sweet rumble of Cal's voice breaks me apart, I stand on my own, pushing myself away from the tree. I can do this. I can do this. I'll leave Abe here and hoof it back to town. I'll find someone—*anyone*—and they'll take over and I'll never have to worry about it again. Someone else can worry about the problems of the world. I have to find Cal. I have friends to bury.

I've turned to grab Abe to pull him a little further into the trees when I see four people approaching the shack. High Pitch and Low Voice are in the front, glancing nervously at each other, their shoulders brushing together as their lips move, as if they are whispering to each other. My Aunt Christie follows behind them, a determined look on her face. Griggs follows behind her a few feet, the hunting rifle slung over his shoulder, my Colt in his hands. He cocks the Colt back and snaps a bullet into the chamber.

Boom, I think. *Boom. Boom.*

High Pitch and Low Voice reach the shack first and wait anxiously at the door. Christie says something to them, and they shake their heads. She scowls and turns back to the sheriff. She says something to him, but he doesn't answer. He's looking down at the ground and frowning. Christie speaks again, and he holds up his hand, silencing her. I don't know what he's looking at. I can't see from where I stand. He bends over and I can only see the top of his head. I look up the embankment and my heart starts to thud.

Drag marks, down the embankment. Through the mud. He's seen the marks left by Abe's feet.

Christie opens the shack door. She grimaces as she takes a step back.

High Pitch and Low Voice peer over her shoulder.

She says something to Low Voice. He looks tense but steps around her and into the shack.

Griggs stands, looking down the embankment. He sees me. His eyes widen.

I smile up at him.

He jerks his head toward the shack. "Don't!" he roars as he spins.

Christie turns to him, startled.

The shack explodes in a burst of fire much larger than I expected. There's a bright flash, and then a concussive blast hits me like a heated wave. I'm knocked off my feet and onto my back. Rain falls on my face. I open my eyes and see the trees dancing in the sky above me, branches waving in the wind. An arc of lightning. A ripple of thunder, though it might be an echo of the blast, rolling down into the valley. Black smoke starts to smudge against the dark-gray clouds. Leaves and grass press against my back. It's all wet. Everything—

i have is blue

—is wet, and I need to get up. I need to get off my back and up. I have to run. I have to run.

I sit up. My ears are ringing. My eyes are focused, unfocused. Focused, unfocused. I shake my head and push myself to my knees. Up the embankment, fire rages, hissing in the rain as if angry. It sparks in reds and oranges, but also blues and greens. I wonder how hard I hit my head until I remember the chemicals that were in the garbage bags.

I need to leave, but I have to know.

I make my way up the embankment, coughing at the smoke and smell of burning plastic. I slide in the mud, avoiding a burning piece of wood. I pull myself up until I'm at the top. The shack itself has been leveled completely, bits and pieces strewn out in a twenty-foot radius. A piece of the roof has landed on the hood of the truck, the front tires now completely flat.

Run.

A burnt body lies on the ground in front of me. I can't tell if it's High Pitch or Low Voice, but I'm assuming its Low Voice since he was the one who turned on the light. Off to the right, the door to the shack remains somehow intact, and I can see an arm sticking out from under it. I hobble over to the door and lift it. Christie is underneath, and next to her is High Pitch. He groans, but doesn't open his eyes. Some of his hair has burned off, and his left eyebrow, but his skin doesn't appear charred, just red, as if he has a really bad sunburn. My aunt looks the same. I watch as her chest rises and falls steadily. She's alive. I toss the door to the side. I reach down and go through their pockets. There's no phone on either of them. If Low Voice had one, it's burned up like he is.

Run. Please. Run.

I tighten my hand around the knife as I turn to Griggs.

Griggs, the man who killed my father, who killed Abe. Who killed Cal. Griggs, who lies fifteen feet away, his jacket slightly smoking but otherwise looking intact. Bullets for the rifle he's carrying spill out of a pocket where the zipper has broken. I take a step toward him and realize how easy it would be to bury the knife in his throat, to slice his neck from ear to ear until it opens like a bloody red mouth. It would be so very easy to watch his eyes flash open as he gurgles, blood bubbles popping out his lips, painting his face in a spray of crimson mist.

It would be so easy, I think as I find myself standing above him. His skin has pinked slightly, his hat knocked off his head. His hair is plastered wet against his skull. His eyes are closed. There's a small piece of shrapnel sticking out of his right thigh, blood leaking slowly, soaking his pants. But still he breathes. His life is not threatened by injury. He's alive. He doesn't deserve to be. He deserves pain, agonizing pain. He deserves death in all its forms. I can do this. I can avenge the men I love and have lost. I stand above him and raise Estelle's gift high above my head, ready to bring it down on him again and again and again. Once he is gone, this nightmare will be over and I just need to *do it. Do it!*

As I raise the knife as high as I can, I hesitate.

You are not the judge, my father whispers.

You are not the jury, Abe murmurs.

You are not the executioner, Cal says, and it's so loud he could be standing right next to me. A tear slides down my cheek. *You are the protector. You are a guardian. It's time to go home, Benji. It's time to—*

A hand reaches out and seizes my leg.

I look down. Griggs is awake and snarling up at me. I try to step back, but he has a vise grip on my ankle. "I'll kill you," he says, his voice a low rasp. "I'll fucking kill you."

Run!

I jerk my leg away, using my good leg to kick him upside the head. He howls as he rolls away from me… directly toward the hunting rifle he used to kill Cal. He lands on top of it, and I'm already taking off toward the forest. I can still hear him screaming as I jump down the embankment, rolling as I land to avoid putting all the weight on my ankle.

I'm sorry, Abe, I think as I reach him and run right past. *I'm so sorry.*

There's a loud crack behind me that can't be anything but gunfire, and a tree branch above me explodes. I hear Griggs scream after me. I glance over my shoulder.

Sheriff George Griggs tears after me, the rifle in his hands.

mile marker seventy-seven

THE rain continues to fall as Griggs chases me through the darkening woods. Branches slap against me, and I raise my arms to protect my face. Thin cuts form when the wood slaps against my skin. The blood from my damaged wrist has soaked through the strip of shirt I used to tie it off. My ankle and foot are going numb. But still I run.

I know where I'm heading. I run toward the place where much of my life ended, and much of it began again. I run there only because I don't know where else to run. My mind is like a static screen, snowy white and almost incapable of broadcasting. I'm not following logical thought. I'm following my heart, and it's leading me to the river.

I can hear Griggs crashing through the underbrush behind me, booming steps punctuated by shouts and screams. He's going to kill me, he bellows. He's going to kill me like he did my father. He's going to hold me underwater until I stop kicking and my skin turns blue. He's going to cut off my head and mail it to my mother and he's going to *laugh*, he roars after me. He's going to watch the look on her face and he's going to just *laugh*.

I zigzag around a tree just as he fires the rifle again. The bullet smashes into another tree just ahead, bark flying in the air, pitch leaking like black oil. Like the tree is bleeding after getting shot. He swears behind me and starts to move again.

There are times when I'm so far ahead of him I can barely hear him behind me. These are the times I think about taking cover, trying to find someplace to hide, but something tells me to keep going, that I need to get to the river, that everything will be okay as long as I can reach the river.

Other times it seems he's so close I can hear him wheezing as he runs. It's only the terror of knowing he could reach out and grab me that allows me to put on an extra burst of speed, putting more distance between us. If he catches me, I know, I will die in the middle of the woods, and no one will find me again.

I think of many things in the fifteen minutes it takes me to reach the river. I am hyperaware of everything around me, yes, but it's like I've detached from myself, floating high above my own body, tethered to myself only by a thread of brilliant blue.

I remember a time my father broke his leg, when I was eight. He was laid up in the house for six weeks. "Gonna need you to be my right-hand man, Benji," he told me seriously. "Gonna have to be the man of the house for a bit. You okay with that?"

I feel the pocketknife in my hand. It feels like it's heating from within. I wonder at the depth of the love between Abe and Estelle, only now accepting with a rip through my chest that Abe is truly gone. *They're together now,* I tell myself. *Please just let them be together now.*

As another bullet flies over my head, I remember the first time my mother smiled after Big Eddie died. We were working outside, raking up the leaves in front of Big House, putting them into a big pile near the old oak tree. We hadn't spoken for hours when suddenly she stopped and turned her face toward the sky. She dropped the rake and ran and jumped into the leaf pile. She was laughing when she came up, and the smile on her face was one of such heartbreaking beauty I felt annihilated.

I trip and almost fall when I think of Nina.

After I woke up on that third day following my father's death, she was the next person I saw after Abe. She came into the room and sat in the chair next to me, reaching out to grip my hand. I turned my head on the pillow to look at her. With tears in her eyes, she said, "I know your heart hurts, because mine does. But you have to know you'll see him again. One day, you'll see him again."

I hear Griggs roar in anger behind me as I remember a time about a year after my father died. Abe came into the shop under the pretense of having his car checked out, looking uncharacteristically nervous. When I finally asked if he was okay, he told me gruffly that he was just fine, and didn't I know there may be gold in those hills? Estelle always had wanted to go look for herself and see. I nodded, following the routine as always. Finally, as he was about to leave, he turned to me, pointed his eyes toward the floor, and said, "You know you're just about the best friend I've got, right? I know I'm just this crazy old guy, but you're my best friend. Okay?" I nodded, speechless. He left, and we never spoke about it again.

I remember Mary and Christie telling me they were going to move into Big House, for as long as we needed them there. "You two will never be alone," Christie had said. "The Trio will never let you down." I had bunched my fists at my sides, trying to maintain my composure, trying to be the man of the house. Christie had come to me, wrapping her arms around me, holding me as I broke and cried into her neck, saying only, "Thank you, thank you, thank you."

I remember the people of Roseland gathering for Big Eddie's funeral. The church was full, with people spilling out onto the streets. Speakers had been set up so the pastor's voice could reach everyone. Most people kept their heads bowed the entire time. Many had tears on their faces. We stood next to each other, my mother and I, after the service and before the cemetery. It seemed like every single Roselandian waited in line just for the opportunity to touch one of us in some way, either a handshake or a hug. A hand on my shoulder. A kiss on my cheek. "He was a great man," they all said. "He was a wonderful man." Even Sheriff Griggs had shown, wearing a tie. He was one of the last, and even though I wanted to ask him about the status of his investigation, I couldn't find the words. He shook my hand gently and said, "I grew up with your daddy. He's always been a part of my life. I'll never understand why these things have to happen to good people." I nodded and looked away.

But even through all these thoughts, even through every flash of my life before my eyes, as the pieces are coming together to make the whole of who I am, I think of *him*. Falling from the sky. Saying my name for the first time. The look on his face when he ate green clover marshmallows. The way his eyes lit up at the sunrise. The way he made a home for himself inside Little House. The way he held me. "I'm a guardian," he told me. "I'm guarding."

The sound of the river invades my thoughts. I'm close.

I throw a glance over my shoulder. The forest is dense, but I see a flash of clothing through the trees. Griggs is still behind me, twenty, maybe thirty yards. The rifle is still in his hands. I don't know how many times he's fired at me, or how many bullets he has left. It only needs to be one for everything to end. I can't let that happen. I can't let him bury me in the river and get away with all he's done. Everyone needs to know, and I need to be the one to tell them.

I no longer feel my ankle. I no longer feel the cuts and bruises. No burning in my chest, no lumps in my throat. I have remembered enough. I have been hurt enough.

Or so I think.

The ground beneath me suddenly gives way, and I think *sinkhole* before I start somersaulting down a hill instead. My shoulder smashes into the ground repeatedly, and I cry out, stars dancing across the black behind my eyes. I keep my eyes closed as I tumble, wondering just how long I'll fall. *Can't break my leg or it's all over*, I think as my shoulder hits the ground again. *Can't break or I'll die.* Water splashes up all around me. I squeeze the closed pocketknife tightly, not wanting to let it go.

Nothing breaks, at least as far as I can tell. I reach the bottom of the hill and snap open my eyes, staring, dazed, at the stormy sky. Trees sway around the edges of my vision. Rain continues to fall, the wind gusting over my skin. I push myself up, staring back up the hill I've fallen down. I still hear Griggs crashing through the underbrush. Maybe he'll fall too. Maybe he'll fall and break his goddamn neck and this whole thing can be over. I turn my head, my brain screaming at me to get up, to get the *fuck up*. I'm in a clearing.

The clearing where Cal fell.

The clearing is flooded slightly, and for a moment I think it's because the river has risen so high it has overtaken the hill in front of me and is pouring down to fill the clearing, making a lake. It's just the ground, though. The ground is so saturated the water can no longer soak into the soil. It's too much for the ground to handle. It's—

Gunfire. I hear the whine of a bullet more than I feel it. The ground two feet from my left hand erupts with a spray of water. I turn my head. Griggs stands at the top of the hill behind me, cocking the rifle. He aims for me again, and I still haven't risen. This is it. This is the moment I die. I've almost made it to the river. I don't know what I would have done had I gotten there, but I wasn't fast enough. I've failed. I've failed my test, whatever it was supposed to be.

Through the rain and up the hill, I see Griggs smile, squinting down the sight of the rifle. I spread my arms wide, water dripping from my fingertips. "Come on, then!" I scream up at him. "Come on, you fucking bastard! Do it! What the fuck are you waiting for? *Do it*!"

He pulls the trigger.

Nothing happens.

Again. Nothing.

He's empty. He pulls the rifle back with a snarl of anger and starts digging through his pocket to reload.

I run.

The small crater where Cal landed is completely filled with water. I look down as I pass it. Clearly visible through the water are the blue flowers that stretch out into the shapes of wings. They flash an even more brilliant Prussian blue, lighting up the water until I'm sure it will blind me, the outline of wings almost more than I can take. It's just a trick of my exhausted mind, I know, but for a moment I think the wings will rise from the water and Cal will be there, taking my hand in his and making this whole day disappear like it never happened. I'll be swallowed by the blue light and I'll never be scared or sad again.

But, of course, that does not happen.

I reach the opposite side of the clearing as Griggs starts to slide down the hill. He's reloaded the rifle and attempts to aim it at me as I scramble up the wet grass, but he slips and lands on his back, sliding down the rest of the way.

I dig in my feet, kicking the ground with each step I take, trying to create divots so I don't slip and fall back into the clearing. I'm halfway up the hill when the rifle fires again and the bullet hits the ground below my feet. I glance over my shoulder. Griggs is slowly walking across the clearing, taking aim again. I've gritted my teeth against the inevitable shot in the back when the crater again flashes blue. Griggs stutters in his steps, looking down toward the crater. There's another pulse, so dazzling I have to close my eyes against it.

Move!

I start climbing again, ignoring the flashes of bright light behind me, not focusing on the fact that the flowers are glowing in a crater where an angel fell. I dig my hands into the soil above me and pull myself higher up the steep hill. My legs burn as I push. My arms hurt as I pull. Griggs howls behind me as the blue lights begin to fade. I'm almost at the top. I crouch, pressing my stomach against the ground. I push as hard as I can and launch myself up and reach the crest of the hill, clutching the trunk of a tree.

The lights behind me fade out completely.

Griggs is staring dumbfounded at the crater below, rubbing his eyes. Another crack of thunder rolls overhead, and he snaps his head up toward me. Rage roils over his face again, and he raises the rifle more quickly than I think possible. He gets one shot off, and I duck against the tree, the bullet striking the trunk where my head had been just a second before.

He starts after me again.

I dash down the other side of the hill, through the trees. Ahead, the noise of the river is getting louder, until it's an almost unbearable roar. But I don't turn back. I can't. There is no plan beyond reaching the river where Big Eddie died. It'll be enough. It has to be.

As I clear the tree line, I skitter to a stop.

Mile marker seventy-seven lies before me, and the area has changed.

The river is fury incarnate, swollen and snapping, moving swiftly as it tears its way through the valley. It has crested its banks, waves splashing up and over the ground that surrounds the river. Debris floats by: shrubs, branches, a young maple tree, ripped from its roots. The boulder my father's truck struck is partially underwater on the opposite shore, split in two from the night Cal fell. I've never seen the river fill so quickly. Maybe the dam upstream has broken.

A shout from behind me.

I take a step toward the river and then hesitate. There's no way I can make it across. The river's moving too fast, the current is too strong, the water too deep. I can't run along the edges of the river because it has already risen. The only way out is back the way I came, but Griggs is thundering through the woods behind me.

I take another step toward the river and then another. And another. Water begins to rush around my ankles, and I feel the pull of it. I take another step, and the water is so cold my injured ankle goes almost completely numb, blanketing the pain that had started to come back. I stare down at the brown water, unable to see my reflection. The water is up to my calves when I reach the edge of the bank. Another step and the water will be up to my chest and I'll be swept away. *Maybe it's better that way*, I think. *Maybe it's better to float in the river than die at the hands of my father's killer.*

This feels like the dream, though I don't think it is. My father's truck is not in the river. There's no shadowy figure standing on the roadway above, though now I know who it was. There are no feathers. There are no crosses. There is only the sky above, the rain falling down. The river rushing in front of me, hell rushing toward my back.

I turn and face what's coming.

ONCE, when I was six, my father made me angry. I don't remember what I'd done, or what he'd said in response, but I made the decision to run away from home. I waited until the house was quiet that night. I loaded up my backpack with a pair of jeans. Three pairs of socks. Underwear. Two shirts, and a sweatshirt. I also packed a copy of *The Boxcar Children*, sure I could find an abandoned train car to live in and that the book would show me how. I went quietly down the stairs, jumping over the second-to-last one because it always squeaked.

I went to the kitchen and made three cheese and mustard sandwiches. I put them in a paper lunch sack, along with barbeque-flavored Bugles and strawberry Fig Newtons, each in their own baggies. I grabbed two Capri Suns out of the fridge and put them in my bag. I figured this bounty would last me at least three or four weeks, until I could figure out how to hunt for food. I contemplated taking a rifle, but they were locked up in the gun case in the garage, and I didn't know where the keys were, so I packed my sling shot instead. And then, after further consideration, I also grabbed my boomerang that I hadn't quite figured out how to make return just yet. I'd have time to learn.

I left a note (*I'm mad at you, so good-bye FOREVER!!! Don't look for me!!! Love, Benji*) before I left—it felt like the right thing to do. I opened the door into the night and started my journey into the wild unknown.

I'd barely made it to the end of the long driveway before I was sure something was following me. I'd forgotten a flashlight (much to my embarrassment and there was no *way* I was going back to get one) so I couldn't quite see if it was an animal or not. I wasn't scared of the dark, but this dark seemed *darker* than the normal dark. *Maybe it's a bear,* I thought. *Or maybe an otter. That would be kind of neat to see.* I pulled my boomerang from my backpack just in case it *was* a bear and started walking down the roadway again.

The footsteps continued behind me.

I whirled around. "Who's there?" I cried, my voice small. "I've got my boomerang, so don't you mess with me!"

A snort of laughter came from behind a tree. "You should probably learn how to throw it first," my father said. "Unless you're just going to hit me over the head with it."

I scowled. "What are you doing?"

Big Eddie stepped out from behind the tree, wearing his pajama pants and a blue shirt and the rubber boots he kept near the door for when it was raining. "Wondering what you're doing," he said easily. "Going for a walk at night?"

"I'm running away," I said, putting the boomerang back into my bag. "Forever."

"Oh? Is that so?"

"Yeah. I'm mad as hell." I figured I could say that word now that I was a runaway.

He chuckled. "Are you? That's not good."

I glared at him before turning and walking down the two-lane road.

He followed.

"What are you doing?" I said, resolutely not looking back at him.

"Going for a walk," he said. "It's a nice night."

I huffed and didn't say anything back.

I only made it half a mile before I got really hungry. Big Eddie stayed with me the whole way, talking about how pretty the night was, how many stars were in the sky, and did I see the Big Dipper up there? Or Orion's Belt? I didn't answer, but I did look up and find the constellations because he'd shown me how, a long time before. He chattered away about this and that, and I did my best to ignore him.

But eventually I was hungry and figured I at least deserved a break to have part of one of my sandwiches and maybe some chips. The cookies I'd save for later as a treat to celebrate when I found my very own boxcar. I wasn't thirsty yet, so the juice could wait.

I went off the side of the road, through a ditch, and found a nice big tree to sit under. Big Eddie followed me and stood next to me while I dug around my bag until I found the lunch sack. I pulled out one of the cheese and mustard sandwiches and was about to take a bite when I remembered they were his favorite too. I felt bad, knowing that since we'd walked so far, he must be hungry like I was. I only warred with myself for a moment before I said, "You want part of my sandwich?"

He nodded and sat down next to me, putting his back against the tree trunk as I tore the sandwich in half. I handed his half over to him, and he thanked me quietly. And then I figured you can't have mustard and cheese sandwiches without barbeque Bugles, so I gave him some of those too. And that led to Fig Newtons, because you needed dessert after a big meal. And that led to juice because the cookies coated our throats and we were thirsty.

Eventually, my head started to bob. I was tired because it was almost eleven o'clock, according to my *Star Wars* watch. I'd hoped to at least make it to Canada by morning since it was so close on the map I'd looked at before leaving.

And somehow, I found myself in my father's lap, my head pressed against his chest, mumbling that I was running away, that I was mad at him and didn't want to live with him anymore. But he was so big and warm I couldn't fight the waves of sleep washing over me much more and figured I would rest until morning and then start out again.

"I'm sorry," he said, when I was almost asleep.

"For what?" I asked drowsily, because I'd already forgotten.

"For making you mad."

"Oh. That's okay."

He kissed my forehead. "Do you still want to run away?"

I shrugged.

"Well, if you do, can I go with you?"

This surprised me. "Why?"

"Because I'd be sad if you were gone forever."

"Oh. Okay. You can come." I paused, thinking. "What about Mom?"

He sighed dramatically. "Oh, I forgot about her! Well, we just can't leave her, can we. That wouldn't be fair."

"Maybe we should just stay at the house," I said wisely. "All our stuff is there already and it might just be easier."

He hugged me tighter. "That's a great idea," he said. "I'm glad you thought of it."

"Would you have really been sad?" I asked, snuggling back down onto him. "If I'd been gone?"

"Yes," he whispered as sleep began to chase me. "I'd have been very sad. If we were ever apart, I'd miss you every day until we were together again."

"Because you're my daddy?"

"Because I'm your daddy."

I considered this sleepily and came to the only conclusion I could. "I guess you love me, huh?"

"Oh yes. Very much so."

"Why?"

He was silent for a moment. Then he said, "Because there is no one such as you in the world, and you belong to me. I'll believe in you always because you are my son. You're going to be strong and brave, and one day, you're going to be a great man and you will stand for what you believe in. I have faith that you will stand and be true."

I didn't understand, but then I was asleep, so it didn't matter. I was safe against Big Eddie.

I woke briefly, later in the night, to my father carrying me back up the road, my backpack slung over one of his big arms, my head on his shoulder, his hand on my back, rubbing in slow circles as he sang a familiar song. "Sometimes I float along the river, for to its surface I am bound. And there are times stones done fill my pockets, oh Lord, and it's into this river I drown."

He carried me all the way home, and I knew it would all be okay because my father held me in his arms.

GRIGGS points the rifle at me. The river roars at my back. The heels of my feet are on the river's edge. The rain pours from the sky.

"You killed Big Eddie," I say.

"You should have just left things alone, Benji," he snaps at me. "All of this could have been avoided had you just walked away."

"I am my father's son."

He laughs. "And look where that's gotten you! The same place where Big Eddie drowned. It's almost poetic, if you think about it."

"You won't get away with this," I say, strangely calm, clenching my hands in fists at my sides. Abe's pocketknife is still in my right hand. "Others will ask questions. The day you murdered my father was the beginning of your end. Others will come. People will hear the truth."

He narrows his eyes. "The *truth*? The *truth* will be whatever *I* say it is! I've got this fucking town in the palm of my hand, and no one—not *you*, not your *father, no one*—will take it away from me."

"You've already lost," I tell him. "You just don't know it yet."

He tightens his grip on the gun as he takes a step toward me. He's six or seven feet away, seemingly unaware that he's moving closer. Maybe....

Griggs gives me a nasty smile. "Your father cried out," he says. "Even as the truck began to fill with water, it was still clear enough that I could hear him screaming, begging for someone to save him. He only stopped when he started to choke on the river water in his mouth." He takes another step. "I watched, you know. I stood up on the road by the mile-marker sign, and I watched the river overtake the truck until I knew he was dead. And then I left him there. I left him in the river for someone else to find."

Somehow, I smile at him. "You are nothing, Griggs. The world will know you are nothing." I push up the blade of the knife with two fingers slowly, trying not to attract his attention. It catches on my dirty jeans, and I unfold the knife completely.

"Who else have you told?" he shouts, jabbing the rifle in my direction. "Who the fuck have you told!"

There's no one else, but he doesn't know that. "So many people," I tell him. "I wouldn't be surprised if the FBI was already in Roseland. You're fucked, Griggs. You're so fucked and you don't even know."

"You're lying!" he screams. "You're fucking lying!" Another step. One more, and the rifle will be within reach. Grab the barrel, pull it away, and slash him with the knife. I might end up in the river, but at least he'll go with me.

"You thought you were so smart," I say with a laugh. "You thought you would get away with everything. Traynor's *gone*, Griggs. Who do you think they're going to go after for the murder of a federal agent? It's all going to rest on you, and you're gonna *fry*."

He raises his foot... and takes a step back. "Nice try, Benji," he says as chills go up and down my spine. "You almost had me there, didn't you? You were good, but I'm better."

"It doesn't matter," I tell him quietly.

He arches an eyebrow. "And why is that?"

I look him in the eye. "Because I've done what my father asked of me. I've stood. I haven't backed down. I've kept my promise to him."

"Last stand, huh?" Griggs says, looking amused. "To the very end."

I tilt my face toward the thunderous sky and close my eyes. I stretch out my arms away from my body, like wings. When I speak again, my voice is a roar, letting Griggs and Cal's Father hear what Big Eddie has made me into. "I have *faith*! I believe in the *impossible*! If this is my test, then so be it! I have *lived*! I have *loved*! I have *lost*! And I am still standing, you bastard! You fucking asshole! I am my father's son and I am *still fucking standing*!"

"Good-bye, Benji," Griggs says, pointing the rifle at my head.

I open my eyes. A patch of blue sky peeks out from behind a dark cloud.

Something explodes up from the river behind me. I snap my head forward and see Griggs's eyes rise to something above me, his jaw dropping, the rifle starting to shake. Tiny blue lights burst all around me, flying along my skin, warming me from the inside out. There's a beat of great wings, and through the heavy rain I smell earth, deep and rich. A massive presence lands behind me, a strong arm wraps around my chest, pulling me back into a solid mass. Wings rustle as they fold around me, their touch like a caress. There's a breath along my neck, hot and harsh. A furious growl emanates near my ear.

"You have made a mistake," the guardian angel Calliel snarls at the man in front of us. "You have tried to harm what is mine. You have tried to take from me. And now, I will take *everything* from you."

He moves faster than I've ever seen him. One second he surrounds me, and the next he's flying at Griggs, wings outstretched, trying to shield me from any attack. Griggs is able to squeeze off one shot before the rifle is ripped from his hands. I take a stuttering step back, my head suddenly swimming, my legs like jelly. My chest feels like it's on fire. I didn't know a bullet could hurt this much.

Cal tosses the rifle into the river and picks up Griggs by his neck. Griggs struggles weakly in his arms, blood soaking the pants of his uniform where the shrapnel embedded itself in his thigh when the shack exploded. The shrapnel piece is gone. He must have pulled it out himself while chasing after me.

Blue lights begin to spin around Calliel and gather in a swirling vortex off to his right. The black hole opens, and I can hear its whispered promises to float, to have all the cares in the world taken away so we can all just float. Griggs screams in Cal's grip, his eyes going wide at the sight of the black, and he starts kicking his legs, to no avail.

I feel so heavy, but I have to try and stop him. I can't let him do this. Not for me. Not now. Now that he's….

I fall to my knees, the water splashing up all around me. "Cal," I say weakly, a blood bubble bursting from my mouth, popping. The bullet must have nicked a lung. It's hard to take a breath. "Cal, please don't."

He must hear something in my voice, because he turns to me. The anger leaves, suddenly replaced by terror. He throws Griggs to the ground, where he lands with a bone-breaking crash. I start to fall forward, but Cal catches me before I am submerged facedown into the river, twisting me over and pulling me into his chest. My blood flows into the water, a red streak in the gray water. The rain continues to fall.

"No," Cal chokes out. "No."

I reach up and touch his face. He rubs his cheek against my palm. "You're okay?" I ask, coughing. Blood dribbles onto my cheek. Water falls in my eyes. I reach up blindly to his chest, near his shoulder, and find a raised bump of flesh, a bloodless hole in his skin. The groove along his head is deep. He's hurt, he's still hurt.

"I'm okay," he sobs, tears falling from his eyes and onto my face like rain. "I wasn't fast enough. O, Father, hear my prayer. I am but your humble servant. Please hear me. Please help him. I can't lose him. Not like this. Not after everything we've been through. It can't end like this."

"You came back," I whisper as he kisses my forehead, pressing his hand against the wound on my chest to try to stop the bleeding. "You...." It's getting harder to speak.

"You will *not* take him from me!" Cal bellows, rocking his head back.

Griggs rises behind him, my Colt .38 Super in his hand, pointed at Cal's head.

"Griggs," I whisper.

Cal flashes out his right wing, which knocks into Griggs. The gun flies from his hand and lands in the river. Cal growls as the wing wraps around Griggs like a snare, holding him tight. I expect the vortex to return and Griggs to be flung into the black. I don't think I'll have the words to stop him.

But it doesn't come. Instead, Cal brings his wing in toward himself, until Griggs's face is inches from his own. Griggs screams at the black fury on Cal's face. Above his cries, I hear Cal's words. "You are not welcome here any longer." Then the wing snaps away and Griggs is hurled into the river.

He lands with a splash toward the river's center. He disappears under the rushing water momentarily but comes sputtering to the surface. He slams into a boulder whose top is exposed. He finds a crevice and grips it tightly, choking on water as he cries for help. His grip slips, and he's about to be swept away when a massive tree slams into the boulder. The crack of bone is audible above the water and rain. He screams in pain and tries to move. The tree's strong branches have caught on the boulder and it's stuck, pinning him against the rock. He struggles weakly and spits out the rising water from his mouth.

I close my eyes. It's dark again.

"No," Cal moans. "Wake up, Benji! You gotta wake up!"

I hear my father singing about a river.

"Benji!"

I hear Abe telling me he's going to take care of me.

"*Father*!" Cal bawls. "Why won't you answer me! I'm *begging* you! Don't you take him from me! Don't you dare!"

I hear great wings spreading, and suddenly I'm lifted off the ground, rain and wind rushing over my body as the angel Calliel takes flight, hurtling toward the sky.

"Stay with me, Benji. Please just open your eyes."

I want to tell him it'll be okay, that I just need to sleep, but I can't find my voice. I want to tell him how I feel, and that I'll wait for him, no matter what it takes. I'll find him, again. If I go to the place known as Heaven, if it is a real and tangible thing, then I will tear down his Father's door until my voice is heard and we are together again. This, I promise him.

"I love you," he whispers as he weeps.

I know. I love—

I am swallowed into the dark.

the white room

I OPEN my eyes in a stark white room. There is no pain. There is peace, but it feels fragile, hard-won. It feels like it could be taken away with just a word. This thought causes me to ache. Now there is nothing but pain. My chest hurts, though there's no wound there. My wrist hurts, though the skin is unblemished. My ankle hurts, though it's not swollen. My shoulder hurts, thought it has mended.

My heart hurts because it is broken.

"Just breathe," a strong voice says.

I can't help the bitter tears that fall. It's not fair. It's not fair.

I turn my head, pressing my ear against the bright white floor.

The archangel Michael sits in a white chair, looking strangely dapper in a deep blue pin-striped suit. His leg crosses the other at the knee. His white wings spread out behind him, almost blending in with the room itself, but they're just off enough to be noticeable. They're a beautiful thing, the feathers shiny and silky smooth. Michael himself is as handsome as I remember. There's an empty chair next to him.

"Breathe, Benji," he says kindly. "I know it's difficult, but I need you to breathe."

I need to get away from him. I need to get out of this place. I push myself up, ignoring the twinges in my body, almost blinded by tears. I gag and taste river water at the back of my throat. I press up against the walls, sliding my hands along the smooth surfaces, trying to find a catch, a handle, a door, anything that would allow me to escape this room. I go from corner to corner, again and again. Michael says nothing as I circumnavigate the room. The only thing in the room that's different, aside from the chairs and Michael, is the faint outline of a child on one of the walls, like their shadow has been flash-fried into the wall.

Eventually, I can move no more, and I stop, leaning and panting against the wall, sweat dripping from my brow. Michael looks at me and nods to the empty chair beside him, then sits back and waits.

"Am I dead?" I ask him finally, unable to look him in the eye. "Did I die?"

Michael hesitates, as if unsure how to answer. Or as if he doesn't want to answer. "It's close," he finally says. "It's going to be up to you, I think. You have been tested greatly, Benji. But it is not over. Not yet."

"Why me?" I say, wiping my face. "Why is he doing this to me? What does he want?"

"Who?"

"You know who."

He sighs. "My Father."

I say nothing.

He gestures to the chair next to him. "Sit, Benji."

I almost say no just to be defiant, but I don't have the energy. The glaring white of the room is starting to give me a headache, and I can't stop my eyes from traveling to the burnt outline of the shadow on the wall. It looks so small.

I nod once and sit in the chair next to Michael. It's surprisingly soft, and I sink into it. "What is this place?" I ask him.

"The room?"

I nod.

"It's… hmm. Well, to be honest, Benji, I don't know *what* this room is, not exactly. It exists for moments such as these, when an individual needs to hear something or learn something that may be hard for them to understand, to point them in a direction they never thought possible. But that's really all I know. I don't know how it came to be or why certain people are able see it. Like you have."

"What does that have to do with me?" I ask, pointing at the child's outline on the wall.

He watches me for a moment, rubbing his chin. "Nothing," he says finally. "Or at least I don't think it does. Though," he says, frowning, "I don't know why it's still there. This room usually resets each time it's used. Do you remember when I told you about the darkness rising, spilling over from another plane of existence?"

"Yes." With people who could manipulate earth and water. Fire and wind.

"Time moves… differently over there, compared to the other levels. Sometimes it slows, other times it speeds up, but it never matches anywhere else. Guardians aren't allowed there, at least not of the angel variety, and it's run by a being that thinks Itself a god. Even *the* God, though I hope It hasn't sunk that far. A false deity is a terrible thing and can only lead to an ending constructed of a wave of fire."

"I don't understand."

"That image, that burnt image of a child, was meant for a man named Seven who might be the key to not only saving his world, but the ones on every level above and below him."

"Who is the child?"

Michael closes his eyes. "One who has the power for great destruction growing within him. It remains to be seen what side he will choose. In the end, though, the boy will burn. We just don't know how."

"I don't understand what this has to do with me," I say hoarsely.

"Indeed," Michael says, quirking his eyebrow. "But here we are, nonetheless, in the White Room, as it's called. Only a few have come here and even fewer have left with an understanding of *why* they've come here. While it's meant to show a being the way, it usually ends up offering only confusion."

"What about Seven?" I ask, almost rolling my eyes at the name. "Did he leave understanding?"

"I hope so, for all our sakes," Michael says. "But let us focus on other matters for now. You, in particular. Do you know why *you're* here?"

I hazard a guess. "I was shot?"

"Yes, yes, but *why* were you shot?"

"Griggs had a gun pointed at me, and he pulled the trigger."

Michael sighs. "There is that, yes."

I narrow my eyes at him. "Did you know this was going to happen? When you touched him? Did you know?"

"No, Benji. I didn't. As much as I'd like to think I have that much foresight, I did not know. It comes with the concept of free will. A billion tiny actions could have led to the specific moment of you and Griggs at the river. It could have been set in motion long ago, and nothing could have disrupted the design of it. That's the paradox, you see, of the design: it's like a spider web, and once caught, it is hard to shake."

"But it *is* possible," I mutter, saying the words he doesn't.

He smiles, his eyes sparkling. "Some say so. And that's where you come in. Regardless of how caught in the spider's web you are, you've still managed to break free, at least partially. That's something beyond anything I've seen."

"I don't know how I did it, though," I admit. "I haven't done anything different than I've normally done."

"Haven't you? Think, Benji. Think of all that has occurred to bring you to here, to this *now*. What have you learned? What has this taught you?"

"My father...." I stop.

"What about your father?" He's curious, and I wonder if he doesn't know much more than I do.

"Your Father," I say. "What has he told you about me?"

Michael's eyes cloud over, but the look is gone only a second later. "Father seems to have little to say on the matter, though I was able to recover Calliel's lost memories."

I'm stunned. "How?"

He tips his head in my direction. "In due time, Benji. Now, what about your father?"

"My father was a great man."

"Yes, as you've said before. But what *made* him a great man?"

I am careful with my answer. "He was kind. He was loving, and not just to me and my mom, but to everyone around him. He was honest and brave." I shake my head, hearing the way my voice cracks. "He stood... oh God, he stood and was true when he saw something wrong. All he wanted to do was make everything okay for everyone. He was the one who chased the dark away when it got too close. He was the one who made me think everything would be okay, even if there was a chance it wouldn't. He had this way about him that even when you were at your lowest, you'd feel his arm on your shoulder and hear his smile in his voice and you knew, you just *knew,* it would be okay." Tears stream down my face, and I can do nothing to stop them. "He always did the right thing, no matter what it took. Even if it meant—" My voice catches in my throat, and I don't think I can finish.

"Even if it meant what, Benji?" the archangel asks me kindly.

No, you bastard. You son of a bitch. I won't say it. I can't say it. Please don't make me. I want to go home. I just want to go home.

"Benji?"

"Even if it meant sacrificing himself," I choke out. "Even if it meant he wouldn't be coming home, he had to do the right thing. He couldn't stand by and watch the world go bad. He always had to do something to right the wrong. He always had to make a difference, to make it better."

"And who did he do that for?"

"My mom," I say, unable to hold back the sobs. "My aunts. His friends. His family."

"And?"

"Me," I whisper.

"Yes, Benji. You. He knew what it meant to sacrifice because of what you taught him by being his son. You enabled him to be a father and to know the true meaning of love, for what is love without sacrifice?"

"I never asked him to do that!" I cry at Michael.

"That's just it: you didn't *have* to," Michael says, folding his hands in his lap. His wings shudder slightly, the white feathers rustling. "The act of sacrifice is by its very nature a selfless act. One cannot sacrifice unless one is doing not for himself, but for the greater good. Your father knew this, Benji. He knew it more than most people."

"It's not fair," I mumble at him.

He gives me a sad smile. "It never really is. That's the funny thing about life. The moments of joy and wonder may be far and few between, but when they arrive, they are more glorious because of their long absence. The trials and tribulations you must go through to reach that glory are a test to make sure you can appreciate what you are given." He pauses, looking away. "May I tell you a secret, Benji?"

I nod, only because I don't know what else to do.

"I told you once that I was jealous of my brothers, that I vied for my Father's affections because I felt that he didn't have enough to share with all of us. How would he notice me amongst all my brothers and all the levels of humanity? Jealousy is an emotion that leads to sin, as one begins to covet what another has. I sinned in the name of love, and it was a dark thing." He looks back at me. "But I learned something, even being so young and brash. I eventually understood that my Father loved me just the same, as he did everyone else; that it wasn't any more or any less. Because there were so many, he couldn't love any one of them more. It would not have been fair. Do you understand?"

I nod.

"But you. It's different with you. Your father did not have anyone else. He had no one else to share his love with, at least as a father does with a son. Benji, I might not know your father personally, but I have seen the design. I have seen the pattern, the shapes. Your father loved your mother. He loved his friends and this tiny little town from which you both came. But his love for you made all the rest pale in comparison."

I hang my head.

He leans forward and puts a hand on my leg. "It's not meant to make you sad, nor is it meant to be a slight against your father. His love for you is a powerful thing, like the brightest beacon in the dark." He leans back. "There was a man who died shortly before your time. His name was James Baldwin, and he was a beautiful man. An old soul. A poet. I admired him for what he did and what he tried to do to help change the world. He wrote something once that I will remember for eternity. 'If the relationship of father to son could really be reduced to biology, the whole world would blaze with the glory of fathers and sons.' It's lovely, isn't it?"

I am unable to speak. I think Michael knows this. I turn my head and look at the charred outline of the child against the wall. I wonder what this child's father thinks about who he is.

"We are tested," Michael says. "Every day we are tested so that we might know faith and love. It might not always seem fair, but it is the way of things. You are going to be given a choice soon, Benji, and it will be more difficult than anything you've ever faced. For some reason, my Father has decided to see what you are capable of."

"I thought you hadn't spoken to him. To your Father."

He smiles. "Not directly. But I hear his whispers, and I recognize his design. I've known him a very long time, Benji. I know who he is, and I know the choices he makes. I may not always agree with them, but I know my Father. He's not always as mysterious as he sometimes likes to think he is."

"What do you want from me?"

He looks startled. "This is not something I am asking of you. This is...." He struggles to find the right words. "This is not an attempt to influence your free will, because that is something you will always have. The right of choice. *That* can never be taken from you, nor should it be. It helps define who you are and who you'll become. I merely mean to level the playing field, so everything is out in the open and you can make an objective decision."

"About what?"

"You'll soon see. I told you I've seen Calliel's memories."

"Yes," I whisper.

"Would you like to know what I saw?"

Do I? I don't know. I've received answers to questions, more than I ever hoped to find. I know what happened to my father. I know who killed him. I know the name of the betrayer from my family. I know my father died attempting to do the right thing. I know he loved me. I know that on the brink of death, he met with the angel Calliel and pulled from him a promise to watch over me specifically, to protect me when the time came. And whether or not he felt it before he fell, Cal loves me, I know. Completely and fully. I would do anything for him. If this would help Cal, then I need to listen. He needs me as much as I need him.

"Yes," I say, my voice clear.

He watches me for a moment, as if gauging my sincerity. As much as I want to quake under his gaze, I don't move until he nods. "I've told you that we're all tested. Has Calliel told you this as well?"

"Yes. He said that all angels are tested to prove their faith. He said that since he's newer at what he does, your Father might test him more."

"Our Father is nothing if not consistent. What Calliel told you is true. We are tested regularly. I wish to make sure that you understand that our Father is *not* questioning our faith in him. He's an old thing, set in his ways. He knows we have faith, but he wants us to *prove* it whenever he asks it of us. Often he'll give us two different paths, and we must make a choice about which path to follow. Think of it like contained free will. While we have the option to choose the path, whatever way we choose already has a set course, a predetermined construction in the design."

"So no matter what you choose, the outcome of that choice is already decided?" I ask. "That doesn't sound like much of a choice at all."

"And it's not," Michael says. "Not really. But it's presented as such. Most of us are much smarter than that and can see it for what it is. While the path beyond the choice may be veiled, the outcome is usually easy to discern. The design is a grand thing to behold, to see the way the paths reverberate out through the whole of it."

"What was Cal's test?" I ask, suddenly not wanting to know. "How did he fall?"

Something flashes behind Michael's dark eyes, but I don't know what it is. "Calliel is the guardian angel to Roseland, Oregon," he says. "He is the youngest angel in all of On High. Normally, when new townships are incorporated, they are enfolded into an existing angel's territory to protect. One day, our Father let us know that a new angel would be created, and that his name would be Calliel. This was cause for celebration, and, I admit, consternation, as no new angels had been created for millennia. He was given Roseland and its people, and while he may have fumbled at times, he was good at what he did." Michael shakes his head. "To be honest, he reminded me of me when I was his age. Overprotective of his charges. Desperate to please. Incapable of corruption.

"He existed quietly in this part of the world, on this plane of existence. He loved the people he watched over as he was supposed to. And that love was as it was supposed to be: a distant thing, a faraway thing that could never become more than that. But that changed."

"Who did it change for?"

"You're not *that* blind to the way of things, are you?" Michael asks with a smirk.

"*Me*?" I say incredulously. "You're talking about *me*?"

He cocks his head at me, an action so like his Strange Men I get goose bumps on my arms. "Of course I am. Who else would it be?"

"I… just… I don't know."

"From the moment you were born, Calliel watched you. It was a simple thing, at first. You were one of his charges, and he cared for you. He loved as he should. But then you began to grow, and those feelings changed. You have to understand, in terms of angels, Cal is still considered a teenager, if you will. He doesn't have the tight rein on his emotions that one in his position should have. There have been a few small instances in the past that have come to this, but they've always been corrected on their own as such things are unrequited. We are not meant to love."

"That's… so sad," I finish lamely. "You can love your Father and the people you watch over, but you can't ever get close to someone?"

Michael's eyes turn wistful for a moment, and I wonder if there's a story there. "It's the way of things, Benji. But Calliel changed that. He broke away from the pattern, the design. He allowed it to become something more. So Father did what he always did. He tested him."

"How?"

Michael's eyes burn darkly. "He gave him a choice. Either save your father and allow the man named Griggs to die, or allow your father to die and Griggs to live."

Of all the things he could have said, what he *did* say is what I expected the least. I grip the arms of the white chair as anger begins to well in my chest like a bloom of fire. I want to leap across at the angel and put my hands around his throat until he takes it back. I want to tear the White Room down until it's nothing but rubble underneath my fingers. I want to find God and make sure he pays for everything he's done.

But most of all, I want to find Cal and tell him to return to On High. I want to tell him to never come back, to forget he ever knew my name. And after that, I never want to see him again, and I will find someplace to float off into the darkness. It's the only way to keep me from killing him myself.

The White Room begins to shake a little, the walls and floor vibrating. I think I hear whispers all around me, but I can't tell above the blood roaring in my ears. Michael doesn't move, his eyes still on me, waiting.

"Why?" I manage to say.

"Because that is how my Father works. The tests aren't ever something simple, with a choice to be made that won't matter in the long run. What would be the point of such a thing?"

"This is my *life*!" I snarl at him. "This isn't some fucking game!"

Michael's not intimidated in the slightest at my fury. That sad smile makes an appearance again, as if he's trying to show he understands what I'm saying. But he can't. He can never know. He follows his Father blindly while the rest of us struggle to make sense of even the simplest of things. *It's faith,* Cal/Big Eddie/Abe whisper. *It's faith pure and simple. Sometimes, oh* sometimes, *you're not* meant *to understand.*

"It's not a game," Michael agrees. "And maybe I was a little harsh when I said it as such when we first met. I did not know then what I know now."

"What happened?"

Michael hesitates.

"Tell me!"

"Father revealed the whole of the design to Calliel," he says. "The outcomes of his decisions, however far down the line they could go. He gave Calliel the choice of who to save on that day."

"Why didn't he save my father?" I croak out. "Why did he choose to save Griggs?"

"Sacrifice, Benji. It all comes back to sacrifice. Choices are never meant to be black and white. By saving your father, he would ensure he would have lived a long and healthy life, that he would have been by your side for decades to come until one day, at the age of ninety-eight, he would have died peacefully in his sleep, surrounded by you, your partner, your children and grandchildren. He would have been so loved by the family you would have had."

"And by saving Griggs?"

"By saving Griggs, he potentially ensured the survival of humanity."

"*What?*"

Michael looks down at his hands. "Should the business of the Elementals on the other plane of existence resolve in the way we hope and all the worlds be saved, there will come a time, a hundred years from now, when there will be the possibility that a man will rise in the East on this plane with the intent to destroy all he sees. His fate will be decided by a simple action by George Griggs. Two years after your father died, Griggs helped save a young woman involved in a car accident. Because of him, she lived and will go on to give birth to a daughter. That daughter will grow up and give birth to a son. That son will save another woman from a fire, who in turn will live and give birth to twins. And so on and so forth, down the line, until the necessary opposition will rise against the man in the East, and humanity will have a fighting chance.

"My father revealed more of the design to Calliel than he ever had to anyone before. Calliel was left with a choice of whether to ensure your happiness or to make sure the world has a chance at survival should this dark man rise, long after you've already gone."

"He punished him," I say bitterly. "What you're trying to say is that he punished him for loving me."

"*Sacrifice*, Benji. It all comes down to *sacrifice*. And while the decision was difficult on Calliel, he made the only one he could, the only one an angel in his position *could*."

"And it had nothing to do with jealousy?" I snap at him. "Cal saw my future if my father had lived. You said I had my own family with me when my father died. Cal was obviously not in it. You don't think that influenced his decision at all?"

Michael looks at me sharply. "Does anything you know about Calliel suggest pettiness?" he asks, his voice hard. "I know you're angry, and I know it hurts, but think carefully before you speak, child. You're not a stupid boy, so don't act like one."

Ashamed, I look away. He's right. Of course he's right. Calliel doesn't have a selfish bone in his body. But even though it's not fair to *him*, I still can't find a way to soothe the anger burning through my veins. *He could have saved my father. Cal could have saved Big Eddie and I would have had him for a lifetime.*

"Why did he fall, then?" I ask.

"Because of your grief, Benji. Calliel was finding it harder and harder to live with the consequences of his decision. He broke protocol by making a promise to your father, one that was not his to make."

"What promise?"

"Think, Benji. You know. You've seen this. You've heard this. You've been there. It was in—"

the river

"—your dreams. You've been getting closer and closer every time, and you finally heard what you were supposed to hear."

I close my eyes and in the dark, I remember the river:

You have to protect him. If you are who you say you are, if you are a guardian angel, if you've been watching us all this time, then I'm asking you. No, I'm begging you. Do your duty. Guard him. Protect him with everything you can. Never take your eyes off him and let no harm come down on him. Do you promise me?

Big Eddie, I—

Promise me! You fucking promise me! This is my son! *You fucking promise me!*

I promise.

"He promised to protect me," I whisper.

"He did, but it was more than that. He is a guardian, Benji, and he would have guarded you anyway. But he was bound to his promise because Big Eddie meant it more than being a guardian. And Calliel knew that when he made the promise. He knew what it meant to accept a dying man's last wishes. He loves you, yes, more than I think I've ever seen before, but he fell to keep the promise he made to your father."

My mind is spinning, and I am dangerously close to being overwhelmed. There are too many emotions running through me all at once. I feel detached, and I can see everything Michael has told me swirling in me like a great storm. It's a massive thing, an angry thing, but every now and then there's a flash of blue, mixed in with all the black and gray and red. It's small, but it's bright, so very, very bright. I latch onto it, and the warmth I feel from it is like nothing else I've known.

"So he fell?" I ask, closing my eyes to see the blue lights.

"Yes," Michael says. "It's part of our limited free will, the choices that we can make. Metatron made that decision. And now Calliel."

"You keep saying free will," I tell him. "But it sounds like anything but."

He laughs and I open my eyes. "Semantics," he says with a wave of his hand.

"So what is my test? What decision do I have to make?"

He opens his mouth to answer, but then his eyes blacken completely and he rocks his head back slightly, his mouth dropping open. His wings shudder violently, and impossibly (*improbably,* I manage to think) a flash of light begins to spin above his head. I realize I'm looking at the faint outline of a halo. His lips begin to move as his eyes twitch back and forth toward the ceiling. The whispers from the walls of the White Room get louder and louder until they sound like the flow of a river. I cover my ears with my hands and bow my head as the White Room erupts in brilliant light.

And then it's over.

I slowly open my eyes as I lower my hands. I look back up at Michael, who is rubbing the sides of his head. "What the fuck was that?"

"That," he mutters, "was my Father."

I gape at him. "You just spoke to him? To *God*?"

He chuckles. "More like he spoke and I listened."

"What did he say?" I am *sure* I don't want to know, but I can't stop myself from asking.

"That I've said enough," Michael says ruefully. "That instead of telling you, it's time to show you." He shakes his head. "Unexpected, to say the least. I don't think this has ever been done." He stares at me hard. "What is it about you? Who *are* you?"

The whispers in the White Room quiet. All that's left is the sound of my ragged breaths. "I am Benjamin Edward Green," I say. "I am my father's son."

He stands suddenly, his wings flapping up behind him. He's a commanding presence as he holds out his hand toward me. I think of my father as I stand and take his hand. "Where are we going?" I ask the archangel.

"Away," he says. "There is a man who needs your help. A choice needs to be made."

"Why? Why must we always make choices?"

"Because my Father has commanded it." His wings begin to close around us, to capture us in a cocoon. I glance one last time at the child's shadow burned into the wall and send a single wish to him and the man named Seven. I wish for their happiness and that they can know peace, whatever it might take. Michael's wings close completely, and the White Room is gone.

"Who needs my help? What am I supposed to do?"

Silence.

"Michael?" I whisper in the dark.

A hand on my shoulder. "Yes, little one?"

"What's going to happen to me?" I sound so small. I feel so small.

He sighs, and when he speaks next, his mouth is near my ear. "You are being given a great gift," he whispers. "One most people will never receive. You must cherish it, and do your duty as a son. It's time for you to stand, Benji. It's time for you to stand and be true."

Everything flashes white.

the river crossing

I FEEL the sun on my face, warm and beautiful.

I hear the sounds of the birds in the trees, bright and sharp.

A breeze ruffles my hair, like a caress, carrying with it the perfume of summer.

A river flows somewhere in the distance.

I open my eyes.

I stand on a two-lane road, the asphalt cracked, the double yellow line down the center faded and chipped. A bee buzzes past my face. I follow it as it floats up and down until it lands on a green sign on the side of the road. The sign reads:

77

"No," I mutter. "Not here. Not again."

No one answers me.

I turn around to tell Michael to take me from this place, but I'm alone.

"Michael!"

No response. All I hear are the sounds of a normal, sunny day in the middle of nowhere.

This angers me.

"Why am I here?"

I spin.

"What do you want from me?"

"Take me home!"

"Why do I have to choose!"

"*Michael!*"

My voice echoes over the valley. I stop, throat dry and heart sore. My chest rises and falls rapidly. I don't understand why he'd take me to this place. I don't understand why I have to come here. This place is sadness. This place is loneliness.

This place is my grief.

I look down to the river.

It runs softly, beautifully. The water is a crystal clear blue. It laps gently at its banks. It does not feel threatening. It is not—

A man is crouched on the riverbank near a large cracked boulder. His massive back is to me, his face hidden. He lets a hand drift in the water. He's a big man, bigger than any man I've ever seen. He must be the biggest man in the world. In his chest must beat a great heart that pumps furiously to keep such a man alive. His dark hair is cut short, almost shaved completely, like my own. He's staring down at the river as if looking at his reflection. I…. He….

Oh, my heart. Oh, my soul.

I need him to turn around, but I can't find my voice.

Impossible, I think. *Improbable.*

I take a step toward him and then stop.

"Dad?" I whisper.

As if he can hear me, the man turns to look up to me. His green eyes shine like fireworks across a dark sky. Edward Benjamin Green, Big Eddie, my *father,* smiles up at me.

"*Dad!*"

And then I'm running. I'm running as fast as I can toward him, and everything around me slows and bleeds together and I—

am five years old, and he laughs a big laugh because no one laughs like my father. None laugh like him, and it is such a joyous sound, a happy sound, an amazing sound that my heart swells until I am sure it will burst. I

—leave the road, my feet crunching in gravel and dirt, and I—

am ten years old, and my father shows up to pick me up at school unexpectedly. He walks in, having to lower his head so it doesn't hit the doorjamb. I am worried at first, thinking something is wrong at home. But then he grins at me and winks, speaking quietly with Mrs. Norris. She laughs, and he beckons me with his hand. He steers me out of the classroom and out the door and we spend the rest of the day fishing off the old covered bridge. My

—feet hit the grass, and he starts to rise from his crouch and he—

asks me to hand him a wrench while he curses under his breath without looking up from underneath the hood of the Ford. I'm thirteen years old and scowl at his big hand engulfing my own when I hand him the wrench, wondering when I'm going to get my growth spurt so I can be big like Big Eddie. Somehow he knows what I'm thinking because he turns back to me, a grease smear on his nose, and says, "Only the size of your heart matters, Benj. The only thing that matters is"

—that I reach him as soon as possible. I feel like I could fly down the embankment. I feel like I'm—

dying. I feel like I'm dying as I stand under cloudy skies in a place called Lone Hill Memorial. I feel like I'm dying because I'm one of hundreds moving toward a waiting stone angel emblazed with fifteen words that mean nothing, that don't even begin to show the measure of the man they are supposed to represent. People hover nearby. My mother, the Trio. Abe. Rosie stands to my left, next to Doc Heward. So many others. They're all waiting for me to break. They're all waiting for me to shatter into a billion pieces. How can I explain that I already have? How can I explain that there is nothing left to me but dust and shadows and memories that rise like ghosts? They can't know. They couldn't possibly.

But that is not this moment. All that matters at this moment is the weight on my shoulder as I help carry my father up the dirt path to where the stone angel stands, her arms outstretched. All that matters is I can feel the corner of the coffin digging into my skin, the pain bright and vivid. All that matters is that I carry my father so he can sleep.

We reach the hole in the ground, perfectly dug and fitted with the lowering device. A member of the funeral home rushes over and points out quietly how the coffin should fit against the device. This makes it more real, and I almost refuse, wanting to tell everyone to go home, that I've changed my mind and I will not leave him here. Abe must see the look on my face, because he steps to my side, putting his hand on my shoulder and whispering soothing words in my ear that I can't quite make out. I nod and there's a count to three and we set my father down.

Later, after we're all seated, my mother clutching my hand, Pastor Thomas Landeros says, "Into the ground we lower a man who was a husband. A father. A friend, both to us and this community. God's plan may not make sense to us right now, and it may even make us angry, but rest assured there is a reason for all things, even if that reason is hidden from our eyes. Isaiah forty-one verse ten reads: 'Fear thou not, for I am with thee; be not dismayed, for I am thy God; I will strengthen thee; Yea I will help thee. I will uphold you with the right hand of my righteousness.'"

Fuck you, God, *I think.* You fucking bastard. Fuck you....

We stand, and people sing a hymn behind me. Their voices carry and wash over me, and I realize I am not broken completely because yet another part of me fragments. A tear falls down my cheek. The singing gets louder in my head, and I float along the river because I'm bound to its goddamn surface, and these stones fill my pockets, and it's into this fucking river I drown. I weep as I lay a single blue rose on top of the casket, my mother's hand at my back. Tears drop onto the oak lid, and I feel my knees begin to buckle. They give way as the coffin starts to lower into the ground, and I let out such a scream, such a howl of heartbreak and loss that everyone in the crowd shudders and sighs, bowing their heads and I—

can't get to him fast enough, I can't get to him fast enough, I can't get

—over the fact that I'm graduating high school. It's an odd feeling, really, that I've survived to get to this point. But when they call my name and I hear the roar from my family, I grin and walk across the stage. I accept my diploma and flip the tassel. I take a deep breath and walk down the steps. Later, we all throw our caps in the air, relieved and scared that this part of our lives is over.

My father is the first to reach me, running almost full tilt, and I freeze. I freeze, because for a moment, I think he had died in a river when I was sixteen, drowned after his truck flipped into the Umpqua. I have the feeling of being split, a duality that threatens to tear me apart. But then it's gone because he's laughing that big laugh and hugging me tightly, spinning me around in circles like he used to do when I was a kid. "You did it," he whispers in my ear. "Congrats, boy, you did it."

In one world I reach the bottom of an embankment, running toward my father while trapped in the memories of another world that never happened.

I'm twenty-four when I come home to Big House for Christmas. I'm nervous because for the first time, I'm not coming alone. I knock on the door, dusting snow

off Jeremy's hat as he winks at me. My mother opens the door and smiles at me widely, leaning in to kiss me on the cheek. She shakes Jeremy's hand before laughing and pulling him into a hug. Big Eddie waits just off the doorway, looking imposing as all hell, big arms crossed, a stern look on his face. My boyfriend Jeremy (who I might just be starting to love) quakes a little in his designer boots but holds his head high and reaches out to shake my dad's hand. My dad just stares at him until Jeremy drops his hand awkwardly. I roll my eyes and punch my dad in the arm, and it's all he can take before the façade breaks and he welcomes Jeremy with open arms.

I'm twenty-eight when Jeremy asks me to marry him.

I'm twenty-nine when my father stands beside me as my best man, trying his best not to cry as Jeremy slides a ring on my finger.

I'm thirty-two when I tell Big Eddie he's going to be a granddad. The look on his face is one of such wonder I can't seem to catch my breath.

I'm thirty-three when Jamie is born, all pink and perfect. Big Eddie is the first to hold him in his arms, telling him he's so happy to meet him, that the world is such a beautiful place.

I'm thirty-six when Hailey is born and we bring her home.

I'm thirty-nine when Big Eddie calls to tell me he has cancer. I hang up the phone, my world crashing down around me. I book a flight that very night. He's the one who picks me up at the airport, in the old Ford. We stay in the parking lot for an hour as he lets me sob on his shoulder, telling him he can't leave, he just can't. Telling him that I can't make it through this life without him. He holds me tight.

I'm forty when the cancer goes into remission and I remind him that he can't get away from me that easy. He just gives me that slow smile of his and drops his heavy arm around my shoulders, pulling me close.

In the world where the river runs and the sun is shining, I'm almost to him. His face, once adorned with a smile, is now scrunched up as he starts to break. He falls to his knees and opens his arms wide, his eyes bright.

There are so many memories. They rise like ghosts, and I remember stretches of days and weeks and months and years and he's there. He's always there. There are phone calls and visits and celebrations and sadness. There are bright days and dark days. Every emotion humanly possible is felt. But through it all, I realize the gift I've received. Whether or not this is real, I have been given the memories of what life could have been like had my father not drowned in the river.

And still I want more. I push for more.

He's ninety-eight years old when I sit by his bed. Jeremy is with our kids, watching our grandchildren in the hall. I sit quietly with my father in the night. The doctors say it will be soon and that he will not wake up. The others have left me alone so I have my chance to say good-bye.

I try to find the words to say to him that could convey the depth of my love for him. I try to think of a single thing to say that would show him what he means to me. I rest my head on his arm, rubbing my forehead against his skin. I might have imagined it, but for a moment, there seems to be a hand on my shoulder and a breath on my neck and I think that everything is blue. But then it's gone.

Finally, I say to my father words he'd said once to me. "There is no one such as you in this world, and you belong to me. I'll believe in you, always." I squeeze his hand and give him fifteen words that mean everything. "It's okay to sleep now, Dad. I know that one day, we'll be together again."

As if waiting for my permission, he slips away only moments later.

There is a world where he sleeps under an angel made of stone.

There is a world where he passes quietly, watched by the one who loves him the most.

And these two worlds collide, pulling in toward each other, rushing and rolling, combining until I can see *everything*, until I can feel *everything*. I feel the *life* of my father. I feel the *love* of my father. I feel the *loss* of my father, and it happens over and over and over again. There is the world that actually happened. There is the world that *could* have happened. I think this might be what Michael spoke of, and I cherish every moment of it even as my heart shatters again and again.

Every memory flashes before my eyes. Every single moment we did and did not share. All of these memories are pulled down to a single point, the tiniest possible space. There's an instant where it's black and silent, and then it explodes outward, arcing through this world and every other. Wave after wave of my past and future washes over me, and I see all possibilities. Every path not taken. Every shape. Every pattern. Every design.

And this. Out of everything, I beg you to see this:

This is the world where the river runs wild. This is the world where I leap the last five feet, unable to take the distance between us any longer. I hear the beat of massive wings, I hear the earth singing, I hear all the planes of existence holding their breaths for just one sweet, freeing moment. It is in this moment that I break through the surface of the river and come out on the other side.

And for the first time since he died five years before, I crash into my father, and he wraps his arms around me, and oh my *God,* I am home. I am home. I am *home.*

WE STAY like this, for a time. My head on his shoulder as I tremble, arms tight around his neck. He puts one arm around my back, the other pressing the back of my head with his big hand. I don't even try to hide that I've broken down, sobbing into his shirt, clutching at him. He tries to whisper soothing things to me, but his voice keeps cracking, and I can feel my hair getting wet from where his cheek rests.

What strikes me first, aside from the fact that this is actually real, is the way he smells. If I'd tried to remember it even an hour ago, I wouldn't have been able to. Not completely. But now? Now it's everything I remember from my childhood. It's wood smoke, it's clean sweat, it's grease, it's wintergreen, it's hard work. It's all the things I remember about him all wrapped up into something that is distinctly Big Eddie. I shudder at the thought.

Finally, he speaks, and the sound of his voice is almost enough to set me off all over again. "Let me look at you," he says roughly. "Just let me look at you." He pushes me back, cupping my face, roaming his gaze over me as if to catalogue every little thing he can. His hands are shaking as he wipes my cheeks. He tries to smile, but it breaks and his face stutters again. He closes his eyes and takes in a sharp breath. He drops his hands to my shoulders, and his grip is biting. He opens his teary eyes again. "Benji," he says, and I try to wrap my mind around the fact that I can hear my father say my name again. "Benji."

I weep for my father.

TIME passes, though I can't say how much. I don't know if it matters, or if I even can find the heart to care. It's deceptive, this place. The sun never seems to move from its position overhead, though I'm sure hours have gone by. The wind always blows sweetly, and the river babbles more like a brook than the Umpqua I know. The grass is the brightest green, the water the clearest blue. The trees seem to reach up to the sky, and the mountains are snowcapped, like they're covered in clouds. It's picturesque. It's perfect. It's not real.

What is real, though, is the weight of my father's arm on my shoulders. We sit side by side, our pant legs rolled up, feet in the water. The water's cold, but not so much it's unbearable. The sun is warm, chasing away any chill. We haven't really spoken yet, so overwhelmed the words aren't taking shape. It's like all my synapses have fired at once, and I can't form a single coherent thought. Everything is sensory—the warmth of his arm across the back of my neck, the smell of pine and oak, the sound of birds and bugs, the light refracting off the scales of a salmon when it jumps out of the water, the taste of the drying tears that have tracked to my lips.

I have so much to say, so of course I say nothing. It's not as if I'm scared, or as if I'm unsure of what I want to say. I want to tell him everything. I want to go through it all, day by day since I last saw him, leaving nothing out, so he can know the minutes and the hours he has missed. I want to tell him about Mom and how strong she really is. I want to tell him about Nina and how she might be the only one who understands why I missed him as much as I did. I want to tell him about Mary and how she kept us all together. I want to tell him about Christie and her betrayal. About our best friend Abe, who asked me to look away. About anyone and everyone he's ever known.

But most of all, I want to tell him about Cal. I want to tell him about the man I love and the man I hate. I want to feel rage, I want to clench my fists and hurt something. I want my father to see just how much I hate the angel Calliel for taking from me what was rightfully mine, the consequences be damned. Fuck Michael and his beliefs about faith and sacrifice. Fuck Cal and his decisions. Fuck God and his games.

So much to say. I say nothing.

"How are you, Benji?" my father finally asks, his voice light and happy. It's such a ridiculous question I can't help but laugh out loud. And even though he may not understand, my father starts to laugh just the same. Such a big fucking sound. "Okay," he says, chuckling. "That might not have been the best way to start."

I grin at him, my anger temporarily forgotten. "It was the *only* way to start. I'm okay, Dad. You?"

He smiles faintly before looking back out at the river almost longingly. I don't quite get the look, but I ignore it for now. "I'm better now," he says softly. "Better than I have been in a long while. It's been quiet here, since the others left."

I feel a chill at his words. "What others?" I ask, looking around. There's no one else in sight, and it doesn't seem like anyone else is watching us.

He shrugs. "Just some people came and went," he says. "I only talked to one of them. He was a… an odd man and he wanted me to go with him, but I couldn't. I don't think he understood, but I had to stay here. So he left."

"Why here? Why didn't you just leave?"

"I tried," Big Eddie says, squeezing my shoulder. "I tried to walk home, but…."

Tears well in my eyes yet again, and I brush them away. "You couldn't make it?"

He nods. "Every time I started walking down the road, I would get tired. I would need to sit down to rest, and before I knew it, I'd be asleep. And every time I woke up, I'd be right here again. I tried everything. I tried running. I tried sleeping before I left so I wouldn't be tired. I tried cutting through the forest. I tried going the other way. It didn't matter. I'd make it maybe half a mile, right before mile marker seventy-seven changed to seventy-six or seventy-eight, and then I'd have to stop."

"What about the river?" I ask. "Did you try crossing the river?"

He tenses immediately, and I want to take the words back, though I don't know why. "No," he whispers, unable to look at me. "I never crossed the river. That's what *he* wanted me to do, and I just couldn't."

"Who?"

"He called himself the River Crosser. He took the others across the river in this little boat, but I couldn't go. I just couldn't."

Through the fog and haze, I hear the Strange Men, both light and dark, whispering in my head about crossing. I can't quite remember what they said. It's lost, at least for now, as the haze swallows it again. But that's okay. It doesn't matter.

"I'm glad you stayed," I say, leaning my head on his shoulder. I try to ignore the unease that starts to prickle my skin.

"Me too," he says quietly.

We're silent for a time. Then, "Dad?"

"Yeah?"

I don't think I'll be able to get the words out, but I have to try. "Why did you have to go?"

And when he speaks, I already know the words he's going to say. I already know because I've said the same things to Michael. I've said the same things to Michael, and he told me things in return. About my father, about Cal. About the design of the world. About Seven and the child's shadow on the wall. But I can't seem to get his final words out of my head, about receiving a gift and my duty as a son. I am supposed to stand, but I don't know for what. I am supposed to make a choice, but I don't know what that choice is.

"I didn't want to leave you," my father says, looking down at the water. I follow his gaze and see his reflection in the water staring back up at us. "That was the last thing on my mind. I just... I couldn't just sit by and let these things happen. I couldn't let Roseland be taken over like I knew it would be." He frowns. "I overheard Griggs and Walken talking one day, and I just couldn't let it go. It wasn't right."

"You made a sacrifice," I say, understanding my own words for the first time. Hearing them from him is different than hearing them from Michael or myself. It actually means something; it has truth behind it.

"Although I wish I hadn't, now."

I'm surprised at this. "Why?"

"Because it took me away from your mom. It took me away from Abe. It took me away from my life and everything I had in it. But most of all, it took me away from you."

"I was angry," I admit hoarsely. "For a long time."

"I know. I could feel it. I could feel it here, like a storm was brewing somewhere far away."

"I'm sorry."

He snorts. "You shouldn't be the one apologizing, Benji. You didn't do a damn thing wrong. I know these last few months have been hard on you."

I'm cold again, and it has nothing to do with the water. "Dad?"

"Yeah?"

"How long do you think you've been here?"

He frowns again, lines forming on his forehead. I can tell he's thinking, because his tongue appears between his lips, a thing he's done since I can remember. He twitches his fingers on my shoulder and moves his lips, like he's counting, or at least trying to. It's taking longer than I think it should, and the unease gets stronger.

"Four months?" he finally says, sounding dubious. "Maybe a little bit longer?"

I shake my head, not trusting myself to speak until I have some sense of control. I swallow past the lump in my throat. "It's been five years," I say.

"No," he whispers. "That's impossible."

It's improbable, a voice whispers in my head.

"Trust me, it's not," I say, trying to keep the bitterness out of my voice. "You... died five years ago."

"It's... you're twenty-one now?" He sounds shocked.

"Yeah."

"I've missed... I...." He slowly drops his hand from my shoulder as he looks back to his reflection in the water.

"You didn't know?"

He shakes his head. "The River Crosser, he told me time could be a bit... funny here. I didn't listen to him because there were other things on my mind. He warned me about a lot, I guess. I just didn't listen. I had to...."

"Had to what?"

"Protect you," he whispers. "I had to make sure you were okay. I was so scared for you, Benj. I was angry with myself because I couldn't be there to protect you like I wanted to. I tried to do the right thing, and it got me...." He stops himself before he can say the word we're both thinking. "I didn't do my job as a father. My priority since you were born has always been you, and I let myself get distracted. I'm sorry, Benji. I'm so sorry."

"It's not your fault," I tell him. "You did what you thought was right."

"But you said you were mad."

I shrug, looking away. "I was. Maybe I still am. But... I don't know if it's at you anymore. I don't know if I can be mad at you when you're sitting right here next to me." I take a deep breath, steeling myself. Even though I know his answer, I still have to ask. "Did you miss me? Because I sure missed you."

"Every day, boy," he rumbles as he wraps his arm my shoulder again, pulling me tight. "Every damn day, which is apparently longer than I thought. A second hasn't gone by when I haven't thought of you."

"That's why you stayed? When the others left?"

"Yes," he says simply. "Are you really twenty-one now?"

"Yeah."

"My God, you're a full-grown man."

"I guess so."

Silence.

"Dad?"

"Yes, son?"

"I heard your promise. To Cal."

"I know. I tried very hard to show you."

"The dreams? That was you?"

He sighs. "Sort of. I tried to show you as much as I could."

I scowl, anger rising again. "And he tried to keep me away from you. Cal always pulled me out of the river. He didn't want me to see what you were trying to show me."

My father looks stern. "As well he should have. It wasn't all me, Benji. Those dreams. It was the river too. Cal was only doing what I had asked of him. To protect you as much as possible. I couldn't control it as well as I thought I could. He saved you from drowning. He saved you again and again and again."

I don't reply.

But this is my father. He knows me better than anyone. "So that's what I was feeling," he says in awe.

"What?" I say, my face flushing.

"You love him." It's not said as a question.

"Dad...."

"Well, shit."

"Yeah."

"He's... a nice guy."

I can't help the laugh that comes out. "A nice guy?"

"Does he love you back?"

I nod. "I think so."

"He better."

"I don't know if I can do right by him."

"I raised you, didn't I?"

"Well, yeah."

"Then you'll do the right thing, Benji. You always will."

My eyes start to burn again. "I'm losing him," I say through the tears. "When I thought he was gone, it felt like I'd lost everything all over again. He's... Dad, he's made me feel alive for the first time in a long time. He's sweet, and kind. And smart. And everyone loves him. He had such reverence for the Ford you would have thought he helped to build it too."

"Maybe he did," Big Eddie says slowly. "I gathered he'd been around for some time."

"But he can't stay," I say, my breath hitching in my chest. "He can't stay."

My father pulls me closer. "Why?"

"Because he'll die. Angels can't stay where we are. He has to go back."

"Says who?"

"I do!" I say angrily, trying to pull away from him. He doesn't let me go. "I couldn't take it if he died too. My heart couldn't take it."

"It will," he tells me. "It will because I've raised you to be strong and brave. I've raised you to always think of others before yourself."

I'm incredulous. "I *am*! I don't want him to die!"

"What does *he* want?"

"I don't...."

"You've never asked him, have you?"

"No, sir."

"I'll bet if you did, he'd tell you exactly what he wants. It seems to me if he wanted to go back, he would have already. If he wanted to avoid any risk at all, he could have. But he didn't. He took a chance."

"Because he promised you," I remind him sadly. "He wouldn't even be here if he hadn't promised you."

Big Eddie sighs. "You don't know that. He could have chosen just the same. We all have a choice, Benji, with everything we do. And if you ask him, I'd bet anything he'll tell you he wants to stay. And even if it means he dies, don't you want to say you had what you could with the time you have left? It's better, Benji, to have something burn brightly for a short time than to never have it at all. But that may not even happen. You just have to have faith."

"In what?"

He smiles. "That everything will be okay. If he believes in you, then you need to believe in him. Nothing's written in stone."

"I don't know if I can do this without you," I say, starting to break again.

"Hush," he says, resting his chin on my head. "There's still time."

We say nothing for a while after that, just sit there, content with each other's reassurance that somehow it'll all be okay. He never removes his arm from my shoulder. Our feet kick the water. He ruffles my hair. I breathe him in, and he does the same to me. After a time I hear him humming, and I can't help but go along with it. He finds his words and we sing together: "Sometimes I float along the river, for to its surface I am bound. And there are times stones done fill my pockets, oh Lord, and it's into this river I drown."

There's that sense of duality again, like I'm being pulled in two different directions, like the road ahead splits into two different paths. One is safe and certain, the other scary and unknown. But it helps to see.

I understand now, I think. I understand Michael's gift and what I must do, the choice I have to make. This was never about helping me. This was never about my grief or pain. This was never about the anger, the loss, the love, the betrayal. It's about nothing that I thought it was. It's not even about me.

This is about my father. It's about this man, this big man who sits beside me, who I will compare everyone to for the rest of my life, should I choose to go that direction. It's about this man who would not cross the final river so he could go home because he loved his family above all else, and he couldn't see them hurt, no matter the cost to himself.

That's because it's all about sacrifice, Michael whispers. *The world will blaze in the glory of fathers and sons because they know it's about* sacrifice. *What a person does for the greater good defines who they are. A man should never be measured by how full his life is, but what he is willing to give up in order to protect those he loves. He must do so without regard for his own self. That is a measure of a man. That is worth more than any combination of fifteen words that mean nothing.*

"I saw things," I tell him quietly. "Beautiful things. Memories of things that could have happened. They rose like ghosts and I saw it all. I thought it was a gift...."

"But?" Big Eddie prods gently.

I think before I speak. "But it's not. That wasn't the gift. It wasn't, because it wasn't real. It never happened. It was part of the design never used."

"Then what were you gifted?"

"You," I tell him, and he smiles at me with watery eyes. "Here, this moment. This chance. I was given you because in my heart, that is what I wished for the most. Not even for you to be alive, not for things to not have happened the way they did, not really. All I ever wanted was to just have a few moments where I could sit right next to you and feel you here, so I could tell you how much you mean to me. How much I love you for being my dad."

"Benji, don't you think I know?"

"I know. I know you know. But please, just listen, okay?"

He nods, looking pained.

"I have this moment. I have this great moment, something most people will never get. Not while they still have a chance to live. Not when there is still hope to return. So I have to say thank you." My voice breaks on the last word, but I push through. "Thank you for being my dad and thank you for making me who I am. Thank you for loving me and accepting me. Thank you for protecting me and making sure I could stand on my own two feet. And if anyone ever thinks me brave and strong, if I ever stand again for what's true, it'll be because of you. It'll be because you are my father, and I will always be my father's son."

He looks off to the river, his eyes brimming. "There has never been a father prouder than I am. I hope you know that, Benji."

"Yeah. I know."

"You're not going with me, are you?"

I shake my head even as my heart breaks further. "No. I think I'm here to tell you it's okay now. It's okay to let go. It's time for you to move on." I shudder. "There are others who need me. There are other people I have to help." I hate the words. I hate everything about them. Even as they spill from my mouth, I want to take them back. But I can't, because that's not what he taught me. That's not what it means to be his son. It's about sacrifice.

He nods. "It's the river, isn't it? I have to cross the river."

"I think so."

"I'm scared," Big Eddie Green says, holding me close. "I shouldn't be, but I am."

"I know," I choke out. "I'm scared too."

"Benji?"

"Yeah?"

"Will you help me?"

And this is it, here, this moment: this is my last chance. This is where I could say I'm going with him. This is where I could say I'm tired, I'm so very tired, and I don't want to go back. This is where I could say we'll cross all the way together. That we'll be side by side for the rest of time, and that will be all that matters.

But I don't. I say none of that. I say none of what is tearing my head and heart to shreds, because there *is* a part of me that wants to cross with him. There's a subtle whisper that I think has been here since I arrived, and it causes me to ache because it's singing me home. It's nothing like the voices in the black. It's kind and soothing, telling me all will be well, that the world can be a wonderful place, but sometimes it's okay to just leave it behind and come back home. I don't know how my father has been able to ignore it for so long.

So instead of saying what part of me wants, I say the only thing that matters, because I am not here for me. I am here for him. "Always," I tell my father, who sighs in relief.

We sit then, just for a bit longer, with what time we have left. As if our words were what it was waiting for, the sun begins to move slowly across the sky, the day pushing toward night. It's subtle at first, but the river begins to move more rapidly, the waves growing bigger, the water level rising. I feel my father start to shake again, and instead of allowing him to comfort me, I shrug his arm off my shoulders and wrap my arms around him. He sighs and leans his head down against mine as we watch the river rise.

"I'm tired, Benji," he says. "Don't know how I got so tired."

"I know," I reply, kissing his forehead. "It's okay, though. Just a little longer. You only have to go a little longer."

"The water is moving so fast," he murmurs.

"You're stronger than it is," I say, gathering my courage for a final time. We have to go.

"I'll miss you," he whispers, and it's like I'm six. It's like I'm six years old and trying to run away but knowing I will always come home because *he* is my home. "Every day we're apart, I'll miss you until we're together again."

"Because you're my daddy?"

"Because I'm your daddy," he says faintly, smiling at the memory.

"You must love me, huh?"

"Oh yes. Very much."

"Why?"

The river rises and begins to roar.

"Because you're everything. Benji, I'm scared. I'm so scared."

"I know. But I'll be with you. I promise."

"Even here at the end?"

"Even here at the end."

And because if I don't do it now I never will, I stand, pulling my father up with me, his arm around my shoulder, lifting and holding his weight against me. He moans quietly, and I choke back the sob that threatens to rise. He leans against me as the sun disappears behind the mountains and twilight begins to fall.

The first step's the hardest, as it always is. The first step is filled with doubt and trepidation. The first step makes you want to stop and reassess, to make sure you're going about this the right way, doing the right thing. The first step is where choices are met with determination, because every step after will be easier.

And so I take it. I take that first step for my father. For myself. That first foot forward is followed by the other, and my father has no choice but to follow me or be left behind. For a moment, I think he *won't* follow, but he does. Of course he does. Big Eddie is strong and brave. He's the biggest man in all the world. He is the smartest, the funniest, the greatest man alive. He's the reason the sun shines in the sky, the reason the stars come out at night. He is the greatest man in the world because he is my father, and I can see him no other way. So of course he steps forward. Of course he moves along with me, beside me for that first step and the ones that follow.

We reach the riverbank and I'm sure we'll hesitate. I'm sure we'll pause to make sure we're doing the right thing. But even as the thought forms in my head, my father steps down and into the river, the swift water rising to his knees.

I follow him in.

"Benji," he gasps. "You can't...."

"Until the end," I say.

He nods, and his head comes back to my shoulder. We step together.

What follows is hard. The current is stronger than I've ever felt before. The river mud sucks us down with every step we take. The water splashes up into our faces, blinding us, choking us. And still we push on. My father's breath is ragged in my ear, and my chest feels like it is burning. But still I push on, for him. For him, I would do anything.

The river reaches my shoulders by the time we're halfway. And it's at this halfway mark that the whispers from the other side get louder, more inviting, more calming. They are calling me home, telling me all it takes are just a few more steps and I'll be home, my father will be home, and we'll be home together. Isn't that what I want? Isn't that what my heart desires?

It is. It is. It is.

"No," my father croaks. "No. Not now. Not yet. It's not your time."

River water splashes up into my face, urging me on, and I try to pull him toward the whispering voices.

"No," he says, sounding more sure. He grunts as he pushes himself upright, the water to his chest. He pulls his arm from around me and turns me to face him. When I look up at my dad, his eyes are shining such bright green. He looks stronger than before, and I know that look. He's made up his mind, and there will be no other way.

"You're going back now," he says as the river batters us both. "It's time for you to turn around and go back."

I begin to panic. "No. No! It's not. It's not time! There will never be enough time. I'm going with you! I'm going with you, and I won't look back! Please don't make me. Please don't leave me here. I can't do this without you!"

He shakes his head. "You can't go with me," he says. "You know you can't. It's not your time. It's not meant for you."

"Just don't leave me alone again," I moan. "Please."

He cups my face in his hands. "You listen to me, boy, and you listen good. Are you listening?"

I nod, and even the river fades because all I can see is him.

"You are my *son*," he says fiercely. "You will never be alone because I will *always* be with you."

"You promise?" I cry.

"I promise with all that I have. Now go *back*."

"Dad." I don't know what else to say.

But he understands anyway. "I know. I'll see you again. I swear, one day, I'll see you again."

And he pushes me away. Not knowing what else to do, I take a step back. And then another. And then another. He watches me and waits, the river slamming into his massive frame. It's a struggle, but I make it back and haul myself out of the river and onto the cool grass.

And as the stars come out above, and as the moon glows brightly in the sky, my father turns and faces the other side. He takes a deep breath… and pushes on. Every step he takes is one closer to the other side. It gets harder for him as he gets closer. The waves wash up and over him, the river trying to sweep him away. There's one moment where he stumbles and I think he's going to go under, but he manages to keep his balance and takes another step.

And another.

And another.

Away, away, away from me.

And then he reaches the other side and pulls himself up and onto the bank. We both collapse on our sides of the river, lying on our backs, catching our breath. The stars are so bright. So blue. Everything here seems to be blue, and I know it's almost time for me to go home. I've been given a gift. I've made my choice. I've done my duty as a son. For him.

I sit up and look across the river.

My father stands, watching me.

I don't know how much time passes then. But we watch each other, a river separating us, taking one last look while we can. I don't know when we will see each other again, but I cling to the promise that we will. I pray. I have faith. I have hope.

Then suddenly he smiles and looks over his shoulder. I know someone is calling to him, someone I can't see or hear. I wonder who it is. He turns back to me, and the smile fades, a conflicted look coming over his face. He takes a step toward the river. I do the only thing I can do, to ensure he goes.

I say good-bye.

I raise my right hand in his direction. A small wave. I ache.

Big Eddie nods slowly and raises his hand in return.

His smile returns and he lowers his hand, and with one last look, he turns away. Above the river, I hear him shout in joy. It sounds like he cries, "Abe!"

And then he's gone.

I SIT for a time, in the dark, watching the other side of the river. He doesn't come back.

Finally, I rise to my feet. "One day," I say with a small smile. "One day."

One more time, I must stand.

I turn away from the river, and everything explodes in white.

the fallout

I OPEN my eyes and I'm back in the White Room.

For a moment, I panic, sure I will be trapped here forever, that I was meant to cross with my father and since I didn't, I am now in limbo. I'm sure, in that split second of rising terror, that I'll be nothing but a burnt shadow on the wall, a vague mystery for all those who will follow my footsteps into this place.

"It's okay," a soothing voice says. "Benji, it's okay."

Is it? Is it really?

The confusion on my face must be clear, because the voice says, "Oh, baby. Oh, sweetheart. You're okay now, you're fine. And I love you. Everything will be okay." Then, quietly, "Go get the doctor. Hurry. Now."

The room comes into sharper focus. Not *the* White Room, but *a* white room. Soft fluorescent lighting overhead. Eggshell ceiling tiles. The subtle tang of ammonia. The hiss and beep of machines. A blurred face, hovering over my own. A cool hand brushes against my brow.

My mother. Lola Green. The most beautiful woman in the world. I have so many things I need to tell her. So many, many things.

I try to smile at her, but there's something in my throat. My eyes widen. I start to panic. I start to breathe heavily. The machines beep loudly in warning. I'm gagging. My body starts to shake, and I can't stop it. Pain rolls over me in crushing waves. I hurt everywhere. My body. My heart.

Cal. Cal. Cal.

I try to make her see with my eyes, try to tell her what my soul is screaming for. She looks scared and she's yelling at someone over her shoulder, and then she looks back down at me, telling me it's okay, to calm down, that everything will be fine.

Cal, I try and tell her. Cal.

But then I'm in the dark again.

I'M COGNIZANT on what I'm told is my fourth day in the hospital. Apparently, my right lung collapsed after being shot, hence the need for intubation to clear all the rising fluid in my chest. I was Life-Flighted through the storm and taken to Eugene, where surgery was performed on my lung and to remove the bullet from my chest. I woke up on the third day and had some sort of panic attack then collapsed back into unconsciousness for another eighteen hours.

My right wrist was shredded from the pocketknife. I am told I will have heavy scarring on my wrist unless I would like to consider plastic surgery. I wave the offer off tiredly. I don't care what my wrist looks like. It's now heavily bandaged. The stitches itch horribly. No one will help me scratch it.

My ankle is severely strained. I have contusions in varying shades of greens and yellows, blues and purples, covering my entire body. Cuts on my legs and arms. My nose is running, and I have a wet cough I can't seem to shake.

And that's the biggest concern, I'm told. The potential for pneumonia. It's no wonder, the doctors say, seeing as how I was found in the river in the middle of a storm by a passing motorist who then drove me back into Roseland. They'd seen a flash of my clothing and had almost continued on but stopped. I say nothing to this, casting only a casual glance toward my mother, who looks away. We both know that's not what happened. The risk for infection is quite high, though, the doctors say, and I'm not exactly out of the woods yet.

The path of the bullet was, I am told, miraculous. Aside from nicking my lung, it bounced off a rib, breaking it in the process, and embedded itself in muscle. It didn't strike any other organs or any other bone. The doctors can't figure out how a shot from a rifle didn't cause much more severe damage at such close range. I'm told I must have a guardian angel on my shoulder.

The doctors leave, telling me I'll need plenty of rest, though I have quite a few people waiting to speak to me.

The room is covered in balloons and flowers, stuffed animals and cards. My mother tells me it seems like everyone in Roseland has sent me something, and that there's been quite the stream of visitors to the hospital here, though they've all had to stay out in the waiting room. There were always at least five or six of them, and they seemed to take turns. It's a funny thing, she says, how close our town really seems to be. She grips my hand tightly as she says this.

"Mom?" I ask her tiredly. "What's going on? Where's Cal?"

A tear rolls down her cheek.

Dread fills me. "Where is he?"

A shuddering sigh. Then, "He's dying, Benji."

The storm hit faster than they thought it would, back in Roseland. One minute it was just cloudy and overcast and they were all enjoying the festival, and the next it was like Heaven itself had opened up and poured down. The rain, my mother says, was a frightening thing, cast almost sideways by the roaring wind. The gusting wind itself blew down Poplar Street, knocking over signs and breaking windows. The booths and displays for the festival were toppled almost immediately. Most of the town was at the festival, and the majority took refuge in the church, the rest in the Grange. It was strange, some whispered, how the wind had seemed to blow them directly into these places. Some tried to leave but turned back when it became impossible.

There were concerns that the river would rise too high and flood the streets. Sandbags were placed out along the church and the Grange as a precaution, just in case floodwaters began to chase after them.

My mother was in the church, with Mary and Nina.

The power flickered on and off before finally just staying off. Candles were lit as people huddled together, listening to the storm rising outside. My mother was panicking, not knowing where I was. She tried calling me many times, but eventually the signal cut out and her phone was useless. Mary and Nina tried to calm her, to let her know I was obviously with Cal and Abe and that we'd be okay. Christie, they said, would also be okay because she was at Big House.

There had been nothing to do but wait.

And pray.

My mother says she prayed that day. She prayed for the first time in a very long time. Pastor Landeros was leading a quiet service for those who wanted it, but my mother wasn't listening. She was sitting toward the back, looking at the beautiful stained glass window set high on the other side of the church. It was a circle of so many whites and greens and reds and yellows, with St. Jude Novena in the center, a red beard, long flowing robes of green and brown. And blue. So much blue.

Her grandmother had taken her to this very church on many occasions when my mother was a child. She remembered a prayer she'd been taught when she asked who that man in the glass was. *That's St. Jude Novena*, her grandmother had told her. *And he has a special prayer, one made for your darkest hour. But prayers are not like wishes, my child. They won't always come true. But if you pray hard enough, surely someone will listen, and that, my darling, is what prayer is all about.*

So my mother prayed, and recited the prayer of St. Jude Novena.

Most holy apostle, St. Jude, faithful servant and friend of Jesus, the church honors and invokes you universally, as the patron of hopeless cases, of things almost despaired of. Pray for me, I am so helpless and alone. Make use, I implore you, of that particular privilege given to you, to bring visible and speedy help where help is almost despaired of. Come to my assistance in this great need that I may receive the consolation and help of heaven in all my necessities, tribulations, and sufferings, particularly that my son is safe from harm so that I may praise God with you and all the elect forever.

I promise, O blessed St. Jude, to be ever mindful of this great favor, to always honor you as my special and powerful patron, and to gratefully encourage devotion to you.

Amen.

Seven minutes later, the doors to the church blew open with a great crash. Wind and rain flew into the church. People shouted and screamed. And then all fell silent when the impossible happened.

An angel entered the church, deep blue wings spread wide, water dripping onto the floor. He had a panicked look on his face as he looked from side to side. "Help," he croaked out. "I need help. Someone, please. Help me. He's hurt and I can't fix him. Please." He looked down at the body he carried in his arms. "He won't wake up. Please just wake up. Please, Benji. Just wake up."

My mother gives me a fragile smile now, from her place next to my hospital bed. "You'd have thought," she says, "people had seen angels all the time with the way things happened next. Doc Heward ran forward and made him lie you down. I was holding your hand and crying so hard I couldn't see straight. Others came forward and offered to help. Rosie got blankets. Mary got the first-aid kits. Jimmy brought fresh water, and the Clarks went back to try and radio for help.

"But it was Nina who went to him first. Our little Nina. He stood, off to the side, watching the doc work on you. His eyes never left your face, not until she came over to him. She walked right up to him and reached up to touch his face. He closed his eyes and sobbed, just once, his whole body shaking."

Everyone fell silent then, watching the tiny woman touch the gigantic angel. The doc continued to work on me, but even he glanced out of the corner of his eye.

"Oh, Blue," Nina said finally, her voice quiet. "You are in so much pain."

"My heart hurts, little one," Cal choked out. "I cannot lose him. Not now. Not ever. I would be lost."

"What does your Father say?" she asked.

"Nothing. He has forsaken me." His voice was bitter.

Nina smiled up at the angel. "He would never forsake you. You just aren't listening."

The angel trembled… and then he collapsed.

"Where is he?" I demand now, horrified. "You didn't bring him here, did you?" I can only think of him being locked in a room while having experiments performed on him by people who need explanations, who need everything broken down to exact science rather than being able to believe in the impossible. "Please tell me he's not here!"

My mother shakes her head. "No, baby. We didn't. He's still in the church. The doc has been watching over him. Hell, the whole town has been watching over him. But there's not much more the doc can do. He's fading, Benji. Cal's fading. I'm sorry. I'm so sorry." She has tears in her eyes when she finishes.

I'm still so very angry, though I don't know if the anger is directed toward him anymore. I don't know how it could be, but part of me still feels the need to place blame. Part of me feels none of this needed to happen, that Cal shouldn't have been put in the impossible situation of deciding between the lives of two men. My father didn't need to die. So many things didn't need to happen but did because of God. Because of his games. Because of his design.

I love you, Cal had said.

"I need to see him," I mutter. "He needs me." I make to get up from the bed, but my body is one gigantic ball of pain and I can barely move. I groan as I force my way through it, but my mother leaps up from the chair and pushes me back down.

"You need your rest," she says sternly. "I swear to God, if you try to leave here and something happens to you because of it, I will never forgive you."

"If he dies while I'm here," I say to her coldly, "I will never forgive *you*." And in my secret heart, I know this to be true, no matter how dark it makes me feel.

She flinches and looks away.

See me, I pray to him. *Cal, see my thread. Please hold on. Please don't leave me. I need you.*

But anger continues to rise. At her. At my father. At God and Michael. And at Cal. Mostly, at him.

Sleep takes me only moments later.

MANY people want to speak to me the next day. Doctors, therapists. Nurses and radiologists. They all have questions as they poke and prod me, as they take my blood or wheel me down to yet another test. I'm lucky, I'm told repeatedly. Only a few more inches to the left, and the bullet would have pierced my heart. So lucky, they sigh. I could have died, they say in hushed voices. It's a miracle.

Many people want to speak with me the next day, but none more than the FBI.

Turns out a man named Teddy Earle was found wandering near Old Forest Highway with some surface burns on his skin. He was dazed and slightly confused. He said that his friend had been burned to a crisp, that his boss was gone when he awoke. He was taken to a clinic in Jackson County, and when they found crystal meth in his pocket, they called the police. Police came (thankfully, I was told, not the Douglas County Sheriff's office) and Mr. Earle was interviewed. Turns out he had quite the tale to tell, dropping names most could not believe. A psychopath named Jack Traynor. A dead arrestee named Arthur Davis. An FBI agent named Joshua Corwin. A sheriff named George Griggs. A mayor of a small town named Judd Walken. The woman in charge named Christie Fisette.

And, of course, a man named Edward Benjamin Green. Big Eddie, to his friends.

The storm cleared and four different law enforcement agencies ascended the mountain to the caves Earle had pointed them to. They found remnants of a large methamphetamine operation up there. They found the body of Mr. Earle's associate, a man named Horatio Macias. They found the body of one Abraham Dufree, pulled away into the forest. Eventually, they found the body of George Griggs, who had drowned in the river, pinned up against a rock by a tree.

Mayor Walken fled the day of the storm. He made it as far as Glendale, forty miles down the road. His car was found overturned in the river. They thought he survived the impact, but might have drowned when the water rose too high. He must have lost control, they said.

Jack Traynor was found a day later, washed up on the banks down river five miles away.

My Aunt Christie was found the day before I woke up. Her body was deep in the woods, huddled up against a large rock. It was unclear exactly how she died, but most likely it was from exposure. It appeared she'd gotten turned around while trying to escape into the woods. Water, I was told, had filled her lungs. Like she had drowned. They didn't know how that had happened.

I told those who asked what had happened, leaving Cal out of every part of it. I told them about Traynor trying to run us off the road. I told them how Abe had saved us by shooting Traynor in the head. I told them about how Griggs and my aunt had shown up only moments later. I told them about my meeting with Corwin, and how Griggs and Christie tried to use Abe to find out if I'd told anyone else. I'd told them, my voice breaking, how they'd shot Abe right in front of me.

I told them about my escape, the explosion, my run through the woods. I told them how Griggs had followed me, and that he shot me, only to slip and fall into the river. Did I remember who found me? No. Did I remember getting taken back into town? No. Did anyone in town remember who had brought me in?

Apparently no one did. Just some stranger, the agents were told. Some stranger who passed right on through and didn't leave any information.

Small towns take care of their own.

"You're lucky to be alive," an agent named Nathan Rosado told me once the interview was done. "Most wouldn't have gotten away like you did. You did a very brave thing, even if you had no business trying to go up there in the first place." But his admonishment was soft, and I saw he was impressed. I knew I'd corroborated almost everything Mr. Earle had told them, and Agent Rosado told me that most likely I wouldn't have to testify, seeing as how almost everyone involved appeared to be dead. "There will be more questions, though," he said. "But those can wait for now."

They left me alone after that, for a time. No one from town had been in my room to see me, though I knew some of them were nearby. I didn't want to see them, not yet. I wasn't ready to face the questions they would have, about the angel that slept in the church. I wasn't ready for those questions, because I didn't know what answers to give. I needed to see him first. I needed to get the fuck out of this damned hospital. I needed to see the man I loved.

And my anger grew.

These thoughts were interrupted when my mother came back into the room shortly after the FBI agent had left. It was only then that it hit me how hard this had to be on her as well. Not only had she lost her husband, she'd found out her sister had ordered it done. Whatever I was going through, she was experiencing almost the same. She looked tired, dark smudges circling her eyes. Her hair was frazzled and pulled back into a loose ponytail. Her clothes looked wrinkled and slept in.

I knew we were survivors, she and I. I knew we'd have to pick ourselves up from the dirt yet again. If we didn't, then we'd be nothing and blow away. So much of life demanded sacrifice, I knew, and the only way to make it through was to take one step at a time, one day at a time. She needed me to help her back up, and I was the only person left who could.

So for the moment, I stopped planning my escape when she wasn't looking. I stopped trying to figure out a way to get to Cal before the day was over. I started thinking about more than just myself and what I needed. She came back into my room and I opened my arms, and there was a stutter in her step, a frown on her face that turned into something more. She cracked and rushed over to me, and as she shattered, I ran my fingers through her hair and told her it'd be okay, that it'd be all right. I told her that even though it may not seem like it, one day, we'd be okay again.

There was a brief moment when I almost told her about seeing Big Eddie again. I opened my mouth to spill the words, wondering what, if any, comfort it might bring her. But a second later, I closed my mouth again. It didn't feel right. It didn't feel fair to her. I didn't want her to know that he'd been trapped by the river for five years while trying to protect me. Maybe it was guilt. Maybe it was something more. I don't know. Maybe I *will* tell her. One day.

"How do you know?" she sobbed into me, clutching at my arms. "How do you know we'll be okay? The world has gone to shit and everything is broken! How do you know? *How do you know!*"

"Because I have faith it will," I whispered back. "And because I have faith in you. There's no one I know who is stronger than you. It might be rough, and it might seem unfair, but we'll be okay. I promise you we'll be okay."

My thoughts strayed to Cal, and I felt like a liar. If something happened to him, I wouldn't be okay. If he left me, I knew I would find the river and once again be adrift.

With those thoughts came the seed of doubt that sprouted quickly.

A final test.

I'M AWOKEN from a nightmare by a touch to my face, a finger dragging along my cheek. I open my eyes. It's dark in the room, the only light coming from the door that's cracked open. My heart thuds painfully against my chest. I'm convinced it's Griggs here with me in the dark and that he's going to take me into the White Room forever.

But then my eyes adjust and my nightmare flees. Nina is standing over me, touching my face, poking my cheek. This is the first time I've seen her since I've been in the hospital.

"Are you awake now?" she asks, her eyes shining in the dark.

"What time is it?" I ask her.

"Not too late," she says. "Not too late for a lot of things."

My mind is still fuzzy. "What are you doing here?"

"Big House and Little House are empty," she says quietly. "So many things are gone. Even Mary feels it. We came here to see Lola. I came here to see you." She looks down at my arm and touches the needle for the IV at my wrist. Her eye follows the tubing until it reaches the machine pumping me full of God knows what.

I smile up at her. "It's good to see you." It's not as hard to breathe as I thought it would be.

She nods and then pulls the needle out of my hand with a quick jerk, the tape catching on my skin.

"Nina! That fucking hurt!"

She frowns. "Language," she scolds. "We don't have much time."

"For what?"

"You. We need to leave."

She pulls me up to a sitting position, ignoring my groans. "And go where?"

My aunt stares at me as if I'm stupid. "Blue needs you," she says. "Can't you feel it, Benji? He's almost gone. He needs you."

I feel cold. And what's worse is, I hesitate. Removed from the situation by a few days, I've allowed my anger to rise unchecked. And this time, it is *all* directed toward him. He had a choice to make, yes, and he was tested by his Father, oh yes, but he could have done something. He could have done something more. He could have stood up to his Father and said no. He could have done everything in his power to stop it from happening. He could have saved my father.

Or, Michael whispers, *he could have promised him to watch out for his only son for the rest of his days. Or he could have fallen to earth to protect this son. Or he could have cared for this boy. Or he could have fallen in love with him and treasured him above all else, even though it was so close to blasphemy it endangered his mortal soul.*

"Nina," I say, hedging.

She stops and stares at me hard.

I look away.

"Oh, no," she says. "You don't get to do this. You don't get to say no. Not now. Not after all he's done for you."

My mind is beginning to clear, and it hurts to think.

"That man loves you," she growls at me, squeezing my hands tightly. "And he needs you, Benji. Just like you need him. You can't stay here. You can't keep hiding. This is just another white room and you know it. If you wait too long, the choice will be made for you."

I snap my eyes to hers. "How did you…."

"It doesn't matter. You must hurry."

"I'm tired," I say. "I'm tired of everyone telling me about choices. I'm tired of having to make choices. I'm tired. The choices I make don't matter. Nothing I do matters. How can it? God can just take everything away whenever he wants, so how the *fuck* does anything I do matter? It's just a *game*, Nina! It's all just a fucking game!"

She flinches away from me as I finish, but it doesn't last long. Her gaze filling with steely resolve, she leans over and brushes her lips against my cheek. "Then you fight," she whispers harshly in my ear. "You fight for what you believe in. You *fight* for what's yours. He would do it for you—he already has. The only real person in the world who can know what a father can mean is dying, Benji. He's dying, and he needs you."

"I can't," I whisper, the fight draining out of me. "I can't watch that happen. Not after everything I've seen. "

She stands back, the lines around her mouth pronounced in anger. "It's not always about you," she says coldly. "You may think it is, and maybe since Big Eddie died it has been, but not now. Not anymore. You've allowed yourself to drown in your grief, thinking only about yourself. You've been selfish long enough, Benjamin Edward Green. Big Eddie raised you better than this."

Her words might as well have been a slap across the face. "You don't have any idea what I've been through," I say with a scowl.

"No? So I didn't feel pain when Big Eddie died? I don't feel heartache knowing my Christie was the cause of it? I don't know grief now that my own sister is dead?" Her voice breaks, and her eyes fill with tears.

"It's not...." But it is. It is the same. It's all the same. Every single piece. Every single part. She's right. This isn't what my father taught me. These aren't the lessons I was supposed to learn. Seeing him on the other side of the river as we said good-bye should have been enough. Michael was right. I was given a gift, one that most will never get to have. And I've thrown it back in so many faces. I hang my head. If this was another test, then I don't know if I've failed yet or not.

"You haven't," Nina says, and not for the first time, I wonder if she can read my mind. I wonder at my little aunt and how she came to know so much, how she can see what others can't. I wonder just what exactly she is. "There's still time. Not a lot, but enough. You must hurry."

"People are going to see how I'm dressed," I remind her.

She nods. "Thought of that. Couldn't grab your clothes because Mary would know what I was doing, so I just took this." Only when she starts to shrug out of it do I see she's wearing a big coat that almost engulfs her completely. She helps me put it on, and for a moment I smell the heartbreaking scent of earth.

"I thought this went down in the Ford," I say softly, touching the fabric of Big Eddie's jacket. There's a sharp pang in my head and heart because I smell earth again and think I see a flash of blue.

"It was in Little House," she says quietly, putting my other arm through the sleeve. "Hanging near the door."

I don't know how that's possible, because I'm certain it was in the Ford. As a matter of fact, I *know* it was. It was sitting on top of the bench seat, behind my neck, when the truck flipped. I don't remember seeing what happened to it after.

Nina says nothing as she waits.

Do you believe in the impossible? Big Eddie whispers.

I do. I do believe in the impossible.

"How am I going to get there?" I ask, easing myself off the side of the bed with a groan. I feel dizzy as I stand, whatever drugs they've given me for the pain causing my head to swim.

She stands next to me, puts her arms around my waist, and allows me to lean on her. "I took Mary's keys from her purse when we got here," she said, grunting. "I felt bad, but then I whispered I'm sorry and so I think that makes it okay. She and Lola are drinking coffee in the cafeteria, and I told them I had to use the bathroom. We have to hurry."

"You can't drive," I remind her as we move toward the door.

"It's a good thing you can," she says.

"Uh, I'm slightly high from the pain meds."

"I'll be there to keep you okay," she says. "And I think God will too."

I don't know how to respond to that.

"Plus, there's coffee in a thermos in the car."

Great. I'm sure the judge I'll have to stand before when I get arrested for DUI will be okay with me having drunk coffee while high after breaking out of the hospital to go save my guardian angel boyfriend, all precipitated by my aunt, who has Down syndrome and may or may not be some kind of psychic. Or something.

It hits me again that my life might just be a little strange.

IT TAKES us almost ten minutes to get out of the hospital. Nina is taking her covert mission seriously and stashes me in empty rooms or supply closets every time someone walks by. She smiles widely at them and hums to herself, waiting for them to pass. As soon as they do, she drops the act and grabs me again, pulling me toward the elevator.

It's empty when we get in, and the time is displayed electronically above the buttons for the floors: 8:17 p.m. She hits the button for the first floor, and I rest up against the wall, buttoning the big coat up the front so it covers the hospital gown I'm wearing. The coat hangs down to my upper thighs. It should be okay as long as no one feels the need to scope out my bare legs and feet.

The elevator moves down and then stops suddenly on the third floor. We hold our breath as the doors open. There are voices right outside the door, but it sounds like they're distracted. I move away from the wall and hit the close button repeatedly when I hear someone say "Hey, hold the door!" I don't, and it slides shut before anyone can see us.

"This is ridiculous," I say to no one in particular.

The elevator reaches the bottom floor and Nina helps me out. Instead of walking out the front, she pulls me toward the side doors, leading me to the parking garage. There's no place to hide me anytime someone passes, so I stand as tall as I can, clutching the coat around me, smiling and saying hello to everyone who passes. We get a few strange looks, but no one tries to stop us.

Finally we're out into the garage, and the rain-scented air hits me in the face. It's cold outside, and my feet are numb against the pavement. Nina pulls the keys out of a pocket and starts clicking the fob. Eventually, there's an answering beep of a vehicle.

Christie's SUV sits a few spaces down, lights flashing.

I stop. Nina was right. I've been selfish. I've thought too much of my own grief and not what anyone else might have gone through. Seeing my aunt's SUV sitting in front of me hits me like I didn't think it would. She betrayed not just me and my father. She betrayed my mother. She betrayed Mary. And she betrayed the little woman standing so fiercely next to me, who is determined to hold me up, determined to help me get home to the man I love before there's nothing left but memories that rise like ghosts.

I sigh and put my hands into the pocket of the coat. My bad hand touches something small and cold. I pull the object out as Nina fumbles with the door. A small pocketknife. The handle is red. A small inscription on the side: *I love you, my husband. Forever, Este.* Estelle's gift to her husband Abe. It was in my hand when I was shot. It fell into the river as I fell. It was lost to the rushing waters. As was the coat I wear.

"Nina?" I ask as she helps me into the driver's seat. "Where did you say you got the coat?" I sound hoarse.

"I told you," she huffs, pushing my legs in. "It was hanging on the coat rack just inside Little House." She hands me the keys and shuts the door in my face.

She hurries around the back of the SUV and is climbing into the passenger side when something else hits me. "How?"

"Hmm?"

"The SUV."

"Yes?"

"Why don't the police have it? Wouldn't they have impounded it?"

"You would think so," she says with a smile. "Strange how these things work out."

I stare at her.

"Coffee?" she asks me sweetly. "We've got an hour drive ahead of us."

IT'S as we ride through the dark that I confess. "I saw him."

"Oh?" Nina says. She waits.

"Big Eddie. I saw him again. At the river."

Silence.

"I'm sorry, Nina."

She seems startled. "For what?"

"You know. Christie."

"Yes," she says quietly, looking out the window into the night. "Those who live have always lost. What was three goes to two. But that's okay. There's *always* two." Her voice gets a little funny at the end.

"Nina? Are you okay?"

"Felix," she whispers. "Oh, Felix. Turn away. Turn away, please. It is not a god It never was a god." Then she shudders as she shakes her head.

I glance at her, concerned. "Who's Felix?"

"Did he cross?" she asks, ignoring my question. Her voice sounds clear again. "Did you help Big Eddie cross?"

Oh, my heart. Oh, my soul. "Yes," I whisper. "He crossed."

"I wonder," she says, "if Christie will too. If God has enough forgiveness in his heart."

I take her hand in mine.

FOR the first time in a very long time, I pass mile marker seventy-seven and I do not slow.

I do not stop.

AND here, at the end of things, I show you this:

Five days have passed since the storm hit, but Poplar Street is still littered with debris. Large tree branches pile up on sidewalks. Broken windows are boarded up, waiting to be replaced. Puddles of water still remain in the shadows of buildings.

I drive slowly down the road that is my home.

Rosie's Diner survived and is still standing, though it's closed up tight.

Big Eddie's Gas and Convenience looks none the worse for wear. There's a pile of debris off to the side, and the whole front of the store has been swept clean. Someone has taken care of it for me. Maybe my mother. Maybe Mary or Nina. Maybe someone else entirely. I don't know.

All the other businesses are still standing. They're all dark, but they're all still there. Roseland might have been struck by what is now being called the worst storm of this century, but it has survived. It has rolled with the punches. It has known sacrifice, but what is love without sacrifice? It has taken all of this on and it has survived. Its foundations might be shaky, and it might not be in the same shape it once was, but it has survived.

And it has also kept a great secret.

Our Lady of Sorrows blazes ahead, bright, like a beacon in the dark. It calls to me. It sings to me. Voices whisper to me out in the night, like I'm still trapped in the White Room, now gone black. *Here,* they say. *Here he is. Here he is, coming to change the shape of things. This is a pattern of impossible endings. This is a design of improbable beginnings. O, joy. O, wonder. O, behold, for it is miraculous.*

I see people standing off in the shadows, almost hidden because the streetlights are all burned out. They watch as I drive by. I know they can't see inside the vehicle, but I feel they know who it is just the same. As I pass them, they step out onto the road and begin to follow us on foot, step by step, until I see hundreds of people behind me, their heads bowed low, hands folded in front of them. I see people I've known all my life, people I've laughed with, people I've cried with. I see people who helped to pick up the pieces after I shattered away into the wind. It seems all of Roseland is here, watching, waiting.

"What is this?" I whisper, unable to process what I'm seeing.

"It's been like this since he came," Nina says softly. "They've all waited for you. They've all prayed for you. And for him. For Blue."

"This is going to get out," I say, sure of my words. "This won't stay secret for long. Someone will talk, and they'll descend on Roseland. They'll come here with their questions and their cameras. Their scalpels and their knives. They won't understand. They won't understand who he is. It won't matter what he is to me. They'll try and take him away."

She watches me curiously. "Not here," she says. "Not this place. Roseland is… different. The people here are… different. We protect our own. Now that everything is out in the open, we protect our own." She sighs and looks back out the window. "The eyes of everyone were here for a few days. The news people with their cameras and their reports of this poor little town. Such tragic things happened to them, they said. Drugs and deceit. Betrayal and heartbreak. They told the story, and then they left. There are always stories to be told, I think. Elsewhere. Every day. It was just our day, and now it's over. He was protected."

"Why?" I ask, as we approach the front of the church, the crowd behind me bigger than I would have ever thought. "Why are they doing this?" I pull into a parking space in front of the church and turn off the SUV.

She puts her hand on top of mine. "Because they know love. They know sacrifice. They know miracles *do* exist, and they must be protected. They must be cherished." She removes her hand. "We protect our own," she repeats.

"I don't know if I can do this," I say, the doubt in my voice evident. "Why me? Out of all the people in the world, the *worlds*, why me? Why this moment? Why now? I'm no one. I'm nothing."

"You're the one Calliel chose to love," my aunt says, her sweet face breaking into a sad smile. "If that's not enough for you, I don't know what else could be."

"I love you," I tell her. "I love you so very, very much."

Her eyes fill with tears and her lip quivers. "Oh, I know," she says. "And I love you more than the moon and the stars. Secret?"

"Yes. Yes."

"Cross your heart?"

"Hope to die."

"Stick a thousand needles in your eye." She looks away and takes a deep breath. "I think everything was leading to this," she says quietly. "I think this is the real test. For you. For Blue."

"I'm scared."

"But loved."

"Yes."

She opens the door.

I stare after her for a moment, trying to catch my breath. I hear people shuffling outside the SUV, waiting for me to exit. The church is so bright.

I open the door.

The crowd sighs. All of their eyes are on me. No one speaks. They watch. I'm unsure of what to do. I don't know what's expected of me. I don't know what they want me to say.

Then, a familiar face pushes her way through the crowd.

"Welcome home, Benji," Rosie says, pulling me gently into her arms. "Oh, honey. I am so happy to see your face."

"Rosie," I breathe, trying not to wince at the pain in my chest.

"Your mother called," she says in my ear softly, so no one else can hear. "She called in a fright, said you'd gone missing from the hospital along with Nina. I told her there's no other place you'd be going. She asked me to stop you from entering the church before she got here. Can I do that? Can I stop you?"

"No. You can't. I can't wait. Not now. Not when I'm this close."

She nods, pulling away, brushing at the tears in her eyes. "The doc's in there," she says. "With him. Pastor Landeros is in there too."

"How is he?" I ask, searching her face. "Cal. Is he? Is he…."

She shakes her head, crumbling as she's pulled away by Suzie Goodman. I hear her gentle sobs as she falls back into the crowd.

Dad, I need you. I need you so bad right now. Please, hear my prayer.

"I am going to ask something," I say, my voice stronger than I think it would be. "I am going to ask something of you. Of all of you. Please. Let me have this moment. If this is supposed to be… good-bye, then I ask that you let me have this moment. Please."

The mob sighs again, and my words are carried in hushed whispers throughout the crowd. No one says anything against me. I knew they wouldn't.

I turn and face the church and take the first step toward the light. I do not become lost in thought. Memories do not rise like ghosts, stabbing me like knives. All that matters, and all I focus on, is the angel who awaits me in the church. All my thoughts are with him.

I reach the steps, and they creak under me as I mount them. I count them. There are seven, though I am not surprised. It seems fitting.

The whispers from inside the church grow louder, until they sound like a rushing river. I press my hands against the massive doors, and they vibrate against my fingers. The vibration rolls up my arms until my whole body shakes, and I hang my head. In these vibrations and whispers are songs of grief and loss, of heartache and people forgotten. In these songs are words of sorrow and pain, of regrets never gone, of aches that hurt as if they are new.

But.

There is hope. There is faith. There is belief that maybe, just *maybe*, everything will be as it was and as it should be. It's a thread that wraps itself around my heart and soul and tugs on them gently. It calls for one who can be strong. And brave. It calls for one who can stand true.

And there is no one it wants more than me.

I push open the doors. They groan mightily as they part. A warm light washes over me, and the whispers cease. The songs fade. Silence falls.

I step into the church, and the doors close behind me.

o lord, hear our prayer

I STAND in the narthex of the church, the entryway lit by hundreds of candles stretched along the wall. This is the light, I realize, the light I'd seen upon approach. The power must still be out all over the town, and the brightness, the beacon, was the candles that had been lit. Hundreds of them. Thousands.

I cross the narthex and enter the nave. The pews have been removed. It looks like there were halfhearted attempts to set up booths for the festival inside the nave, but the project was abandoned, possibly when the storm became too great. Candles line these walls as well, giving off heat but not overwhelmingly so. They reflect the stained glass lining the nave, the colors flickering so much it appears the saints are alive. As if they're walking with me, blinking their eyes, opening their mouths. No sound comes out. But still they walk with me, or so it seems.

I take another step.

Past the end of the nave is the aptly named crossing, the middle of the north and south transepts. Past the crossing is the chancel, elevated from the crossing. The chancel leads to the altar. High above the altar, St. Jude Novena stares down at me from his stained-glass window. He looks as if he's holding me in judgment with his frank gaze. Shadows dance along his face from the candles below. I swear I see him move.

There are three people on the altar. Doc Heward stands facing me, his hands at his sides, his face pale and drawn. He looks older than I've ever seen him. His thinning hair sticks out every which way. His clothes are wrinkled. He has dark circles under his eyes. His hands tremble at his sides.

Pastor Thomas Landeros stands on the other side of the altar, head bowed, wearing a black Roman cassock. Thirty-three buttons fall down the center of the cassock. I asked him once, after the Christmas service when I was young, why there were thirty-three buttons. It seemed like such an odd number to me. He told me it symbolized the thirty-three earthly years of Christ. I asked him how anyone could know this. He said it was what was written. I asked him how he could trust something passed down. He said it was a matter of faith.

He moves his lips as if in prayer, his hands folded near his chin. I can't hear what he's saying aloud, if anything, but for some reason it chills me. I wonder how long he's been at this, wonder what this has done to his belief, his faith. Does he think this is a reward for his service? Does he see this as proof of his faith? Or has this shattered every notion he's ever had about the way the world works? To say you have faith is one thing; to see evidence of it with your own eyes is something else entirely.

But it's the third figure that captures my attention. It's him I see the most.

Lying on a white cot with a blanket pulled up to his chest is the guardian angel Calliel. Blue lights flicker around him weakly. His wings disappear then reappear, the long feathers draping across the floor. The smell of earth is heavy and sweet. His skin has a sickly pallor to it, almost yellow in the candlelight, in his own lights. His eyes are closed, and his breathing seems labored. One breath in, held, then released. It takes a second, two seconds, three seconds before he breathes in again.

I'm moving even before I know I am. I run across the nave. I reach the crossing, the name not lost on me. For a moment, I think it will turn into a raging river that I will be forced to cross. It doesn't matter. I would. I will do anything to get to him.

But it doesn't. The stone crossing remains as it always has. My footsteps echo through the church, my bare feet slapping against the cold ground. I reach the steps that lead to the chancel. The red carpet feels rough against my soles. I'm at the altar before the doc can speak, though I feel his eyes on me, a subtle intake of breath that heralds the beginning of speech. The breath releases without any words as I fall to my knees beside Cal. Closer now, I can hear Pastor Landeros mumbling under his breath. His words sound Latin.

But above his prayer, I hear the slight rattle in Calliel's chest with every breath he takes. It's a subtle clicking that seems to sound like a shotgun blast in my ears. I take his hand in mine and lift it, brushing my lips against the cool, dry skin. It might just be my imagination, but I swear the blue lights become brighter, just for a moment. I choose to believe they do. I choose to believe he knows it's me, even with how far under he seems to be.

His eyes are moving rapidly under his eyelids, as if he's searching for something there, in the dark. I place my hand against his brow, and he takes in a deep breath, his chest rising, pressing against the blanket, against the white bandage on his shoulder. He lets it out with a sigh and his eyes become still. I brush my thumb over the groove in the side of his head. Feathers flutter around me. My heart hurts.

"Can you fix him?" I ask, my voice echoing in the empty church. "Can you do anything for him?"

Doc Heward looks down at his hands. "Benji, I don't know *what* I'm doing," he says, his voice scratchy. "I don't know anything about this. I've... removed the bullets. I've closed the wounds. He has... organs. Just like us. They were damaged, and I tried to fix them as best I could. But... they're the same? As us? How is that possible? I don't...." He rubs his hands over his face. "I've given him antibiotics. There's no infection. There's nothing there. Everything is fine."

"Then why won't he wake up?" I rub my hand over the stubble on his head, just as he likes. I ignore the tears on my face.

"I don't know," Doc Heward says, sounding like he's losing control. "I don't know. He should be getting better. His eyes should be open, and he should be talking and... Benji. I don't know. I don't know what to do. He's dying, and I don't know why. This is out of my league." He gives a bitter laugh. "I don't know why," he says again. He takes a step back.

I do. I know why. I know why his eyes aren't open, why he's not talking. I know why his wings can't seem to stay and why his blue lights are getting weaker and weaker. It's close.

"Leave us," I say quietly, never taking my eyes from Cal. "Please."

The doc makes a sound of protest. I shake my head just once, and I hear his footsteps as he walks away slowly.

Pastor Landeros stops his mumbling. He looks at me like he's just now aware of my presence. "Benji?" he whispers. "When did you…." He glances down at Calliel then back at me. "Do you know what this is?"

"This is my friend," I tell him.

"It's a miracle," he breathes. "I've never…."

"Not now, Pastor," I say, shaking my head. "Not now. I know this is your church. I know this is your home. I know this is an affirmation of your faith. I know this is everything you've ever hoped for. Everything you've ever dreamed about. But this is my friend. I need you to leave us alone. Please."

He takes a step toward me and gently touches the top of my head. "It's more than that," he says. "It's so much more than that. It means we are never alone."

And then he leaves. I wait until I hear the doors of the church shut behind them.

"Okay," I whisper. "Okay."

I don't know what else to say. Actually, I *do* know what else to say, but I can't seem to find the power to say it. I can't seem to form the words to say what I really want, how I really feel. It seems like everything depends on what I'll say next, that this final test is the most important one.

How do you say what's in your heart if your heart is something you haven't known for years? How do you give yourself completely when all you've done is bury yourself in grief? How do you come back from the dark when it's all you can remember?

"I don't know," I say, my voice cracking. I hang my head and grip Cal's hand tightly. "I don't know what to do. I don't know where to go from here. I thought I was the strong one. I thought I could be brave. I thought I could stand and be true, just like what was asked of me, but I don't know if I can. I'm scared. I'm scared I won't be good enough. I'm scared I can't be courageous enough. I'm scared I can't do what's expected of me. I don't *know* what's expected of me. I just know I don't want you to leave. I don't want you to go away. I don't want you to cross the river, because I'm not done with you yet. I haven't had enough of you, not even close. I don't think I ever will, even if we could go on forever. I need you to come back. I need you to come home. I need you." The sound of my voice dies in the church.

I wait.

Nothing happens. Of course nothing happens.

My anger rises. I drop Cal's hand. I look up at St. Jude Novena. He is not God, nor did he ever claim to be. But aside from the unconscious angel in front of me, he's the closest thing I've got. "What do you want from me?" I growl up at the stained glass. "What do you expect me to do? Do you want me to fall to my knees and beg you? Well, here I am!" I raise my voice until it's a shout. "Here I am! Right here! Right here in the middle of your fucking design, your goddamned pattern! I'm begging you. I'm begging you with all that I have. I've done everything you've ever asked of me, so you fucking give me something back. You give me something in return!"

The saint does not respond. God does not respond.

My ire grows. "I'm *sick* of your fucking games! None of us have deserved what you've done! You take and you take and you take, and you give *nothing* back! You dangle any chance at happiness right in front of our fucking faces and then you snatch it back right when we think we can have it for our own. I don't *care* if love is sacrifice. I don't *care* if that's the only way we can recognize it. I *know* what it is, I *know* what it can do, and I won't let you take love from me. Not again. Not anymore. He's *mine*, you bastard. He doesn't belong to you—he belongs to *me*."

My voice echoes throughout the church: *me, me, me, me*.

St. Jude flickers in the candlelight. *Me*, he seems to say. *Me, me, me*, he seems to mock.

Then the doors fly open behind me. I turn, expecting God himself to walk through the doors, eyes blazing, preparing to strike me down for speaking to him like I have in his house. It's what I deserve. It's what I'm owed.

But it's not him. It's not God.

It's my mother.

"Benji," she cries, rushing toward me. I can't find the strength to take a step toward her, but it doesn't matter. Soon she puts her arms around me, pulling me close. She sobs quietly in my ear, scolding me, telling me I can't scare her like that again, that she was so scared because for a moment, she thought I was gone. *Really* gone. Gone so she would never see me again, gone just like Big Eddie was gone, and didn't I know her heart couldn't take that? Didn't I know I was all she had left?

"I had to come," I tell her. "I have to be with him."

She pulls back, kissing my forehead, my eyes, my cheeks. "You don't get to leave me too!" she shouts in my face.

"Okay. Okay."

I let her hold me for a bit longer, and it's only then that I realize my anger has waned, and I am just hurt. Every part of me hurts inside and out. She rocks me back and forth gently, humming something lightly in the back of her throat, and I focus on the sound. I pick up each and every note in her voice, following the thread of the music until it becomes my father's song. She's singing my father's song to me. I wrap my arms around her.

"I saw him," I say for the second time tonight. It comes out unbidden.

She stops humming. She grips me tightly, but she doesn't pull away. "Where?"

"The river. Michael took me to the river. After I was shot."

"And he… he was there?"

"Yes. Oh, yes. He was there. He was so big. He was so much bigger than I remembered. Do you remember how big he was? Bigger than mountains. Bigger than the sky. He...." My throat closes.

She quakes against me. "Did you get to speak with him?"

I smile into her hair. "I got to say everything to him."

"Was he happy? Is he happy now? Please, Benji. Please tell me he's happy now!"

I remember the grin on his face. His happy shout. *Abe*, he'd said. "I think so," I say. "I think he's okay now. He crossed the river. I made sure of it."

"Oh, Benji. I miss him so much."

"I know. But we'll be together again. One day."

"I know, baby. I know."

"He... told me...."

She pulls back and cups my face. She's so beautiful, my mother is. So goddamned beautiful. "What?" she asks. "What did he tell you?"

You just have to have faith.

In what?

That everything will be okay. If he believes in you, then you need to believe in him. Nothing's written in stone.

I pull away from her hands and turn back to Cal. I fall to my knees again beside him and lean down, brushing my lips against his. The blue lights flash brightly again, and his wings are solid beneath me for seconds before they start to flicker again. I pull away only just, our lips still pressed together. "Do you believe in me?" I ask him quietly.

There's no answer. Just the lights. Just his wings.

But it's enough.

I reach back and hold out my hand to my mother. There's no hesitation on her part as she steps forward. I tug her down gently until she settles beside me. There's no fear on her face, being this close to him. There's no trepidation. If anything, she smiles sadly as she reaches up and fixes the blanket on his chest. She lifts it up and pulls it higher, but not before I see the larger bandage covering his stomach. I remember the look on his face, then, right before he fell. Anger. Pain. Love.

So much love. And it was for me. It was mine.

My father was right. Nothing is written in stone.

I do the only thing that's left to do. I take my mother's hand in my own. "Will you pray with me?" I whisper.

She looks unsure as she glances from me up at St. Jude Novena and back again. Something shadows her eyes, and I wonder who she's thinking about. Is it her grandmother? Big Eddie? Cal? Me? I don't know. I don't know if it matters. If she says no, that will be okay. I'll do it on my own. I'm not leaving this place until I've had my say.

I wait.

She doesn't make me wait long. She sighs and leans over, kissing my forehead. "What should we pray for?" she asks.

I can't help but feel this is the most important question of all. I know what I think I want. I know what I *should* want. I know what's right for me. I know I could pray for all different things. But I also know what my heart wants, and my heart pulls all those others together until they take their own shape. Until they make their own pattern. Their own design.

"The power of choice," I say, looking down at Cal's sleeping form. "We need to pray for the power to choose what we want, and the strength to make that choice. That even though the world might be dark, and we might be crawling on our hands and knees, we can always choose to come home and find it light again."

My mother brushes her eyes as she nods. "Benji?"

"Yeah?"

"How... how did he look? Big Eddie?"

"Like the most wonderful thing I've ever seen," I tell her, smiling through tears.

She gives a watery bark of laughter. "He was pretty great, wasn't he?"

"The best there was. He loved you, you know. With his whole heart."

She weeps quietly. "I know. I know. The both of us. Benji?"

"Yeah?"

"We're going to be okay, right? After this? After all of this? You and I?"

I understand now that she needs me. She needs me as much as I need her. We've been knocked down, beaten and battered, had brushes with insanity and death. I've pushed her away for so long, but she and I are the same. I am my mother's son.

"One way or another," I tell her, "we'll be okay. After all of this, we'll be okay. We'll sit and watch the sunrise, and I'll tell you everything I've heard. All of the things I've seen."

She nods. "I'd like that."

I take her hand again, and she squeezes my fingers tightly. I don't let go of her as I lower my head. I close my eyes.

And pray.

I'm not going to be very good at this. I haven't been very good at a lot of things. I've lied. I've cheated. I've disrespected my parents. I put my own needs before those of others. When Big Eddie left, I only worried about how it affected me. I didn't worry about the others. I was selfish. Self-centered. I took to the river and let myself float on its waters. I didn't care if I drowned. I didn't care what became of me. I was hurt, I was angry, and I didn't care what that meant for the future. I just wanted everything to stop. I was too much of a coward to commit the ultimate selfish act... but I thought about it.

A hand drops on my shoulder, squeezing once and drifting away. I keep my eyes closed.

There were times I wondered just how easy it would be to fill up my pockets with stones, oh Lord, and walk into the river and let myself drown. I wondered how hard it would be when the river closed over my head and the light became murky and I opened my mouth to inhale the water. It would have been easy, I think. It would have been hard, I know. But it would have stopped the pain. It would have taken me away from my head and heart. It would have only taken moments for it to be over, and that seemed easier than a lifetime of agony.

More touches, to my shoulders. My face. My hair. My back.

But he came, when I was at my darkest. I prayed him down from the sky, and he came in a flash of blue fire that lit up the heavens. I know he came by his own choice, but he came because I called him. He came when I could no longer take the weight of the world on my own. He came when I needed him the most. He came and saved me from myself, saved me from the waters that rose up to my chest and over my head.

The shuffle of feet. The whisper of voices. So many whispers.

He made me believe I was stronger than I ever thought I could be. He showed me how to chase away the dark. The sun rose every morning because he made it so. He broke me down into tiny pieces and then picked them back up and shaped me into something... different. I understand now, I think. We're tested. We've always been tested, and we always will be. It's not meant to be cruel. It's not meant to be some dark malevolent thing, even though it might seem like it. We might not always understand why things happen the way they do. We might not always agree. We might hate it. But they happen regardless. We could allow ourselves to become buried by it. Or... or we can rise above it, learn from it, and allow ourselves to see something more. I want to see more. I want to see more so badly I can taste it.

More and more footsteps. Tears. Sighs of relief. Of reverence. Beauty. Truth. I am touched over and over again, until my skin vibrates from it. I don't think I can take much more without breaking.

My father told me it's better to have something burn bright for a short amount of time than to never see it burn at all. If that is true, then so be it. I will have loved with my whole heart. With my whole soul. I gave as much as I was able, though it might not have been all of me. I can see that now. I can see the burden he was to carry. I can see the fear and loneliness in his own heart. It weighed on him. It held him down. But still he pushed on. Still he cared for more than just me. He cared for all of us. He cared for us because we are his. You gave him to us, and even if you take him back, you can never take that away from us. We will remember the time, however short it was, when we came alive. When we felt the fire in our chests, the wind in our heads. The earth beneath our feet and the water against our fingertips. We will remember him always.

But what if....

What have I been taught? What have I learned? I don't believe this is a game. Not anymore. Michael said he didn't understand why me, why God had picked me to do what he's done. He didn't understand why this tiny little part of the world, so insignificant in the grand scheme of things. His focus is on the destruction of a world

I don't know, of a mankind that can manipulate the elements. A world of a child flash-burned into a wall of a room so white, of a man named Seven who might be the one to save us all. He didn't understand what importance we might have. And maybe, in the long run, it won't matter. Maybe that's the point. Maybe the point of all of this is not what will happen in the future, but what will happen now.

And what happens now? Maybe Michael knew more than he realized. Maybe he knew all along when he said love is nothing without sacrifice. *The act of sacrifice is by its very nature a selfless act*, he'd said. *One cannot sacrifice unless one is doing not for himself, but for the greater good. Your father knew this, Benji. He knew it more than most people.*

My father knew. He knew about the greater good. He knew about what the cost could be.

And so do I.

I open my eyes.

St Jude Novena stares down at me, alight with such beauty that I tremble.

I caress my mother's hand before I gently let it go. I stand. And turn.

Hundreds of people have filed into the church, filling the nave until they are shoulder to shoulder. The church is completely full, and I can see the doors at the narthex are open, and even more people fill the streets. I see them all—my friends, my family. Neighbors. People I've seen almost every day since I can remember. I see my town. I see Roseland. Some of them have their heads bowed, hands tucked under their chins. Others have their arms spread like wings, palms and faces toward the ceiling, mouths moving. Some look fearful. Others are crying. Still others are watching me closely, as if waiting for my next move, waiting for me to speak. But I can feel it. Even if they're not all the same, I can feel them. They're praying. Almost all of Roseland is praying. If one prayer is but a whisper, then this must be a roar to the heavens. These are my people. This is my home.

And if it can't be his, I won't let him disappear into the dark.

I turn back to St. Jude Novena.

"Michael," I say, my voice strong. I hear people raising their heads, a rustle that reminds me of wings. "I know you can hear me, hear all of us. I know you're listening. I know now what you meant. In the White Room. I know what you meant when you spoke of what love really means. You gave me a gift, or your Father did. You gave me what my heart wanted. You allowed me the moment to say good-bye. And I will remember what you did for the rest of my life."

I take a deep breath. "But I also know that gifts come with a price. I know that all things demand sacrifice. We have a choice. We have free will. The design is not fixed. The future is not set in stone. You have made your decision, and you have helped me make mine." I look down at the angel. My angel, my guardian. The blue lights are flashing brighter now, and his wings have returned, solid and sure. I reach down and rub my fingers over the feathers. They feel like home. They feel like hope. He deserves this. More than me. I lean over and kiss him gently. "I love you," I whisper.

And then I stand, my shoulders squared, my head held tall. I am bigger than I ever felt before. I am stronger. I am braver. I am true. I will give up my heart to save his soul. "Take him home."

The crowd behind me gasps as my mother struggles to her feet, grabbing onto me, asking me *why*, crying *why*. But I don't back down. I don't turn away. I don't allow myself to be pulled into the throngs of people behind me and carried away. I ignore their cries, their tears, their anger and fear at what seems like my betrayal. The angel Calliel deserves his chance to be free of this place. Where he can hear his Father's voice, even if it's just a whisper. Where his soul will thrive.

I raise my voice. "You hear me, Michael? Gabriel? David? Raphael? He can't stay here. He can't. I won't allow it. Not for me. Not with all that he'll suffer. You take him back. Love is nothing without sacrifice, and I am willing to sacrifice *everything* for him, even if it means I'll never see him again. Take him back to his Father. You take him home!"

Nothing.

"Michael!"

The cries of the town silence behind me as a white light explodes in through St. Jude Novena, illuminating the church in a fierce glow. It's a warm thing, a curious thing, and all of Roseland holds its breath. They can feel it too, just as I can. It's coming because it heard me. Heard all of us.

The light is blinding as it lowers to the ground at the back of the altar. It touches down, and the light begins to fade. Standing in its place is the archangel Michael.

He offers me a sad smile. "Benji," he says with slight a nod of his head. "It's good to see you again, child."

"Michael," I say in return. My mouth feels dry.

Michael does not look at Cal; instead, he seems interested in the townspeople who have gathered in the church. "What an odd little place," he says. He cocks his head at the crowd, and as one they take a step back. "Hello."

No one replies.

This doesn't seem to bother him in the slightest.

Cal stirs fitfully, and I think he's about to wake. I put my hand to his forehead. He's burning up. His skin is slick with sweat. He jerks beneath my hand, his face contorting in pain.

"Hush, brother," Michael says. "Not yet."

As if that's all it takes, Cal stills. He sighs deeply but doesn't wake.

I hear my mother moving until she's standing in front of us, as if she can block Michael from Cal and me. If I know anything about her, she'll try. I can't allow that to happen.

"What an odd place this is," Michael says again to the town. "On the outside, it looks like everywhere else. You go through your lives, day by day. Some of you pray. Some of you don't. Some of you have damaged faith. Some of you have too much. Some of you have lied and stolen. All of you have hurt someone unintentionally. Some of you have done so with malicious intent. There is deceit and heartache and anger and selfishness. There is rampant sin. There are actions that go against my Father. I know, because I have looked. Since I have become aware of this place, I have looked. This place is no different than anywhere else in the world as far as I can see. There are secrets here that would destroy others if they got out. But you still all live *here*. In *this* town. This... Roseland. What is it about this place? And about this boy?"

His gaze rolls over the crowd. "One day, all of you will stand before your Creator and you will be judged for how you lived your life. On whether or not you showed kindness and compassion. On the purpose of your being and how you fit into my Father's design. I wonder, though... here, now, if this will be your defining moment? Prayers are always heard, whether they are answered or not. Every day. Every person. Every single one. They *aren't* all answered, not even the majority of them. But there's a fundamental difference between saying a prayer and praying. One is recitation, the other comes from your soul. And in this church... I heard nothing but souls. Every single person here, and on the street outside, did not pray for themselves. You did not make personal requests. You thought about those of yours who you have loved and lost, and you bowed your heads. You prayed for an angel and a boy. For them to never be parted. Why is that?"

"Because they're ours," a voice says, sure and strong. I pull away from Cal and look out onto the nave. The crowd sighs as it shifts, the whispers picking up again.

Nina steps forward until she reaches the small steps to the altar. Michael looks down at her, a curious expression on his face, his white wings twitching as he stares down at the small woman before him.

"Are they?" he asks her kindly. "And why is that, child?"

"Because *we've* been the ones who have tried to hold them together when they started to break," Nina says.

Rosie steps forward. "*We've* been the ones who held on when they shattered anyway, trying to hold the pieces together as best we could."

Doc Heward raises his voice. "*We've* been the ones who swept up the pieces and put them back together."

My Aunt Mary moves to stand by her sister. "And they did the same for us. Every day. They did the same for us. You asked why. The answer is because we *could*. We *chose* to do it."

"Not all of you," the archangel says. "Not all of you chose this. Some of you chose a dark path instead. Some of you chose pain and anger. Some of you chose yourselves over the good of your people."

"And they're all gone now," Nina says, hanging her head. "Even Christie."

"Even Christie," Michael echoes. He steps off the altar, toward Nina. The crowd takes a few steps back, pressing into one another as they try to move away from Michael. They're in awe, yes, but they're also scared of him. I can't blame them. He's accused them all of sin while also telling them they've done something he's never seen before. It's intimidating.

He stands before Nina and brushes the knuckles of his right hand over her cheek. "You know," he tells her, "none of what happened was your fault, child."

"Then whose fault was it?" she asks, her voice cracking. "If your Father is who you say he is, then why does he let such things happen? Why does he let us hurt? Why would he take people away from us? Away from each other?"

Michael doesn't answer her. He's waiting for something. He's waiting.

For me.

"Sacrifice," I say. The crowd turns its attention back to me. "It all comes down to sacrifice." I step toward Michael. My mother immediately goes to Cal's side. She holds onto his arm as he starts to jerk again.

"Yes," Michael says, still watching my aunt. "Always."

"Well, then, there is only one explanation," Nina says.

"And what is that?"

She pulls her shoulders back and narrows her eyes defiantly. "Your Father is a bastard," she says. "He takes what he wants, and he's a bastard for it."

The crowd moans. Mary tries to pull her sister away, but Nina shakes loose. She crosses her arms over her chest and refuses to move.

Michael looks amused. "Is that so?" he asks.

"Yes," she spits out. "We give and we give and we give. We give all that we have, and it never seems to be enough. For every moment of happiness we have, there are always two things more that threaten to take it away. For every good, there is evil. For every love, there is hate."

"Everything needs its opposite," Michael tells her gently. "It creates order. Balance in the chaos."

"*Fuck* your balance!" she cries at him. Startled, he takes a step back. "Fuck every part of it! We've had those we love taken from us so unfairly. We've survived everything that has been thrown at us. It's time we got something back in return. No more sacrifice. Not today."

He gapes at her. "Child, do you know who you speak to?"

"Do you?" she retorts.

"Nina," I say quietly. "It's okay. I can't let him stay here. I can't let him die."

Her eyes fill with tears. She rushes past Michael and up the steps to the altar, throwing herself at me. I catch her in my arms and bring her close. I don't know how much time I have left. "You listen to me," I whisper harshly in her ear. "This will hurt. This will break us, but we've been broken before. We can put ourselves together again." I try to say more, but my words feel like lies.

"Okay," she cries softly. "Okay."

"My Father is not a cruel being," Michael says to the town. "I don't pretend to know why he does everything he does. But I choose to believe there is a purpose to all things." He turns to face me and takes the short steps back to the altar... and moves past me.

"Calliel," he says, standing before the guardian. "Are you ready?"

As if waiting for this, Cal opens his eyes. I want to go to him, but I can't move. I can't even take a breath. I've made the only choice I could. I am sending him home.

"It's time to go," the archangel says.

"No," Cal croaks. "I won't. I won't leave. I won't leave them. Roseland. All of them. And him. I will never leave him. Go now, brother. Leave."

Michael glares at him, his patience seeming to wear thin. "You realize," he says, "that I could wipe out this town and its people with a single thought? I could send wave after wave of those things Benji calls the Strange Men here to burn this place to the ground." His eyes turn black. "I am an archangel, one of the Firsts. I am the leader of On High, and you do not get to make demands of me, guardian." Even though no real physical change overcomes him, his aura is something palpable and dark. It's like he's grown ten feet taller without even moving.

The people of Roseland shrink back.

"No," Cal says, trying to sit up. A grimace of pain shadows his eyes. My mother tries to hold him down, but he's too strong for her. I find myself moving before I can even think about it. I'm at his side only for a second before he shoves me away roughly. His eyes are only for his brother. "I won't leave. Not now. Not ever."

"Cal," I choke out. "You can't. You can't do this for me."

He ignores me. "Michael—"

Michael's wings flash brightly as they snap open. A blazing halo appears above his head as he roars at me. People in the crowd scream, but they do not try to leave. If anything, they surge forward, pushing their way in between Michael and me. They form a circle around Cal and me, and while their eyes are alight with fear, and while their chests heave with ragged breaths, they don't back down. They don't move.

"This is our town," Rosie growls at him. "And Benji and Cal belong to us. Cal is not yours. Not anymore."

And as quickly as it came, the white lights around Michael fade away. His wings settle. His halo disappears. His eyes lighten. "This town," he says as he chuckles ruefully.

And then it all comes charging back. His wings snap out to their full length. They flash a blinding light. The halo spins furiously. He rocks his head back and his mouth falls open, the cords in his neck straining against his skin. A great wind begins to rush over us all. The crowd around me tightens its circle, and Cal presses his head against my stomach. I wrap my arms around his head and hold him tight. My fingers brush over the groove caused by the bullet, and I know how close it was. I know how close this is now. "Until the very end," I whisper.

The lights fade.

The winds die.

The crowd breathes around me.

Michael sighs.

"What did he say?" I ask him. "I know you just spoke to him. What did he say?"

The crowd parts as Michael walks toward us. I grip Cal tighter. He digs his fingers into my skin as Michael approaches, dragging his wings along the floor. He stops in front of me, glancing between Cal and myself. "I was tested," he says roughly. He looks pale.

"Did you pass?"

"I don't know." He looks down at his hands. "We don't always know the answers right away. Sometimes we never know. Things... things are changing. He...." Michael trails off, looking unsure.

"He what?"

"He has a message for you."

Goose bumps break out over my arms, and I swallow past the lump in my throat. "What did he say?"

I have faith. I have faith. I have faith.

"He said... he said he wants you to know that those we love are never really gone." Michael closes his eyes. "We may not get to see them like we used to, and we may not even remember what they sound like, but they will always be with us. Do you understand?"

My mother and some others around me begin to weep openly. Mary puts her arm around my mother's shoulders and whispers quietly in her ear. "I understand," I tell him. "Do you?" I don't believe the message was meant for just me.

Michael's eyes are bright when he opens them. "I think I do," he says.

I nod. "Is that it?"

He looks down at Cal. "No," he says softly. "Everything is changing."

"Then we face it," I tell him. "We face it head-on and we don't look back."

"I think I can see it now," he says, raising his gaze to mine. "Why he chose you."

I shake my head. "I'm nothing. I'm no one. I'm just one person."

"No, Benji. You are so much more. You have changed the course of Heaven." He takes a step back and closes his eyes, tilting his head back and taking a deep breath. "Brothers! I call to thee!"

There's nothing at first, and it gives me time to panic, knowing, just *knowing* that Michael has called for reinforcements, that he's going to take Cal away while others descend upon Roseland, destroying everyone and everything in their path

Then there are bright flashes of gold and purple and black. The people of Roseland cry out as they raise their hands to cover their eyes. I hold Cal against me, refusing to let go. If this is to be our last moment, then I want it to be with him.

The lights fade. I open my eyes.

Three more angels stand before me, next to Michael. The first is a fierce-looking man with black wings and black hair. He's bigger than Cal, even, almost as big as my father was. He has a scowl on his face as he looks around the church, his dark eyes flashing in what looks like anger. He appears to be dressed for battle, his chest heavily plated in armor, gauntlets on his wrists. A sheathed sword hangs at his side. "Raphael," Michael greets him.

He turns to the next man, who is slender and gorgeous. His hair is a cascade of blond curls, his eyes bright blue. His golden wings appear smaller than those of his counterparts, but he makes up for it with a wicked twist of a grin. My heart thumps lightly in my chest, an observance of true beauty and nothing more. "David," Michael says.

The last man is staring interestedly at me and Cal. When he catches me staring at him, he gives a little wave, a big smile adorning his face, revealing even teeth. He brushes a lock of his long white hair out of his face and flutters his bright purple wings. Earrings that look like they're made of stone hang from his ears. "Gabriel," Michael says.

Oh fuck. More archangels.

My eyes get wider at each name mentioned, and Cal gets more tense. He starts to pull himself up. I try to stop him, but he ignores me. He leans on me, putting one arm over my shoulders, wrapping the other around his middle, holding his stomach as he grimaces. It's obvious he's trying to push himself between me and the other angels.

"Well, this is certainly new," Raphael grumbles, looking pissed off.

"It's better than appearing in a vision surrounded by fire," David says, looking at all the people who are watching him. He preens a bit for the crowd. "That usually scares everyone off."

"I think it's just you," Gabriel says. "People like seeing me." He starts shaking hands with everyone around him. Rosie looks dumbfounded as purple feathers brush over her face. Nina laughs in unfettered delight.

"What have you done?" Raphael accuses Michael.

Michael snorts. "It wasn't me. You can trust me on that. Benji did it."

All their eyes turn to me. "Uh. What did I do?" I ask them nervously.

"Changed the shape of things," Michael says, though he doesn't sound upset, just resigned. "Calliel will be the first, but surely others will follow. You are more, Benji, than the sum of your parts."

"The first what?" Cal asks.

"The first to be given a choice," Michael says.

"The big guy upstairs must be getting old," David says, sounding bored. "He's lost his marbles."

Gabriel shrugs. "Maybe he just knows something we don't."

David rolls his eyes. "I think that's a given."

"We don't have time for this," Raphael says. "A war is coming. The longer we're gone, the further behind we get."

"Patience," Michael says. "We don't even know if it will be our war yet to fight."

"You may have forgotten Metatron," Raphael snarls at him, "but I haven't. I know what our brother is capable of. He's a ruthless bastard who thinks he's a god. His corruption will soon overflow and spill into the rest of the worlds. You have missed news from the front lines, Michael. The Split One has crossed into Metatron's field. Even Father himself cannot say what will happen. The timetable has shifted. This is different from all the times that it has happened before. You know it is. Its own Firsts won't be able to stop It again. The seventh time will be the last."

"We wait," Michael says firmly, even as he pales further. "We agreed to wait. To give them all time. But you are right. We must return."

They all turn to look at Cal and me. The people of Roseland try to crowd in front of us again.

"Calliel," Michaels says. "You are to be given a choice. You may return to On High and continue to be the guardian angel of Roseland. The people and everyone in the town will be yours as your duty dictates. It is the reason you were made, and these people are your responsibility. Father will be there, as he's always been."

"Or?" he asks.

"Or," Michael says slowly, "you may choose to stay. You will no longer be an angel. You will be human. Your halo and wings will be stripped. You will no longer be able to return to On High. You will age. You will bleed. You will get sick. Eventually, you will die. How you live your life from here on out will determine what happens then. Another angel will be assigned to Roseland, though it won't be given priority. Our resources are stretched thin as it is. There may be times Roseland will not be guarded, though I know not of Father's plans for this place during those times."

"What's the catch?" I ask even as my heart begins to race. There has to be one. It can't be that easy.

Michael watches me with shrewd eyes. "Calliel will not be able to speak to our Father for as long as he lives. Even in prayer, even in the quietest moments, our Father will not be there."

"You bastards," I whisper. "Oh, you fucking bastards. I've already made the choice!"

None of the archangels flinch. "We are tested," Michael says. "Always. That was yours, to show you could know the true meaning of sacrifice. My Father has seen your heart, Benjamin Green. He has seen it well. Your time is done. This is meant for Calliel."

I turn to Cal. His eyes are closed, his lips drawn in a thin line. His jaw is tense. My nose rubs his cheek, the red stubble prickling wonderfully against my skin. I know what his Father means to him. I know the way he ached at being cut off from him after he fell from On High. I know the pain he carries with him at the loss of the one who made him. I know better than anyone else. I know because of the choice I almost made sitting next to the river with my own father. I know the feeling of separation. Of loss.

I could beg him to stay. I could whisper in his ear how much I love him. I could plead with my eyes that I am nothing without him. But I can't. It's not my choice. I can't tell him what I want, because it's not about me. It's about him. It's all up to him. I won't blame him, no matter what decision he makes. His Father means more to him than I ever could. I know because of what Big Eddie is to me. It's impossible, this choice. It's improbable.

Part of me wants him to go, just like I said.

There's another part, though, one that rises within me. Another part that whispers, *Oh, my heart. Oh, my soul. Please stay. Please stay with me. Don't let me go.*

As if he can hear my thoughts, he turns and brushes his lips against mine. An arc of electricity shoots down my spine at the subtle scrape of his mouth. He leans his forehead to mine and opens his dark eyes. They are endless. I try to smile. It doesn't work.

"If my Father is what I must sacrifice," the angel Calliel says, "if that is what he asks of me, then so be it. I choose humanity. I choose Roseland. I choose these people." He kisses me again as a tear slides down my cheek. "I choose you, Benjamin Edward Green. I will always choose you."

"Are you sure?" I ask, my voice cracking. "Is this what you want? Your Father... you can't just give that up. It's not fair. He's your home. You can't do this. Just for me. You can't. I'm not—"

"No," he breathes. "*This* is my home. These people are my home. This place. And you. Benji, I do it for you, but I do it more for myself. I do it because I can finally make my own choice." He pulls away from me, and I almost whimper at the loss. He turns to face his brothers. "I choose to stay," he says, his voice clear and strong. "I choose to stay, for I am home. Father, I am *home.*"

Michael nods tightly. "Brothers," he commands, "it's time."

Cal takes a step away from me, and the crowd around us clears. The archangels surround him, like the corners to a square. Cal bows his head and brings his folded hands to his chest. He closes his eyes and breathes deeply.

The angels hold out their arms toward each other, completing the square. Their wings snap open wide. Halos appear over each of their heads, Cal's the brightest of all. It glows with such a fierce blue light it takes my breath away. I almost want to stop them, to end this. He's giving up everything he is. And for what? Me?

You are everything, my father whispers. *Impossibly, improbably, you are everything. To me. To your mother. To him. I've taught you, boy. I've taught you true. Now it's time to stand and accept what is yours. He has made his choice. And you both will be loved for as long as you live and beyond.*

Big Eddie is right. He always is. Cal is my responsibility.

And I will cherish him.

I hold myself tall, ignoring the aches and pains, the sweat on my brow. I don't turn away from the lights growing brighter here in the church. The crowd around me begins to back up again, trying to get some distance from the air that starts to swirl around the five angels. Cal still has his head bowed, and he's moving his lips. The archangels upturn their heads and close their eyes. "O, Lord," the archangels say as one, "hear our prayer."

Everything explodes in vibrant color, as if the church is in a kaleidoscope. Many fall to their knees in veneration. There are tears on almost everyone's faces, but they're ones of joy, of rapture. They are witnessing a miracle, here, in our little town, and they cannot look away.

And here, at the end, I show you the humanizing of the guardian angel Calliel.

The roaring wind gets louder, the lights almost impossible to look at given their brightness. Cal drops his hands to his sides and his head falls back. When his eyes open, they're glowing white, as if he's alight from within. His wings extend completely and he rises from the ground, his toes dragging against the carpet and then lifting off completely. He continues to rise until he's level with the stained-glass image of St. Jude Novena. His halo spins impossibly fast. His body is arched so far back it looks painful. His hands and feet fan out, each digit straining.

And then a soft light comes from St. Jude Novena, as if the window itself is emitting the glow. The colors of the stained glass refract and pour out onto Cal as he starts to spasm. The wind whips through my hair as I take a step forward toward the archangels, my eyes never leaving Calliel above me. Someone tries to stop me, tries to pull me back by my hand, but I shake loose and continue forward.

It starts with his wings.

The tips of his wings begin to fall away, like they're crumbling and turning to a bright azure dust, pulled into the storm that rages inside the church. Cal's mouth falls open in a silent scream as his wings dissolve further. His halo begins to expand, growing larger and larger until it's wider around than he is. For a moment, I think the center of the halo will go black, and he'll be sucked into the black for choosing this world over his Father. I think this whole thing has been God's great joke upon us, one last punch in the gut before he sends my whole world crashing down.

But it doesn't happen. Cal's wings have dissolved completely, and blue light fills the church as the crumbled feathers are sucked up with the wind, catching a downdraft and falling toward me. I close my eyes as the dust hits my face and rolls down my body. All the pain in my body is soothed, and I feel him there, in me, in my head and heart. I feel the connection with his mind. He's scared now, scared of what's happening, scared he won't be able to keep me happy. He has doubts, and they're such a human thing that my breath catches in my throat. But the one thing he does not doubt is me. The one thing he does not regret is becoming human.

Even as I heal and feel him within me completely, I press back toward him and the dust rises again, caught in an updraft, flying up toward him. It travels around his body, wrapping around him front and back, rising up until it passes over his head. He spasms again as it leaves him, clenching his hands to fists at his sides, snapping his head back and forth. I cry out, but he doesn't seem to hear me. What remains of his feathers spins above his head and shoots through the halo. Nothing appears out the other side. Once the blue dust is gone, the halo shrinks back in on itself, collapsing until it falls into nothing. The light of St. Jude Novena fades away. Cal is lowered from the ceiling, the winds beginning to die as he descends. Weak blue light circles him, and all I can think of is how he first came to me, a flash of fire falling from the sky.

His body relaxes as he floats toward the ground, spinning until he's facedown. He lands on the floor on his knees in the middle of the archangels, and they sigh as one and step back. The wind is gone. The lights are gone. His wings are gone. His eyes are closed, and he takes short, shallow breaths, the only sound in the quiet church. He collapses on his hands, his head bent toward the floor of the church. He twists over and lies down on his back.

I take a hesitant step forward. "Cal?" I whisper. I reach him and drop to my knees, my hands shaking as I reach out to touch him. I let my fingers trail over his face. "Cal?"

He opens his eyes. "Benji," he says, his dark eyes filling with wonder. "I feel... different."

I worry. "Different good or different bad?"

"Different different."

"Do you hurt?"

"No."

"Are you sick?"

"No."

"Then what's wrong?"

"My heart," he says, reaching up to touch my cheek. I nuzzle into the palm of his hand. "It's never been like this. I never thought it could be like this. It aches, but it's so good. It's better than anything."

I understand, I think. He's not sick. He's not in pain. He's not wounded. His heart aches because he's human. It aches because it's full. "You're home," I tell him gently, leaning down to kiss him once. He wraps his arms around me and holds me down against him, my face in his neck.

"You still hurt?" he asks me hoarsely.

"No. Your feathers. They... helped me too."

"I asked him for that."

"Asked who?"

"My Father. Benji, I saw my Father. I spoke with him. I walked with him."

Michael crouches down on his knees, staring down at us, a quizzical look on his face. "Father spoke to you?" he asks carefully. The other archangels look just as interested.

"Yes," Cal said.

"What did he say?"

Cal sighs. "He told me there was no one such as me in the world and that I belong to him. He told me he'll believe in me, always. He told me he'll miss me every day we're apart, but that one day, I would see him again."

I close my eyes to keep from breaking.

Michael sighs. "Maybe one day I'll be able to understand him."

"Highly unlikely," David snorts. "I doubt any of us will."

"No matter," Gabriel says. "What's done is done and can't be undone." He blushes for a moment as Michael glares at him. I wonder at it, but don't ask.

"This is just the beginning," Raphael says, looking disgusted. "Wait until On High hears what Father did for Calliel. We're going to be losing angels left and right! How the hell can we be expected to win this war if we have no one left to fight should we be called to do so?"

Michael stands as I help Cal to his feet. "It doesn't matter," Michael says, looking up at St. Jude. "Father has made his decision. The design has changed. If others choose to fall, then it will be done. We have to put faith in him that he knows what he's doing. He would not have made this decision now if he didn't think we could survive." He looks back to us. "If the time calls for it, Calliel, I may ask you to stand with us. I pray it doesn't come to that. But in case it does, I will come for you again."

I feel cold as I grip his hand tightly. "Not without me, you won't," I snap at Michael. "He's mine now. He goes, I go."

"Benji—"

"I'm not asking you. I'm telling you."

He nods, unable to meet my eyes.

"Will it be soon?" Nina asks suddenly. I'd forgotten that all of Roseland surrounds us. I look out over the crowd. They look dazed and tired, confused and elated. Exactly how I feel.

Michael looks at her. "What was that, child?"

"Your war," she says. "Is it coming soon?"

The other three archangels share glances. Michael doesn't look away from Nina. I wonder what he sees in her. I wonder if he knows she is different, in the best sense of the word. "I don't know, little one," he says finally, his wings drooping. "I think so."

"Will you fight? All of you?"

"If we're called to. If there's no other hope." The other archangels nod.

"There's *always* hope," she insists. "There is always hope, and you must remember that. You are *not* alone in this."

Michael's eyes widen as he takes a step back. "Where did you hear...." He shakes his head. "This town," he mutters. "What is it about this town? Who *are* you people?"

No one answers.

"Michael," Raphael growls. "It's time to leave."

"It's been… interesting," David says, tipping a salute at us.

Gabriel surprises me by rushing over and pulling me into a hug. "Thank you," he whispers. "For allowing us to choose. Maybe one day when this is over, I can find my own redheaded daddy." He kisses me on the cheek, and I gape at him as he prances away.

Then only Michael stands before me, and I can't yet tell how I feel about him. "Good-bye," I say finally, unable to think of anything else.

He nods. "Benji," he says. He turns to Cal. "I hope you don't live to regret this."

Cal leans over and kisses my forehead as I help him to his feet, then rubs his nose against my scalp. "Even if I do," he says, his lips against my skin, "I will remember this moment, because this moment will have made it all worth it."

"I'm sure it will," Michael says slowly. He turns and walks back to his brothers, and then he looks out at the crowd. "Keep him safe," he calls out gruffly. "Or you'll answer to me."

And with that, the world explodes in color, and the angels are gone.

Silence falls over the church again as everyone seems to hold their breath at once.

It is Nina (always and forever Nina) who speaks first. "This has been the strangest start to a summer I've ever seen," she says, looking around. "I wonder what will happen next year?"

And with that, the dam breaks and the crowd surges up to me and Cal, and there is love, and there are tears. There is laughter, handshakes, and hugs. There are moments of breathtaking joy. These are my people. This is my town. This is my home. And for the first time in a very long time, it feels complete once more.

the sunrise

IT TAKES us a while to escape the throngs of people who want nothing more than to hear our words, to touch Cal and welcome him home. They want him to know they'll protect his secret until the very end. They want him to know they love him. They want him to know he'll always be welcome in our little town. They kiss him and me over and over again.

My mother, Mary, and Nina are the last. Mom pulls down the neck of the scrubs I wear, trying to find the bullet wound on my chest. It's gone. She pulls the bandages off Cal's chest and stomach (taking a quite a bit of hair with it, if his yelp is any indication) and his wounds are gone as well. "I don't...," she says, shaking her head and taking a step back. "Why does this all feel like a dream?"

I don't know how to answer that, so I just hug her tightly against me then reach around her to pull in Nina and Mary. We hold each other for a time and then let go, standing in a circle with our foreheads together. "Secret?" I ask.

"Secret," they all whisper as they watch me.

"Cross your heart?"

"Hope to die."

"Stick a thousand needles in your eye." I sigh. "I have so many things to tell you. Things I've seen. People I've spoken to. What I've learned and what happens next. But you're... you're all my family, and I think I'd forgotten that. I'm sorry. I just...." I can't finish.

"We know," Mary says, tears in her eyes. "It just took you some time."

"We've always known," Nina says with a sniffle. "We knew you'd find your way back."

"And we've been here waiting," my mother says as she weeps. "Waiting for you to come home."

They kiss me and hug me, then do the same to Cal. After that, we are alone. And without a word, we know where to go. He puts his hand in mine, and we leave the church behind.

IT'S the wee hours of the morning. We haven't yet slept. We're sitting on the roof of the house my father built. I'm sitting between Cal's legs, my back pressed against his chest. He's wrapped his arms around me and holds me close. I feel his breath on my ear.

For the first time in a long time, my mind is not cluttered with questions. For the first time in a long time, I feel like I can breathe without the weight of the world on my shoulders. For the first time in a long time, I am at peace.

"It feels different today," he says, kissing the top of my head.

He's right. It does. I tell him so.

He accepts this with a gorgeous smile.

Then I realize I *do* have a question. "Cal?"

"Yes?"

"Your Father."

He sighs. "My Father."

"Was he… was he what you thought he'd be?" I don't want the answer for me. I want the answer for *him*.

He takes his time before he speaks, as if he's choosing his words carefully, but that's okay. "He was more," he finally says quietly. "He was so much more. I don't know if I can find the words to describe him. He was everything all at once. Beauty, life, horror, death. Love. Everything."

"Sometimes words can't show the measure of a man," I say, thinking of my own father.

"Yes. Oh yes. Even if he's not a man. But it doesn't matter. I thanked him, in the end."

"For what?"

"For this place. For these people. For you. Most of all, I thanked him for you." He takes a deep breath. "Are you scared?"

I don't hesitate. "Yes, but not of you. If there's anything I'm sure of, it's you. All the rest we'll take as it comes. Together. If we're called to fight, we'll do it together."

Moments before we see the sun, Cal says, "I love you."

"I know," I say as I smile. "I love you too.

"What happens next?" he asks. He doesn't sound worried.

I kiss him sweetly and feel him press his tongue against mine. He curls his hand around the back of my head, and I feel like fire. I pull away, but only just. "We live," I tell him before falling back into the kiss.

The sun rises over the mountains, bringing with it the dawn of a new day. And it's enough.

MY NAME is Benjamin Edward Green, after my father, our first and middle names transposed. People call me Benji. Big Eddie wanted me to carry his name, but felt I should have my own identity, hence the switch. I don't mind, knowing it will always bind us together. It's a gift, and because of him, I've been able to find my life again.

I've been able to find meaning in all the colors of the world. Because of him, I've found my home.

This is at once the end and the beginning.

This is the story of my love of two men.

One is my father.

The other is a man who fell from the sky.

When TJ KLUNE was eight, he picked up a pen and paper and began to write his first story (which turned out to be his own sweeping epic version of the video game Super Metroid—he didn't think the game ended very well and wanted to offer his own take on it. He never heard back from the video game company, much to his chagrin). Now, two decades later, the cast of characters in his head have only gotten louder, wondering why he has to go to work as a claims examiner for an insurance company during the day when he could just stay home and write.

He lives with a neurotic cat in the middle of the Sonoran Desert. It's hot there, but he doesn't mind. He dreams about one day standing at Stonehenge, just so he can say he did.

TJ can be found on Facebook under TJ Klune.

His blog is tjklunebooks.blogspot.com.

You can e-mail him at tjklunebooks@yahoo.com.

Also from TJ KLUNE

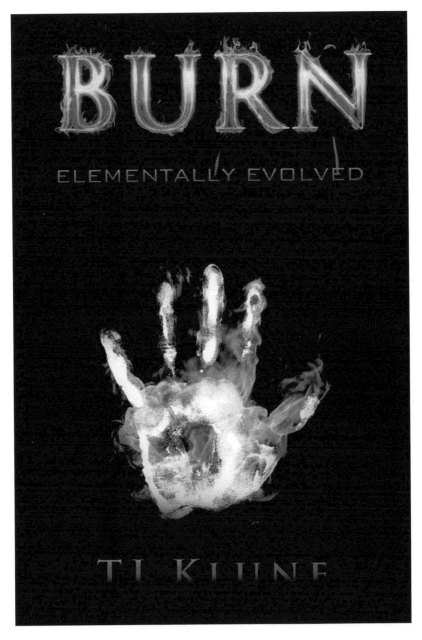

http://www.dreamspinnerpress.com

Also from TJ KLUNE

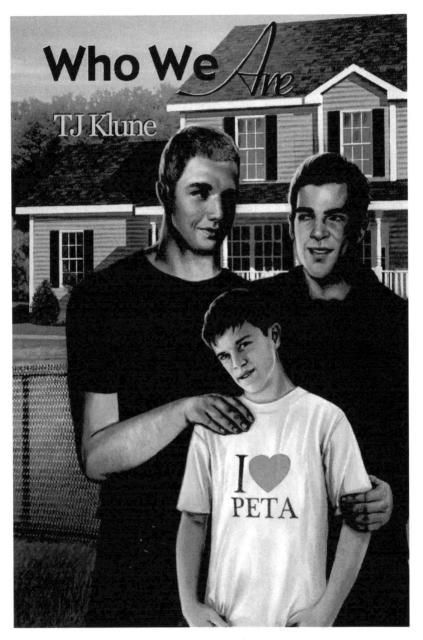

http://www.dreamspinnerpress.com

Also from TJ KLUNE

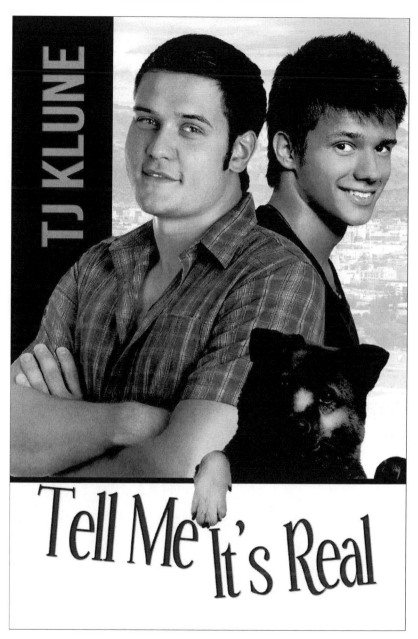

http://www.dreamspinnerpress.com

French translation

http://www.dreamspinnerpress.com

Printed in Great Britain
by Amazon